Made for Breaking

Lauren Gilley

ISBN-13: 978-1491010136

MADE FOR BREAKING

Prologue

"Not everyone has the stomach for killing."

Sly had told her that once. *"Most people, when they get right down to it, can't look a man in the eye and pull the trigger. It's cold, cold shit killing someone. You gotta go away in your head somewhere. It isn't something to be proud of."* He'd said it on her parents' front porch while he ate peanuts and tossed the shells into the flower beds. The look he'd skated to her, eyes the blue of a winter sky, had suggested he didn't think *she* had the stomach for it.

He'd been wrong.

"You can't do it, Lis."

Her hands, small as they were, held steady around the grip of the Smith & Wesson revolver. Her palms weren't clammy. Her arms didn't shake. This gun was on old friend: her first time at the range, Dad's hands clapped over her ears; shooting cans off the hitching rail beside the old barn; the smell of WD-40 and house oil on a stained beach towel at the kitchen table. Holding it stripped away her smallness, her helplessness.

"How do you live with it?" she'd asked Sly over peanut shells.

He'd shrugged. *"I never put anyone in the ground who didn't deserve it."*

"Lisa!" Someone called from the front of the house. Drew. She heard the thump of running feet.

She only had a moment. If she waited, if he reached her, it would be too late. If she was going to do this, it had to be now.

3

"That 'both eyes open' thing is bullshit," her uncle had told her down by the hitching rail. So Lisa closed one eye and centered the sights on the man lying at her feet.

He screamed.

She pulled the trigger.

1

Six Years Ago

"Are you sure about this, sweetie?"

Her dress was ivory and strapless, with a sweetheart neckline that complimented her small bust. It hugged her slender waist to her hips and then the bottom widened into an airy confection of layered tulle.

In the mirror, her reflection stared back. Calm. Composed. She wore the lightest layer of foundation and powder over her porcelain complexion. Dainty pink blush. Smoky eye shadow chosen to bring out the vivid green of her large eyes. Her mahogany hair was swept back off her forehead with a crystal headband and fell down past her shoulders in a dark tumble of curling iron-created twists. Her grandmother's diamond solitaire necklace caught the light each time she drew in a breath and her chest swelled above the bodice of the dress.

Lisa thought she looked like a bride. Even if she didn't feel like one.

"Well, you look fantastic," her maid of honor, Morgan, called from the side table where she was pouring herself another glass of champagne. The hotel suite that had served as the bridal dressing room was still in a shambles from the bachelorette party the night before: confetti, streamers, obscene party favors and liquor everywhere. Morgan had been sipping her hair of the dog all morning, her blue eyes puffy and bloodshot.

Ignoring the compliment, Lisa turned away from the mirror and faced her mother. Cheryl wore her own dark locks up in a knot at the back of her head. Her gold mother-of-the-bride dress was fitted, low-cut, and heavily beaded with little crystals. *"You sure you're not the sister of the bride?"* Lisa's father had joked.

Lisa smoothed her hands down her skirts and smiled, anticipation quickening her pulse. "I'm fine, Mom."

But Cheryl pursed her lips and fussed with Lisa's necklace. "It's not too late, you know. No one would blame you." Her equally large, thoroughly brown eyes were full of doubt. "This is one of those things people are gonna talk about forever."

"Good."

"Good!" Morgan echoed, tipping back her champagne flute and nearly stumbling over the hem of her yellow bridesmaid gown in the process.

"Well." Cheryl sighed, then a smile touched her lips. She laid a gentle knuckle under her daughter's chin. "If you're gonna go out, might as well go out swinging, huh?"

"That's what I figure."

A light knock sounded at the door and Lisa's father, Ray, poked his head in the door. "We all set in here?"

"Yes," they all said in unison.

They rode down in the elevator together, Morgan holding a hand against the side of the car, listing hard to the left. When they reached the lobby and the doors slid open, Lisa felt another tingle of excitement as they crossed in front of the expansive front desk and her skirt whispered over the sleek marble floor. A summertime Saturday at noon, the Atlanta Ritz Carlton was full of tourists moving in and out of the glamorous hotel. Eyes and smiles followed the foursome as they progressed through the lobby. Lisa answered congratulatory wishes from strangers with smiles and *thank yous.*

When they reached the hall that led into the ballroom, her cousin Johnny and Uncle Mark were waiting, both looking ridiculously dressy in their dark suits. "We know we're supposed to be sitting down already," Mark said with a sun-lined smile so much like his brother's it made Lisa want to chuckle. "But I wanted to see you one last time while you're still a Russell." Mark and her father had the same green eyes, the same strong nose. But Mark was quicker to laugh, more apt

6

to find the humor in life. She hugged him and then her cousin who'd been raised almost as her brother.

"I love you, baby," Cheryl said, pulling her daughter into a hug. And then she whispered, "Good luck," in Lisa's ear.

Mark took Cheryl's arm and led her into the ballroom.

"Knock 'im dead, girl," Morgan said, a drunken smile plastered on her pretty face as she handed Lisa her bouquet of white roses. "Literally." Then she let Johnny lead her inside.

The string quartet struck up "The Bridal March" and Lisa offered her dad a smile as she slid her arm through his. "Alright, Dad, let's hear it," she said with a little laugh.

Ray Russell's hair was thinning on the crown of his head, and the sun had pressed lines in his tan face around his dark eyes and mouth. He had one of those thin, straight, aristocratic noses and deep-set eyes that made him look stern, foreboding. His stoicism had made him a legend in the courtroom. And his dark scowls had made him an adult to be avoided by her friends growing up.

But when he smiled – like he did now, when the deep grooves between his drawn brows smoothed and his dimples popped in his cheeks – he was no longer Raymond Russell esquire; no longer the defense attorney who left prosecutors sweating in their bad suits, but her daddy, and on a day like today, she was praying he continued to support her decisions the way he always had.

"Lisa-baby," he said with a sideways twitch to his grin as he stared down at her. "Why do I get the feeling you're about to do something we're all gonna regret?"

She smiled back at him. "'Cause I probably am."

He sighed. "I was afraid of that. 'Kay." He covered her hand with his and began to tow her forward. "Let's get this over with."

The wide double doors of the ballroom were open and through them, Lisa could see the spectacle of ivory and yellow that stretched before them. Bamboo chairs flanked a white carpet that had been sprinkled with rose petals. Gauzy sweeps of tulle decorated the end chairs of each row that were closest to the aisle, clusters of lilies, daisies, and roses secured with silver bows serving as the focal point of each bundle of fabric. Overhead, the chandeliers dripped with crystals that fractured the light into a million dancing points of color, and ornate candelabras on heavy silver stands flanked the walls, their flames adding a rosy warmth to the room.

One hundred and fifty guests in their cocktail finery twisted in their chairs as Ray and Lisa stepped onto the carpet. Murmurs of approval rippled through the crowd. Women dabbed at their eyes with tissues.

Lisa's eyes went to the front of the room, to the altar that was a white rose trellis surrounded by dozens of potted ferns and flowers and more candelabras. She saw her lone bridesmaid swaying dangerously on her heels, fanning herself with her bouquet. She saw the five groomsmen, her betrothed's pack of smiling, idiotic friends who were whispering amongst themselves up in front for all the guests to see. Nick had a big zit coming to a head in the middle of his nose and it looked beet red and oily under the chandeliers. Kevin had a hickey peeking out from the neck of his white dress shirt that could have been seen from space. Will looked her up and down, sneering. Steve was staring at a girl in the crowd, making what he thought were sexy faces at her. Damon was drunker than Morgan.

And then, standing beside the pastor, his hands clasped loosely in front of him, his lean, handsome face split with a dazzling white smile, there was Tristan.

For one moment, just one, Lisa's stomach lurched and she tightened her hand on her dad's sleeve as anxiety spiked inside her, squeezed the air out of her lungs.

Before Tristan, she'd never told a man she loved him. Before Tristan, she'd never entertained the thought of marriage. They'd met at the gym a year ago and as she'd hopped off a treadmill, her sweats clinging to her damp body, her hair falling out of its topknot, he'd given her a wolf whistle and charmed his way right into dinner with her.

Before Tristan, no man had told her how beautiful she was, how sweet she was, how lucky he felt to be close to her. Cheryl had worried herself into a frenzy over the notion that

Tristan was newly divorced, but Lisa had tried to make her understand that his ex-wife had been scheming and heartless, had cheated on him, and that in the wake of that devastation, he needed Lisa. He'd told her he loved her feisty side; that she always kept him interested.

Before Tristan, she'd thought that someday, someone might fall in love with her. And when he said as much, she'd fallen hard: a base jump off a daring cliff with no chute.

He smiled at her now, his dark eyes full of pride, of admiration...*for himself*.

Before Tristan...she'd been stupid as hell.

Lisa felt her father's head come down close beside hers as they stepped up onto the dais and Tristan moved to her other side. "We love you, little girl," Ray whispered into her ear, and it was the shot of courage she needed, the fortifying knowledge that chased her nerves away; smoothed her pulse and left her breathing evenly.

"Who gives this woman?" the pastor asked in a deep, strong baritone that resonated throughout the ballroom.

"Her mother Cheryl and I do," Ray said.

Lisa turned to press a kiss to his cheek, to give him one more smile. The close-lipped grin he offered said the same thing it had every time he'd boosted her up into the saddle as a little girl: *Don't let me down*. She didn't plan to.

With one last squeeze of his hand, Lisa let her dad go and a perfect calm settled over her as she faced forward again and put her hand in Tristan's. She didn't feel nervous as the pastor began to welcome the guests and laud the significance of the day, the ceremony. She stared at her fiancé, her partner, her lover, and felt a cold prickling at the back of her neck, an iciness that seemed to spread, to pour through her veins until she may as well have been a marble statue in front of him. When he moved this thumb in slow circles against her palm and smiled a warm, intimate smile that had once made her melt, she felt nothing behind the iron veil she'd pulled down around her mind and heart. *Never again*, she thought to herself.

9

"At this time," the pastor said, "if there is anyone who feels that there is cause for this man and this woman not to be wed – "

"Can I say something?"

There was a collective intake of breath out in the audience. Tristan's hand tightened on hers in an almost punishing way. Lisa met his gaze with a challenging one, and for the first time since she'd met him, she saw his suave calmness give way to uncertainty.

"Uh…" the pastor stumbled. "If you…"

"Thanks," Lisa drawled. Just the act of opening her mouth had sent another electric jolt of boldness through her, and with deliberate movements, she withdrew her hand from her fiancé's and reached down amid the delicate white roses of her bouquet. "Tristan. Baby," she said, fingers closing over the scrap of lace she'd hidden amongst the stems up in her bridal suite. "Something fell out of your jacket pocket at the house the other day."

His eyes followed her hand as it withdrew from the bouquet, and then they goggled out of his head when he realized that the pink lace between her fingers was a pair of panties.

Another, louder gasp filled the room.

"Oh, shit!" She was pretty sure she recognized Johnny's voice.

Tristan reached toward her, but she stepped out of range. Something like panic creasing his handsome face, he leaned as close as he could, brows scaling his forehead. "Lisa, *what* are you doing?" he whispered.

"I'm giving you a chance to explain," she said in a calm voice.

To her disgust, he blinked, and then seemed relieved. "Okay, okay." He waved his hands in a gesture that suggested he thought she was being unreasonable, but that he would gladly defend himself. "You've got it all wrong, baby. You see, what happened was – "

His words ended in a startled grunt as her bouquet connected with the side of his face.

10

Chairs screeched back across the floor.

"Lisa!" someone cried.

Tristan brought a hand to his cheek, a finger probing the small, bloody scratch where a forgotten thorn had nicked his skin. His eyes flashed dark and full of anger. He opened his mouth to speak, but Lisa cut him off.

"You lying *son of a bitch*!" she snarled at him through her teeth. "Did you think I was that stupid? Huh? You thought I wouldn't find out?"

"Get him, girl!" Morgan whooped.

Tristan lowered his hand and stepped back, beginning to collect some of his dignity. He managed a sneering smile. "Yeah," he said, loud enough for the ballroom to hear. "I thought you were just that stupid."

She hated that the words stung, so she tightened her veil of coldness, scrambled to erect a wall for extra fortification: a thick, impenetrable, stone and steel wall that would keep out not only Tristan, but *all* men.

"Well, from now on." She had no idea how she kept her voice from shaking, but she did. She lifted her little chin and managed to look down her nose at him though he stood a head taller. "You can put your itty-bitty dick wherever you want to, 'cause I don't want a damn thing to do with it anymore."

Amid gasps and shouts, cries and dirty looks, she turned and found her father's quiet almost-smile.

Never again, she thought as she stepped down off the dais and marched down the aisle, unmarried. At nineteen years old, Lisa Lee Russell was done with love.

Five Years Ago

"Does your client have any physical evidence to submit? A video tape maybe? Security footage?"

From across the high-gloss polished surface of the mahogany table in the conference room, Ray waited for opposing counsel, Steven Sheridan, to produce some factual basis for the lawsuit. He had taken on this charitable case as a favor to his brother only because he'd known litigation would fall to pieces during discovery.

"No." Sheridan sighed and shot a dark look toward his clients, Mr. and Mrs. Peters, the owners of Peters' Motors where five pre-owned Cadillacs had been stolen on Ray's clients' watch. Sheridan looked like a man who longed for more intelligent clients.

"Then I'm not sure what we're doing here, Steve." Ray leaned back in his plush leather chair, fingers drumming on the table. "Your clients have changed the damages sought three times now and – "

"They stole 'em!" Mrs. Peters burst out. "I know they did! Look at 'em, the smug little bastards, they - " Sheridan shushed his client with a look and Ray made a soothing gesture with his hand for the benefit of the men on his side of the table.

Edward O'Dell and Sidney "Sly" Hammond were far from innocent. The two mechanics had escaped grand theft auto charges in three states and had been at it again; only this time, their victims were only seeking damages in the form of the cars' value, claiming the two crooks had allowed the cars to be stolen since they couldn't prove they'd done the stealing themselves.

"That's not what this lawsuit's about, Mrs. Peters," Ray said. "You're suing for my clients' negligent acts that supposedly resulted in the theft of your property."

The woman's face turned the same shade of bloody orange as her hair. "I know that!" she snapped.

Ray sighed. "Steve, we both know this is never going to trial…"

In a matter of minutes, the Peters went from irate, to crestfallen when they realized their case wasn't even strong enough for Judge Judy, let alone Russell & Carillo. When they were alone in the conference room, Ray turned toward his clients.

"I'm not the charitable type. And this was one hell of a favor. You do realize both your asses belong to me now, right?"

He caught Sly's blue gaze. The man looked carved from stone, but one corner of his mouth lifted in an attempt at a smile.

Eddie snorted. "Yes, sir."

Four Years Ago

"I've got an idea."

Ray lowered his newspaper and took stock of his younger brother across the kitchen table. Marcus still had all his hair – probably because he had nothing stressful on his plate that caused it to fall out – and his green, Russell eyes were dancing this morning. "Another one?"

"This one's a good one."

"That's what you said last time."

"I know, but this time, I mean it."

With a sigh, Ray folded up the paper and pushed it to the side, picking up his steaming coffee mug instead. Beyond Mark, Cheryl stood at the stove in lemon yellow capris and a white button-up blouse, yellow pumps, looking like June Cleaver as she slipped on a pair of potholders and crouched to pull a baking tin of homemade bread from the oven. Her kitchen was a modern chef's masterpiece of stainless and black granite: Mexican tile floors, custom cabinetry. When she turned to give him a look over her shoulder that said *humor your brother*, he saw the diamonds around her throat he'd given her, the studs that glittered in her pretty ears, and would have done whatever his brother asked if she'd just keep giving him those looks.

"Alright, let's hear it," he said.

A smile stretched across Mark's still-boyish face. "I wanna open a garage, the guys and me. Custom classic car restoration. Just a small place, really focus on quality over quantity. You know how I always wanted my own place..."

"News breaking today that Georgia attorney Ray Russell is being disbarred. This comes on the heels of Russell's escape from obstruction charges during his latest case. He may have avoided arrest, but he did not, however, keep his job…"

Lisa pulled the hood of her light, fitted sweatshirt up over her head and turned away from the Best Buy electronics display where two dozen high-priced TVs were filled with images of a perky, blonde reporter telling the camera that her father was no longer allowed to practice law. Tears burned the backs of her eyes and she blinked at them in vain, sympathetic pain for her father filling her up.

With her head bowed, eyes trained on the toes of her boots, she didn't see Missy Albright until she was nearly colliding with her.

"Watch where you're going!"

Lisa's head snapped up, hood slipping off her dark hair, and she was not properly composed for a run-in with Missy. Missy who'd spread rumors about her in high school, who'd worked relentlessly to turn a whole generation of girls against her out of spite and jealously. Missy who'd married Tristan just three months before, the two of them making a beautiful picture in the Sunday paper.

Today, the tall, long-legged blonde was in a denim mini skirt and furry Ugg boots, a t-shirt with the word *delicious* printed across the chest. She had the fashion sense of a fifteen-year-old, and a fake-and-bake tan. She sipped an iced coffee through a trademark Starbucks green straw and looked completely disgusted to have been bumped into by Lisa.

"Sorry," Lisa managed and side-stepped the blonde.

Missy huffed. Then laughed. "Heard about your dad," she called to Lisa's retreating back. "Whatcha gonna do without Daddy's money? You and the rest of the Beverly Hillbillies gonna go back to the mudhole you crawled out of?"

"How's Tristan?" Lisa whirled around, her smile more of a snarl. "He found wife number three yet?"

The blonde was such a good actress that, even if the jab had affected her, she didn't show it. Her painted lips curved in

14

a false smile. "There's that temper," she purred. "Tristan always hated that, you know. It's so…trashy."

Trashy? Trashy?! When Missy looked like a stripper who'd just gotten off work? A half a hundred insults boiled up behind Lisa's tongue, but a sharp glance from a passing employee kept her quiet.

Ashamed, aching inside, she turned and headed toward the front of the store, Missy's laughter echoing behind her.

The rain had been falling steadily since dawn. They'd lugged boxes in the rain, had toted mattresses and hauled furniture in the rain. Now, as evening painted the gray sky with another layer of darkness, Lisa lingered in the front door, staring out at the weed-choked lawn. The wide, deep porch with its Doric columns and high ceiling had once been beautiful. Now the paint had peeled up in thick strips like scabs off a wound, exposing natural wood tones and rotten places. Wisteria had claimed one column and rode it all the way up, its violet blooms vibrant against the dying house.

It smelled dank and full of mildew inside. They had put buckets out to catch ceiling drips. Cobwebs with spiders big as Shelob filled up every corner; green mold clung to baseboards and globes of lamps. Upstairs, the sounds of footsteps echoed like gunshots on the hardwood.

Lisa went outside, her boots thumping over the boards of the porch as she walked toward her dad.

Ray had one shoulder propped against a column, staring out into the heavy mist that hugged the world, the water that beaded on every leaf and branch.

She didn't remember her grandparents' house like this. In the pictures, when Martha and Harry Russell had been alive, the place had gleamed: a birthday cake of white clapboard on a plate of crisp green lawns full to bursting with flowers. But it had been empty since before she was born, and it was abandoned, rotting, and haunted.

"What are we gonna do now?" she asked, just loud enough to be heard above the soft pattering of the rain.

Ray gave no indication that he'd heard, but she thought his shoulders bowed when he sighed like an exhausted, defeated man. "We're gonna start over," he said. "That's all we *can* do."

2

Present Day

The outdoor security lights were on timers and clicked off at exactly one-thirty a.m. every night...morning...whatever. Lisa was too tired to be nitpicky about the details because it was *three*-thirty and she was piloting her truck up into the drive and pulling all the way around the house to her usual parking space in front of the carriage house. It was dark back there, the tall trees holding hands up above the drive, creating a deeper dark than that of night. The white clapboard of the rear of the house seemed to glow, and even though it was now full of people and furniture and fresh air perfumed by cleansers, flowers and laundry detergent, at times like these, it still had the air of a haunted mansion about it: The kind of place where ghostly confederate soldiers wandered the halls, moaning and rattling chains and doing whatever it was that ghosts did.

It was an effort to drag herself out of the truck. And she toed off her platform sandals with one arm braced against the tailgate, feet too sore to make it to the back steps. *I bet this is what a stripper feels like,* she thought as she massaged her arches. All the bartenders and waitresses at Double Vision had a dress code: heels, super-short cutoffs, and a pushup bra if Mother Nature hadn't been generous enough. By the end of her shift, the bra was digging into her ribs, her feet felt like someone had run railroad spikes through them, and her cheeks were stiff from smiling.

It could have been worse: her tips could have been in her panties and not in her purse.

Sandals dangling from her fingers, she hiked her bag back up her arm and tiptoed barefoot across the dew-dampened driveway, biting her tongue each time she stepped on an acorn. She paused once she'd gained the comfort of the screened-in back porch and greeted her dog. Hektor missed nothing, and he'd known the sound of her engine, the whisper of her feet over the ground. His nub of a tail was wagging as he greeted her with sleepy eyes and a yawn. Lisa scratched behind the Doberman's cropped ears until he went back to his big dog bed in the corner. She unhooked her bra, pulled it out through an armhole of her tank top and stuffed it in her purse. She stowed her shoes on the rack by the door beside the guys' boots and then noticed there was a light on inside.

Her mother was in the kitchen, the lamp tucked beneath the cabinets up on the counter casting a muted glow that didn't reach into the corners of the room. Cheryl sat at the long, rustic table, a silk robe open over terry cloth pajamas, her hair up in a clip, dark strands loose around her face. She glanced up from the open sketch pad spread before her and looked toward the door.

"Hey, sweetie." Her voice was thick with needed sleep.

Lisa should have gone upstairs, but at the moment, any resting place on her trip between back door and bedroom was welcome, so she managed to take the seat across from her mom. "Hey." She propped a hand beneath her chin, eyelids flagging. "Can't sleep?"

"Struck with inspiration." Cheryl turned the sketch pad and slid it across the table. An outdoor kitchen stared up off the page: a white pergola over a stone patio that was outfitted with a stainless sink and grill, burners, an oven, a dishwasher, a wine cooler. A peninsula of rustic, stacked stone served as a bar, ringed by stools.

"Very man cave-y," Lisa said, passing it back. "I like."

"Yeah?"

"Yeah."

Their interior design business had started as a guilty wish for both of them. Then they'd started talking about it. It wasn't off the ground – they had yet to take on a client – but it was a constant topic between them. Lisa wasn't as hopeful as her mother, hence the pushup bra and the steady gig at Double Vision, but sometimes, late at night – morning – staring at her

18

bedroom ceiling, she dreamed about their business cards, their full appointment books, and most of all, their reputation. She wanted to have a *good* reputation for once.

She was hopeful, but not optimistic.

"I talked to Patty Smyth today," Cheryl said, spinning her pad back around and taking her pencil to the sketch again. "She's interested in having her husband's office redone now that they're both working at home."

"Hmm." Lisa picked at her peeling red fingernail polish and didn't tell her mother that Patty Smyth had made vague hints about hiring them for the past year, none of them ever coming to fruition. When she glanced up, Cheryl was staring at her, nose wrinkled.

"You don't think it'll happen."

"I dunno what I think," she admitted.

"I wish you'd stop doing that."

"Doing what?"

"Being so much like your father."

A smile touched her lips. "Just what every girl wants to hear."

"Truth hurts." Cheryl returned the smile, then was overtaken by a yawn that Lisa could tell she tried to stifle.

"You should get some sleep, Mom."

"You too. Shower first, though. You smell like a bar."

"What's wrong with you?"

Lisa pushed her mirror-lensed aviator shades up her nose with a knuckle and squinted at her cousin through them. She felt the wrinkles between her brows and at the corners of her mouth, and didn't care. "I got three hours of sleep," she croaked, "that's what."

Johnny Russell – Mark's youngest, and the only one of his two children he actually ever saw – had gone from pudgy kid to lanky young adult in the past couple of years. At nineteen, he was proud of the dark scruff on his chin and had developed an addiction to muscle shirts and hair products. He had a hip propped against the desk, arms folded, and was much too alert and perky for her tastes at eight-something in the morning.

"Did you work last night?"

She bit the tip of her tongue instead of pointing out the stupidity of his question. The computer was on and she swiveled her chair toward it in the hopes he'd take his inquiring little ass elsewhere. He was more a brother than a cousin to her, but for that reason, he got on her nerves.

Lisa took a sip of her coffee and tried to toss her functioning brain cells into her day job. Work orders had been dropped onto the desk, scattered, and now she had to put them in order and then key them into the electronic spreadsheets that she couldn't get any of the guys to use. Her Uncle Mark was a genius when it came to the cars, but paperwork eluded him.

"Did you hear?" Johnny asked, moving around the desk so he could plop down into the chair across from her.

"Don't know," she said as she shuffled the work orders into a tidy pile and scanned the topmost to determine its date.

"We got the Trans Am."

"You *what*?" Lisa's head snapped up and her hands dropped, paperwork forgotten. She pushed her shades on top of her head, the news doing what caffeine had failed to: wake her up. "Are you serious?"

A wide grin stretched across his face, making him look like his father. "You wanna come see it?"

King Customs was a small garage: two bays, an office squatting beside it on a narrow lot between a gas station and the beginning of a strip mall full off cafes and nail salons. It had started as "King of Customs," Mark's one streak of braggadocios pride, but had been shortened because no one seemed to want to use the "of." Alpharetta real estate was pricey and hard to come by, so the grand vision of a teeming shop had been whittled down to something more affordable, something manageable. Ray had funded the project and Mark was still in the process of paying him back – a feat that seemed impossible due to the slow nature of classic car restoration.

The morning was already muggy and sticky with humidity as Lisa followed Johnny through the connecting door from the office into the first bay. Both roll top doors were open and one of the guys had Bad Company playing on a radio, the song muted by the sound of passing traffic. Eddie and Sly were having their morning smoke break – soon to be followed by a mid-morning smoke break – and Rico was rifling through a Craftsman tool chest.

But the Trans Am sat, waiting to be fawned over, silent, full of promise.

Its original color was impossible to tell because now it was covered with rust and Bondo. It lacked wheels, tires and a windshield.

"Damn," Lisa murmured, stepping down into the bay and circling the ruined Pontiac. "What's under the hood?"

"Take a look." Sly's voice drew her attention. The mechanic ground his smoke out on the heel of his boot and nodded toward the car. In the shade of the garage, his eyes almost seemed to glow. His face was, as it normally was, a flat mask that gave nothing away. Maybe it was the eyes, maybe the short chestnut hair, his love of white t-shirts, but Lisa thought it was his aloofness that had always brought Steve McQueen to mind when she looked at the man. Sly was cool where most were egotistical…lazy too, but cool.

With no regard for her nails – they were short, the polish was peeling, and she didn't mind getting her hands dirty – she worked the release open and levered the hood up. She sucked in a breath.

"Is this a four-fifty-five?" It was a mess of dusty coils, snakes and geometric shapes, but she'd flipped through enough of her uncle's manuals to know the engine for what it was.

"Yep," Johnny said proudly, stuffing his hands in his jeans pockets. "It's a seventy-six, got the original Pontiac V8 in it." The kid's smile stretched ear-to-ear. "Can you believe it?"

"No," she said, honest, feeling a smile steal across her own face. "Where the hell did he find it?"

21

"Some old dude had it rotting in his back yard," Eddie said with a chuckle. "Guy had no idea what he was sitting on."

"No kidding." As her eyes roved over the Trans Am's innards, she gave an internal nod of satisfaction. Her Uncle Mark and Johnny had been talking about having one of these since Johnny was old enough to understand what they were. There'd been a time, when Ray had been working out of a plush Alpharetta law office, that he'd tried to track one down for his brother. Mark had refused – he'd lived off Ray's charity enough already, he'd said. Dreams weren't worth a shit if you didn't reach them by yourself.

"She'll be pretty," Eddie said, then shot Johnny one of his killer grins. "Ten-four, good buddy."

"Shut up."

Lisa lowered the hood with care. "It's beautiful. At least, *it's gonna be*." There were grunts of agreement. "Where's Mark? His baby's here and he's not?"

Sly gave away the tiniest of smiles. "He and your dad had an appointment."

"I don't really know what to make of this, *Padre*."

Our Lady Catholic Church of Cartersville was not the small city's most popular Catholic church. It sat in the middle of a lawn that was really a field, amongst a clearing off a skinny road that slithered its way through pastureland like a young rat snake. Beneath a heavy drape of power and phone lines, the church sprouted up out of the grass, its single steeple threatening to get them all electrocuted. The grounds hosted a cemetery ringed by a chain-link fence, a gravel parking lot, a series of outbuildings that served as storage for the lawnmowers and church vehicles. Father Morris lived at the back of the property, in a white cottage that was his rectory.

Ray sat in a ladder-backed chair at Father Morris's kitchen table. Mark was beside him, Father Morris across from him, the cleric's back to the bay window so that the incoming light streamed around him like a halo. Above the holy man's

22

shoulders, Ray watched morning hang over the lawns, and waited for a response.

Father Morris had made them coffee and laid it out on the table. Then he'd rechecked the door locks, paced across his tiny, spotless, dated kitchen, and finally pulled a flask from a small drawer beside the stove. He'd spiked his own coffee and had thrown half of it down. The eyes he lifted were braver than they had been before.

"You were a well-renowned attorney," the priest said at last, sighing. He couldn't have been much older than Ray, but his hair was white, the lines around his eyes deep and full of shadows.

"Past tense," Ray said. "I haven't practiced in three years."

Father Morris nodded, but his gaze didn't waver. "But a man doesn't lose his skills because he stops practicing."

He shared a glance with his brother. Mark shrugged. "No offense, Father," Ray said. "But I don't go to church for a reason: I was never good with all that speaking-in-metaphors, life-lessons shi…crap."

"I'm not doing either, Mr. Russell. I invited you here so that I could ask for your help."

"My *help*?"

Father Morris took another fortifying sip of his brandied coffee and then pushed the mug away. "People talk, Ray." His tone took on a new edge, a casual insistence that had nothing to do with his position, like the priest parts of him had been sloughed off in an instant. "Just because I'm a man of the cloth, it doesn't mean I don't hear the gossip. I know you boys lend a hand when it's needed."

Ray snorted. "Ya hear that, Mark? We sound downright charitable."

"I'm *very* charitable," his brother said with a laugh.

Father Morris didn't smile. He stared at them, face stern.

"What've you heard?" Ray softened his voice. He needed this kind of business – this under the radar, word of mouth reputation building, but if he was going to stick his neck out, he wanted the cause to be worthy.

"I know you were hired to keep Cynthia Abbot safe during the trial of her rapist," the priest said. "I know you're the reason Bryan Stanton was in violation of his parole when the police picked him up." He sighed. "I might not approve of the methods, but I know you help people who need it."

"And why" – Ray studied the other man – "would I do that?"

"It's what ended your career. A man has a hard time letting go of his principles. He does what he can with the resources at his disposal."

"I'd say you're right, but I don't have any principles, Father."

The priest tipped his head. "We can disagree on that."

Ray felt his brother kick at his leg under the table and turned toward him. Mark had a terrible poker face and his opinion was plain in his green eyes: he thought they should see what the *padre* wanted.

What would Cheryl say? he thought to himself. But he knew. His wife had given him a long, level look when she'd guessed the truth about Bryan Stanton. *"That man doesn't belong on the street,"* she'd said in a voice that had been stronger than his confidence. Every time he thought about the ramifications of what he was doing, he thought about that look in her dark eyes. He might not have had any principles, but Cheryl did, and everything he'd ever done, he'd done for her.

He tapped his fingertips on the table and Mark turned away, nodding, understanding. "Father Morris," Ray said, turning back to the clergyman. "What can we help you with?"

3

"How much?"

"Father Morris estimated close to forty grand worth of electronics."

"Shit." Eddie rubbed a hand down his carefully groomed, dark goatee and shook his head. "How's a piss poor church like that get a hold of that kind of money?"

They stood in the parking lot of Mark's shop, Ray, Eddie and Sly all gathered around the hood of Ray's black Dodge truck where Ray's day planner was spread open. To a passerby, they looked like three car guys talking shop. And they were...in a way.

"Donations," Ray explained. He unfolded the rumpled list Father Morris had given him. "Every TV, every laptop, every iPod – all of it donated by church patrons and the good people of Cartersville." There was an itemized accounting for every donation, though names had been omitted. "Once word gets out, Father Morris thinks his flock will assume the worst."

Sly snorted, though his face never changed. "That the church stole it."

"Sold it on the black market." Eddie shrugged. "Worse has happened. Coulda been little boys who – "

Ray cut him off with a sharp look. Of the two car thieves he'd rescued from the penal system, one had the brains, one had the beauty. Eddie had looks in spades, the little shithead, but with the exception of how to bag a woman for the night and how to hotwire a car, there wasn't a lot else rolling around between his ears.

"Church volunteers were going to make a drop at Just Like Home – that charity group – today. Everything was loaded up in a van. Father Morris found the garage door open this morning, the van gone."

His guys waited. Sly had a knowing look in his almost-translucent eyes. The man was downright spooky when he wanted to be. He had cold eyes. Dead eyes. They followed you.

"The Piper," Eddie said, nodding. "If someone's boosting electronics, chances are they'll move it through him."

"Or he'll at least know about it," Sly corrected.

"I thought we could head over to the fights tonight. Kick over rocks and ask questions. That kinda shit."

Both the others nodded. Eddie's cell chimed to life in his pocket and he stepped away to answer it, his wide, white grin giving away the caller's identity as female.

Sly lifted his shoulders in a shrug, as if to excuse his friend's behavior. "I'll make some calls and find out where the fights are tonight."

"Fights?"

Ray cringed at the sound of the female voice behind him. Lisa had mastered the art of sneaking long ago. Her penchant for cowboy boots with loud, wooden heels extended back to her elementary school days and when she was angry or excited, or proud of her boots, they clacked loudly as she walked. But she'd also learned how to walk up on the balls of her feet so that she was silent as a little wraith. And the brat had obviously been too curious to help herself when she'd seen them out at the truck.

He turned, sighing, and faced his daughter. Lisa had an innocent smile pasted on her face, one that she knew was effective. "Don't even try it," he warned, and the corners of her mouth turned up in a true grin. "And no. No fights."

They'd made the mistake of taking her a time or two before, and though it hadn't ended badly, she'd garnered way too much attention for his tastes. There was nothing like seeing drunken gamblers leer at your daughter.

Her smile fell. "Are you letting Johnny tag along?"

Yes. "No. He's not twenty-one."

"Pretty sure the Masters of the Pit Fight Series isn't legal anyway, so a little underage gambling never hurt anybody."

Damn. So much for logic. "You're not going."

Lisa sighed and folded her skinny arms over her chest. "If we argue about this, we'll just waste ten minutes because you know you'll let me go."

She's too bold. He should have been tougher on her. She'd always been too bold, even as a kid. "Not happening."

He watched her eyes move toward Sly, who might have been holding back a smile. "No, no, no, don't look at him. He can't help you."

"Dad."

"Lisa."

"I'll just go by myself then."

"You won't know where it is tonight."

She pulled her bottom lip between her teeth and stared down at the toes of her boots, frustration pressing lines between her drawn brows.

"Why do you wanna go so bad anyway?"

"I just do." Because she was an only child and had served as both son and daughter. Because they'd been to rodeos and fishing tournaments, softball games and bowling nights together. She'd always been a bit of a tomboy. And despite the hoop earrings and all the eyeliner, she worked Mark's garage because she loved cars. And she wanted to go tonight not – for the reasons he did – to gain some kind of intel, but because she liked boxing.

Ray could feel his resolve crumbling. He glanced at Sly and saw a laugh dancing around in the guy's eyes. Ray wondered if it was as shameful to be manipulated by a daughter as it was by a wife. He didn't think so, but wasn't sure.

"We'll see," he told her, and Lisa dipped her head in final acquiescence, turned and headed back toward the office, boot heels clacking this time.

She paused halfway there and twisted her head over her shoulder. "That means yes, doesn't it?"

"Yes."

She grinned and kept walking.

***

27

The Masters of the Pit was one of those events that didn't technically exist. Flyers were stapled to telephone poles and tacked to the insides of diner windows and pinned on college corkboards outside dorm halls. You called a number, and someone on the other end asked for a password. If you knew the word, you were given another number, this one that connected to a prepay cell phone whose answerer gave you the location of that week's fights. At each meet, new passwords were agreed upon and new prepay cells were bought. For an event so secret, it managed to grow week by week.

This week, the GPS led them to the given address: an abandoned metal barn out west of Atlanta, in the middle of some nowhere field. The fights had turned the place into a circus.

Cars and trucks had flattened the grass in a wide half circle around the open entrance of the barn. Bright, yellow light poured from the building and it highlighted hastily put together concession stands and t-shirt vendor tables. People would hawk anything at these sorts of events – from keychains to cigars to bootleg DVDs.

Lisa zipped up her summer weight sweatshirt and pulled its hood up over her head. Her long dark hair still spilled out around her shoulders; it wasn't as if she could hide the fact that she was a girl, but it never hurt to add a little mystery about herself. At least, that was her logic. Standing between her cousin and Eddie, Mark and Sly and her dad in front of her, they moved into the barn amongst the swaying, squawking crowd. The gamblers and spectators were laughing and jostling one another, arguing about the night's outcomes, spitting tobacco juice into the dirt. The air stank of cigarette smoke, sweat, and something that reminded her of scum off the top of stagnant water.

Inside, the ring had been set up in the middle of the floor and bodies were packed all around it, waiting impatiently. Ray raised an arm and pointed toward one of the tiers of bleachers that flanked the ring and they headed that direction. There were a lot of spectators who wanted to be close enough to feel the flying blood and sweat on their faces, but Lisa was glad that her dad, like her, wanted a good vantage point from which to really observe the fighters' moves.

They found a spot up at the very top of the bleachers. Lisa wedged in between Johnny and Eddie; the three "elders," as Johnny called them, sat one seat down in front of them.

"Do you know anything about who's fighting tonight?" Lisa cupped her hand around her mouth and leaned into Eddie to be heard above the din of voices that swelled around them.

"This is some kinda semi-finals," he shouted back. "Winners here move on to next week's fight."

"What do they win?"

He cracked a grin that did devilishly handsome things to his face, put dimples on either side of his smile. "Bragging rights?"

She rolled her eyes. "Only men would compete for *that*. You'd have to pull out a purse for me to stand up and get my teeth knocked in."

"I don't wanna watch chicks fight. Too much hair pulling and shit."

True. She nodded and straightened.

There were no programs or schedules of any kind. No announcer. But when a knot of four men started pushing their way through the crowd toward the ring, a cheer went up. Lists and betting books started coming out of people's pockets and the first two contestants slid through the ropes, their trainers taking up posts in opposing corners. The ref clambered up into the ring, red-faced and panting, and waved his hands for quiet. The noise only lessened partially. He screamed the names of the opponents, a bell was struck, and it began.

Lisa scooted forward on the bleachers, elbows on her knees, eyes trained on the fighters. As adrenaline tickled her stomach, she wondered again if maybe she should have been born a boy.

In the dim glow of a security light, Andrew Forester sat on the lowered tailgate of a truck, listening to the pulsating roar of humanity just on the other side of the barn walls while his hands were being wrapped.

"I don't expect to be embarrassed tonight," Ricky said, because that's what Ricky *always* said. He wound another strip of white tape around Drew's knuckles and pulled until Drew swore he felt his bones shifting beneath the pressure. "We are not losers. My boys *do not* lose."

Dark out in the country was different than dark in town. It swallowed a person up. It was full of strange night sounds: owls or coyotes…and something that screamed. Something he'd never heard before, but put goose bumps down the back of his neck. Other fighters paced across the trampled grass of the field, warming up with their shadows, imagining the fights to come in their heads.

Drew tried to do that – tried to push out all the sounds of voices and crickets, tried to visualize the ring, the man he would fight. But Ricky liked to hear himself talk. So Drew watched the wraps go round and around his knuckles, listening.

"Two more weeks after this." Beads of anxious perspiration glittered on Ricky's forehead as he reared back into the path that the security light cut across the property. "Two!" He held up two meaty fingers, eyes bugging white and bloodshot from his head. "You know what it means when we go legit?"

Yes, boss. But he shook his head.

"Vegas!" The trainer's teeth were gapped and crooked when he smiled. Someone had put a fist in his mouth years ago and he'd never bothered to have them fixed. "'Cause you know what's in Vegas?"

Yes.

"UFC headquarters."

To Drew's knowledge, Ricky had zero experience training Ultimate Fighters. The closest he'd ever come was watching it on Pay-Per-View. But Ricky was convinced that because it was popular – and it was – that it meant bigger media coverage, bigger money, better sponsors. And while all of that was true, Drew wasn't so stupid that he believed he could go from underground boxer to sponsored cage fighter overnight.

"You'll like that, won't ya?" Ricky put his hands on his fat knees and leaned down low so they were on eye level. His breath stank of the Philly cheesesteak he'd had earlier: onions and cheese. "Huh?" he pressed when he got no answer. *"Won't ya?"*

He talked to his fighters like children. Or maybe more like dogs. Drew hated that Kung-Fu, kicking and biting UFC shit. He was a boxer, end of story.

But he nodded. "Yes, boss."

"Good." Ricky reached up and slapped him across the top of his head. "Then sack up. You haven't won anything yet. You go in and you win *tonight*. Then you've got work tomorrow. I'll call you a winner when you are one. When you *deserve* it."

The only thing worse than the idea of moving to Vegas to become a Tae Kwon Do head-kicker was knowing he had to work the next day.

But he nodded again. "Okay."

4

Fighters were animals. And in Lisa's mind, that was not a wink-and-a-nudge suggestive comment; it was just a fact. As the two men in the ring traded jabs, they ceased to be human in her eyes. She sized them up like horses at auction, watched the muscles and tendons jump beneath their skin, estimated the speed of their striking arms. No matter how evenly they were matched, one was always just that much quicker, stronger. Lisa liked figuring out which one that was early in the game. She made silent wagers with herself. While the rest of the women in the stuffy, overcrowded barn hung off men's arms or looked for men to take them home, *she* watched the action.

"The guy in the red shorts is stronger," Johnny said beside her.

It was true. His shoulders looked too wide to fit through a doorway. His biceps were as big as hams – solid, strong hams, not fleshy hams like on the woman who owned the deli next door to King Customs.

"Blue shorts is faster, though," she told her cousin. That was true too. She'd been watching his strikes for five rounds; his arms didn't swing away from his body, they lunged, lightning fast, and then snapped back. His blows weren't as hard as his opponent's, but he ducked those. He was like a dancer, always a half a step ahead, his feet stepping more lightly across the mat.

"I wanna put money on Red," Johnny said. He touched Mark's shoulder. "Dad, I wanna do that."

"It'll have to wait till we get back," Ray answered him, twisting around. "Eddie, can you sit with them?"

"Yep."

Johnny's face fell. "Where are you guys going?"

32

Mark stood and turned to face them, knuckling the stiffness out of his back. "To see a friend." He offered his son a smile. "We won't be long."

"Can I come?"

No, Lisa knew the answer before Ray shook his head. Johnny was still a kid...and though that frustrated him, at least he would grow up, whereas she would always be a girl. Tonight, Eddie was the appointed sitter for kids and girls.

He didn't look happy about it, either. "Thanks, guys," he called as Ray, Mark and Sly trooped down the bleachers.

"So not fair," Johnny muttered under his breath.

Lisa sighed and bumped her shoulder against his. "Life's not fair. Watch the fight."

Something Ray had learned before he was disbarred, before law school even – when he and Mark had been long-legged teenagers growing up in Cartersville and dreaming about bigger cities and bigger things – was that certain events drew in certain types of people. An illegal boxing match was just the sort of thing to bring all sorts of nefarious types crawling in on their bellies like the roaches they were.

Which, if he thought about it, wasn't a fair assessment of some of his favorite vagrants. But when he thought of Simon Piper, roaches always came to mind.

He'd called himself "The Piper" so long it had finally stuck. He thought of himself as someone who had some sort of control over the tumultuous, chaotic world of bootleg merchandise. He was a small fish in a huge pond. But no one could tell him that. Ray found him standing at the back of a knot of men on the far side of the barn, near the open back doors. Stick thin and half a head taller than everyone surrounding him, Piper was easy to spot. To compensate for the bald spot on top of his head, he wore the rest of his hair long and tied it up in a greasy ponytail that trailed over one shoulder. He was constantly sweaty – which Ray attributed to a drug habit – and even in the dim light of the barn, there was a wet sheen across his forehead. He wore a Harley-Davidson t-shirt with the sleeves cut out and cargo pants. It was an outfit Ray had seen him in more than once.

"Piper."

At the sound of his name, his head swiveled on his neck like a bird's might, saucer-wide eyes finding Ray as he and the others moved through the crowd. "Ray..." He didn't look happy to see them.

"How's it going, Pipe?" Mark asked. Ray had no idea where his brother found these big, toothy, seemingly genuine smiles, but Mark wore one now. He approached Piper first, offered a hand for the tall man's shake.

"Fine." The Piper never looked at Mark; he'd deemed him non-threatening. His eyes moved to Sly – who was taking up a watchful stance at the edge of the crowd, looking for ears that might be listening – and then came back to Ray. "Help you boys with somethin'?"

Ray and his brother traded places, Mark sliding in front, creating a barrier between Ray and the con man, putting just that much of a wall around their conversation. "What if I needed to get hold of high-end electronics?"

Piper shrugged, scratched at his patchy mustache. "'Fraid I wouldn't know anything about that. DVDs, CDs, I'm your man, but – "

"Who would I talk to then?"

The match in the ring ended as the fighter in the blue shorts sent his opponent spinning back against the ropes and then to his knees. Red Shorts didn't get back up and the voices in the stands swelled, cheers and boos drowning out all other sound.

Ray felt the tall man lean closer to him. "People are talking, Russell," Piper said. "They say you're nobody's friend."

"Nobody's anybody's friend, and you know it. So..." He lifted his brows in a blatant demand.

The crook held his gaze a moment, then looked away with a sigh. He shrugged. "I don't know anything...but if I did, I'd say you oughta talk to Ricky Bullard."

"Who?"

"He's got a man in the fights tonight. You'll see him in a bit – won't be able to miss him."

Beer sloshed over the sides of the plastic cup as Johnny passed it to her, the liquid running down over her hand. Lisa set the drink on the bleachers beside her and sucked the spill off the web between her thumb and forefinger before it could get sticky. "Thanks, cuz," she said with an eye roll as she picked the beer back up.

"Hey, you shoulda seen me down there," he defended himself, handing over Eddie's beer and then sitting, sucking the foam off the top of his own. "All those people pushing me around and I didn't spill a drop."

"Till you got up here."

He made a face.

"Leave him alone," Eddie said, which drew two dark looks. Lisa had watched him charm his way into the pants and skirts of so many girls, but when she stared him down, Eddie glanced away. His swagger had no effect on her and he knew it. "Next fight's about to start," he said, pretending he hadn't just tried to give her an order.

Lisa smiled internally. Ray called her a brat when she used her sway over one of his guys, but she'd seen the smiles he'd tried to hide. *Never again.* She was never going to let a man shape her life again, and her dad was proud of that.

"*Coming into the ring –* " The ref had a bullhorn now and he yelled through it. He turned to one side of the ring, arm stretched out to showcase the man climbing between the ropes. "*The Monster!*"

And the man looked like a monster: a big block of a head with a nose that had been broken so many times it was only a blob of flesh in the middle of his face. He had a thick, Cro-Magnon brow and a neck like a tree trunk. She didn't envy whoever was going up against him.

"The names these guys come up with," Eddie snorted. "Real creative."

35

"You expected boxers to be creative?" Lisa asked.

He made a sound of agreement.

"And daring to stand up against him tonight," the ref continued. *"Standing five-eleven, weighing in at two-hundred pounds...the Lynx!"*

"Shit, it's Rocky and the Russian," Eddie said. "Gonna be a slaughter."

"Well they said 'Lynx' and not 'mountain lion,'" Johnny said, laughing at his own joke.

As Lisa watched the man who'd dubbed himself "The Lynx" climb into the ring and straighten to his full, unremarkable height, she knew his weight had been embellished by at least twenty pounds. He was fit and tight; exercise had shredded every ounce of fat from his body and he was an impressive display of carved muscle and tendons. But he was not the brute his opponent was. And even if he was quick and strong and more skilled than anyone else in the barn had been tonight, he didn't look like a man who could take down The Monster.

As Lisa watched the two fighters come to the center of the ring and touch gloves, Monster sneering around his mouthpiece, she felt a tiny coil of fear twist in her stomach. It was such an odd sensation, it took her a moment to put a name to it; she realized that, though The Lynx was nothing but a pair of silky shorts and red gloves to her, she was suddenly afraid she might witness a man get killed in the ring tonight. It was an intoxicating kind of fear, the kind that invested her in the outcome of this match.

"Ref might as well call it now," Eddie said.

Lisa scooted forward, hands clasping together in her lap. "Let's wait and see."

"Ricky Bullard?"

"What?" The man was nearly as wide as he was tall, the thick rolls around his waist testing the elasticity of his white tank top and sweatpants. He had two meaty arms hooked over the top rope of the ring and swiveled a neckless, splotchy face in their direction. He was even uglier than Piper had indicated, his teeth gapped, his nose a bulbous nightmare, more white hair spilling over the neck of his shirt than there was on top of his head.

"Can we talk a minute?" Ray asked.

The trainer scowled. "I got a guy in the ring! Not now."

Ray flicked a glance toward the match that had just begun. The problem with these underground things was that there weren't any regulations, which meant unequal opponents were pitted against one another, as was happening now. "He won't be in there long," Ray said. "It'll just take a minute."

"I said no!"

Ray felt a hand clap down on his shoulder and knew it was Mark before he turned. "I'll handle it," his brother said. "You're grinding your teeth again."

He didn't argue, but nodded, and Mark climbed onto the ropes beside Ricky Bullard, a smile lighting up his face.

Ray shook his head. "You know," he told Sly, who stood silent sentry next to him, "of all my clients, I never had to work at getting my brother off light. No one can stay pissed at Mark."

Lisa was transfixed. Eddie and Johnny's voices faded into the din of the crowd. She was aware of cheers and yells, but she didn't really hear any of them. Her eyes were beginning to water because she refused to blink. Lynx was *good*. Lynx was better than that, he was *talented*.

He approached the fight like a dance. The lumbering Monster was his partner and he anticipated every step, every strike, every parry. He didn't just move his feet and throw jabs at the other man, but controlled his entire body; every muscle was mastered, every move deliberate.

She chewed at her bottom lip as he ducked a vicious swing and then popped up faster than Monster had expected, landing a hard blow to the guy's jaw.

Something wet hit her knee and went dribbling down into her boot and she realized she'd squeezed her beer until the plastic cup cracked. With a disgusted face, she set the ruined drink down at her feet and swept her eyes back up to the action.

"I can't believe this," Eddie said, a touch of awe in his voice. "This guy's actually gonna – "

"Don't say it," Lisa cut him off. "You'll jinx him."

"He's the guy," Mark confirmed as he joined them again. Ray and Sly had moved beyond the crowd and stood in the open doorway of the barn, where lamplight met moonlight and where a breeze relieved some of the stinking heat of so many humans pressed together. They smelled as bad as a barn full of animals would, Ray thought.

His brother shoved his hands in the back pockets of his jeans and shrugged as he came to a halt. In the shadows, he could have been twenty-years-old for all the lines that showed on his face. He always brought literal meaning to "little brother." "Said we could meet up this week to talk about 'transfer.'" He rolled his eyes and cast a glance over his shoulder to where Ricky was red-faced and screaming at his fighter – who was actually winning the match. "Dumbass used about fifteen words he didn't know the meaning of."

Ray snorted. "Stupid's good. We can work with stupid."

"Who stole the van?" Sly asked. "I know his fat ass didn't do it."

"He's got a crew. At least, he said he did. And at least one of 'em's the man he's got in the ring."

Ray glanced up toward the ring and saw the smaller fighter, the one he'd assumed was at a severe disadvantage, hammering his opponent with a deadly-fast combination of punches. "Using his fighters to boost church vans," he muttered. "Now I've seen it all."

**

38

When the last match had been fought and the loser dragged away unconscious, the bleachers emptied in a matter of seconds. Enraged and delighted bettors grouped together around the ring, haggling over winnings, shoving at one another. The air was cloudy with smoke and the smell of spilled beer and sweat. Lisa didn't argue when Eddie looped an arm around her shoulders and steered her out of the barn and back into the welcome coolness of the night. The field came alive with humans and trucks, headlights slicing brightly through the dark.

"Be glad your old man wouldn't let you bet," Eddie said to Johnny as they found a spot in the shadow of the barn in which to wait for the others. "You'd be what, five hundred in the hole?"

"Shut up." Johnny waved him off. "Would not."

Lisa tuned them out as they continued to give each other shit. She scuffed a booted toe through the dirt and reflected on the scene that she couldn't shake out of her head; of all the matches she'd watched tonight, it was Lynx standing over the huge, fallen Monster that she saw every time she blinked.

She wasn't easily impressed – by anyone – but she hadn't expected to see a boxer of that caliber fighting in an underground gambling match. She admired raw talent, in all its forms.

When her father, uncle and Sly emerged from the barn, she pushed herself away from the wall she'd propped against, ears pricked. Ray didn't talk about certain things in front of her, like the "business" he and Mark discussed in their office back at the house, but she always hoped to catch meaningful glances and hints of conversation. She watched Sly and Eddie trade some silent communication with a look.

"Dad." Even in the shadows, she watched his face change, saw his features shift into the mask he wore when he was her father, transitioning away from his lawyer face, his working face, his intimidating face. It always stung a bit to think that he had to be different people, that he didn't trust her the way he trusted the guys. "How much did you win tonight?"

He twitched a smile as he moved forward through the others and put an arm across her shoulders, leading the group back toward the truck. "None. I wasn't betting tonight."

"You shoulda bet on that Lynx guy," she said. "That was...amazing."

He snorted and she didn't know what he meant by it.

It was always the same after every fight: as the adrenaline bled out of his system, Drew was left with an achy, empty feeling that had nothing to do with sore muscles and lucky punches. When his opponent lumbered out of the ring, clutching his bloodied face, he wasn't filled with a sense of pride or accomplishment. Drew was good at what he did, but he wasn't The Lynx any other time save those few minutes when his life and livelihood were dependent on his performance. When the action stopped, the excitement went away.

"How's the hand?" Ricky asked from behind the wheel.

Drew flattened his palm against his knee and watched his fingers tremble. "Fine," he lied. He knew Ricky didn't want the truth, only some version of it.

"Good." The tires hissed as they pulled off the gravel drive and back onto a real road. The headlights cut a path through the dark, showing them the way back to civilization. Ricky offered no praise or gratitude for the victory Drew had just won; instead, he cleared his throat and said, "I think I found someone to unload the new merchandise on. You'll meet them Wednesday."

And he would. Because it didn't matter how many men he took down in the ring. Out of it, Drew wasn't a fighter. He wasn't much of anything, really.

5

Lisa had an unconscious sleeping routine: she always ended up facing the window, on her side, the covers pulled up to her chin, one hand beneath the pillow, the other fisted up on the sheets beside her head. The encroaching, gray light of dawn had pulled her up out of sleep only minutes before, but she knew it was time to get up when she felt something cold and wet press against the side of her hand. A smile touched her lips.

"What?" she asked, voice a croak.

There was a soft *thump* and the mattress dipped. Lisa cracked her eyes and Hektor's sleek, seal-like head was a dark wedge in the shadows of her bedroom. He had his chin rested on the sheet and when her eyes opened, he responded, nub of a tail wagging, tall, lean body wiggling. He snorted and rooted under her covers. Who needed an alarm clock when you had a ninety-four pound Doberman?

"Is it time to get up?" she asked, as per routine, and the dog withdrew his head and backed up. He snorted and then executed an elaborate stretch that ended in a yawn and an impatient snap of his teeth. "Okay, okay." She sat up, waited for her vision to clear, then flipped back the covers while her dog pranced happily around the room.

Hektor – named after the fabled Hektor of Troy – had been a present from her parents. Their first year back in the old Russell family house in Cartersville had been one of empty pockets and hard adjustments. With the exception of Morgan, all of her friends had disowned her after she'd admitted to them, that, since her father had been disbarred, they could no longer afford to stay in Alpharetta. Leaving Tristan's cheating ass at the altar hadn't helped her social situation either. So she'd thrown herself into work: a waitressing gig, a bartending gig, a summer or two as a horse camp volunteer. She'd slaved over the house with her family, breathing new life into the warped wood and haunted halls. The place would never be a posh mansion, but it had a certain amount of old South charm to it.

Six months after the huge change in all their lives, Ray had come home with a thirteen-week-old puppy in his arms that was as long-legged and clumsy as a foal. His freshly-cropped ears had been taped up and he hadn't slept through the night the whole first week, but Lisa had been in love. Hektor was her baby, her guardian, her – as pitiful as it sometimes sounded – friend. He forced her to have a routine, which was good. Otherwise, there had been times she thought she might have gone crazy.

"I'm coming," she told him as she stepped into a pair of flip-flops and cinched her light robe around her waist. The house was full of original hardwood floors and poorly insulated to boot, so even in summer, it was cool at night. Lisa rubbed at her arms on her way across the room, fighting off a chill. Her mother said she was always cold because she was too skinny, but she didn't believe that. She was sticking with the haunted-house-cold-pockets theory.

This early in the morning, the house was full of whispered sounds: running water from down the hall at her parents' room, the dull droning of Johnny's radio, Uncle Mark rifling through drawers in the bathroom. The upstairs was a large horseshoe hall with a sitting area at the top of the stairs. As Lisa followed her dog, she glanced through the unadorned windows above the little cluster of chairs on the balcony and could still see a sliver of moon visible in the rapidly-lightening sky.

Hektor's nails clicked on the wooden staircase that curved down and around to the first floor, Lisa's flip-flops slapping loudly behind him. Ground level was shrouded in deep, black shadows, the wingback chairs in the sitting room looking almost humanoid to her cautious eyes as she went to the front door and punched the release code into the alarm system's keypad. The motion detector chimed as she let Hektor loose and then closed the door again. She locked the deadbolt before she returned upstairs; Ray had raised a prudent child, but *not* a frightened one.

Cheryl was coming down the stairs as she ascended, also in a robe, her own flip-flops made out of fleece so they made no sound. For one moment, Lisa was struck by how twin-like they seemed. *You're turning into your mother faster than you thought*, she told herself, but then shook the thought away.

"Bagel or toast?" Cheryl asked, pausing. The soft bit of color on her eyelids, even in the shadows, proved she already had her makeup on, and her hair fell in soft, perfect sheets around her shoulders. Southern women got up and put their faces on, by God.

"Apple," Lisa said, beginning her climb again.

"Ugh, you're not going to go on another of your diets, are you? Because, honey, you really can't stand to lose any more weight."

"No," she lied, still climbing.

By the time she'd gathered clothes for the day, the bathroom was free, though fogged up with rolling clouds of steam left over from Uncle Mark's shower. The humidity was already going cold and the showerhead leaked with a sick-sounding *plunk* every three seconds or so. Lisa set her clothes on top of a clean towel and tried to ignore the little bristles of hair and shaving cream scum her uncle had left behind that morning. Every day she cleaned the bathroom, and every day the boys messed it up again.

This morning she scrutinized her reflection in a way she hadn't done in a long, long time. She primped and applied her sheer lipstick twice, frowned and couldn't get her hair to twist the way she wanted it. She was not usually this self-conscious.

An image from the night before, of the Lynx cartwheeled through his mind without warning. What would a guy like that – what would *he* – think of her hair this morning? Why did she even care?

"You're being stupid," she told herself with a scowl that turned her brows to angry dark slashes over her green eyes.

"Yep, you always are." Johnny pushed open the cracked door and shuffled in behind her, his reflection staggering past hers in the mirror.

"You could knock, you know," she scolded.

"Could, but won't."

"Well hurry up. You're supposed to be at work the same time I am."

The others were all in the kitchen when she went downstairs. Someone had let Hektor back in the house and he was laying half under the table, gnawing on a rawhide chew. Cheryl was at the stove, trying her best to live up to Southern housewife stereotypes, steam curling up from the skillets she stirred; Lisa smelled eggs, bacon and potatoes. Her stomach rumbled, but she picked a granny smith apple out of the basket on the counter and sat down next to her dad.

"Morning, sweetheart," Uncle Mark greeted her. He was only a few years younger than his brother, but he looked even younger than that. He was tan and dark-haired, his eyes green. They almost could have been twins. "You're not eating?"

Ray gave her a sharp look.

"I'm making food," Cheryl said, turning away from the stove, her expression perturbed. "You're eating."

Lisa rolled her eyes and earned an elbow from her dad for it. She bit into her apple with a loud *crack* and let her gaze wander across the kitchen – she'd become an expert at averting her eyes, pretending to be fascinated by the décor when her father and uncle had to whisper some bit of something important under their breath.

Their kitchen here in the old house was nothing like the one they'd had in Alpharetta. Old, antebellum houses tended to have small kitchens by comparison and this one was no exception. It was a narrow rectangle that mirrored the shape of the long, plank table they'd situated between two walls of cabinetry. The cupboards were original and had been painted and lined with contact paper, retrofitted with new hardware, but they still looked almost antique. The countertops were butcher's block. A single window above the sink overlooked the side yard where Cheryl had planted her herb garden. The floor was linoleum meant to resemble marble. The appliances were new, but were white, not the posh, modern stainless of current kitchen fashions. Lisa had seen her mother wipe a tear from the corner of her mascara-lined eye on the day the fridge had been delivered, her one show of weakness.

It was not a glamorous kitchen, but it was comfortable. Lived-in and loved. And like all kitchens in the South, it was the hub of their household; the place where all the important conversations happened, where visitors gathered and meals were shared.

A plate landed on the table beneath her nose and the smell of finely-chopped potatoes cooked with sautéed onions turned the apple to lead in her mouth. She took another bite anyway.

"So, Uncle Mark."

He twitched his dark brows and the movement put creases in his forehead.

"Have you got parts lined up for the Trans Am?"

He swallowed and nodded, a smile breaking across his face. "Some of them. And I think I got a lead on a new rear axle."

She returned the smile, feeling some of his excitement for herself. "When you redo the paint are you going to – "

"Put the eagle back on? Absolutely."

"Thing's a hick-mobile," Ray said, but he grinned. "You couldn't give the damn thing to me."

"Good, 'cause I'm not gonna."

"Eat," Cheryl said, sitting down across from Lisa.

"I'm eating."

"Eat the *carbs*."

All of them living together wasn't so much a choice as a monetary necessity. And sometimes, Lisa just wished she could have a moment without someone else's voice in her head. Eat more, don't drink too much, get enough sleep, be careful…it never ended.

Ray could tell there was something his wife was having trouble holding in all through breakfast. She'd been asleep when he'd climbed into bed the night before, and downstairs already when he'd awakened, but there was a storm brewing behind her dark eyes and he was glad she waited until they were alone, Mark and the kids headed for work, before she let the reins slip through her fingers.

"You took Lisa to the fights last night, didn't you?" she said without preamble, her head titled down toward her plate, but her eyes locked on his.

There was really no lying to Cheryl – she never bought it and it only intensified the argument. Not that this was an argument yet, but Ray knew it could turn into one if he wasn't careful.

"Yes."

She pressed her lips together into a thin line and sighed through her nostrils. "She's a girl, Ray."

"Huh. Hadn't noticed."

"Don't even start that," Cheryl warned. She didn't raise her voice, but there was a knife edge to it. She set her fork down and leaned back in her chair, pegging him with a look that left him wanting to squirm in his chair; he didn't. "You know what I mean."

He set his coffee down with a sigh. "Aren't you supposed to take up her feminist torch? Tell me how I shouldn't treat her like a girl?"

Cheryl clicked her long, red-painted nails against the table top. "She *is* a girl." She gave him a sharp look. "A very petite, very pretty girl, and I don't care how much she likes cars or boxing or any of that; if she falls in with the wrong kind of boy, if she gets drug off to – "

Ray cut her off with a wave. He knew what she was getting at: Lisa was little and had the upper body strength of a toddler. "She's still on her single crusade."

"But – "

But that wouldn't much matter if someone tried to snatch her. "I know." His voice was firm. "I know, alright? We never left her alone." He shook his head, frowning. "I try to keep her away from shit like that." Cheryl raised her brows. "But she listens about as well as you do."

She held his gaze, unblinking, for a long moment, then a smile finally curved her lips. She turned away, presenting him with her graceful profile. Her long, straight mahogany hair was pulled back at the crown of her head and fell free at her shoulders, chin-length strands floating around her face. Her eyes turned from chocolate to amber as she faced the light coming in from the French doors. "I'd deny that," she said, "but it's true."

Ray smiled. Sometimes, like now, he saw her without the lines that time and sun had pressed into her pretty face, without the worries she had as a wife and mother. She was twenty-two again and trying to hide a smile because he'd told her she was every bit as stubborn as her father, who refused to acknowledge their marriage and was trying to press an annulment on them.

"I just worry about her," Cheryl admitted, glancing at him again. "I hate that bar job she has – it's only two Lucite-heeled steps away from stripping and I just..." She heaved a tired-sounding sigh. "I never wanted her to struggle. The way we did."

"Everybody struggles." At least his daughter wasn't struggling the way *he* had: no parents, an irresponsible little brother with bad taste in women. "Lis is fine."

47

6

Drew had never been into the bar scene. He was on a strict training diet comprised of lean proteins, vegetables and lots of water. Every bite he put into his mouth was designed to build muscle or keep fat at bay; his body was a temple and all that – well, not really, but it *was* his livelihood. Because of that, he didn't drink much; it was just sugar and carbs and a headache he couldn't afford to have.

But tonight, one of Ricky's other fighters, Josh, wanted to stop off at this place he'd been talking about for weeks. They'd made a run out to the warehouse to check inventory, and without a way home besides his feet, Drew couldn't protest when Josh turned the van into a parking lot so full that people were pulling up onto curbs and medians. The long, dark building in front of them was massive and windowless, the only light coming from an orange neon sign above the door that labeled the place as the Double Vision.

"They're s'posed to have seriously hot girls workin' in here," Josh said as he threw the van in park and killed the ignition. They were double parked behind another car, but Drew didn't caution him against it. "Or," Josh chuckled, "maybe you could give a shit."

Drew met the other boxer's gaze across the van, the whites of the guy's eyes shining in the darkness, teeth gleaming as he smiled nastily. *Asshole*, Drew thought. He stared him down until Josh became uncomfortable enough to look away and climb out of the van.

The lot was full of people: patrons coming and going, smokers out for some "fresh" air, and what Drew guessed were underage kids hoping to slip into the door when no one was looking. There'd be no sneaking for them, he realized, as they approached the door. Josh had talked about Double Vision as if it were some dive bar, but it was now obvious that this was a nightclub that had been *modeled after* a dive bar. Bouncers with headsets stood stationed on either side of the door – burly, well-over-six-foot meatheads in STAFF t-shirts – watching a knot of bearded, leather-clad biker types who lingered on the sidewalk.

They were out in the suburbs, not downtown, so there wasn't a line wrapped around the building. But one of the bouncers halted them with a raised hand the size of a dinner plate and asked to see IDs.

"Really, dude?" Josh asked as he dug for his wallet in his jeans pocket. "We look underage to you?"

"Just policy," the bouncer said in a voice that sounded like a diesel engine turning over. He'd most likely been a fighter at some point. His broken nose gave testament to being hit, and his size led Drew to believe he'd done more hitting than what he'd received.

"You too, cupcake," the other bouncer said, and Drew pulled out his wallet, flashed his license and followed Josh inside the bar.

The interior was everything the exterior was not: a riot of color and sound. The doors opened up onto an elevated platform that seemed to stretch to the left and right and go on forever, most likely wrapping around the whole perimeter of the club. Tables and couches served as seating for patrons who'd obviously wanted a more intimate setting than the main floor provided. At their feet, wide, wooden steps inset with lights led down to a crushing sea of humanity.

The bar was a monolithic wooden rectangle at the heart of the structure. Ringed by stools, draped with colored Christmas lights and centered around a pyramid of liquor bottles. A half a dozen girls worked behind it in short cutoffs and halter tops, pouring draft beer and rattling cocktail shakers, all of them coiffed, painted and smiling.

To the right of the bar, pool tables and a stage marked a gaming area. A dance floor, round tables and booths filled up the left wing.

Drew turned his head side-to-side three times, and noticed something different on all three passes: the karaoke machine, the photo booth, the beer pong setup, the stripper poles. Double Vision was an odd cross between a frat boys' paradise and an old west saloon. He saw cowboy types and preppy jocks shuffling around in the crowd below.

"Really?" he asked, giving Josh a sideways look. "You just had to come in *here*?"

"What? It's great!"

Drew didn't argue – he wasn't big into arguing – and followed Josh as he descended the stairs and then wove a path between bodies on the main floor. They found two empty stools at the bar and of course Josh hopped on the one beside the hot blonde in the denim miniskirt, leaving Drew to sit beside the fat trucker-looking guy in the CAT t-shirt.

A bartender was in front of them the moment their asses touched their seats, little white cocktail napkins at the ready that she set before them. "What can I get you gentlemen to drink?"

She was on the small side – no doubt she was wearing the same platforms as the girls Drew had seen walking out amongst the crowds – and she was thin, fit-looking. Her tan arms and legs were lean and tight with muscle. She looked like someone who spent time outside, who got real sun and not tanning bed rays, who liked exercise, and oddly, that was what he noticed about her first. Then he registered the thin, delicately-boned face, the big green eyes. Her long, dark hair was pulled back in the front and fell loose down her back in big twists. Her voice had sounded genuine enough, but her eyes were guarded, her expression one of polite, but forced, interest. Drew made a living out of reading other people, anticipating their moves, their thoughts, no matter how hard they tried to disguise them, and this girl looked like she'd rather be anywhere but behind this bar, serving drinks.

"Lemme get a gin and tonic," Josh said, and Drew watched the bartender's eyes move toward his fellow boxer.

"Okay." She dipped her head in acknowledgment, but there was something about the twist of her small smile that made Drew want to grin too. *Bitch drink*, he'd thought the second the order left Josh's mouth, and he wondered if the girl thought the same. "What about you?" She flashed him a bright white set of teeth and a big dose of fake sincerity.

"Beer. In a bottle."

She lifted her brows and tapped chipped, red nails on the bar top. *What kind?* Her stance asked.

"Just whatever's closest."

Her lips parted and she looked like she was about to speak, but then something flashed across her face, some thought that narrowed her eyes and cocked her head to the side. She looked him over, all of him that was visible from her side of the bar, and then nodded. "Good way to end up with Pabst Blue," she said, and moved away.

Lynx. It was him – the boxer she'd marveled over just the night before. Lisa had caught a glimpse of two men standing at the top of the stairs, just a chance flash of clear sight in which she'd registered two men entering the bar, and she'd wondered if maybe the fighter had been one of them. She'd dashed the thought instantly, chalking it up to another mental hiccup akin to her critical self-assessment in front of the mirror that morning. But now that she'd seen him up close, on a stool just across the cracked wooden bar top from her, she was certain her mind wasn't playing tricks on her. And she was also certain she cared *waaaay* too much that this guy had come into Double Vision.

A wide, stainless-topped island held the liquor in the center of the bar and she went there first to mix the G&T. "Hey." One of the other bartenders, Trish – a thickset redhead who carried her weight well and detracted from it with teased hair and bold accessories – sidled up to Lisa. "You got any limes over where you are? I'm out and these bachelorette bitches I'm 'tending are going through the Cuervo like crazy."

"Maybe." Lisa twisted around mid-pour without spilling so much as a drop of gin with the intention of checking the plastic tub of lemons and limes stowed beneath the bar top over at her post. Instead, her eyes went to Lynx.

"Ooh," she heard Trish say and felt a light elbow in her ribs. "He's hot."

She hadn't been actively thinking that, but at Trish's comment, she reassessed the boxer. He didn't have the typical roadmap of broken facial bones that most fighters did. The little bump halfway down the ridge of his nose looked genetic rather than the result of a break. His dark hair was buzzed so close to his scalp it was only a shadow on top of his head. He had surprisingly big, dark eyes, not the slanted pig eyes of a dumb jock.

And then she almost smiled when she realized she'd looked at his face first and that Trish had probably been drawn by the bundles and cords of taut muscle visible beneath his shirt.

"I guess," Lisa said, noncommittal, as she faced her task again, finishing off the drink with a little splash of tonic water.

"You guess you have limes or you guess he's hot?" Trish smiled and waggled her auburn brows. Her eye shadow was the same color of blue as her halter top – her halter top that flashed enough cleavage to make a man's eyes pop out of his head. Sourly, she reminded herself that Trish was feminine and bold and hot, whereas she was not – she was just a skinny girl who loved cars, who, besides, wanted nothing to do with men right now anyway – and the frown that had been threatening fell away.

"I've got limes," she said. "Lemme get these orders filled and I'll bring you some."

"'Kay." As Trish returned to her post, a wide smile painted on her face, she swayed side-to-side as she walked, keeping time with the Mötley Crüe song that crackled through the speakers and pulsed up through the floorboards.

Growing up, Lisa had never tried to compete with other girls. She was addicted to nail polish and loved makeup, had her own particular fashion code, but she'd never tried to be sexy like the other girls, never tried to outdo any of them. Here at work, with her padded bra and uniform heels, she felt like she was being forced to compete...and coming up short. The thought was as effective as a bucket of ice water dumped over her head; as she dropped a swizzle stick into the mixed drink and grabbed a Bud from the cooler, she smoothed her expression into one of serene indifference. She approached her customers without any real interest. So Lynx was a damn good fighter – that was all he was.

"Gin and tonic." Lisa set the drink on its napkin and earned a nod from the blonde who'd ordered it before he returned his attention to the girl beside him. "And for you." She couldn't stop her smile, so she turned it into a smirk instead. "Beer. Whatever was closest."

"Thanks." The boxer had a deep, deep voice. A raise-the-hair-on-your-neck, don't-want-to-hear-it-in-a-dark-alley kind of voice. It gave Lisa pause, held her in place just long enough that she watched his eyes lock onto hers without so much as one inappropriate glance at what her pushup bra was doing for her chest.

Dangerous, she warned herself, even though she didn't break eye contact. And the danger had nothing to do with him and everything to do with her own sudden wish that she was a better flirt.

"Do I know you from somewhere?" he finally asked, frowning. The expression pulled his brows tight over his eyes, made him look more threatening.

"No." She twitched a quick smile and forced her eyes away. "We've never met. Excuse me."

In an almost rude haste, she pulled the tub of citrus from beneath the bar and did an about face.

She *did not* rush away from the boxer, she reasoned. She slowed her steps purposefully, putting some hip action into her walk as she made her way toward Trish. And she *did not* keep her eyes down as she moved around to the other side of the bar and pretended to search for a bottle of Patrón.

Lisa shuffled bottles around until she glanced up through the gaps in the glass pyramid and saw Trish in front of Lynx and his friend, winding a lock of red hair around a finger, one wide hip propped against the bar. She was laying the charm on thick, and Lisa felt both relieved and agitated.

Disgusted with herself, she untied her apron and stowed it beneath the bar. "I'm taking my break," she told a fellow employee, Jackie of the giant fake breasts and streaming platinum hair, who passed behind her.

"You're gonna miss the Roundup!" Jackie called to her retreating back in a sing-song voice.

"Good."

The Double Vision was a zoo at all times. Even on a dead night, the place was packed with humanity, and tonight was far from dead. Most of the girls took their breaks out back, in the dark shadows beside the dumpster, with a cigarette and pilfered beer. The actual break room was a dimly-lit, grungy dungeon of a room and Lisa only stayed there long enough each night to both stow and retrieve her bags. She didn't smoke and the back alley that stank of garbage had no appeal for her, so she skirted around the dance floor and up an illuminated set of steps to the catwalk that ran around the perimeter of the bar. There, she climbed further up a narrow staircase that was roped off from the public, up to the glass-walled booth where DJ Twist spun live five nights a week, though most patrons assumed the music ran on a preset loop without any human involvement.

Trevor Stiles sat behind the built-in electronics panel that controlled every aspect of the music he played – bass and treble, volume. There were black lights and disco balls that operated off switches he could flip. Lisa had long ago given up trying to figure out the function of every knob and dial of his station.

"Hey, T," she greeted, dragging a wheeled chair over beside his and plopping down into it once she'd sealed the door behind her.

"What up, girl?" Trevor was six-three and as skinny as a broom handle. His mixed Hispanic and black heritage had left him with skin the color of milk chocolate that looked a shade darker up here in the deep, dark confines of the DJ booth. He wore his hair in short cornrows that ended at the base of his skull. Tonight, as on all work nights, he was dressed in baggy dark jeans and a long, Affliction look-a-like shirt that

54

had the Double Vision logo done in bleeding orange letters surrounded by artistic swirls and leaf patterns. His headphones were hooked around his neck, the Rihanna song that was playing out in the bar sounding tinny and far-away as it whispered from them.

"Nothing." Lisa was straddling the chair and she folded her arms over the back of it, chin resting on her crossed wrists. "I'm on break."

He grinned, white teeth flashing, and turned back to his instrument panel. "You just happen to go on break right before I flip the Roundup switch?" He chuckled.

"They don't need me in the T & A parade down there," she said with a disdainful snort.

Trevor laughed again. "You sure? You can still make it down there if you want."

"Nope. Flip away."

As he stopped the track currently playing and began punching buttons, Lisa's eyes swept out through the window to the shuffling crowd below. The regular lights dimmed and the black lights came on. The disco balls dropped. Colored lights began revolving, throwing spots of red, blue and yellow across the floor. Trevor pulled the mike on its little stand over in front of his face and Lisa chuckled as he donned his announcer voice.

"You guys know what time it is?"

Even through the walls, glass and wood, she could hear the roar.

"Alright, girls, you ready for a Roundup?!"

Lisa had no idea why this ridiculous, over-the-top, cheesy tradition had begun. Probably because the bar's owner wished he owned a strip club but couldn't get the license approval and wanted to push the limits as much as possible. But whether she disapproved or not, the Roundup was going to happen. As the opening guitar strains of Jason Aldean's "She's Country" flooded through the speakers and echoed off every flat surface in the place, bartenders and waitresses alike abandoned their posts and rushed to form a rough line that stretched from one end of the bar to the other.

Trevor pushed the mike away and hooked his headphones around his neck again, still smiling as he reclined in his chair. "It's a beautiful thing," he said, more to himself than to her.

"It's a stupid thing," Lisa countered.

She knew the dance by heart – of course she did – she'd had to learn it as part of her interview process when applying for the job. So in her head, she counted off beats and imagined herself spinning and dropping and shaking her ass along with her fellow employees. It wasn't that raunchy; the choreography wasn't even worthy of a child's theater production, and most of the girls were poor, poor dancers, but the male customers only seemed to care about the possibility of a wardrobe malfunction. And all the sultry looks the girls tossed over their shoulders between moves.

"There a reason you're extra uptight tonight?" Trevor asked. When Lisa glanced at him sideways, his grin was still there, but it had become probing and thoughtful. "Your bitch-ass boy didn't come back in here, did he?"

She had to grin, just for a moment. Several weeks before, Tristan had come in, and he'd been sure to toss verbal barbs at her across the bar for the benefit of his laughing friends. They'd been cheap, unintelligent barbs, but they'd stung all the same. "No," she assured, glancing back out through the window again. "I just..." *might have a mild crush on a total stranger who is no one I need to ever meet* "...dunno," she finished lamely.

He shrugged. "You can stay up here till you figure it out, then."

Drew threw back three beers over the course of the two hours he suffered inside Double Vision. He didn't really suffer, but he just didn't care about the place. Josh got cozy with the girl he'd been sitting beside and disappeared for a while, leaving Drew to let his eyes wander over the crowd. The little brunette who'd brought him his first beer never came back, and he found himself thinking that was a shame because he would have liked to see her participate in the group line dance or whatever the hell it was. She looked like she could move – lithe and fit – and would have done the routine better justice than the wiggly redhead who served his drinks the rest of the night.

"Where'd you go?" he asked Josh when the guy finally returned to the bar.

The blonde boxer threw back the last of his drink that he'd left on the bar – Drew secretly hoped someone had drugged it, thinking it was a chick's drink – and jerked his head toward the door. "Got a call from Ricky." He had to nearly shout to be heard over the music as they began making their way toward the staircase.

Drew lifted his brows in surprise as he stepped between two girls who were clearly drunk and dancing together. One of them made a grab at his arm, but he slid out of her grasp. "Really? What'd he want?"

"That guy you're supposed to meet tomorrow. Russell?" They reached the bottom step and started to climb.

"Yeah?"

"Rick says he used to be a lawyer."

"So." Ricky sold stolen merch to all kinds of buyers, even high-and-mighty lawyer types.

They paused at the top of the steps and customers coming in had to break around them, some throwing them nasty looks. Josh gave him what he thought was a very pointed, meaningful glance. "He doesn't want you to meet him tomorrow night. He says show up at the guy's shop instead – some garage in Alpharetta. He'll email you the address."

Drew frowned. "Why? And why didn't he call *me*?"

"Dunno." Josh shrugged and moved toward the double front doors, leaving Drew to follow.

Outside, the night was as dark and thick as swamp water, though it smelled faintly of honeysuckle and largely of exhaust fumes. The dull glow of street lamps kept the stars from being visible and the sky was a dull blanket thrown over the world. Patrons weaved between cars, laughing and talking loudly.

"I'm calling him," Drew said as they headed toward the van.

Josh shot him a scowl, his pretty-boy face drawing up in a not-so-pretty way. "Do what you want. Just tellin' you what I know."

The roundabout message delivery didn't sit right with Drew at all. He was a straightforward kind of guy – he met the people he was supposed to meet, delivered the product he was supposed to deliver without question and without incident. Ricky should have called *him*, rather than going through Josh – who couldn't be trusted with anything. And Ricky should have stuck to protocol, or at least offered some sort of reasoning for the break…

Something caught Drew's eye across the parking lot and he couldn't say what it was until he halted and pivoted toward it. There was a dark Ford truck parked beneath a streetlamp and there was a girl standing beside it. She closed the partially open truck door and hiked a bag up on her shoulder, turning to head back toward the bar. She was dressed like the waitresses and bartenders, in short cutoffs and a yellow halter top that showed a lot of skin. He registered the petite frame and long, thin, tan legs. The flash of dark hair that looked coal black in the shadows as her locks flipped over her shoulder and fanned across her back.

It was the brunette who'd brought him his first beer and he was again struck by how much he liked looking at her. A smile touched his lips as he watched her fidget with the straps of her bra and make a face. She paused to bend forward at the waist, her hair tumbling like a waterfall, and adjusted her bra, top and breasts before straightening.

Her head came up and even across the shadowed parking lot, he knew she saw him because she stopped mid-stride, a platform sandal hovering over the asphalt.

Her expression changed – self-conscious or nervous or just plain curious, he couldn't tell – but then she started forward again, her steps quick and ground covering, athletic.

Drew watched her until she was back to the sidewalk, and by that time, she was nearly jogging in her haste to get back inside.

He frowned, released a sigh through his nostrils. There were two types of women he came across in his line of…"work": the ones who loved him for purely physical reasons, and the ones who were terrified of him. It looked like this girl fell under the terrified category, and that was a shame…

"Dude!" Josh called. "You coming or what?"

"Yeah."

7

Hektor looked like a dead dog, flopped on his side on the asphalt of the parking lot, unmoving, soaking up morning sun. If Lisa squinted, she could see his ribcage swell with each breath and knew he was alive. She smiled. She didn't bring him to work every day because the patrons of the shops on either side of them, though separated by grass medians, were terrified of the Doberman. The deli bitch next door had threatened to call animal control one afternoon when Hektor had wandered over into her parking lot after a scrap of dropped sandwich.

"He's supposed to be in the office with you," Ray commented as he stepped in through the connecting door from the first garage bay.

Lisa had her feet propped on the desk, reclining in her swivel chair, and tipped her head over the back of it so she was looking at her dad upside down. He was in jeans and a short-sleeved plaid button-up that he wore open over a black t-shirt. Though it had been three years since he'd worn a suit and tie to work, Lisa still half expected to see him in Armani with Gucci wingtips when she glanced his way at the garage.

"He likes the sun," she countered, and sat back up in the chair, looking out at her dog over the pointed tips of her Tony Lama cowboy boots.

"He's gonna get heat stroke."

"Nope. He's smarter than Johnny."

Ray snorted; Johnny had taken a nap in the backseat of a car two summers ago and had to be rushed to the ER for IV fluids after a literal bout of heat stroke. "I coulda killed that little shit that day."

"Almost didn't have to."

"True."

She listened to his boots on the gritty tile as he moved around the side of the desk. He crossed to the window and blocked her view, presumably looking at Hektor. "Slow day?" he asked, nodding toward her very non-busy pose, the flying toasters screen saver that was up on the computer.

Lisa took note of the casual way he propped a shoulder against the wall and knew it was a ruse: He might have been a high-priced attorney once upon a time who made a living fooling other people, but he couldn't fool his family. Blood recognized blood. "Classic car restoration's not exactly in high demand."

"True."

Lisa frowned and pulled her boots down off the desk, sitting fully upright. "What's up?" she asked. It wasn't like Ray to repeat himself, unless it was to make a point, and he looked too distracted at the moment for that to be the case.

He stared out at the parking lot. Lisa followed his line of sight and saw that a car had pulled in and that Hektor had gone to greet the driver. The driver who had the door open and was contemplating whether it was smart to climb all the way out.

"Why don't you take an early lunch? And take the dog with you," Ray said. It didn't sound like a friendly request.

She stood, the wheels of the desk chair clacking as they rolled across the tile. Through the window, she watched the car's driver finally get up the courage to wave Hektor away and stand. Lisa knew who he was in an instant. She slowed down the whirring gears in her brain, took stock of the unremarkable late model blue Impala he was driving, the navy t-shirt that was visible beneath the halves of his unzipped hoodie. *It's too warm for a sweatshirt,* she thought to herself. But then her eyes went to his face and she stopped prolonging the inevitable conclusion that the boxer who called himself The Lynx was giving her dog a wary glance and starting toward the office.

"Shit," Ray muttered, shoving away from the wall. He didn't run and he didn't look panicked – that would have been too out of character – but he crossed the office in three strides.

"Stay in here," he told her, voice clipped. "When he comes in, don't get up. Tell him none of us are here."

"Dad." Her pulse kick started in her ears as she read his sudden urgency. "What's going on?"

"Nothing you need to worry about." He paused halfway out the door and gave her a commanding look over his shoulder. "*Do not* get up," he repeated, and then disappeared into the garage.

Lisa half rose out of her chair, and then sat back down, cursing her own obedience but too startled to do anything but listen. A glance out the window revealed that Lynx was drawing closer, Hektor trailing at his heels, hackles up, ready to leap on the stranger if need be. The office ran perpendicular to the garage bays and gave the building a shortened L-shape. The front door was glass, but tinted, and she knew Lynx couldn't see her through it. So she took a moment to compose herself, hands on the desk, deep breaths moving in and out through her nostrils with measured slowness. To her left, past the water cooler and mini fridge, the partially open door that led into the garage gave her ears access to an unusual silence. The radio had been switched off and the momentary surge of voices that had stirred up at Ray's entrance had quieted as well. There were no clangs and bangs, no whines of air hoses and hydraulic lifts. The garage had gone dead as if with a flick of a switch.

She wasn't afraid of the boxer – as strongly as he'd fought in the ring, there wasn't anything outwardly threatening about him – but her stomach sank as he reached for the door handle, a kind of dread she couldn't name catching her breath. She had the sense that something bad was about to happen, and hated that the sensation was so vague as to be *bad*, and not more certain than that. But she took one more deep breath and squared her narrow shoulders as Lynx pulled open the door and stepped into the office.

The boxer hesitated a moment, the door propped against his shoulder, to let his eyes adjust to the dimness of the office. Hektor took the opportunity to slide past the guy's leg and come in, his nails clicking against the tile. He came to Lisa's side at the desk and sat, ears pricked, watchful.

"Hey." Lynx stepped fully inside and let the door swing shut, the little chime above sounding again. "I'm looking for –" She knew he recognized her then, because his eyes widened to the size of half dollars, the dark chocolate of the irises looking almost black in the shadows. *He has nice, good-sized eyes*, she thought. *When he's not freaked out.* She hated little pig eyes on horses, and on people too, apparently.

"For...?" She pretended she'd never seen him before in her life, hoping that, given how dark it had been in the bar the night before, he would start to think maybe he'd never seen her before either.

"Um..." He reached up to scratch at the back of his head, the bunching of the muscles in his arm visible even under his sweatshirt. "Is Ray here? Ray Russell?"

Lisa wondered, idly, if her father ever took for granted the fact that she would cover for him at all times. "No," she said, and made a deliberate show of swiveling her chair toward the computer, hands going to the keyboard.

"Oh." She snuck a glance from the corner of her eye and watched him wipe the confusion off his face. When he spoke again, he was more composed than he had been – her coldness had had the intended effect. "When's he gonna be in? I need to talk to him."

"Don't know." She could sound like a real bitch when she wanted to, as Eddie and Sly often pointed out to her. "Pretty sure he's not coming in today."

She heard his sneakers shift on the tile. "Doesn't he work here?"

"No, he owns the place." In a feat of acting that made her both proud and remorseful, she did a slow half-turn and forced her eyes to move up from his shoes to his face in a way that would appear almost disgusted. "Unless you have business for us – which, judging by that soccer mom thing you drove in here, you don't – then I'm gonna have to ask you to leave."

He didn't back down right away, and for one tense moment, Lisa started to worry that he would fight her on it. But finally, he afforded her one last hooded look – which could have been the result of a bruised ego or disbelief – and left, Hektor settling down on the floor with a little grumble once he was gone. Only once his car was turning back onto the street did her dad reappear.

"Good job." Ray's voice startled her. She'd been staring through the window, watching Lynx leave, and whipped her head around to see her father striding casually back into the office, hands in his jeans pockets. Mark followed him, his garage shirt with his name sewn over the breast pocket unbuttoned over a white undershirt, toweling his hands on a greasy rag.

"What was he doing here?" She wasn't so quick to take the praise and pretend like nothing weird had happened.

Ray didn't look at her, but stared out the window, a frown pressing deep grooves in the skin around his mouth. "Musta been some kind of miscommunication."

Uncle Mark turned and offered her one of his patented smiles.

Lisa sighed. "Something shady's going on and no one's gonna fill me in, are they?"

Ray spared her a quick, hard to read glance. "Nope. Now how 'bout you take that lunch break we talked about."

"Apparently our new friend Ricky is more resourceful than we thought."

"A lot more." Mark had taken Lisa's seat at the desk and put his oil-spattered boots up on the blotter, the chair groaning in protest. "So much more that I'll bet each of you a hundred bucks we've got the Piper to thank for our visitor today."

Sly nodded from his position leaned back against the fridge, his arms folded.

"I keep telling you guys Simon Piper is not worth trusting," Eddie said.

64

Ray sat on the edge of the desk, listening to his brother and employees without really hearing them. Their arguments made sense, but none of them had any revelations that hadn't already crossed his mind.

He had not once, not ever, invited any activity that so much as *smelled* criminal onto the lot of his brother's garage. King Customs was a completely legitimate business – not necessarily a profitable one, but there was nothing conspicuous going on. He'd practiced law too long to think that lines could be blurred without consequence. Helping out a church – whether he got paid for it or not – had nothing to do with the classic car business.

At least, that's what he'd fooled himself into thinking. Seeing a hired thug come onto the lot had planted a tight, hard knot of doubt in his chest. That, or he was having heart palpitations…but either way, they had a problem.

"I'm calling Father Morris," he said, lifting his head to find Eddie in the middle of a comment that he squelched. He and Sly might have been car thieves in a former life, but they'd been SEALs too, and they had some respect for authority. Ray stood. "He's gonna have to find someone else to get his shit back for him."

"Ray," Mark said.

"It's too big a risk."

Mark dismissed Sly and Eddie with a look. They left without protest and closed the door behind themselves. Ray thought maybe he should give them a raise, despite the lack of profits.

"Okay." Mark pulled his boots down off the desk and sat forward, elbows braced amid the stacks of paperwork Lisa hadn't finished yet. "Since when do you think anything's too big a risk?"

Ray snorted, and then stood when he realized Mark was serious and was giving him that annoying little brother stare that demanded an answer. He shoved his hands in his pockets and took casual steps toward the window, stalling until he turned and put his back against a file cabinet; he stared at his shoes until he no longer had any excuses. Mark was still

65

looking at him, his green eyes full of genuine wonder. *How has he lived this long and still stayed so…?* Ray groped through his mind for a word. His brother wasn't naïve per se, or ignorant, delusional. He just always seemed to take things at face value. That, and he had this unshakeable faith that Ray could always find a way out of every sticky situation.

"Some hired meathead," he said, "came into my business today. *Your* business. With my little girl. You know how many prisons I've been into? How many of my clients were in orange jump suits and handcuffs? That put *me* at risk; but when this Robin Hood shit is coming into my personal life, trying to reach out and touch my family…" He shook his head. "That's *too big* a risk."

8

Sly had spent the majority of his thirty-five years taking orders from someone else. He was used to it. He was good at it. It didn't bother him. Ray was his boss, the man who cut his paycheck, but it was easy to slip into a mindset in which he was his CO too.

Despite the radio, he could stand at the grill of the 1970 Mustang Fastback he was working on and hear the dull murmur of voices coming from the office. Eddie had his head down, his hands black with grease as he stripped old, dead parts out of the Ford, but he heard too. For all his money spent on hair products and obnoxious sneakers, the guy was still the Eddie O'Dell who'd jumped out of planes and executed top secret raids. He always heard, he was just smart enough to keep his thoughts to himself.

When Ray came out of the office and into the garage, scrubbing a hand over his short, thinning hair, Sly stepped away from the car and put his back against a metal shelf stacked with boxed air filters. Ray's eyes followed him.

"Everything alright?"

Ray gave a short, curt shake of his head. "I'm pulling the plug on this church thing."

Eddie bolted upright and smacked his head on the underside of the Mustang's raised hood. "Ah, shit," he hissed. "Mother..."

"Why?" Sly asked.

His boss's expression was uncharacteristically defeated, shaken almost. Sly didn't understand: He'd seen the boxer come by, and he wasn't impressed with the guy. So he could hold his own in the ring - that didn't mean shit out in the real world.

As if he could feel the calculating stare that was aimed at him, Ray shed all outward displays of emotion, and went to prop a hip against the fender of the Trans Am. He camouflaged his worries so well most of the time that Sly thought he would have made a better lieutenant than lawyer.

Either way though, he shouldn't have been giving up this easily.

"Boss," Sly said, and earned a backward look thrown over Ray's shoulder. "We can handle Ricky Bullard." And on his part, that wasn't bullshit. "If you still wanna do this, we can keep it from coming back home."

Eddie must have recovered from his fatal blow to the head, because he chimed in with, "We can."

"Ray." Mark's voice echoed from the office door behind Sly. "The girls won't get hurt. I swear."

"Oh, you swear?" Ray crossed his arms over his chest, stress threatening to put permanent furrows between his brows. "And how're you gonna make sure of that, little brother?"

The title was said with such contempt that Sly wondered, had his own brother spoken to him like that, if he'd have been able to resist taking a swing at him. But Mark put his hands in his jeans pockets and propped a shoulder in the doorjamb. "This is small potatoes, bro," he told Ray with a placid almost-smile smoothing the lines on his own face. "How many big-time assholes have you dealt with? How many *real* bad guys? You can help this church out. They have no one else to go to."

"Who?" Johnny had gone around back to search for a misplaced box of electric motors and now stood in the open roll top door, box in hand, staring at all of them curiously.

"No one," Ray finally answered him after a long stretch of silence. "Everybody back to work." He headed back for the office, but paused when he reached Sly. His green eyes bored holes into him. "Do not screw this up," he warned in a voice just above a whisper.

Sly inclined his head in the barest of nods. "Wasn't planning on it."

***

Hektor rode home that evening standing up in the small backseat of Lisa's truck, his head wedged in behind her headrest so the tip of his nose was pressed to her cracked driver's side window, breathing in the smells of their travels. Lisa propped her forearm up against the hot window glass and rested her head against her knuckles, set upon by late afternoon sleepiness and a general dissatisfaction for the day as a whole. She watched Alpharetta – and all its boutiques, coffee shops and expensive luxury cars – fade into more humble suburbs, then into pasture as she headed home. Her home of the past three years. To Cartersville. The degradation she could do without, but despite the difficulties in overhauling her life, she missed nothing about Alpharetta, or its people.

Her mother, who worked as a receptionist in a Cartersville dentist's office, was home before anyone else, as usual, and she was in the front yard as Lisa pulled into the drive, a garden hose snaking through the grass like a long, black mamba as Cheryl watered her dozens upon hundreds of flowers. Lisa parked behind the house in her usual slot – if she didn't, someone would come raid her keys out of her purse, move her truck and put it where it was supposed to be – and opened the rear suicide door so Hektor could hop down. He didn't so much hop as bound onto the pavement and took off at a gallop around toward the front of the house.

"If only I had your energy," Lisa said with a shake of her head as she slung her purse over her shoulder, shut the doors, and followed her dog at a more dignified walk up the drive and around the wide front porch.

Cheryl glanced up as she came across the yard, then her eyes went back to the yellow lantana she was tending. "Hey, baby." The sun was inching toward the horizon and its buttery, golden light caught the water streaming out of the hose and turned it to liquid crystal. Cheryl had changed into old jeans cut off at the knees, garden clogs and Ray's Allman Brothers t-shirt tied at the waist, her hair piled up on her head with a clip. "Good day?"

"Depends." Lisa found a dry patch of grass and plopped unceremoniously onto it cross-legged, her bag beside her. Hektor had been sniffing through the flower beds but came to her, snuffled at her face and then stretched out at her side. "What do you consider good?"

"That bad, huh?" Cheryl let her thumb fall away from the end of the hose and the water pressure slackened to a drizzle.

Lisa put her elbows over her thighs and rested her weight on them with a skyward sigh that ruffled her long, overgrown bangs. "Dad treats me like I'm five."

"Have you been acting five?"

She snorted. "No more than usual."

Cheryl grinned and knelt in front of the pine straw-stuffed bed that ran along the foot of the porch. Her dedication to her plants bordered on obsession. Ray complained about it frequently, but the results were spectacular. "You know how he is," she said as she began pulling weeds with careful fingers.

"That's the problem." Lisa sighed again. "I think he…" She trailed off, chewing at her lower lip, unsure if she should be gossiping, even with her mother.

"You think what?"

The thing that she'd been thinking for a while now. Lisa flopped onto her back, the grass springy under her, the tips prickling at her bare arms. She felt almost like she'd be betraying her dad, even if she was only speculating, and even if she was only talking to her mom. It wasn't even as if she knew anything. She just had suspicions. But suspicions, as she'd learned with Tristan, had a way of eating at a person.

"I think he and the guys" – she squinted, eyes watering beneath the assaulting brightness of the cloudless sky overhead – "are involved in some really…*not legal* things."

There was a pause. Lisa lifted her head a fraction, straining to see her mother.

Cheryl was still plucking weeds from amongst her lantana. "Guys being…?"

"Uncle Mark. Sly. Eddie. Maybe Johnny…I dunno."

"And by *not legal* you're thinking…what?"

70

"I don't know, Mom." She let her head fall back, hair rustling against the turf. "I just...nevermind."

Cheryl's garden clogs brushed through the Bermuda and then her face appeared in the sky some five-feet-four-inches above Lisa's. She twitched a sideways smile. "You always were a good secret keeper."

Lisa frowned. "I'm not keeping any secrets."

Cheryl's smile widened. "The CIA couldn't crack you, baby."

She retreated, but Lisa continued to frown. Secret keeping or not, every fiber of her being was screaming with the need to talk about what had happened at the garage that day. But she couldn't bring herself to open her mouth and start spilling. Maybe it was better to be left out of the loop, to stay home and do girly things and go nowhere near the underground fights. Then she wouldn't be having this dilemma.

Cheryl reheated leftover homemade veggie soup for dinner and slathered a baguette with butter that she sliced up and served on one of her grandmother's favorite serving platters as a side. Johnny and Mark contributed heartily to her attempts at conversation, but her husband and daughter were awkwardly quiet. They weren't fighting, because Cheryl could always tell when they were at odds, but both seemed preoccupied.

Lisa helped her clear the dishes and clean up the kitchen until Cheryl saw her yawning and finally sent her away. "Go read, sleep, listen to music, whatever. But unwind before work, sweetie." Poor baby – as everyone else wound down for the night, Lis was just prepping for job number two. She worked too hard, neither of her jobs anything that resembled a career. It was times like these when Cheryl wished so hard that her interior design business might take off that she had to bite her lip to keep from screaming; she wanted better for her baby than bartending and paper shuffling. Better for herself too, if she were honest.

Alone in the kitchen, or mostly so, she listened to Ray's stocking feet move across the linoleum and held out a hand for his sweet tea glass without glancing up from her sink full of dishes. The dishwasher was running, but wasn't large enough to handle all the dinner aftermath, so she was finishing up by hand so she didn't come downstairs to a mess in the morning.

The damp, condensation coated glass was pressed into her hand, but then she felt his arm slide around her waist, his palm flattening over her stomach. A smile tugged at the corners of her mouth as she put the glass beneath the foamy water and picked up her sponge.

"Trying to make up?" she asked.

"For what?" She felt his chin on top of her head.

"Am I supposed to be unhappy with you?"

"You tell me."

"Okay, enough with the word games, counselor." She bumped his arm with her hip, moving him a step back, and rinsed the glass. "We talked about Lisa this morning. So why did she come home in a mood?"

Ray sighed and pivoted around so he was leaning back against the counter beside the sink. "She's a girl. Isn't that what you were telling me this morning?" He lifted his dark brows. "Girls have moods."

A different father with a different daughter might have been able to chalk this up to "girl problems." But Ray and Lisa were too close, and too much alike, for that to be the case here. Cheryl gave her husband a pointed, sideways glance before she returned her attention to her task. "Ray." She dropped her voice a notch, despite the loud rumble of the TV coming from the living room. "You and I had a conversation three years ago." Another glance told her that a frown was pressing lines into his face as he stared at the opposite bank of cabinets. "About keeping work and home separate – "

"I'm doing that," he cut her off, his voice hard. "Things are separate."

*To be so smart...*She cut off the tap, dried her hands on a dishtowel and turned to face him, one hand on her hip, the other propped on the counter. "Clearly, you weren't listening then." His gaze lifted to meet hers, bristling with challenge. "When you take Lisa to those damn underground fight clubs, that's putting her in physical danger. That friggin' bar job she has…" She exhaled in a loud, tired rush. "But she's tough enough to know *why* you go to those fight clubs."

He looked like he wanted to protest.

"Don't lie to her and treat her like a child," Cheryl said more gently. "She's a smart girl, babe. She'll be your biggest fan in this crusade you've got going on." She smiled. "Like me. And you won't have to worry a day about her talking to people she shouldn't."

"I know that."

"Then *tell her* you know that. She just wants to make you proud."

"He still hasn't shown."

From the other end of the cell phone connection, Ricky made a sound that reminded Drew of the one made when you turned a two-liter bottle of Coke upside down and let it all go pouring out at once: a sick gurgling sound that could have been a burp or a puke or God knew what else. "He'll show," the trainer insisted and then released what was definitely a burp. "Mighta been too scared to meet you today, but he'll show tonight. Pipe says he don't like bein' seen in public. Rich asshole thinks he's untouchable."

"Yeah, well…" Drew cast a glance down the long, empty stretch of concrete and asphalt to his right. "I'm just askin' to get picked up out here. And I got a van full of – "

"Just shut up and wait," Ricky barked. "Call me when the drop's done." And then a dial tone buzzed in Drew's ear.

With a sigh, he snapped the cheapo prepaid flip phone shut and slipped it into the pocket of the light windbreaker he wore over his t-shirt and jeans. It was a warm night, but he'd been told, and believed, that dark clothing with sleeves did a better job of hiding a guy who wanted to stay hidden.

He was parked along the back side of a long row of warehouse businesses. A tire store, several furniture wholesale places, a feed store and an industrial lighting place rented slots in the low-slung, metal-sided, ugly structure that ran parallel to a twin building in the middle of a sprawling parking complex, the structures looking very much like chicken houses. Drew had nosed the van up to a loading dock at the lighting place where, ironically, the streetlamp was on the fritz and a circle of darkness hid him, and his van of stolen electronics, well. He stood leaning against the van and, through a stand of baby pine trees, he watched the road and wondered if each passing set of headlights belonged to a cop.

The man he'd tried to go see earlier today, Ray Russell, who was clearly related in some fashion, even if just professionally, to the girl from the bar, was thirty minutes late to their meeting.

The girl from the bar...

Drew's thoughts wandered toward her even though he didn't want them to. He knew nothing about her save for the fact that she obviously had two jobs and obviously didn't want anything to do with him. But seeing her in the daylight, in camel and tan cowboy boots, her hair in a ponytail, a Braves t-shirt hanging loosely off her shoulders, he'd confirmed what he'd suspected the night before: She was really pretty. Hot, yes. Cute, sure. Was she the kind of girl he found sexually attractive? Double yes. But she was pretty too in a very honest way that had clashed with the cold, unreadable look in her green eyes today when she'd sent him away. Most girls couldn't keep from flirting, but she apparently could...

A sound pricked his ears and sent his head swiveling around on his neck. Just a quiet whisper of a noise that he couldn't even be sure he'd heard. Drew cussed his lack of focus as he scanned the shadows around him. His eyes bounced around in panic, so quick that he almost missed the contrast of a darker, blacker, more defined shadow as it moved amongst the darkness.

"Hey – "

His voice turned into a grunt; his teeth snapped together; he tasted blood in his mouth. His body went rigid. Fire raced along every nerve ending, and then he felt nothing, not even when he saw the world tilt crazily as he went crashing to the pavement, as stiff and unmoving as a rake handle. He blacked out before he landed.

Sly pocketed his Taser and withdrew a plastic zip tie instead, kneeling beside the immobile body at his feet. The Lynx might have fought mightily in the ring, but with fifty-thousand volts of electricity coursing through his body, he'd fallen like all the rest. With military precision, Sly pulled the man's wrists together behind his back and secured them with his makeshift cuffs. In his experience, taut, biting plastic were easier to deal with than traditional handcuffs. He didn't have to keep up with a key.

"You're getting rusty," he said as he stood.

Eddie emerged from the darkness behind the van, his ski mask pushed up onto his forehead, mouth curled in disgust. He scratched at his goatee. "We didn't have to *Tase* him, dude."

Sly peeled up his own mask. "Check the van."

Eddie was a better pick-pocket than mechanic – and he was a damn good mechanic – and he had the rear doors of the utility van open in seconds. "Shit," he swore. His flashlight came on with a click and Sly watched its beam dance across a very small cache of what appeared to be iPods and iPads. "This isn't all of it."

Sly nodded. "See? Had to Tase him."

Eddie turned around, still frowning. "Ray's gonna be pissed."

"He'll get over it. Come on, help me load him."

9

"Wake him up."

He registered voices through a hazy barrier of consciousness before his head was doused with something cold. Grogginess fell away in an instant, all his sensory receptors coming back online at once. Drew blinked away the water – he licked his lips and was thankful to realize that the cool liquid pouring down his face and into the neck of his shirt was just water – from between his lashes. He didn't panic, but he was overcome by the sudden knowledge that he needed to wake the rest of the way up. When he lifted his head, the world tilted, and he knew that he hadn't just been stunned, but injected with some kind of sedative too. A Taser didn't knock you the hell out like whatever was giving him double vision and sending him lurching forward against...

Ropes. He took a deep breath and felt them digging into his chest, his arms. He flexed his biceps and felt his wrists fight the biting pressure of whatever held them.

Calm, calm, calm he told himself. He relaxed, though it was an effort, and blinked until his eyes were clear. But it was still too dark to see much of anything: a section of earthen floor with a film of algae growing on it, a rough-hewn wooden wall, a rake and a broom hanging on it, a swinging bare incandescent bulb on a chain. The smell of decaying vegetation shot up his nostrils as he took his next deep breath through a nose that dripped water. And the ropes tightened and slackened with each contraction of his lungs.

"Welcome back to the world of the living," a man's voice came from somewhere behind him. "I was starting to think you'd OD'd."

On what? Drew wanted to know. His head weighed a hundred pounds on a neck too weak to lift it, but he managed to do so anyway. His vision still swam, but he was able to pick out more details: two metal trash cans in a corner, a John Deere riding lawnmower. He sensed that he'd been here before – it smelled familiar, it *felt* familiar – but his reeling mind couldn't put a name to the place.

"Wha – " His tongue was stuck to the roof of his mouth and he swallowed, the insides of his cheeks feeling like dry, cracked leather. "What are you doing?" He craned his neck around as far as he could, which wasn't far given the post-Taser full-body cramp that was rapidly taking hold of him, and saw the sleek, black glimmer of a vehicle to his right. And three figures standing just within the edges of his vision, their faces unclear.

Ricky's van, he recognized the car. It had been pulled into what was obviously a garage or a barn or a…storage shed. *Oh shit.* The church. The Catholic Church in Cartersville where he and Josh had lifted the van full of electronics. The electronics he'd intended to sell to…

"Oh shit," he groaned aloud.

"Yeah, 'oh shit.' Or in your case, *stupid* shit." Booted footsteps made soft thumps over the dirt floor as one of his captors circled around in front of the chair. "What kind of dumbass robs a church?" The speaker came closer, flirted with Drew's line of sight, then his footfalls retreated and moved slowly back around to the other side of the chair. He was smart; he wasn't going to let himself be seen.

"That was a question," he said, and Drew felt the need to test his bonds again, the ropes digging into him.

"What was?" He could feel his pulse picking up, hear it drumming in his ears. He was still loopy from whatever they'd used to drug him, and the cottony feel of his mouth made him think they'd forced it down his throat – ketamine or Rohypnol most likely.

"What kind of dumbass robs a church?" the man repeated. Drew didn't respond, though he wanted to. "You. The answer would be *you*, apparently."

It wasn't my idea, he answered in his head. *I'm not this guy.* He didn't steal parishioners' donations or sell stolen shit out of the back of a van. At least, he hadn't ever thought he'd be doing that. But he needed the money, and Ricky was his trainer, and fighting was all he was good at...Men in his position always said they didn't have a choice. He did, probably, but the choices hadn't been good ones.

"Where's Ricky keeping the rest of the stash?" the man asked. "Or did he sell it already?" A beat of silence passed – a silence that was filled with the sounds of night insects beyond the shed walls and the stink of mildew – and then the questioner sighed. "We don't want you, or your fatass boss. Just the goods."

Ricky was going to be furious. He was going to turn so red, and that vein would pop out in his forehead; he'd stutter and spit as he talked, ranted, screamed. Drew could imagine the stink of his hot breath as he got in his face. He hated Ricky. How many times had he wondered what it would be like to break the rest of his teeth? To put his fist in the middle of that jowly, mottled face?

But whatever else Drew was, he wasn't a rat. There was no coming back once you'd squealed. So he sat, silent, willing to wait this guy out.

"Not talkative then? That's fine." He heard a snap, like fingers, and then footsteps again. A man stepped in front of him. Drew didn't get a good look, but he registered dark hair and a goatee, a shapeless black sweatshirt. And then a hand slapped duct tape over his mouth and the man was gone again.

He'd seen it done in the movies, but he hadn't been prepared for the sudden sense of suffocation, the urge to scream at the top of his lungs. He took a deep breath, told himself not to be a bitch, and forced his muscles to relax.

"We'll be back in a while," the original speaker said. "Maybe after you've had some time to yourself – after your whole body's gone to sleep and you've got piss running down your leg, you'll be ready to chat."

The light was extinguished and a dark, cool, complete blackness doused the parts of the shed he could see. Drew listened to three sets of boots leave, the door shut, and then he was alone. In the dark. With nothing to do but wait.

Ray watched the sun come up through the many-paned, lace-curtained windows in Father Morris's kitchen. The priest had seemed anything but surprised to find them on his doorstep – undoubtedly he'd seen the headlights down at the shed behind the church and his remark on Ray's text had confirmed as much. What do ya know: a clergyman who was up to speed on cell phone technology.

As the first pale fingers of pink lemonade broke over the horizon, stabbing through an indigo jungle of clouds and stars, the pine-and-linoleum rectory kitchen smelled like strong coffee and loaf of cinnamon bread the Father had slid into the oven upon their arrival. Canned lights in the ceiling illuminated a small, tidy room full of potted ferns and an impressive collection of wrought iron crosses mounted on the wall between a cordless phone and a hutch full of serviceable white crockery. It was the same kitchen where Ray and Mark had first met the priest, but at dawn, it felt less like a meeting place and more like a man's home, the priest himself less like a client and more like a host.

Ray glanced across the table and took note of Eddie, who seemed locked in a staring contest with a statuette of the Virgin Mary. He lifted his brows in slight amusement and then turned his attention to the priest. "We'll have him moved before anyone knows he's here," Ray assured.

Surprisingly, Father Morris hadn't argued when he'd learned that one of the men who'd stolen his donations was being held hostage in his maintenance shed. He lifted his shoulders now in an almost delicate shrug. He was not a large man, and seemed even smaller dwarfed by a terry robe with slippers poking out from beneath the hem. But he had one of those peaceful expressions on his face that Ray thought was mandatory of all clergy. "Keeping him here doesn't worry me so long as your…questioning…proves useful."

"It's always 'proved useful' in the past," Sly said, and Ray picked up on a hint of pride in his otherwise neutral tone.

Father Morris gave another little shrug and opened a drawer along his bank of cabinetry, pulling out a pair of oven mitts that were too flowery even for Cheryl's kitchen. "It's just…" His eyes flicked upward, moved across the four of them, before he turned toward the oven. It had been a very pointed trail-off-and-glance move, one Ray had seen executed many times in the courtroom.

"It's just what, Father?" he asked.

The bread came out of the oven and the hot smell of cinnamon came swirling through the room like it was being fanned in their direction. Ray's stomach growled.

"Sometimes." The priest set the steaming baking dish on a cutting board in the middle of the peninsula and pulled off the mitts, another of those practiced, pointed looks sent toward the table. "I've found that guilt can be more persuasive than force."

"You ever seen somebody get water boarded?" Eddie asked. "No guilt there, and it's pretty damn effective. Er…friggin' effective." He pulled a face.

Mark chuckled.

"No disrespect," Ray said, "but we got this covered."

Father Morris went to his outdated, but spotless white fridge and withdrew a little ceramic plate of butter and a jar of Smucker's. Ray had an idle wonder if the man worked on the side as a butler as he watched him pull a tray from a cabinet and begin loading it with napkins and plates and butter knives. Had Father Morris been anything other than a priest, Ray would have waved off his offer of hospitality – something about having a man play waitress for him was unsettling.

"Well, if you change your minds," the Father said, "I'll be glad to help."

There were two of them, his questioners. One was the guy who'd had the duct tape before. He was distinctive enough that he should have kept his face hidden: the Mr. *GQ* looks, the goatee, the little white scar in his left eyebrow. He didn't look like any thug Drew had ever met, but he had the trash talk down pat.

The other guy, the one who said little but did a lot of staring, was the spooky one. He looked like Frank Bullitt from that old movie of the same name, those eerily light eyes watching with an intensity that rivaled all the chaotic bloodlust of the men Drew fought against. This man's violence was calculated and practiced. He was threatening even at rest, even though he sat on a stool, watching, doing nothing.

"I'm gettin' real tired of asking this," GQ said with an elaborate sigh. "Where" – he enunciated each word like Drew was an idiot – "does Ricky Bullard keep his shit stashed?" Drew was so soaking wet, he might as well have been in the pool for hours. Water – cold water – dripped off the tail of his t-shirt and saturated his jeans; it trickled down between his socks and the clammy skin of his ankles. These two had the Guantanamo Bay routine down to a science.

"You might as well put that towel on my head again, boys." He wished his voice sounded braver and less exhausted. At this point, he wasn't giving Ricky up just on the principle of being difficult. He had a fleeting wonder if Ricky would do the same for him. He doubted it. "'Cause I ain't saying nothing."

"You heard him," Goatee said, twitching his brows. "Let's – "

A knock from somewhere behind Drew cut him off, and a moment later, a shaft of sunlight opened across the floor; Drew could feel its warmth against his back.

"Our good padre's getting tired of this," a voice – the initial voice from the night before – said, and Drew tried unsuccessfully to twist around and get a look at him. "Take a lap, guys."

The two inquisitors backed off with one last frigid glance from the blue-eyed man. He listened to their boots leave, watched their shadows blot out the light a moment, but the door remained open, and a moment later, a new figure came circling around the chair. This one walked rather than stalked, his steps slow and almost gentle. He wore some sort of soft-soled shoes that sucked faintly at the earthen floor that had been turned to muddy soup during his water torture.

The newcomer moved slowly, like a man afraid he might startle an aggressive animal. His face, though, showed no sign of apprehension as he stepped fully into the light. He was not very tall, not even five-ten, with white hair and a neat gray mustache. Thin and soft-looking, he was dressed in acid wash jeans he'd dug out of a time capsule somewhere and a polo shirt with all the buttons buttoned, the tail tucked in neatly. He carried an orange Home Depot bucket that he turned upside down and then sat on, hands resting on his knees. Maybe Drew was having hallucinations at this point, but he could swear the man brought a sense of calm order into the shed with him. He offered a small smile.

"Hello."

Drew blinked.

"I'm Father Morris."

Oh shit. Drew's father had been an atheist, or maybe he'd sought religion in the bottom of a bottle, but his mother had been Catholic. Devout Catholic. Being in the presence of a priest made him suddenly, ashamedly guilty. Not to mention, he'd stolen from this priest. He averted his eyes, staring down at the murky water that had puddled on the floor.

"This is my church," Father Morrison continued. "Did you know that?"

Drew nodded – it just seemed wrong to ignore a holy man.

"So." His expression became one of disappointment, like a parent addressing a misbehaving child. "You knew you were stealing from a church, then?"

If guilt was a motivator for Drew, he wouldn't be in this position in the first place. If a priest thought he could put some holy-roller bullshit over on him, have him recant his sins and all that, then he was very, very naïve.

At least, that's what Drew told himself to bolster his resolve. The truth was, he was crumbling fast. He'd been more loyal to Ricky than the guy deserved. No way would Josh have held out this long. Drew had come to the breaking point. He was being driven to collapse by the water that had chilled him to the bone. The extreme fatigue. The shakes that must have been some sort of aftereffect of what they'd dosed him with. A church thief deserved no less, he reasoned. But he was thinking more and more that he had absolutely nothing left to lose. He was going to jail anyway; he might as well not prolong this misery longer than he had to.

"Can I ask you why?" Father Morris wondered. "What's gone wrong in your life, son, that you would stoop to this level?"

Drew sighed, the ropes again cutting into his chest, preventing him from drawing in the deep breath he needed so badly. "Look," he said through chapped, tape-burned lips. "I don't wanna do this anymore."

The priest lifted gray brows expectantly.

"I'll tell you where the rest of the stuff is."

"Well I'll be damned," Mark said when Father Morris emerged from the garage. "Shoulda sent you in from the start."

The priest offered a brief almost-smile. "I think he was close to admitting it already. I didn't have to push too hard."

Eddie was smoking and took a hard, angry drag, exhaling through his nostrils. "He just didn't wanna cave to us," he said, smoke rolling off his tongue. "Jackass."

Sly shrugged.

"I think," Father Morris said, meeting Ray's gaze, "that he might even be willing to help you retrieve the goods. He's not really a bad sort, I don't think."

Sly and Mark snorted in unison at "bad sort."

"Help us retrieve?" Ray asked.

The priest's smile widened. "That's what I'm paying you for, isn't it?"

Ray had to grin. "You know, Father, you make me *almost* wanna come to church."

10

Back when Cheryl Russell had still been Cheryl Peake, when she'd helped her parents farm fish, she'd had no comprehension of chivalry. Richard Peake had been more a warden and slave driver than father, and there was no love between him and his wife. Cheryl had always been knee-, and waist-, and chest-deep in algae filled water, catch net in hand, wrangling the trout and catfish from the warm, muddy, man-made ponds where they matured. She'd reeked of fish and slime and had worn her hair boy-short back then, when she was a skinny teenager. She'd watched her father harass her mother until April was no longer even a woman, just a pair of hands and a set of brown, downcast eyes.

She'd had no idea how a man was supposed to treat a woman until Ray had come into her life. The afternoon of their meeting was a treasured, perfectly preserved, crystalline memory she carried around like a worn photo in her back pocket. Sixteen, lanky, all elbows and knees, a hank of almost-black hair falling over her eyes, she'd stood in line at the Seven-Eleven, a box of powdered donuts in one hand, an orange juice in the other, a wad of cash clenched between her fingers. She'd been in cutoffs and a mud-spattered white t-shirt that hung off her narrow frame. And when she watched him come through the door, the bell above jangling, she'd wanted to take her dirty, short-haired, fish-farming self and get as far away from him as possible, because girls like her did not pass in front of boys like him without suffering some scathing remark or other.

But he'd smiled at her, the boy with the green eyes, and asked if she was "the Peake girl," and if she knew how famous her family's fish were. He'd been lying, of course, but she'd smiled. And after weeks of smiles, more than smiles, she'd started to think that maybe not every male in the world was like her father.

Ray had been the first one to give her flowers and though he now cursed her obsession with the things, and knew she had a yard full of them, he still had florists bring her arrangements for random occasions.

"Flowers came for you!" Jean, one of her fellow receptionists, commented as they passed in the narrow back hall of Dr. Carmichael's office.

"Already?" It was just ten after eight.

"Yes, and they're gorgeous!" Jean flashed one of her dazzling smiles as she shouldered through the door and out into the parking lot, a flash or morning sunlight flaring before the door closed again.

Cheryl stepped into the small break room – it was really more like a closet with a microwave, mini fridge and shelves to hold their purses – put down her bag and slipped her summer weight cardigan on over her scrub top. Wondering if Ray was apologizing for their truly rather benign conversation the night before about Lisa, she stepped back out into the hall and headed for the front of the office, past open, empty exam room doors. Dr. Carmichael and some of the hygienists were having a powwow in the waiting room and Cheryl threw up a hand in greeting as she passed.

While it might not have been her dream job, her receptionist position had become a comfortable, stable environment in which to work. She liked all the other girls and Dr. Carmichael was a grandfatherly sort, who gave good Christmas bonuses and made all of them feel needed and appreciated. The reception desk was a chest-high wall and laminate countertop that separated the waiting area – a sea of vinyl chairs and potted plants, glossy magazines on glass tables – and the neat rows of filing shelves where patient records were kept. As Cheryl pushed through the swinging half-door, she spotted an explosion of color at her station and smiled.

He outdid himself this time, she thought, as she pulled her rolling chair out of the way to more closely inspect the arrangement. White lilies, yellow roses and eucalyptus springs jostled together among red tulips and baby's breath. Each bloom was more incongruous than the last, but it all somehow seemed to work. She would never have put together such a collection, but it made her chuckle.

"Those are lovely." Dr. Carmichael's voice pulled her attention. "From your husband?"

"I'm sure." Cheryl plucked the card from the plastic tongs. "He's always trying to make up for something or other." She flipped the paper square open, read the message, then read it again, her smile faltering.

It wasn't from Ray.

All the pretty colors for a pretty girl, it said, and Cheryl knew without a second thought that it was much too cheesy and trite to have been written by her husband. Ray did not do puns or rhymes or anything even remotely stupid when it came to romantic gestures. There was no name listed, either, which made the fine hairs on the back of her neck suddenly prickly.

"Everything alright?" Dr. Carmichael asked, and Cheryl realized that she was frowning in earnest, chewing at a corner of her lip.

"Yes," she lied, and folded the card back up. She gave her boss a quick, tight smile that seemed to reassure him and then sank down into her chair. *Probably nothing,* she reasoned, and started to trash the card. But at the last moment, she tucked the paper into the mug that held her pens. Better to be safe, because sorry always sucked.

"You know those lists that get put together? 'Top Ten Companies to Work For' and that kinda thing? Yeah, you are so not helping this be one of those places."

Lisa counted to five in her head – because ten would have been pushing it – and still couldn't seem to drum up a pleasant expression for her cousin. "Johnny," she said around a sigh, pushing her still-damp hair behind her ears. "I don't run this shop, your dad does, and if he was here, I wouldn't have to bitch at you. So take it up with him." The phone rang yet again, proving her point. "Where the hell is everybody?"

A quick sadness flickered across his face, the look of a child who'd been left out of some fun activity. He shrugged, scrubbed a hand through his gelled dark hair. "Dunno. Maybe you should try their cells."

"I did. *Four times.*" She picked up the phone and missed his answer beneath her rote "King Customs" greeting.

"Hey, this is Big Tom Elson from over at the Big E-zee Ranch and I was calling to see if…"

Lisa rolled her eyes as she listened to the man's request. The Big E-zee Ranch was actually five acres of abundantly landscaped pretend farm where "Big Tom's" daughter rode her fat pony around in a circle. Hfelt the need to refer to himself as "Big Tom" at all times, often in the third person, like he was trying to make his own nickname happen. Regardless, he had an obsession with classic cars and he both provided them with and referred business, so they humored him.

"*Big Tom?*" Johnny mouthed from across the desk with a grin.

She nodded, then aimed a pen toward the open garage door. "*He wants his Mustang by end of the week!*" she mouthed back, and watched his brows scale his forehead. He left in a rush, nearly tripping over his gangly legs.

In the span of time it took her to assure Tom that the guys could work miracles on his old Fastback and that it would be ready for pick-up in just two short days – an impossible feat if her crew didn't drag their asses into the shop – she watched through the window as a florist's van pulled into the lot. It parked up close by the office and a uniformed employee wrestled a monster flower arrangement out of the back. The delivery driver had both hands wrapped around a massive glass vase that spewed particolored flowers in a spray that he couldn't see over the top of. Realizing he was likely to crash into the door, she hurried to her feet and moved around to open the way for him.

"Thanks," he said as the bell above jangled and he came into the office. He was a young guy, maybe her age, skinny, his arms looking taxed as he tried to hold up the flowers. He huffed a tired breath. "These are for Lisa Russell. Where should I put them?"

87

"On the desk. Oh, here, um…" She hooked a hand in the mouth of the vase, wincing as she felt a missed rose thorn catch her skin, and helped steer him in the right direction. "That should be good."

"Man," he said as he stepped back. He looked even younger without a tangle of flowers in front of his face. His cheeks were mottled from exertion and Lisa had to bite back an amused smile. "Are you Lisa?" he asked.

"Unfortunately."

His face twisted like he wasn't sure what to make of that comment, but he pulled a narrow clipboard from its place tucked into the waistband of his uniform black pants and asked her to sign for them.

"Who're they from?" she asked, casting a glance up at the strange ensemble of colors poking out of the vase as she scribbled her name on the appropriate line.

"No idea." He took the clipboard back. "Guy paid in cash."

That bit of information left her frowning. Lisa did *not* get flowers, except from her dad or uncle on Valentine's Day, and that was after she'd repeatedly asked them not to do it. She certainly didn't get huge, random bouquets midweek from cash-paying customers. When the deliveryman was gone, she reached out to pass her fingertips over the smooth petals of a yellow rose. It wasn't the prettiest grouping of flowers, and most of them were unfamiliar to her. Her mother would have known, but she was flower-handicapped.

The card was a folded square on a plastic stake and she withdrew it. Inside, a single line stared up at her. *All the pretty colors for a pretty girl.* There was no name, no signature. Lisa flipped it over twice and could come up with no clues as to the sender's identity. The words though…were either those of a hormonal teenage boy or a creepy old dude. Very tacky.

"Whose flowers?" she heard Johnny ask behind her. She startled, just a bit, and scolded herself for it. She'd been staring at the card so intently that she hadn't heard him approach and it had rattled her.

"Mine," she said, turning around to face him.

He scrunched up his nose. "Who would send *you* flowers?"

"You're so sweet."

"No, I just mean…" He twitched a grin. "What's the card say?"

She handed it to him and Johnny frowned. "Dude, what is this?"

"Pretty lame, huh?"

He lifted a grimacing face. "How 'bout strange. Guy sounds like a serial killer. You're so preeeeettttty," he said in an affected, breathy voice that brought a chuckle out of her throat.

"Oh my lord, get back to work, you moron."

He passed the card back. "Can't. Gotta order a part for the Mustang. It won't be ready by the end of the week."

The sleeves of his sweatshirt covered the ligature marks on his wrists, the angry red furrows where the rope had chafed his skin raw, but the hooded black sweatshirt drew its share of looks in the middle of a summer mid-morning at IHOP. Drew felt their waitress's eyes move over him as she topped off his coffee and moved on. She was one of those standard waitress types, in her early forties with a mop of curly red hair, glasses, and a brace on one wrist that told a story of carrying too many heavy trays. She hadn't stared at him, but she'd been curious, he could tell.

Across the table from him, Bullitt – his name was really Sly – was in a much more suitable white t-shirt, his sunglasses hooked in the collar by one earpiece. He had coffee too, but hadn't ordered any food. The sunlight streaming in through the plate glass window to his right gave his eyes an almost translucent, ice-like quality. Drew had initially thought, and still believed, that of the four men he'd met that morning, this was the most dangerous.

Which, in a way, put him more at ease. He could respect a dangerous person. True danger, not just a put-on illusion of such, was all about control and self-possession. This Sly was not the go-crazy-and-shoot-up-the-place kind of scary.

No, he was too composed for that. He was professional. Collected. He was also staring at Drew and waiting for an answer.

"I dunno," Drew finally said with a shrug. "There's not a lot of trainers out there. Most of 'em suck. Ricky at least pushed me."

The other man's brows lifted a fraction, putting creases in his forehead, animating his otherwise expressionless face. "Pushed you in the right direction?"

"No." He had to be honest about that. "Not all of the time."

The barest hint of a smirk touched Sly's mouth, but he took a sip of coffee and didn't comment.

Drew's breakfast arrived on the waitress's good arm: ham, two eggs over easy, hash browns, toast, and a blueberry muffin. Screw his damn diet. It all smelled heavenly and he couldn't get his silverware unrolled fast enough. He shoveled an entire egg into his mouth and chased it with orange juice before he took a breath, forced himself to eat more slowly, and turned his attention to the man across the table from him again.

"What did Ray mean about a job?"

Sly dug something out of a back pocket – a card – and slid it across the table. Drew pulled it closer to him while he chewed a corner of toast and read the glossy script printed across the card's front.

Raymond Russell
Business Security Solutions

There was a cell phone number and a P.O. box address listed.

"What's that supposed to mean?" he asked, returning to his breakfast. "I thought he was a mechanic now."

"He owns the shop," Sly said, "but he don't work on cars. Lawyer types don't go grease monkey." It almost sounded like there was a smile to his words, but only for a moment. When he spoke again, his voice was back to its neutral, flat tone. "It's just like the card says: we provide security.

90

Sometimes that means working a party. Sometimes it means what we did today."

Drew snorted.

"Ray's got some old guilt shit he's working out. I dunno. But he's making decent money, so I can't complain."

What was decent? Drew wondered. For a man subletting a room and some bathroom time in a crappy apartment with a roommate he couldn't stand, even minimum wage would have sounded "decent."

The muffin broke open under his fork and steam curled up from its crumbly innards. The blueberries in it were huge and leaked purple juice down onto the plate. "How'd you get hooked up with him?" Drew asked before he shoveled too big a bite into his mouth. He was *starving*. Hungrier than maybe he'd ever been.

The white sunlight showed the shadows at the corners of Sly's mouth when he made a go at a smile. His eyes looked like ice. "That's not a story fit for kids."

Drew frowned and swallowed.

"How old are you?"

"Twenty-seven."

"You ever been in the Service?"

"No."

"Then you're a kid." He took a swallow of coffee that said he'd offer no more information on the topic. "Ray's a good guy," he said. "Mark's better. They take care of their people."

"And you're one of their people?"

"For now."

Ray had told him to go to breakfast with Sly, that things would get explained, but so far, he still felt like he was watching a movie that everyone understood but him. This was all still so vague and shadowy. He needed subtitles or something, and the thought was making him more frustrated by the second. "So lemme see if I got this right," he said, putting his fork down with some effort. "You guys pick me up, drug me, date rape – whatever the hell – and then I cry 'uncle' and you're ready to sign me on?"

The first genuine smile touched Sly's lips. "Now he's getting it."

"Why though?" He had raised his voice and knew it, saw the elderly couple sitting behind Sly shoot him curious glances, but couldn't seem to help it. "Why would he wanna hire me if he doesn't even know if he can trust me?" A passing waitress who stared at them openly forced him to drop his voice to an angry hiss. "I'm a rat, remember?"

"Oh, I remember." The smile fell away. "Everybody rats at some point or other. That's not important. Ray takes on security gigs that call for either a special skill set, or big muscle. If nothing else, you're muscle."

"I'm not an idiot." Drew scowled.

"You kinda are. Come on board, take the job, get away from that bastard you're working for, or don't. It doesn't matter to me."

"I'm a fighter." It felt like a stupid protest, a reminder this guy didn't need – he'd seen him fight in the barn that night.

"I know," Sly confirmed. "You come to work for Ray, chances are you *will be* fighting."

Getting away from Ricky sounded…wonderful, he had to admit to himself with an internal sigh. He really did hate the man.

But on the other hand, he knew Ricky. These guys were a mystery. A violent, torturing-for-information mystery.

Drew knew which direction he was leaning – both options involved a certain risk that he'd end up in jail or dead – but it was hard to admit defeat. "You water board me, then you offer me a job," he said with an unhappy smirk as he picked up a piece of burned bacon.

Sly shrugged, and slid out of the booth. "It's nothing personal. It's just what I do." He dropped a handful of bills on the table and put his wallet back in his pocket. "Think about Ray's offer." And then he was gone, striding between the booths like a character out of a sixties movie.

***

"Finally!" Lisa pushed her chair back as her father and uncle stepped into the office. "Where've you guys been? I've been having a Big Tom crisis," she said, rolling her eyes. So far, the parts company had been evasive about getting back to her with a quote or delivery date. Big Tom had called twice more, each time more anxious than the last. Johnny and their current – affectionately dubbed – "shop rat," Rico, were impossible to motivate on her own. And even worse, she'd lapsed into more than one staring contest with her flowers, racking her brain for possible senders.

"Don't worry, sweetheart." Mark came over to the desk, smiling as always, and dropped a kiss on top of her head. "The cavalry's here."

Ray's glance was more amused than sympathetic. "Don't act like you couldn't handle it."

She made a face; he was right.

"Ooh." Mark turned, hands in his back pockets, and nodded toward the flowers. "Yours?"

The bouquet seemed to be relaxing, the tightly packed stems bowing out to the sides so the blossoms fanned in an impressive display of color. They were gorgeous, and seemed to be enjoying the AC and fresh water she'd put in the vase. Still, every time Lisa looked at them, she frowned. "Yeah," she said. "But I have no idea who sent them."

She watched Ray pluck the card from its tongs and saw his brows knit together as he read the single, stupid line. She wasn't prepared for the way his head whipped in her direction, his expression suddenly hard and guarded. "What'd the delivery guy say?" His tone was clipped, the words snapping off his tongue in a way that left her sitting up in her chair, feeling like a child in trouble.

A quick glance to her left revealed that Mark's posture had changed; he was picking up on his brother's mood change. "He said the guy paid in cash. No name."

"It was a guy?" Ray demanded. "He said that? He knew it was a man?"

Her heart kicked up behind her breastbone; he was making her nervous. "He said 'guy,' but I didn't ask if he knew *for sure*. Dad, what – "

"Hey, Ray." Sly poked his head in from the garage, incoming sunlight highlighting the gold in his hair and the white in his blue eyes. "I think our friend followed me back from breakfast."

Now doubly confused, and wondering if this "friend" was related to the flowers, Lisa swept her eyes out through the window and saw a dark blue, late model Impala cruising to a stop beside her dad's truck in the parking lot. The Lynx.

"What the hell is going on?" she asked, but no one answered; the guys were already halfway out the door. With a sigh, she deflated against the back of her chair. "No one tells me anything."

11

It wasn't too late to change his mind. Sure, he'd gone to the apartment and thrown all his meager belongings into two duffel bags. And yes, he'd left Josh a voice mail to inform him that he was moving out. But as he watched Ray and Mark Russell coming across the parking lot toward him, a last, desperate dread tugged at him. Moving away from one bad situation and into another, possibly worse, one wasn't a positive life change. And there weren't words to describe how infuriated Ricky was going to be. And Josh. And the other guys. He wasn't just making friends here, he was making enemies too.

But Drew stood rooted, and then the Russell brothers were upon him and it was too late to do anything but accept that he was about to make a very big, maybe bad, decision. "You came," Ray said. He sounded neither surprised, nor expectant; he was just stating a fact.

His brother Mark was smiling, barely, but his eyes sparkled with a humor Ray's lacked. "Glad you came," he amended. "You're doing the right thing."

Drew couldn't help it: he forced a humorless chuckle. Right? He'd passed right years ago, and this certainly wasn't it. "I don't think Ricky's gonna feel that way."

"Ricky is a small-time idiot who isn't gonna do shit," Ray said in a voice that could have been a snarl. "There's bigger, meaner assholes out there than him."

The remark sounded personal, at least that was Drew's interpretation, but he made no comment. With a defeated sigh, he shoved his hands in his jeans pockets. "How do we do this, then?"

"Where'd you get that car?" Ray asked.

Another sigh. "Ricky."

"First, we ditch it. Then we start the paperwork."

***

"Smoke?"

Lisa waved away the pack of Marlboros that Sly tilted in offering. "I quit two years ago and I'm not getting started again."

"I quit every day," he said, shaking one out for himself and sticking it in the corner of his mouth while he searched for his lighter in his jeans pocket. "But then I forget I can't, so…" The Zippo clicked on with a soft sound and he touched the flame to the cigarette with that air of resigned familiarity that Lisa found somehow comforting. All the men in her life had their own little quirks and flaws – they were refurbished rather than new and shiny – and she had learned long ago that a man with visible faults was more trustworthy than one who kept them hidden and secret. He'd probably die of lung cancer, but Sly always looked at-home and likeably grungy with a smoldering cigarette between his fingers.

Again, she pivoted, hand braced on the rough plaster of the wall beside her head as she peered through the window of the closed door that separated garage from office. Her father and uncle were at her desk, The Lynx standing across from them, looking twitchy. He kept scrubbing a hand back across his short, bristly dark hair and shifting his feet on the tile. Her eyes had raked over every inch of him, from the work boots to the mud-spattered jeans, the baggy black sweatshirt and shifting muscles beneath. And she scowled and chewed unhappily at her lower lip, frustrated at being kicked out of the office, confused by the boxer's presence and the apparent need for him to sign paperwork.

"What's he doing here?" she asked, turning back to Sly, arms folded over her chest.

He exhaled smoke through his nostrils and twitched his light brows. "You think if you ask that enough I'll finally tell you?"

"Worth a shot."

"No it's not."

96

She narrowed her eyes at him and thought he might have been fighting a smile. "I pity the poor woman who marries you."

"Me too."

The door swung open, startling her – all she ever seemed to do anymore was get startled – and Mark stepped, smiling, down into the garage, as disheveled and without worry as always. "That went well," he announced, and though it shouldn't have, the comment turned Lisa's building confusion into anger. A slow anger that sizzled deep in the pit of her stomach, but anger nonetheless.

"What did?"

She could hear the bite in her words, but her uncle didn't react. He gave her a soft, thoughtful look. "Why don't you go in and talk to your dad."

"Because I might as well slam my head against this wall instead."

Mark chuckled. "Go talk to him."

With a sigh, she pushed off the wall and headed through the door he held open. Lynx was leaving the same moment she entered, through the main door, and he cast a look back over his shoulder. Their eyes met a moment, but didn't hold. Lisa knew she was scowling and didn't blame him for moving on without so much as a nod.

Ray was still at the desk, his elbows propped on its surface, hands clasped together in two tight fists. He stared down at the documents on the blotter and his face was rigid with tension, stubble on his cheeks proving her suspicion that he'd been out all night and hadn't been at home for a shave that morning. He'd looked tired just thirty minutes ago when he'd arrived, but now he looked stressed, harried. *Old*. His eyes flicked up to hers, green, like hers, and he motioned toward the chair across from him. "Sit."

"Dad," she said in a rush as she slid into the chair, "okay, some weird shit's been going on and I – " He cut her off with a wave. She tightened her hands on the arms of the chair until her knuckles went white.

"Later," he said, and she wanted to think it sounded like a promise. "Tonight. I'll make it make sense." His eyes lifted up and over her shoulder; she knew he was looking at the flowers that had come for her, which still didn't make any sense.

"Why was *he* here? Lynx?"

"Andrew Forester." Lisa hadn't known his real name, but somehow, that seemed to fit. "He's gonna be working for me."

"As a mechanic?"

"As muscle for the security business."

Which made sense…only it didn't. Not really. Lynx – Andrew, she guessed – was a strong guy, definite bouncer material, but he was also a boxer and someone Ray didn't know at all. Granted, Sly and Eddie had been strangers once upon a time too, but somehow the explanation left a sour taste in her mouth. "I didn't know you were expanding the security business."

"Lis." He exhaled in a loud rush and pinched the bridge of his nose. "Just…don't be difficult, alright?"

The words stung, more than they should have. But she nodded.

"Okay, thanks, Tony." Ray hung up his cell with a *snap* and didn't feel any better. It was six and the sun was a hot, belligerent ball hovering over the tree line. Heat mirages radiated up off the pavement giving the nearly empty parking lot of King Customs all the charm of the Atacama. On either side of the garage, the boutiques and cafes were pulling in their usual dinner business, SUVs and imported sedans swooping around one another like frightened birds. Pedestrians loaded down with shopping bags, clutching iced coffees, their eyes hidden by oversize sunglasses, laughed and talked and strolled up and down the brick sidewalks. It was a sizzling, picture perfect upper class suburban evening, but Ray felt like there was a shadow hanging over him, pulling at him, laughing at him.

Maybe because there was.

"How'd I guess you'd be here?" Mark's voice sounded behind him, and a moment later, his brother joined him on the bench in front of the KC office.

Though Cheryl and Lisa joked about it, they were not twins. Mark was the happy one, the carefree one, the one who didn't worry about much and smiled all the time. Mark was lightness and he was darkness. But they were brothers, and no matter how much Mark smiled, he was more perceptive than anyone Ray had ever met. Ray didn't have to tell him what was weighing on his mind, what was driving him nearly mad, Mark would just know, and after a long moment of comfortable silence, Ray heard the rustling sound of Mark pulling something out of his jeans pocket.

"'All the pretty colors for a pretty girl,'" Mark read off the card that had come with Lisa's flower arrangement. His voice maintained its usual calmness – the man was calmness personified – but Ray heard the layer of tension in his brother's words. "That's what he said, isn't it?"

"Yeah." Ice water went shooting through his veins. A cold, hard knot swelled in his chest, pushing at his breastbone, constricting his breathing. His eyelids closed – he blinked – and in that half-second of darkness, he was in the mahogany and leather courtroom again, the fluorescent tubes overhead droning, someone in the gallery smothering a cough. He saw the board and easel up in front of the witness stand, the photos on it; could hear the papery voice of the medical examiner as he described the mortal injuries that had killed the blonde woman and the little girl in the crime scene shots.

Rene Shilling had been thirty-four, blonde, with a large nose that seemed to fit her face and wasn't unattractive. In the first photo, she'd been posed with her daughter Anna, the little girl a miniature of her mother. The prosecution had shown family photos from a birthday party, Rene behind Anna, loving hands on her girl's shoulders, to drum up sympathy for the victims; it was a tactic that worked well, even on Ray. In his mind, he'd superimposed Cheryl's face over Rene's, Lisa's over Anna's.

And then the crime scene photos had been paraded out for all to see amid gasps and swears. On a sticky, May afternoon, the Shillings' neighbor Linda Peterson used her spare key to let herself into the Shillings' home. The sprinkler had been left on and was flooding the garden, washing pine chips out into the street. And Rene hadn't answered the house phone or her cell. Linda had just been going in to check, she'd said, tears clogging her throat, just to make sure the girls were alright.

She'd found Rene on the living room floor beside the coffee table, her chest on the rug, her face staring blankly up at the ceiling. Her neck had been broken. And all around her, flowers.

Anna was in her bed, her eyes closed, covered in blood and flowers. A note on her white nightstand beside her My Little Pony lamp had read: *All the pretty colors for a pretty girl.*

Ray saw all that in the time it took him to blink, and afterward, the balmy afternoon felt like December. In Montana.

His last case, the one in which he'd turned over damning evidence about his client to the DA, the one that had left him disbarred and shunned, had been the one in which he'd represented Rene Shilling's killer, and husband, Carl. The evidence had been thrown out, though. Ray had lost his job. Carl had been put away on tax evasion charges because the DA had been bloodthirsty and refused to let him walk away.

"Did you call Tony?" Mark asked.

Tony Carillo had been Ray's partner and still represented the family. "Yeah. He said he'd try and find out when Shilling was released. *If* he's been released, he said."

"That case got a lot of press." Mark played devil's advocate. "This could just be a coincidence. And hell, maybe someone really did just send Lis flowers. She's got lots of guys watching her down at the bar. I thought Drew's eyes were gonna bug outta his head."

But Ray shook his head. "That bit about the note was never leaked to the press. What are the odds some secret admirer would write that exact thing on a card? No." His lips pressed together into a firm, thin line. "I don't believe in coincidences."

"Eddie did this? *Eddie?*" Cheryl glanced up and locked eyes with her daughter.

Lisa wrinkled her nose up in disbelief. "No way could he have stayed that straight-faced all day," she argued. Her flowers were sitting on the kitchen counter beside her mother's identical arrangement and she was having extreme doubts about her dad's explanation. "I'm not buying it." A glance proved that Ray was still at the table, his fingers still drumming restlessly on top. "Did he tell you he sent them?"

He shrugged, but Lisa didn't miss the dark look that flitted across his face. "More or less."

Deciding that if he was too concerned about their mystery gifts, he'd tell them, she shared a glance with her mother that said *oh well* and went to the fridge, digging a Coke out amidst the clutter of beers on the top shelf. "So, Dad." She popped the tab and turned around to face him, putting her back against the fridge. His face seemed so heavily lined with some unnamed stress that guilt nearly drove her to withdraw the inquiry, but she pushed on. "Earlier, you said we'd talk tonight."

Cheryl was at the sink adding fresh water to the flower vases and suppressed a snort.

Lisa said a silent thank you to her mother for that one little sound, because she could tell his wife's doubt was what pushed Ray over the edge in a favorable direction.

"Yeah, I guess I did," he muttered, motioning toward the chair to his left that was Lisa's usual seat at dinner. "And you'll just bug the hell out of me 'til I talk to you," he correctly assumed as she sat and put her elbows up on the table in a mirror of his position.

Cheryl murmured an agreement.

Ray sighed. Wiped a hand down his face and looked even more exhausted than he had. Lisa got the impression he hated this worse than the where-do-babies-come-from talk.

Then he looked at her with closed-off eyes and asked, "So what did you wanna talk to me about?"

There was a loud *bang* from the sink as Cheryl dropped the pot she'd been scrubbing. She picked it back up with a muttered word Lisa couldn't make out.

"Dad." Lisa sighed and decided that being subtle wasn't going to work. "Can we please stop playing this game? What's with all the whispering shit at the garage with you and the guys?"

He lifted a single brow that had her slumping down against the table. "Whispering shit" had been pushing it and she knew it, but she was just so *frustrated*. And more frustrating than the actual frustration was the notion that she was worrying over what was probably nothing at all. He was her dad, not her best friend; he wasn't obliged to tell her every little thing about his life and his business.

She'd decided to bury all her I-shoulda-been-a-boy feelings once more and go change for job number two, but his eyes moved away from hers, swinging down like heavy green pendulums to land on the tabletop, and a muscle in his jaw twitched: a sure sign he was about to speak. His words shocked her. "You're a good girl, Lis." He chuckled. "Not always 'good,' really, but no one could ever say that you weren't loyal. Or that you weren't a Russell."

Lisa snuck a look toward her mother but was met by Cheryl's back; she still scrubbed dishes as if she couldn't hear them.

"The security business," Ray continued, "is getting bigger. Word of mouth and all that."

"So that's why you're hiring the Ly...er, I mean Andrew."

He nodded. "That's part of why, yeah. Also because..." She swore she could see the wheels and cogs in his head grinding against one another as he fought the urge to keep whatever he was about to tell her locked away. "He" – another sigh –"is helping us. Your uncle and Eddie and Sly and me: he's helping all of us...help someone else."

Growing up the daughter of an attorney had taught her to listen with more than her ears, to read between the lines more often than she took words at face value. Perfectly normal, perfectly legal "help" didn't involve hushed conversations and underground boxing matches. She recognized all this, accepted it without a backward thought, and took a mental step forward. "That's why we went to the Pit Masters that night, so you could meet him." Her father gave nothing away via facial expression or voiced word. But his eyes said "yes." She frowned. "What did you think I was gonna do, Dad? Run to the cops? Tell them you gamble and hire on boxers? I wouldn't – "

"I know you wouldn't," he said before she could get too insulted. "Trust me: anything I keep back from you, I keep back so you'll be safe."

Lisa nodded. She'd heard as much before – what you didn't know couldn't be used against you. "Soooo," she drawled, "you're saying you guys – "

"Don't always work strictly within the law," he cut her off with an air of finality. "The security business makes money, yes, but it's about more than that." The look in his eyes begged her to understand without asking any more questions. *Leave it at that,* his gaze said.

She glanced to her mother and saw that Cheryl was now leaned back against the front of the sink, arms resting on the counter behind her. She offered a smile and a softer version of her husband's *please understand* face.

And Lisa did understand, really, she did. But she never wanted to wonder if the man she called "Dad" wasn't the role model she'd looked up to her whole life. It was a relief to know that wasn't the case. "You always told me laws and ethics weren't necessarily the same thing," she said carefully, and watched a smile break across his face that was full of approval. "I just don't want to be treated like an idiot, Dad. That's happened to me a lot over the years and…well…" She shrugged. "Thanks for telling me what you did."

103

"Sometimes I wish you could just be one of those mall rats. Clothes and hair and boys and all that," he said, still smiling.

"No you don't."

"No. I don't."

It was a hot night once the sun went down, but there were currents of cooler air in the breeze, like the welcome fingers of a woman against his cheek. Drew dangled an arm through the open driver's side window of Ricky's van and tried to look relaxed. His stomach felt like an angry nest of hornets, but he thought his face was calm enough as he checked it in the side mirror again.

Ricky lived in an ugly little ranch house that had been white once but was now colored by insect remains, red clay spatter and rotting vegetation. The exposed concrete foundation was laced with substantial cracks and the porch sagged, the boards beneath rotten. Holly bushes and some sort of flowering shrubs had grown up in front of the windows, making the place look abandoned. Old beach towels served as curtains. Weeds had choked out all the grass in the lawn. A thick stand of scrub pines and poison ivy had closed the view of the property off from the road, so here, parked in front of the carport, the night was even darker. Ricky's lot felt completely closed-off from the rest of civilization. Drew swore he could feel Eddie O'Dell and Sidney Hammond watching him from their positions across the street. If he pulled out of here without the goods…well, he didn't know if they planned on killing him or tying him to a chair again…or maybe even something worse. But he didn't want to find out. All he had to do was load up and pull out.

"You're an idiot," he told himself, but he flattened his right hand out across his thigh and saw the tremors race up the ends of his fingers. His bones and nerves felt tight, if that was even possible, the old breaks talking to him. Warning him. *You can't fight forever. Maybe not even tomorrow. You need to get away from Ricky,* his conscience said. There was a risk that each punch might be his last, and *that*, above all else, had driven him to accept Ray Russell's offer of a job.

Ten minutes after he'd pulled in, headlights flared in the rearview mirror. Ricky's ancient, shit-brown Cadillac pulled to a rattling, wheezing stop beside the van and died. Drew felt his nerves ratchet up another notch as he watched his former boss pop the door and roll out of the car.

"Where you been?" the trainer called. In the moonlight, his face looked round and glowed with perspiration as he started around the front of the Caddie on stubby, fat legs. "Huh? I been callin' you all day, damn it!"

"Yeah, sorry about that." Drew could hear his pulse thumping hard through the tiny veins in his ears as he climbed out of the van to meet Ricky. Lying made him twitchier than any fight. "My phone died."

"They still got payphones, don't they?" Ricky growled. He propped his fists on his wide hips and spat on the driveway. "Anyway, don't matter now that you're here. Did you make the drop with Russell? I'm gonna need the cash for next week's entry fees."

Guilt tugged at Drew's conscience. Even if Ricky was a mean, worthless son of a bitch, he'd still invested time and money into Drew's training. He had Las Vegas UFC dreams and was putting all his proverbial eggs in the Drew basket. Personality and ethical issues aside, it seemed almost evil to pull one over on Ricky.

"I made the drop," he lied some more. "But Russell wants the rest of your inventory."

There was a flickering security lamp set above them on the county-maintained power pole and though the plastic globe was cloudy and full of dead moths, Ricky's disbelieving sneer was vivid and gruesome. "What? How does he even know there's a 'rest?' *Did he pay you?*"

He felt clammy all over under his clothes. "Not yet."

"What?!"

"He gave me a *down payment*," he covered in a rush, pulling his wallet out of his back pocket. The two fifties he'd been saving were folded up and tucked into a credit card slot, but he pulled them out, willing to take a personal loss if it kept this from getting any uglier. "He's got some buyer dangling and wants to make a bigger sale. He said he'll pay *twice* what our stuff is worth and be able to turn a good profit."

"And I get a hundred bucks for a down payment?" Ricky snorted, flattening the crumpled bills in his palm. "Who's this other buyer? Why would I lose out on that much profit to help this Russell jackass?"

I'm so not cut out for this. "Because we're sitting on a house full of stolen shit." Desperation and logic collided as he rushed to form a reason that Ricky would buy. "Aren't you always saying how we shouldn't sit on hot merch too long?"

The fat trainer gave him a skeptical look, scraping his uneven teeth over his bottom lip.

"We need to get rid of it before the cops start sniffing around."

The reasoning sounded weak to his own ears – no doubt it sounded even weaker to Ricky. Drew's t-shirt was rapidly gluing itself to his chest. He felt a little trickle of sweat go snaking down the back of his neck. *This is what a rat feels like.* Trapped between two factions, both of which had the ability to turn his life to shit, and here he stood, not smart or savvy enough to play the game.

After a moment that felt like an eternity, Ricky exhaled in a loud, defeated-sounding rush. "You're probably right," he said. "When's he want to take delivery? And he better have cash. I ain't no idiot."

It took almost an hour to follow Ricky through his routine of disarming his security system, feeding his four cats, sidestepping what looked like rat droppings as he went down the stained, flattened carpet of the back hallway to the garage. Drew felt as if he counted every one of his own breaths and monitored every word that passed his lips as he loaded the van, stressed to the point of distraction that he'd say something or make a face that gave away his true intent.

When he pulled out of the drive finally, able to breathe again, he saw headlights cut on across the street in the drive of the abandoned house opposite Ricky's: Eddie and Sly. Out of one lion's den and into another.

Two bouquets. Two identical notes. Lisa and Cheryl had been chuckling nervously about the "coincidence" of it. Ray had forced a smile and told them he thought it was Eddie's idea of a practical joke.

But as the clock on the far wall of the kitchen struck one a.m., he sat, shrouded in darkness, staring at the twin flower arrangements up on the counter. Moonlight streamed in through the sheer lace curtains above the sink and made the flowers look like shadows. Snakes. More sinister than the bright blooms they were.

He'd tried to believe Mark before, really he had, but when he'd come home and found his wife with flowers too...the evidence had been too obvious to ignore.

Carl Shilling was out of prison. And he was coming for him. Ray had never been more furious, nor more resolute in his life. No one, but *no one*, threatened his family.

12

Tony Carillo was originally from Jersey, and it would have been obvious to a blind man. He had one of those Italian hairlines, his thick shock of black hair swept back away from his face with a professionally acceptable amount of product, wings of silver shooting over his ears these days. He looked like a fixture in his office in his black suit, crisp white shirt and red tie. The room around him was painted a charcoal gray, white rugs rolled out over the hardwood, black leather couches and chairs with chrome accents grouped around his glass-topped desk. Here and there pops of red complemented his tie: the pillows on the couches, the matting on the framed charcoal sketches on the walls, the leather covers of the law tomes arranged on his modernistic chrome-and-glass bookshelf. Ray had always lacked his former partner's style, though he admired it.

Tony didn't delay things. "I don't have good news." Ray had just settled uneasily in one of the leather chairs across from the desk, a glass of ridiculous cucumber water in his hand that he had no intention of drinking. "Shilling made parole two months ago."

Ray had *known*, but the confirmation was a punch to the gut that left him leaning forward in his chair. "Fuck."

"I would have told you if I'd known," Tony said with an apologetic wave. "But it wasn't my case, so I didn't find out till I started digging."

"I know." Ray took a swallow of cucumber water, winced, wished it was bourbon, and set the glass on the coaster on the edge of his friend's desk.

"Apparently, he was a model citizen in county. He was a shoe-in for parole," Tony went on. "He's working at a La Quinta off 285 in Sandy Springs. Pushes a laundry cart or something. Checks in with his PO routinely, passes all his piss tests."

"Yeah, well, whatever else he was, the shithead was never high," Ray grumbled. He ran a hand over the top of his head, wondering how he had any hair left at all, and furiously racked his brain for explanations to his girls' flowers that didn't involve Shilling.

"Hey." Tony laced his fingers together, light catching the ruby in the ring on his right hand, and propped his elbows on the desk. "Maybe it was a copycat. Someone who knew about the note."

"No one knew about the note," Ray countered with a hard look. "That was never leaked. And Shilling isn't a serial killer – he wouldn't have 'fans.' This *is not* a copycat."

Tony blew out a loud breath. "Yeah, well, no argument here, but I wanted to be wrong."

"Me too."

The oversized, chrome-framed wall clock ticked loudly in the silence that followed. Once upon a time, Ray had been sitting here in this office, his tie pulled loose, a bottle of Johnnie Walker Blue on the desk between them while they celebrated their latest victory. His own office had been next door, a haven of mahogany and potted plants that Cheryl had decorated: his diplomas matted in burgundy and blue on the walls, his little family filling up the picture frames on his desk. He'd spent his whole career defending the indefensible, and in his one, final moment of conscience, he'd managed to put his wife and daughter in danger.

"What are you thinking about doing?" Tony asked.

Ray shook his head.

"Ray," he pressed. "Don't go being the Lone Ranger, now. I've known your girls a long time, and you know I'm worried here, but as your lawyer – "

"As my lawyer," Ray cut him off, "it'll be your job to defend whatever it is I have to do."

Tony narrowed his dark eyes in disapproval.

"And I just hope you're a better attorney than I was, 'cause I don't plan on going to prison."

***

She was wearing a very simple, but very fitted blue tank top with skinny straps. As she leaned forward over a yellow legal pad, writing something that seemed to require immense attention, the silver heart pendant around her neck swung forward on its chain, catching the light, pulling his eyes away from what he could see of her bra down the front of her top. Her hair was coming loose of its ponytail and fell in silky clumps that framed her thin face. She blinked against the incoming sunlight and her lashes flickered, just a ghost of a movement.

Drew had finally learned her name ten minutes before when Sly had given him a flat, serious look and said, "Nobody messes with Lisa." *Lisa.* She was even prettier here, in the daylight, at a desk, with one cowboy-booted foot pulled up in the chair, than she had been at the bar the other night. She'd been sexy in the bar, in the dark, with eye makeup as thick and black as charcoal. But there was an abundance of sexy all over the place. Pretty…truly pretty, was much more rare.

She glanced up at the sound of the bell above the door and for one moment, her green eyes went wide with what he thought might have been shock or surprise; and then in an instant, he watched her pull a great big iron curtain down between them. Her face went blank, her eyes dimmed, and she glanced back at her writing with – if it was fake, then it was damn good fake – disinterest.

He decided to be the one who spoke first. "Hey."

Which he realized was a mistake when he heard the low growl that rose up from behind the desk. A moment later Lisa's Doberman came stalking around the corner, looking like a hundred pounds of solid muscle and curved ivory teeth. Drew had never once backed down from a challenge from a *human*, but dogs didn't use fists and body blocks – and this sonofabitch had a mouthful of daggers.

"Down, Hektor." Lisa's voice was almost bored-sounding. But the dog swiveled his ears in his mistress's

110

direction and then complied with a little groan, settling down on the tile in a wary crouch.

"Hektor?" Drew asked, and the Doberman glanced in his direction, demonic ears pricked.

"With a K." Her eyes lifted briefly – apparently the spelling of her dog's name was important – and then snapped back down.

With slow, deliberate movements, Drew let the office door fall shut behind him and eased around to one of the chairs across from the desk. Watching Hektor from the corner of his eye, he sank down an inch at a time until his ass hit the seat. "Why with a K?"

Either he'd pushed her into annoyed territory, or she'd decided to give up on her charade of being busy. She set her pen down and straightened in her chair, hands braced on the desk. Her fingernails were painted a bright white today, he noticed, right after he got done regretting that when she was upright, he couldn't see down her shirt anymore. Her expression was guarded and wary, the muscles in her slender arms flexed like she contemplated shoving up and leaving.

"Hektor as in Hektor of Troy," she explained.

Thank God for Netflix, was all he could think. "The prince who Achilles killed."

Her brows shot up her forehead. "You read *The Iliad*?" Her disbelief was comical, and maybe a little insulting, but he was willing to let it slide.

"Watched the movie," he admitted. "And I knew someone with a pit bull named Achilles once. Since, you know, he was the one who won and all."

And just like that her eyes were suspicious green slits again. "Hektor was the noble one, though. He fought for his family and his city. Achilles was just a killer."

Drew couldn't remember the last time he'd truly smiled, but there was one tugging at the corners of his mouth now. "I'm Drew," he said, and extended a hand across the desk.

Her mouth twitched to the side, then she accepted his shake with a solid one of her own. "Lisa."

111

"You work at that bar, don't you?"

"Unfortunately."

Why? He wanted to ask her. Russell couldn't be hurting for money *that* bad, and she hadn't seemed comfortable there. But he was halfway convinced she had an active dislike for him, so he decided to keep quiet on the issue. In fact, he was beginning to think he might have prematurely judged the bar scene. If he went back, as a customer, then she'd *have* to be nice to him.

"So my dad hired you," Lisa said, changing the subject in a tactless way that wasn't really awkward.

"Yeah." Feeling both the dog's eyes and the girl's, he leaned back in the chair and made a go at comfortable. "I guess I'm gonna be working security or something."

She almost smiled. "Yeah. Or something." Her look was so knowing that Drew wondered how much she was privy to. Did she know what he'd done the night before? The kind of business her father was involved with?

The bell sounded again and a blast of hot summer air broke their stare-down. Ray came striding into view before Drew could turn around and see for himself. He sidestepped the dog, leaned down to press a quick kiss to the top of his daughter's head, and then fired a sharp glance Drew's direction. "What are you doing here? I don't need you for anything right now." He carried a manila file folder tucked under one arm and crossed the office to a file cabinet. His tone was disinterested and dismissive. "You should go home."

"Um..." This was why Drew had come into the shop, but suddenly, his situation seemed more pathetic than it had before he'd walked in and found Lisa behind the desk. She was watching him now – covertly – and he could feel her eyes. And she didn't bite her lip and bat her lashes like so many of the women he'd known. She *studied.* Ashamed, he admitted, "I kinda don't have a home to go to. I was rooming with one of Ricky's other fighters."

It was silent for a heartbeat...two...

Ray shoved the file drawer shut with a metallic *bang* and did a slow look-around over his shoulder. The angry lines between his drawn brows shifted, became more thoughtful. Lisa was still watching him. "Talk to Sly. He and Eddie rent a house between here and my place. They might have an extra room." He stuck his hands in the pockets of his khakis – he was strangely dressed up today, button-down, belt, nice shoes and everything – and frowned thoughtfully. "How'd you get here, by the way?"

"Um…" More embarrassment. Lisa put a hand over her mouth and he thought she might have been covering a laugh. "I took a cab."

"Can you afford a new ride?"

At this point, he would have rather been kicked in the balls than answer any more questions as to his financial state. "No."

Ray nodded like he'd expected no less. "Guess it's time to put you to work then." He turned to his daughter. "Give us a minute?"

"Sure," she said, but Drew didn't miss her little sigh. She stood, giving him a full head-to-toe look at the supershort cutoffs and her lean, tanned legs and the way they complimented her top half. "C'mon, Hektor." The Doberman rose and followed her from the office with one last warning glance toward Drew. They went out the side door into the garage.

"That's a big dog," Drew said in what was meant to be a severe understatement as Ray took his daughter's place at the desk.

He snorted. "And a big damn problem for anyone who messes with his mama, let me tell you."

That's what Drew had been thinking.

"So." His new boss linked his hands together on top of the blotter, the shiny silver of his no-doubt expensive watch catching the incoming light. "I'm gonna go ahead and get you a pay advance."

Wow.

"And I've got a job for you."

Less of a wow.

113

"A friend of mine" – he pulled a pen out of a Braves mug on the corner of the desk and peeled a blue Post-it off the top of a stack – "is going downtown tomorrow morning and he wants a security detail."

Drew was fully aware of the fact that he wasn't rocket scientist material, nor was he the type of guy who found himself in a leadership role. But logic dictated that unless you were a famous rapper or a foreign dignitary, you didn't need a "security detail" when you ventured into Atlanta. All major cities had the potential to be very dangerous, but people didn't just have body guards. "Who's your friend?" he asked with a frown.

Ray finished scribbling on the Post-it and handed it over. "Meet him here tomorrow at seven," he said evasively. "You can take Mark's truck. Here." He pulled out a drawer on the desk and withdrew a set of keys. "It's the blue Chevy in the back and it probably needs gas." And then the wallet was coming out and bills were peeled from a stack within.

Drew's head was spinning. "Hold on…" Ray's eyes snapped up and they looked so much like his daughter's there was little wonder which of her parents Lisa favored more, and that was without seeing the mother.

"What?"

"Isn't this all just a little…" Drew swallowed, his throat feeling dry. "All-of-a-sudden?"

His face became almost thoughtful. "Well…let's see. I give you a car to use, two hundred bucks, a job a trained monkey could execute, and if you do it right, there's more where this came from. Now, if you take my money, and the truck, and skip town, how long you gonna last on your own?"

Ricky yelled and screamed and cursed and worked five times as hard as this man in the hopes of establishing even a quarter of this kind of presence.

"If you think about it that way, I come out on top under either scenario." Ray twitched a small smile. "So no, it's not 'all-of-a-sudden.'"

***

114

I'm such a lurker these days, Lisa thought as she leaned forward on the work bench on which she was perched so she could watch Drew leave the office and head around the side of the parking lot, a set of keys dangling from his hand.

"You know, I bet if you asked, he'd walk in slow-mo for ya." Eddie's mocking voice drew a scowl. He was working on the Fastback and had black grease everywhere; she even thought she saw it shining darkly in his spiked hair. The knowing, laughing smile he was giving her made her feel about twelve and guilty for no reason.

Her cheeks heated up. "Shut it," she told him, eyes swinging out toward the parking lot again. Drew had already disappeared behind the building which was the reminder she needed that ogling strangers was not on the menu today. She and Hektor went back in the office to the tune of Eddie's chuckles.

Her dad looked like he might have been waiting for her. "Close the door," he said, and once she did, he motioned to one of the empty chairs across from him. Lisa sat, amazed to watch him take the phone off the hook when it rang and leave the receiver sitting on the desk, dial tone droning.

"Is everything alright?" she asked as Hektor pressed his sleek head against her leg and asked to have his ears scratched.

All the menacing poise he'd given off in front of Drew had sloughed off, and in its place was the stressed, tired father she'd spoken to at the kitchen table the night before. He offered her a smile that wasn't comforting. "I'm not sure yet, really."

She forced a hollow laugh. "Well that makes me feel better."

"Sorry." He scratched a hand over his head – she secretly wondered if his thinning hair wasn't self-induced – and gave her a look that begged understanding. "Something's come up. And I don't want to worry you or your mother – "

Her pulse accelerated of its own accord, slamming in her ears.

" – but I also want the two of you to be *very* careful."

"Careful how?"

115

"Just keep your eyes open. Don't be alone anywhere after dark. Be on the lookout for anything suspicious."

Ray was a dad who cautioned at every turn. Burglar alarms and pepper spray and trips to the shooting range – he didn't believe a person could ever be too prepared for all the nasty shit life had in store. But something about the strained note of his voice left her palms clammy. Her chest felt tight. "Suspicious…oh, God, the flowers! Dad – "

"It's fine." He patted the air in a soothing gesture. "It's fine." But his eyes said otherwise, that it wasn't fine at all. "I've got it under control. I just wanted you to be aware."

All the pretty colors for a pretty girl. Kettle drums pounded in her head. *Oh, God.* She had no idea what the flowers meant or who they were from, but looking at her dad, she knew that *he* knew. "How serious is this?" she asked, a quaver in her voice that hadn't been there before.

"I don't know yet."

For the first time, she wasn't sure she was glad for his honesty.

13

Ray's friend Tony – who Drew had learned was also Ray's attorney – looked like he'd walked off the set of *The Sopranos*. Only he dressed better. And smiled more. Their trip into Atlanta had consisted of a stop at a high-rise, the interior of which had been tricked out in marble and glass and could very well have been a museum. He waited in the lobby, as he was told; he rode shotgun in a Mercedes that made him twitchy. He handed a stranger an envelope that felt heavy with cash; stood alone in a deserted parking lot for God knew why, and fielded a barrage of questions about everything from his birthplace to his favorite brand of deodorant.

It was a bullshit security assignment, yes, but more importantly, it was a litmus test.

They were heading north, back toward Tony's Alpharetta office in its beautiful brick building on a street corner surrounded by shops Drew couldn't even afford to look through the windows of. When the lawyer leaned forward to switch the radio off, he shot Drew a look across the interior of the Benz. "Have you figured out what today was yet?"

Drew watched the road through the windshield and tried to look nonchalant. "Yeah."

"Do you really? Or are you trying to save face?"

He'd been second guessed his whole life and it didn't bother him anymore. "You're gonna go back to Ray and tell him whether or not you think I'm a total waste of time and money."

Tony made a soft sound in the back of his throat that might have been a laugh. "Smarter than you look, then." He started to reach for the radio knob again –

"What are you gonna tell him?" Drew turned his head so he was staring at the man's very Italian profile. "You spent half a day with me and suddenly you can tell if I'm decent or not?"

He chuckled out loud this time. "I can tell a lot of things about a man – but not if he's decent."

Drew waited.

"Do I think you're some kind of deranged serial killer? No. Do I think you're a dumb kid who's made one too many bad decisions? Yes." He grinned a quick, sharp, predatory grin that belonged, appropriately, on a lawyer. "I make a living buying people like you second chances. Consider yourself bought."

"Just like that?"

Tony sighed. "Ray does need another guy. Something's come up that's going to make his life more...complicated...so he needs *dependable* employees," he stressed. "If you're good to him, he'll be good to you. Screw him over and, well...I'm advising you do the former."

"...so then I told him that if he *ever* wanted to touch them *again*, he'd have to – " Morgan's overdramatic sigh pulled Lisa's attention from the puddle of caramel sauce she continued to drag an apple slice through. She'd been drawing a map of her bedroom, rearranging her furniture in the sugary goo, and felt guilty for ignoring her friend's current romantic predicament. "Are you even listening to me?" Morgan asked.

"No." She was honest, but managed an apologetic half-smile.

Morgan, on her lunch break from work, was in a billowy, cowl neck purple blouse that flashed a lot of cleavage, gray pencil skirt, her golden hair done up in an elaborate twist and secured with chopsticks. Across from her, in a plain blue tank top, camo cargo shorts and flip-flops, Lisa felt frumpy and gross. It wasn't something that bothered her. Morgan had always been the glamorous one. Besides, Lisa was drowning in thoughts of mysterious flowers and whatever boogeyman had her dad so twisted up. She'd slept poorly the night before and had awakened at four this morning in a tangle of sweat-soaked

118

sheets. She was pretty sure she'd run a red light or two on her nearly hour-long commute to work and hated even the sight of food now, though her stomach churned, empty and full of acid.

Morgan made a face. "Oh. Is this about that whole you being alone thing again? We can talk about something else. I'll bitch about Corey with 'Manda instead."

Lisa had to grin. None of her family liked Morgan – she had a way of being a friend and critic at the same time and was seemingly unaware of the fact – but she was always honest, and Lisa would rather suffer unintentional jabs than put up with the fake nicey-nicey types she'd gone to school with.

"No, sorry, I was just…thinking about something else."

Morgan lifted her brows expectantly and forked another bite of salad into her mouth.

"Just something my dad said. It was stupid." She wasn't getting her friend pulled into this mess, mostly because Morgan kept secrets from no one.

Her friend shrugged and speared a big, slimy-looking hunk of tomato made all the more unappealing by the ranch dressing that dripped off it. "So *anyway*. If I let Corey take me out again, he's got this buddy – Kyle maybe? Dunno – anyway, he's single. Maybe you could come along and we could go doubles."

Lisa thought being involved in a shop class accident sounded more fun, but she managed a somewhat pleasant expression, or so she hoped. "Isn't Kyle the one who spent a week in ICU after he tried to jump over a UPS truck with his bike?"

"I think so. Why?"

Lisa sighed. "If I have to explain it…"

Forcing herself to eat just wasn't working, so she turned back to the Excel spreadsheet that was open on the computer and began double checking the equations she'd entered before lunch; if she overlooked an error, no one else at the shop would catch it.

"What about that Jonathan guy who was at the bar that night?" Morgan was convinced that losing her single status was the key to all things great in the universe. "He was kinda cute."

"You mean the 'duuude, you're kinda friggin' hot' guy? Or the one who wanted a martini?"

"Both were cute."

"Both were idiots," Lisa countered, shaking her head. A glance confirmed that Morgan was trying to hide a smile.

"I just worry about you is all."

"Maybe you ought to worry about *them* and the possibility that people *like them* will actually reproduce and populate the world."

"You're a buzzkill. Seriously."

"I don't really care – "

"Who in the hell *is that*?"

Lisa knew without even looking, and it only intensified the stomach cramps half an apple had induced, for some reason. Morgan had a bit of a thing for Eddie, but the excited, startled sound of her voice smacked of a brand new fascination. Sure enough, when she glanced up and out through the window, Lisa saw that Drew was back from his errand with Tony and had parked her uncle Mark's truck up close to the office. He was in a plain black t-shirt that had probably come from Wal-Mart, jeans and beat-up New Balance sneakers. His dark hair was in need of buzzing but she thought it looked nice a little bit longer. And his arms looked...well, she wasn't going to think about what his arms looked like, because that took her mind in a dangerous direction.

"A bouncer my dad hired." She only had to lie a little – he was working for her dad and he'd more than likely be on bouncer duty at some point – and made a pointed effort to concentrate on her computer screen.

"He's hot!" Morgan hissed like an excited schoolgirl. There was a rustle as she clamped the plastic lid on her salad and dabbed her mouth with a paper napkin. Lisa heard a distinct set of clicks that could only mean her friend was popping a mint and reapplying her lipstick. By the time the bell jangled above the door and Lisa spared a glance in its direction,

Morgan was primped and waiting, sitting sideways in her chair, lashes ready for the batting.

Drew paused for a moment, whether it was to let his eyes adjust to the dimness or because he felt uneasy with two girls and a semi-awake Doberman staring at him, and Lisa felt a little sorry for him. He was just a big meathead idiot who was in way over his said meat head and she couldn't really blame him for not being smooth.

"Hey," he said, and Lisa had to bite back a laugh as she watched Morgan's cat-like smile creep across her face.

"Well, hey there," she purred.

"Um…hey," Drew repeated. He reached up to scratch the top of his head in a move that was, oddly, a lot like one of Ray's nervous gestures, and Lisa's eyes were drawn to the way the muscles in his arm bunched. He wasn't a huge guy, but he had zero percent body fat, and she told herself it was only natural to stare a moment, before she forced her eyes away.

"Can I help you with something?" Her voice wasn't as polite as she'd intended it to be.

"God, you're so rude, Lis," Morgan said. "I'm sorry," she addressed Drew, "she's just crabby sometimes."

Lisa shot a glare at her friend and accidently-on-purpose glanced up in time to catch Drew's smile. It was a little smile, but it made him look anything but threatening. It, for some reason, wasn't the kind of smile she would have associated with someone like him. And it made her uncomfortable – very uncomfortable – and more than a little embarrassed. Which was *stupid*.

"Maybe I can help you." Morgan sounded exactly like a cat who'd gained the power of speech. She uncrossed and then crossed her legs again. If Lisa hadn't known her friend, she might have been ashamed of the display, but that was the thing about Morgan: she had no shame and Lisa didn't hold it against her.

"Actually, I'm looking for Ray."

"He went to lunch," Lisa said, "but he'll be back in a little while."

He shrugged. "I can wait."

She didn't know how to classify the feeling that washed over her as Morgan smiled widely in delight and invited Drew to sit beside her with a pat of her manicured hand on the neighboring chair. Lisa blinked dumbly and struggled to formulate a theory as to why she felt as if there was a stone sinking in her belly. Morgan flirted outrageously with any man who had a pulse, so that was nothing new, and this guy was a slightly-sketchy boxer her dad had hired on, so it wasn't as if she *cared*. She was just irritated, and didn't know why – or, at least, she told herself she didn't know.

"I'm Morgan," the introduction was made, "what's your name?"

Lisa went back to her number crunching and tuned them out, but she noted that Drew was awkward as he fielded Morgan's questions. She couldn't decide if he was intimidated, uninterested, or simply had no powers of flirtation whatsoever. Morgan picked up on it too because she finally heaved a disappointed sigh and got to her feet.

"Alright, girl, I'm out. Good to meet you, Drew." She cast a last hopeful glance his direction as she gathered up her purse and lunch trash.

"Uh, yeah, you too."

Lisa met her friend's gaze and saw her roll her eyes. "Anyway, Lis, call me later. I was serious about that doubles thing. Kyle's decent and it wouldn't kill you to get some action."

"Yeah," Lisa said dryly, "sounds like a friggin' blast."

Once Morgan was gone, the click of her pumps receding across the parking lot, silence reigned, broken only by the clip of Lisa's fingers over the computer keyboard.

"Well," Drew said finally, "she was…" He let the sentence hang and Lisa snorted.

"She tends to have an overwhelming effect on people."

"I guess you could say that."

A glance revealed that his nose was wrinkled up in a comical display of what she could only categorize as distaste. She bit her lip to keep from smiling and focused on the computer again. "She not your type?" *Why did I ask that?*

122

"No, not really."

She bit her lip so hard she thought she might draw blood. *Why are you smiling, you idiot?* she scolded herself. *Stop the damn smiling!*

"What?" he asked.

Busted. Furiously trying to force her face into a neutral expression, she turned toward him…and glanced up over his shoulder through the window where her eyes locked onto a florist's van cruising to a stop in front of the office. Her mouth went dry. Her heart made a gallant leap up her esophagus. "Oh, God."

"What?" Drew asked again, concern in his voice this time. He twisted around to get a look at what she was staring at.

Whoever was sending the flowers, and whatever message he wanted to convey, he wasn't in the van, ready to pop out. He wasn't there on the lot with her. But a chill that felt like human fingers snaked down her spine. She'd been in more than one chick fight, she'd had menacing, violent things whispered in her ear – mementos from Tristan and his friends – but never had anything ever left her actually a little bit afraid like these mysterious flowers.

The same delivery guy from before climbed out from behind the wheel and went around to open the rear hatch doors. Lisa bit her lip again and this time it had nothing to do with a smile.

"What's wrong?" Drew asked, getting to his feet. Hektor growled at him and he shot the dog a wary glance. "You alright?"

"Fine," she lied, watching the delivery boy prop a glass vase full of white lilies in the crook of his elbow as he started for the door. She licked suddenly dry lips. "Can you get the door for him?"

"Sure." He watched her as he sidestepped over and pushed the door open, which made her more uneasy. Having a witness to her discomfort made her feel more vulnerable, which was possibly the worst sensation in the world. But he didn't look away, his eyes feeling obvious and heavy on her as she signed for the flowers, scrounged up a smile for the delivery guy, answered his inquiry as to her having a secret admirer with a weak "guess so," and then collapsed back into her chair.

Eventually, Drew sat back down. "If this is what you're like when somebody sends you flowers, I'd hate to see your reaction to candy."

He meant it as a joke, but she didn't respond, instead leaned forward to retrieve the note from amidst the flowers. She knew what it would say, but read it anyway. *All the pretty colors for a pretty girl.* Goose bumps prickled up her arms.

"Can you excuse me for a minute?"

When she didn't get up, he asked, "Oh, so…you want me to leave?"

"Yeah, if you would."

"I'm not quitting my job."

"I only have three vacation days left and I'm not using them because of some creep."

Ray watched his wife and daughter pace around the living room like two caged lionesses and asked himself how many times he'd counseled a client about the importance of maintaining a daily routine even in the face of threats. Quitting a job or locking yourself away in your home was the fastest way to ensure a stalker's success, not to mention it tended to royally screw up a person's life.

But he wanted nothing more than to brick up every entrance of the house and not let either of his girls see the light of day again.

"Your mother and I can float you some extra cash to make up for your tips at the bar," he told Lisa, and she glared at him so fiercely he thought she might bare her teeth at him and snarl.

He turned to Cheryl. "And you don't make that much anyway – "

"Do not!" she snapped. "Don't feed me that shit about you being able to afford all this off the garage and those stupid bouncer gigs the boys pull off. This is a team effort, Ray!"

"God, why did I not go to college and get a real job," Lisa groaned.

Two identical bundles of lilies in glass vases sprouted from the coffee table and were as disturbing as two live grenades. Well...*almost*. But they were giving Ray heart palpitations none the less.

"I'm trying to keep you both safe," he said through his teeth.

"From what, exactly?" Cheryl demanded. She paused, arms crossed, one leg propped out to the side in a pose that never failed to make him uncomfortable. "From some mystery flower-giver you won't tell us about?"

He scowled. "Yes."

"Do you think we're completely defenseless?"

Not the point! He wanted to scream at her. He would have worried even if they were walking around in plate armor with a gun in each hand.

"I'm taking a shower," Lisa announced with another groan and abandoned her pacing as she headed for the stairs.

"You are *not* going to work tonight," Ray called after her, feeling desperately out of control of this situation.

"I have the night off," she bit back and kept walking.

When she was gone, Cheryl came closer, looming over the coffee table. "What's going on?" she demanded in a low hiss.

He released his breath in a defeated rush and let his eyes linger on the flowers, their pretty white petals and lush greenery. Lying to his wife was too difficult because she never let it go, never accepted the falsities he fed her. He checked to see that Lisa had truly left the room. "You remember my last case?"

Her unhappy expression seemed to freeze. She nodded. "Carl Shilling."

It felt grievous to voice his worries, to put them in her head and make them real for her, so he decided to shave off

125

some of the gory details. "He had a fixation with flowers" - *he spread their petals over his dead wife and daughter* - "and he left a message – "

Cheryl sucked in a quick, startled breath. "But – but, he went to prison, and he wouldn't know us at all..." It wasn't a question, but she was looking for an answer. The anger bled out of her dark eyes and in its place, fear glazed over them.

"He did." *But he got out.* "And he wouldn't know you." *But he wants to hurt me. The note...baby, you don't understand about the note, and Rene's broken neck, and little Anna all covered in blood...*

"Then – " She ran her hands through her hair, realized too late her dark locks were done up in a clip and that she was ruining her 'do; she took the thing out and came around to sit beside him. "Raymond." His mother was dead, so sometimes she liked to fill the role herself. "I know you don't like to scare Lis, but I can handle it. You know who's sending the flowers, don't you?"

Yes. "Not really for sure, no."

She lifted a single brow in challenge.

"I just get worried, is all." She wasn't buying it. "So, please, let me be worried for a little while and I'll...I dunno, send one of the boys to sit on a stool while Lis works, keep an eye on her."

"I guess that could work."

"You're smarter that those women who pretend the world's made out of marshmallows," he said, and she conceded with a nod and a twitchy smile.

"Yeah."

"I'm not being paranoid, I'm being cautious. Humor me for a bit until this blows over?"

Cheryl had a hundred questions shining in her eyes, but she nodded, slid her hand into his. He saw her shoulders sag as she sighed and felt a pang of sympathy for her; he wasn't easy to live with and in truth, it was a miracle she hadn't left him long ago.

***

126

Eddie and Sly's rented house was a ranch with gray wood siding and a brick façade. It was situated on a dead-end road in a nameless subdivision full of tall, well-established trees and forty-year-old homes that were owned by original tenants or what looked to be young families with Fisher Price toys in the yards. It had a chain link fence around the perimeter and a carport instead of a garage, no landscaping, just lawn and concrete front stoop. But it was as neat and tidy as a hospital.

Except for the fridge. There were things *growing* in the fridge. But whatever they were, they seemed to be in an earlier stage of development than the things that had been growing in Josh's fridge.

Drew pushed aside a jar of what he thought were jalapeños and grabbed one of the chocolate protein shakes he'd bought the day before – one was already missing thanks to his roommates. As he stepped back and closed the door of the dingy white Maytag, Sly seemed to materialize in the threshold between kitchen and living room. Drew didn't want to be startled, but he couldn't quite help it.

Sly – continuing to prove that he didn't in fact smile more once you'd spent more time around him – twitched his brows in a look that suggested he knew he'd surprised Drew. He held up his cell phone in one hand. "Just got off the line with Ray. He's got a job for you tomorrow night."

"Really? What?"

127

14

In retrospect, Lisa wished she'd walked her flowers around to the dumpster the moment they'd arrived, and chucked them in, note and all, without telling her father about any of it. Because then she wouldn't have been required to bring a *security detail* to work.

Night had yet to fall, but what was left of the sun was hidden behind the trees, the sky overhead a backdrop of murky blue-gray, the orange neon of the Double Vision billboard flickering ominously against it. A steady stream of traffic was snaking its way into the parking lot, but Lisa's protectors of the evening had managed to find a spot beside hers – oh, how lucky. As she tugged at the too-short, frayed hem of her denim miniskirt, she watched, scowling, as Eddie and Drew climbed out of Mark's old blue Chevy and came around behind the tailgate to join her.

"This is beyond unnecessary," she said, smoothing her hands down the front of her lemon yellow halter top.

Eddie – who'd attempted to dress up in a black button-up and dark, dark jeans – licked his thumb and crouched down to wipe a spot off one of his white sneakers. "You say it all you want, sweetheart, but one of your old man's checks means I gotta disagree with you."

She sighed, miserable, and glanced to Drew. He was more casual in jeans and a t-shirt, and far less comfortable about the whole thing. With his hands in his pockets and his shoulders bunched up, he looked like he'd rather be anyplace else, which struck Lisa as odd. Eddie would have arm-wrestled for the chance to sit around in a bar and watch hot chicks twitch their way across the dance floor while he was on the company clock. Conversely, Drew was staring across the parking lot with worry lines pressed between his dark eyebrows; he turned his head in her direction as if he'd felt her eyes on him. Lisa looked away first – not sure she was at all comfortable with him tagging along; he looked edgy and nervous and like he was taking this much too seriously. Eddie wouldn't bother her – he'd be too busy watching everyone else – but she wasn't comfortable with this near-stranger staring at her all night. Especially not since she was dressed like a piece of meat.

"Well." She slipped the strap of her purse over her head. "Guess stalling won't make this any better."

"You know." Eddie fell in beside her and draped an arm across her shoulders as they walked, leaving Drew to follow. "You have to be here anyway, but me…I'm the one who's had his night ruined."

"You can't make me feel guilty," she said, and meant it.

"You know you'd be chasing tail anyway." He snorted. "Might as well do it with free beer."

"Free?"

"I'm a very important person here."

"No, you're not."

"No, I'm not."

The Double Vision had been monstrous and overwhelming on her first visit, this terrifying crush of humanity and debauchery. Now, though familiar, even comfortable at times, it still felt like six acres of amusement park packed in under a roof. Though the lot was filling up, the interior of the bar looked almost empty. Customers already inside had come early to snag the good tables up on the balcony or favorite stools at the bar. A pair of gray, grizzled biker types were at one of the pool tables. A trio of girls who looked like they'd smiled their way past the bouncers with fake IDs were already into the tequila shots and attempting to dance, much to the amusement of the older men watching them from a nearby table.

The usual.

Lisa started down the wide steps – carefully, thanks to her platforms – to the main floor and headed toward the bar, feeling about twelve-years-old with an escort tailing her. Even if she liked Eddie – which she did – and even if she was fast developing this urge to let her eyes move over Drew – which she was – the idea of them being sent after her, like guard dogs, put spurs in the flanks of her self-righteousness.

Regular people did not have bodyguards. Regular dads called the police and double checked their locks at night and didn't send boxers and dishonorably discharged Navy SEALs to work with their daughters on the off chance that flower-stalkers showed up. Then again…ordinary girls didn't have flower-stalkers, did they? Nor fathers who cared about them so much.

She sighed as she drew up to the massive, free-floating bar and traded waves with one of her fellow bartenders, Holly. She understood her dad's need to play certain things close to the vest. She was just frustrated with the shady life she seemed to be living lately. All the secrets and shifty eyes were getting to her.

"You guys can hang out here." She half-turned and waved to indicate bar stools to the boys.

"For now," Eddie said with a smirk.

Cheryl's yellow million bells had overgrown their pot and tumbled over the side, a waterfall of lemon and green, the perkiest, happiest flowers in all of her garden. She loved her pine chipped beds bursting with perennials, but she loved the pots on the porch too. Delicately, she pinched the dead blossoms off and put them in the plastic bucket she was using for trash/compost.

The sun had just slipped like an orange bobber beneath the dark surface of the horizon, but the porch lamps offered plenty of light for her task. Behind her, she heard the ice cubes shift in Sly's glass. She could smell the butter and garlic of the leftover pasta she'd reheated for him.

"Dinner good?" she asked, pausing to wipe the perspiration from her forehead with the back of her gloved hand. She felt her feathered bangs get stuck along her temples.

"Yup."

She'd always liked Sly. Mark was the happy one and Eddie the one who always said things he shouldn't. But Sly was the quiet one. Lisa had a theory about quietness: it didn't mean a person was stupid, only that he was listening better than everyone else. And that was true for Sly. He saw things other people didn't see, heard things others were too loud to pick up on. It was the reason he was here alone, and why Ray had felt the need to send two men with Lisa; Sly was twice as effective as everyone else.

"You know, something about being guarded makes my evening less relaxing," she joked.

He snorted.

"Ray's being paranoid about all this."

"He's good at that."

Her legs sore from crouching, she sat back on the porch planks and stretched them out in front of her, arms draped over her knees. "You're smart." She turned her head so she could see him sitting in one of the white rocking chairs against the wall. He lifted a brow in acknowledgment. "Tell me something: how worried should I be about all this?"

"I'm sitting here watching you pick dead flowers...how worried do you think you should be?"

Cheryl sighed. "Good point."

"I'm not going to ask you what you're doing with this," Tony had said as he'd passed Ray the index card, "but for Christ's sakes, don't get yourselves arrested. Or get *me* arrested."

Tony's worries had been all for naught; Ray was perfectly capable of comporting himself in a professional, polite manner. Certainly.

At least, that's what he told himself as he walked through the automatic sliding glass doors and into the air lock at the La Quinta Inn and Suites where Carl Shilling worked.

As was typical of most hotel chains, the air lock opened into a lobby with tan tile floors and decorated with affordable furniture that had been designed to look more expensive than it was. Ray glanced over the dark wood and green upholstery of the chairs, saw open double doors to the left that probably led into a small dining room where continental breakfast was served, ahead to the elevators, and finally to the right where two young women in blazers stood behind the registration counter.

The women – and they were girls, really, younger than Lisa – were flipping through magazines and talking animatedly with one another, lots of hand gestures and "oh my God"s thrown in for emphasis. By the time Ray reached the counter, he'd come to the conclusion that some celebrity or other had dumped some other celebrity or some such bullshit. It was after nine and the lobby was a ghost town, so neither employee seemed all that eager to set aside their gossip and tend to business.

"Yessss." The brunette put an extra S or two on for emphasis. "She actually dumped him for *Derek Whitley!* Can you believe that?"

"What? *No way!*" The blonde grabbed for the magazine, but froze, purple-manicured nails stuck like claws in the air, and glanced up at Ray and Mark. "Oh, um, hi. Just a sec." She raked her purple nails back through her hair, gave her head a little toss, and straightened her green blazer. "'Kay. You guys need to make a reservation or something?"

Ray almost wanted to smile. Almost. "No. Actually, I checked out this morning, but I'm afraid I left a bag behind. I was wondering if I could look through your lost-and-found."

The girls traded looks. "Yeah," the slack-jawed brunette finally said.

"The janitor staff keeps up with that stuff," the blonde said. "We gotta have our manager walk you back, though."

"That's fine; I'll wait."

The blonde walked off, presumably to get the manager, and the brunette returned to the magazine.

Mark leaned closer, his voice not even a whisper. "And what if we don't see Shilling?"

"I'm not leaving till we do."

***

Eddie was so not taking this seriously. Drew was so wired he felt sure he'd somehow been plugged into an electrical outlet, and conversely, Eddie was draping himself all over a golden-haired chick in a leopard print dress. While Drew had sipped on a beer, he'd counted Eddie's three Jack and Cokes.

It was annoying. Ray had told them to "watch Lisa," so that's what he was doing. He'd watched her attempt to flirt with a group of college-age boys in what had to be a ploy for a big tip. He'd watched her tug at the hem of her skirt while a comically frustrated expression darkened her face. He'd watched little chips of ice run down the beer bottles in her hands and land on her thighs; and he'd watched the goose flesh erupt on her legs because of it. He'd watched her and watched her and watched her until he had tunnel vision. So long that, as she finished serving a couple their drinks and headed his way, he didn't force his eyes away and try to look casual. She had her elbows propped on the bar and was leaning down in his face, flashing cleavage and a pinched expression, her heart pendant necklace swinging forward on its chain before he could react.

"You're staring at me," she said and didn't sound happy about it. "I mean, really staring. Chill."

"Uh..." He felt like a teenager who'd been busted. "Your dad said to – "

"Well, he's not here and you're freaking my customers out."

"Hey, Lis." Eddie's voice drew both their attentions. "You alright? 'Cause I was thinking..." He jerked a thumb over his shoulder and Drew followed it with his eyes to see Leopard Dress heading toward the dance floor, wineglass in hand.

He was disappointed in the guy. You didn't take payment for a job you were going to flake off on. You just *didn't*.

But Lisa rolled her eyes and nodded. "I think the newbie's got it covered. Go."

Newbie? He waited for it, and it came: her condescending stare. She was on edge tonight, more so than usual. At the shop, she'd seemed in control of her attitude, but here, tonight, she wasn't trying to hide her dislike for him. There were daggers in her eyes tonight.

"I was serious about the staring," she said, and turned her back to him, off to tend to another customer.

Humoring her, he made a slow, visual sweep of the rest of the bar, his eyes feeling overstimulated. The place was a circus. The music – a strange playlist of rock, pop and hip-hop – was so loud the foot rail on the bar vibrated beneath his sneakers, and still he could hear shrieks of laughter and a tumbling swell of voices above it. There were *so many* people, too many to properly make out anyone's face, or to see if there were any questionable figures lurking in corners. At least, Drew assumed he was supposed to be looking for lurkers.

Ray had been vague, apparently, and Sly probably more so. All he'd been told was that he was supposed to not let anything happened to Lisa. Only, what constituted "anything?" And was this anything going to be a big enough problem that he would need Eddie's help? He hoped not, because the guy had vanished into the press of humanity and likely wouldn't be back.

When he looked at Lisa again, he picked up on her defensive posture immediately. The bar was a long rectangle and she stood in the far corner of it, as far away from him as she could be, and was squared off from two male customers. Both looked around her age. One was a half head taller than the other and skinny in an awkward sort of way. The other was tan, dark-haired and had one of those obnoxious male model-type faces, white teeth flashing as he smiled a false, predatory smile. Drew had no hope of knowing what was said, and he couldn't read lips. But Lisa's demeanor had changed completely. Stress lines crimped the corners of her eyes and her arms were folded over her chest. He'd seen her do the lean-and-squeeze all evening in between eye rolls and sighs in an effort to rake in tips, but whoever these guys were, she wasn't willing to play the game with them.

This definitely counted as "anything."

Against his better judgment, he waited until she came back his way to take two beers out of the cooler. "Lisa."

Her green eyes were wide and almost startled as her head swiveled in his direction. She was definitely jumpier than she had been. But she schooled her features. "What?"

"Who are those guys down there?"

She pulled two Coors Lights and popped the tops off along the edge of the bar. "Just some assholes I know." Her tone was clipped. "It's fine."

"Your dad – " he started to protest.

"*Fine*," she cut him off and walked away with a look that was meant as a warning.

Except that it wasn't. No one had ever mistaken him for intelligent – he'd been told the opposite was true his whole life – but there was a difference between smart and dumb. He wasn't dumb. He watched Lisa set the beers in front of the two men and saw the tremor in her hands, interpreted the look on her face as pure revulsion.

The guys – Mr. White Teeth and Mr. Adam's Apple – leaned their heads together and shared a laugh, their eyes on Lisa's retreating back.

When she passed in front of Drew again a few minutes later, he snaked a hand across the bar and caught her wrist. His fingers went all the way around her delicate little bones and overlapped one another, so he didn't squeeze, but held. Whatever pink cocktail was in the martini glass she held slopped out over the side, running down his hand.

"What?" she snapped, eyes flashing.

He didn't back down. "*Who* are those guys? I'm not here to drink. I'm supposed to be watching you."

He hadn't intended to shout, but he must have, because the men sitting on either side of him were suddenly staring, curious, their beer bottles hovering in front of their faces.

Lisa's mouth drew up in a tight, angry bow. "Watch any harder and your eyes are gonna pop outta your head." When she yanked away from him, he let her go, getting showered with pink chick drink again.

The guy to his left, a middle-aged fan of leather bomber jackets and too much hair gel, snorted. "Maybe you shouldn't let your girl work here."

Drew didn't correct his assumption. "No shit." He picked up his beer again and wondered where the hell Eddie was.

15

Lisa had been sure that Tristan's stranglehold on her life had ended the day she left him gaping after her on the altar. As it turned out, the egotistical jackass couldn't stand the notion that a girl had left him, rather than the other way around, and insisted on harassing her when he felt like it. She wanted to say she'd grown accustomed to it, but she couldn't – he was just too much of an asshole for his presence not to bother her.

Tonight, he'd brought his buddy Nick along. Nick who'd always been the gangliest, most awkward of the group of friends, and the one who, through no coincidence, always made Tristan look twice as handsome. He was a geek who had a laugh like the bray of a donkey, and he never missed a chance to hurl it in her direction.

"...I'm just saying," Tristan continued as Lisa carried two pint glasses of Heineken to her next customers and forced a smile for them as she tried to ignore her ex. "We both know you're gonna say 'yes,' so you might as well not say 'no' now."

If she'd been a pot on the stove, her thermometer would have shattered by now. She felt red; hot and red and full of loathing. How had she ever held any affection for this man? She'd told him she'd *loved* him. She'd agreed to *marry* him! How? Just how? What a stupid, naïve little fool she'd been.

Now, she wasn't even bitter, she was just tired. Her hatred for Tristan was not, she told herself with conviction, because she had any residual feelings for the prick, but because she had no room in her life for him or anyone like him.

"I'm not gonna say no," she told him, sparing him her darkest of looks, "I'm gonna say hell no, and you're gonna shut your damn face."

Nick let loose with one of his donkey laughs, his skinny, pimply cheeks turning bright red.

Tristan's smile tightened, but he persisted. "You know my mom always loved you – "

"Your mother hated me!" Lisa halted, though she knew she shouldn't have. She wiped beer and condensation off her hands onto her apron and glared at him. "She always did! So just *stop it.*"

"Don't be sore at me," he defended. "I just think it'd be good for you is all. You spend all your time with those…mechanics…of your dad's and I think you need – "

"I need for you to get the hell out of this bar," she hissed, and hated the smug look that spread across his tan face.

"Only trying to help, Lis."

She ground her teeth together and closed her eyes, willing herself to calm down. *I'm at work*, she reminded herself. *Don't make a scene.*

"Miss?" someone inquired from down the bar and she headed that direction. Three women who looked like moms having a night out ordered appletinis and she walked the long way around the bar to fill their order.

Drew leaned forward to catch her attention as she passed him and she stopped, sighing, wanting to avoid him grabbing at her again. "I know," she said in a defeated voice. "You're trying to do your job."

"I am." He nodded and shot a pointed glance down the bar toward Tristan that was comical in its focus and gravity. He hadn't enjoyed his evening for a second. Had only had half a beer. For a moment, he reminded her so much of her dog, Lisa felt a softening toward him.

Poor guy. "It's fine," she said again, and patted the top of his head before she could change her mind and before he could give her a curious glance. His hair was soft and spiky against her palm.

She *was* fine, but far from pleasant, because when she was forced to circle back around and check on Tristan and Nick – they were paying, after all – the two were whispering, laughing and staring at her in a show of childish gossip.

"Lis," Tristan said when she was close enough to hear. "Stop being difficult. You and me, we're friends." Nick sniggered beside him. "And I want my friend – "

"To come to your wife's baby shower? Are you kidding me?" She controlled her anger and it was a tight ball of nastiness in her voice. "And news flash, dumbass, we're not friends."

Nick turned around on his stool and covered his mouth with his hand, presumably braying some more.

Tristan, full of pretend patience now that they were no longer together, made a *tsk*-ing sound. "Do you *have* any friends?" he asked, looking delighted with himself. "Not too many people out there who'd put up with that temper."

In what alternate dimension would Missy want me at her baby shower? Was what she wanted to scream at him. Instead, she took a deep, somewhat steadying breath, averted her eyes up over his head…and saw that Drew was standing behind him. "Oh, God, *no*," she said. "Do *not*."

"Don't what?" Tristan grumbled, and turned.

Though masterful when it came to false niceties, Tristan couldn't conceal his sudden alarm. Lisa saw his body tense, registered the momentary shock she could see on the half of his face that was still visible to her.

"Do not," Lisa repeated to Drew, and was rewarded with a brief touch of his eyes against hers in which he plainly told her to screw off.

"Dude." Tristan looked the boxer up and down. "Ya mind?"

As much as Lisa might have enjoyed boxing as a sport – when it was contained within a ring with refs and gloves and rules – she had no desire to see it right here in the bar where she worked. "No, he doesn't mind," she said in a rush, but was ignored.

As she watched, Drew scowled. "Leave her alone."

Lisa groaned. Where the hell was Eddie?

"*Leave her alone?*" Tristan repeated. He chuckled. "Are you serious right now?"

Drew's face screwed up and Lisa didn't know if it was because he was embarrassed, or because he was angry. Either seemed probable.

"What?" Tristan went on. "You like her?" He gestured toward Lisa with his beer bottle and laughed. "Trust me, bro, you don't wanna bother."

Had they been anywhere but her job site, Lisa would have backhanded him. She was done. Past done – with this farce of a conversation and everything about Tristan's smirky face. But she was at work, which meant she had to swallow her loathing.

Drew, though…*bless his heart*, she thought in some small part of her very Southern brain that smacked of her mother…he was trying to be a good watch dog. Like Hektor, he had his hackles up and was smelling out a threat. Or, at least, what he thought was a threat. Maybe she should have explained who Tristan was. Maybe she should have allayed his fears with more tact…

Because suddenly Tristan was on his feet and trying to push Drew back away from him, Nick coming to lend assistance. *You idiot*, she thought of Tristan. *What a stupid damn idiot*. Because people who'd been raised and trained to fight had triggers. You did not *push* a boxer.

She was scrambling over the top of the bar, heedless of her skirt and heels and all the reasons she should not be climbing anything, yelling for them to move away from each other. But Drew's fist was already in motion. When it collided with the side of Tristan's face, Lisa didn't know if the *crack* she heard was hand or cheek breaking. Or maybe both.

The night manager was a heavyset, thirty-something, balding man who would have looked more at home at a comic book convention. He walked ahead of them down a hall that, due to its utter plainness, could only have been meant for staff, his key card dangling from a pudgy hand by a Batman lanyard. "What room did you say you were in?" he asked, twisting his head around as far as he could manage on a thick neck.

"Two-oh-three," Ray lied with ease. He had his hands in his pockets and had smoothed his face into a neutral expression. He was just a guy coming to look for his luggage.

The manager nodded and kept moving forward, panting as he waddled. "The housekeeping staff is supposed to bring down any recovered items and then label them according to room number." He shrugged. "Here's hoping, huh?"

The lost-and-found was at the end of the hall, behind a door whose marker proclaimed *Staff Only*. The manager slid his key card through the reader and the lock clicked open with an electronic *beep*. The lights were already on and at first glance, the room appeared to be a storage space for janitorial supplies – metal shelves full of industrial bottles of cleaner and spare mop heads lining the walls. But in the center, two cafeteria style tables were overflowing with personal effects, everything from shaving kits to briefcases to tubes of lipstick. Suitcases had been stuffed beneath.

But Ray didn't let his eyes linger on any of it, because in the corner of the room, sitting at a card table with a microwave on top of it, was Carl Shilling. He didn't see them at first, was staring down into a Styrofoam cup of black coffee. He was thinner than Ray remembered. He'd lost that golden golf course tan and the sun streaks in his dark hair. Now he looked ten years older, gray at the temples, a haggard patchwork of silver stubble covering sunken cheeks. In a green jumpsuit, a mess of keys hooked to his belt, he looked anything but threatening…or even cunning.

But the hairy arms and wrists his folded-back sleeves revealed still looked strong. The hands that had broken his wife's neck were still big and full of death.

"Two-oh-three, you said?" the manager asked. He leaned forward at the waist, his huge belly stopping him short, and began fumbling under the table to check tags. "It'd be under here if it's been found."

"I'll help you look," Mark offered, and Ray watched his brother position himself between the manager and the corner

141

where Carl was sitting, giving Ray the briefest of windows. It wasn't much help, but it was all the help he could offer. He was a good brother like that most of the time.

Ray was glad he'd had a chance to give the man a once-over before he was spotted, because Carl had lifted his head at the sound of Mark's voice, and now his eyes went wide as they found and recognized his former attorney.

"A lotta help you were."

"This isn't my fault." Eddie was so earnest and righteous about the whole thing, it was comical. Lisa might have laughed if she wasn't digging for a first aid kit in the nightmarish clutter beneath the utility sink in the Double Vision break room. "How was I supposed to know he's this big of a dumbass?"

Lisa twisted around – she was halfway inside the cabinet – and saw that Drew was still sitting on the bench between the two walls of lockers, staring at the toes of his sneakers, expressionless and silent. She almost felt sorry for him, for reasons she didn't quite understand. All the tenacity he'd exhibited when he'd not only punched Tristan, but flattened the douchebag back over the bar, had bled out of him. Lisa's manager had come charging in and bouncers had materialized…it had been a huge scene. It had taken no small amount of pleading to get the guys back here in the break room and keep Drew out of the backseat of a police cruiser.

"Whatever happened to leading by example?" she fired back.

A scowl darkened Eddie's handsome face and for a moment, he looked less of a playboy and more the military man he'd once been. Unlike Sly, there were two sides to Eddie O'Dell, and Lisa didn't think either of them were all that pretty, physical traits aside. If he didn't work for her dad, if she hadn't been given unspoken permission to act as his employer when Ray or Mark were absent, she might have bitten her tongue around him. *Might* have, but probably not.

"Nevermind," she said, backing out from under the cabinet empty-handed. "Just go on and do *who*ever you need to do. I'll bring him back to the house."

Eddie held her gaze a moment, his eyes brimming with threats he knew he couldn't and shouldn't make, but then he backed down, leaving with a muttered curse. The door swung shut loudly behind him, the music like a wave as it crashed inside the room and then faded back to a dull thudding from the other side of the walls.

Drew was still a living statue on the bench, his right hand resting on his knee. His knuckles were red with the first kiss of a bruise that would probably turn purple later, and Lisa thought she could see swelling. Tristan's left eye had been a watery slit when Nick had led him from the bar, the tissue around his eye socket broken and bleeding; she didn't doubt his orbital was fractured.

"What happened to the ice I gave you?" she asked as she stepped up in front of him and knelt to look more closely at the damage.

He moved for the first time since sitting down, reaching over for the leaking Ziploc bag of half-melted ice that should have been on his knuckles.

Lisa waited, expecting him to look up at her, to say something, to insist he was fine or tell her to back off or brag or…something. But he kept his head down. She could see his lashes flutter as he blinked, but otherwise he remained motionless.

"Can you move your fingers?" she asked, and they drummed against his knee in response. She saw the tremor race up his arm though. Carefully, as if approaching a startled animal, she reached up and took his hand in both of hers. It was big and heavy and all bones and tendons. When she palpated his knuckles, she heard his breath catch, and she knew why when she felt what reminded her of shattered glass beneath his skin. "You need to go have this X-rayed." Lisa dropped his hand, but stayed on her knees.

He shrugged, and his head tilted up enough so she could see his eyes. He was in pain, probably a lot of it, and his face was strained with the effort of not showing it. "Won't say anything I don't already know," he said.

An old injury, she realized. One made worse tonight. "It needs a cast, or splint at best," she insisted, but not unkindly. She'd really wanted to be furious with him for starting a bar fight, but it hadn't been a brawl, and he hadn't taken any pleasure in it. He looked so miserable now, it was almost endearing.

"Can't do shit with a cast on." He shook his head. "And it won't fix anything."

"Don't try to be macho about it."

"I'm not."

And he sounded sincere. Lisa was fast realizing that the only thing better than watching Tristan get his face ruined was not having to hear a bunch of gloating about it afterward.

She bit back a smile. "Will you at least let me tape it up? And keep the ice on it?"

He shrugged. "Sure."

"Alright, well, there's not shit here, so we'll stop somewhere on our way out. I've gotta feeling your ride won't be waiting anyway."

16

Carl hadn't been a smoker when Ray knew him last, but he was now, hands shaking as he cupped them around the cigarette that dangled from his lips and lit up. With no more than a handful of words, Ray had gained the man's audience, and now the three of them stood in the rear of the hotel, standing in the dewy grass that separated the building from the parking lot. An occasional car slid around the corner, searching for a space, but they had plenty of privacy.

"How've you been?" Mark started the conversation, as congenial as ever. Ray saw the tightness in his brother's face, though.

Carl shrugged. He was a tall guy, taller than both of them, but he'd lost a considerable amount of weight. Physically intimidating before, now he looked like a child could have pushed him over…which, Ray thought bitterly, might be a necessity with this asshole. "I'm working." His voice didn't even sound the same. "I've got an apartment."

"You been in touch with your family at all?"

He had parents and a sister who lived south of Atlanta, but he shook his head. "No."

The major disadvantage of being a lawyer was being limited by the actual law. Here, in the shadows, Ray had no laws to which to adhere. He wasn't going to waste time with court-approved interrogation tactics.

"The flowers, Carl," Ray prompted. "That shit stops tonight, you understand?"

The man's face went blank – he'd always been quite the actor – and he scratched at his graying stubble. "I don't know what you mean. Flowers? What – "

So flooded with sudden rage, Ray might have tackled the guy if not for Mark's hand on his shoulder. He settled for glaring a hole through his lying, wife-killing face. "'All the

145

pretty colors for a pretty girl,'" he recited and Carl's already-pale cheeks went white. Ray pulled his iPhone from his back pocket and scrolled through his photos until he found the shot of Lisa's flowers sitting on the desk at the office. "No one would say that but you," he said through his teeth, showing the picture to Carl. "It stops. Now. If you've got a beef with me, you come after me, but you leave my family out of this."

The janitor raised his hands in a helpless display. A fine sheen of perspiration glittered across his forehead. "Ray, I swear – "

"I don't want your swears. Nothing but shit comes outta your mouth." Ray was aware, in the professional part of his brain that was dedicated to all things impartial and suave, that his legal prowess abandoned him when it came to his wife and daughter. Which was dangerous, but he couldn't seem to control himself at this point. Raymond Russell esquire had abandoned him, and in his place, big brother Ray from Cartersville was doing all the talking.

"This isn't a discussion," he continued, satisfied that Carl retreated a step. "This is me telling you that if you don't back off now, if you keep harassing my girls, I'll put a bullet in you and there's not a damn soul who could find your body."

Carl swallowed, Adam's apple jackknifing in his throat.

"We clear?"

He nodded.

Mark pulled Ray away and across the parking lot before he could say anything else damning. Ray caught one last glimpse of Carl Shilling's stricken face, then he shook off his brother's hand and followed willingly.

"That was subtle," Mark said with a snort as they moved single file between two cars.

"It wasn't supposed to be," Ray said. "Monsters don't understand subtle."

Lisa had traded her heels for cowboy boots in the bar parking lot, and Drew heard her approaching now. She had the hood of her zipped sweatshirt pulled up. A big bag of Twizzlers was sticking out of one pocket and she had a limp one dangling from her mouth like a thin, red lizard tongue while she juggled the rest of her purchases in her arms. He was sitting on the lowered tailgate, waiting, because she'd insisted she didn't need his help. The way she dumped all her boxes into the bed of the truck told him otherwise, though, and he felt guilty.

"Twizzler?" she asked, taking a bite of hers and pulling the rest out of her mouth. She turned around and hopped backward onto the tailgate, booted feet swinging.

Drew had expected her to rage at him after his bar stunt, but she'd been surprisingly cordial. Friendly, even. "No, thanks."

She reached into her other hoodie pocket and pulled out a king size Snickers that she waved in offering.

"Not part of my...program."

She bit off another section of Twizzler and rolled her eyes. "God. You're on one of those training diets where you can only eat chick food, aren't you?"

It sounded ridiculous when phrased that way. He thought of the breakfast he'd had at IHOP that morning of his "interrogation" – definitely not on the diet. "Kinda. But guess I'm done with that now."

She shrugged. "I don't care." The last of the candy was folded into her mouth and, cheeks puffed out like a chipmunk while she chewed, she reached for a box of medical tape. "I was gonna buy a brace," she said, mouth still mostly full, "but that was kinda expensive, so...yeah. Jumbo craft sticks for a dollar. Grab two."

He complied with his good hand, amused that here they sat in the Wal-Mart parking lot, passersby giving them strange looks like they were teenagers loitering so they didn't have to go home.

A silence that wasn't uncomfortable descended as she opened the tape with a wicked looking pocket knife and then framed his knuckles with the craft sticks. Her fingertips were so small, smooth and cool against his burning skin. A shiver went up his spine at the contact. Even this kind of touch felt like an accomplishment, like two steps away from those

147

slender little fingers framing his face as her lips sought his. *Stupid,* he scolded himself.

She'd gone twice around his hand, the tape coming off its spool with loud sounds, when Drew decided that she was in a good enough mood for him to press her for information. "So what's your dad gonna say?"

A thoughtful frown flitted across her face. "It's good to be worried about him, you know. He really does like to have his ass kissed." She snorted. "But he'll probably shake your hand when he hears you hit Tristan."

What a stupid damn name. "Tristan?" he asked. "And we hate him because...?"

Her shoulders sagged as she sighed. Her hands kept working, but the change in her posture was notable. "Tristan Albright." She said the name like it left a bad taste in her mouth. "The douchebag I almost married."

He hadn't expected that. He blinked.

She glanced at his face and then looked away, sighing again. "Yeah, I know." She sounded embarrassed.

"So...you were engaged to him?"

The light was poor, but her grimace was clear. "Right up until I walked away from him in front of the minister."

It was more than a little difficult to imagine her up in front of a crowd in a white dress. Not because it was a bad mental picture, but because the guy he'd punched at the bar had been one of those pretty boy types, and he hadn't figured her for liking those. It was sobering, really. All girls preferred pretty boys at the end of the day, he guessed.

"Anyway," Lisa continued. "I moved on, but he likes to keep torturing me." She finished the wrap job on his hand, ripped the tape in two and secured it, then scowled at what he'd known from the start would be an ineffective solution. "Well, that didn't work." She started peeling the tape off.

"It'll be fine," Drew said. "I'll put some more ice on it and – "

Her eyes flashed up to his, bright green and almost neon in the glow of the street lamp a few parking spaces away. "No, I'm gonna do it," she said stubbornly, sounding more frustrated with her own fumbling than his protests. "It's the least I can do."

He watched, patient, as she tore into boxes of heavy duty foam and tape that were better suited for the job – like the stuff basketball players taped their ankles with – and tried to think of something to ask her that wouldn't piss her off.

She beat him to it. "So when did you break it the first time?"

Drew shrugged and extended his hand at her beckoning fingers. "Couple years ago." The first time around with the foam was so tight his skin felt pulled, which was a good thing, though painful. "Cage match. Guy got me penned up against the post." Sometimes he still dreamed the pain again. After a hard fight, as he drifted between the layers of consciousness, the fire in his hand would roar until he thought he was back in that cage, his bones shattering to bits under his opponent's boot.

Lisa whistled softly as she wrapped. "Cage match? That's…"

"Stupid," he finished for her, and she chuckled. "Yeah. But I needed the money. And, well." He shrugged. "It's the only thing I do right."

She secured the end of the tape down and then smoothed her fingers over her handiwork, which, actually, felt like it might do some good. Regardless, it was better than having a useless, plaster-covered arm for six weeks. "I dunno if it's the *only* thing," she said, a smile lifting the corners of her mouth. "You were pretty good at making Tristan look like shit tonight."

Something in his chest contracted at the praise. Her face, tipped up to his in the shadowy parking lot, was absolutely beautiful. "So I'm not getting fired?" He was only half serious.

"Definitely not."

Done, she sat back, hands falling in her lap, hair sliding over her shoulder and shielding part of her face from view, so only her nose was visible. For the first time, Drew sensed an awkwardness from her. When she was busy, she was totally in control, but now, he swore he felt her putting bricks of ice up between them.

"So, guess we better get going," she said, hopping off the tailgate abruptly. "I'll drop you by the house on my way home."

And just like that, the camaraderie was over.

The house was dark save for one upstairs window when Ray and Mark returned. The small lamp in the kitchen hadn't been visible from the front of the house, but Sly was flipping through a magazine at the big ranch table by its light. He lifted his head as they entered and gave a nod of greeting, then went back to his magazine.

"What'd you find?" he asked.

Mark went to the fridge for a beer. Ray pulled out the chair across from Sly and collapsed into it, hands finding his face and sliding down it in a habit Cheryl always chastised him about. "Shilling was there. And he's good and spooked."

"Spooked?" Sly closed the magazine. "How?"

Mark joined them. "Like Ray was the damn ghost of Christmas past. I swear he was gonna piss himself."

"Or," Ray said, "like he knew he'd been caught."

Sly's glance spoke his agreement, but Mark gave a facial shrug. "Think what you want, but that wasn't the face of a stalker we saw tonight."

Ray scowled down at his hands as he flattened them on the table top. Mark had a point…if he only looked at the surface of their encounter. The hard truth of the matter was that a guy like Carl, who'd fooled a poor, unsuspecting woman into marrying him, into having a child with him, could easily play the innocent when asked about two bouquets of flowers. Monsters had to learn to hide their obsessions and proclivities – it was a survival technique that enabled them to blend into their world, to thrive in it even. Carl Shilling had been a successful businessman, well-loved by family and community. No one had seen the tragedy coming. Which meant no amount of "spooked" under the streetlamp that night could ease Ray's fears.

And they *were* fears. Suspicions were for everyone else, but when it came down to his family, it was terror that ran like chunks of ice through his veins.

"How'd things go here?" he asked, wanting to change the topic even if he already knew the answer.

Sly shrugged. "Fine. The missus and I designed a living room. It's monochromatic," he deadpanned, gesturing toward Cheryl's sketch pad at the edge of the table. His message was code for: *nothing suspicious happened, so stop worrying.* And what had Ray expected? A drive-by? Kidnapping? A brick through the window?

In truth, he had no idea what to expect. Shilling didn't have a previous record, so God knew if this was part of some sick pattern he'd kept all his life. Or if, just maybe, Mark had been right and this was the work of some copycat who knew about the flowers and the note found with little Anna Shilling's body.

"Thanks," he told Sly, and the mechanic pushed back his chair with a nod.

He was out the back door and his bike was grumbling to life in the drive before Mark spoke again. "Do you want my real opinion?"

Ray glanced at his brother with a snort. "Didn't you already give it to me?"

"I don't think Shilling sent the girls the flowers."

"You have a better explanation then?"

"Hell if I know. But what we saw tonight…that just doesn't sit right with me."

And since when are you the perceptive one? he wanted to ask, but kept the thought to himself.

Headlights cut a bright path across the tile as they came flooding in through the windows of the screened-in porch. Hektor had been stretched out asleep in the corner, and rose with a yawn, going to meet Lisa as she entered.

"Hey." She didn't seem surprised to see both of them awake and at the table.

151

"Hi, sweetie," Mark greeted.

Ray was preoccupied with the realization that she was very alone and unescorted. "Where's your detail?"

"Well, let's see." She pulled out a chair and sat, scratching Hektor behind the ears when he laid his head across her knees. "Eddie may or not may not have gone home with some chick. And I dropped your newbie off after I finished taping up his smashed hand."

There were too many things wrong with that statement. "What?"

A smile touched her lips. "Tristan stopped by for his usual game of Giving-me-Shit and your new boy, well…let's just say he's a bit *overeager* when he's been told to 'watch' a person. He broke his hand on Tristan's brick head. Well, *re-broke*, I guess…"

Ray pinched the bridge of his nose, too tired to deal with the explanation properly. "I'm gonna assume you're okay though?"

Her grin widened. "Peachy."

It was after three, which meant Lisa's alarm would sound in less than two and a half hours, but she sat up against her headboard, flipping through her mother's sketchbook. The monochromatic living room done in shades of blue was very chic, but she would have liked to see some pops of an accent color – red maybe. She pulled a pencil off her nightstand and made a note to that effect at the bottom of the page, telling herself interior design was what was keeping her awake as effectively as three cups of coffee.

From his dog bed, Hektor grumbled in his sleep, reminding her of the sound Tristan had made as he'd collapsed against the bar.

The rustle of the breeze as it slipped into her cracked window and tousled her curtains sounded like laughter.

When the sketches proved not to be enough of a distraction, she set the book aside, turned off her lamp, and slipped down between the sheets as the room was bathed in darkness. Moonlight flirted with the gaps between her gauzy drapes, turning her world into a patchwork of blue and gray her mother's room design would have been envious of. Lisa curled one hand beneath her pillow, dropped the other at her side, and closed her eyes…

But sleep wouldn't come right away. And it was *not* because she was thinking about anything…or anyone….she shouldn't have been.

Nope. Not at all.

Never again, she reminder herself, but the mantra was only a whisper.

Behind her eyelids, she saw Drew Forester's hand making contact with Tristan's face. She saw the intense, professional gleam in his eyes, that exact, perfect knowledge of his own strength. She saw the leaping tendons in his arms. Saw the bruises on his knuckles…felt them, the way his skin twitched. She saw his face over hers…felt his arms go around her…felt…

Her eyes slammed open and she exhaled in a shaky rush. She was hot and restless all over now, nipples hard points under her sleep shirt.

"No," she said aloud. *Never again*. But she couldn't shield her dreams, and they were invaded by Drew, once her stir-crazy body finally gave over to sleep.

Drew could feel his pulse thumping in his hand, and he imagined black, damaged blood gushing inside his knuckles, threatening to split his tender, bruised flesh. So heavy and useless, it felt like he was dragging a Christmas ham around on his wrist, and though the pain was tolerable while awake, it was *keeping* him awake now. Lisa's wrap had stayed in place, but it wasn't helping. He needed a brace. Or a cast. Or, like the doctor had said the last time this had happened, an operation.

The thought sent a cold chill sweeping down his spine. He didn't have insurance and certainly not the kind of money it would take to piece his bones back together. He'd been waiting for months now, wondering which swing would be the last.

He was alone in the house, and it was full of creaks and pops. The ceiling fan above his bed made a clicking sound as the blades slid around and it was about as soothing as a leaky faucet. With a sigh, he rolled out of bed, cradling his wounded hand in the other, trying to keep it still, and took the two steps it required to cross the tiny room. He crouched beside his open duffel bag. He had no furniture save the bed, and all his worldly possessions were in bags. He had to fumble through all three in the dark before his fingers closed around the prescription bottle he was looking for. And then he had to hold it between his knees while he worked the top off and shook out two Vicodin. He swallowed them down with a two-day-old, half-empty bottle of red Gatorade and then flopped back down on the bed, silence reigning once more.

Silence didn't usually bother him – he was pretty silent himself most of the time – but after the chaos of the bar, the empty bachelor pad had a coffin-like quality about it. His evening had been nothing like that of the asshole who'd been harassing Lisa. Drew hadn't been out drinking with friends, laughing, pestering girls. Instead, he'd been working. And then he'd come "home" to a place he didn't belong, knowing his new roommates would probably hate him for what had happened tonight.

Don't reach for things, his father had told him once, *you won't be disappointed that way.*

And he wasn't doing that – wasn't reaching – but as he waited for the meds to kick in, he could think of only one bright spot of his night: Lisa's barely-there smile as she'd wrapped his hand.

But in the interest of not reaching, he didn't dwell on it. At least, not once the Vicodin started pulling him under.

17

Could it really be considered oversleeping if you didn't have a reason to get up in the first place? Drew didn't know the answer to that, but he had an internal clock that snapped his eyes open around seven most mornings. And this morning, when he cracked puffy eyelids and surveyed his empty, rented, Cracker-Jack box room with Vicodin-glazed eyes, he could tell it was past seven. He reached to wipe a hand down his face, and pain exploded in his knuckles, shooting all the way up his arm. He ground his teeth and inhaled sharply through his nose, remembering his wounded hand too late. Refusing to go to the hospital didn't mean he shouldn't have gone; he was going to have lots of fun not touching anything with his dominant limb for the next few weeks. Eventually, the bones would knit together in whatever incorrect shape they preferred, but in the meantime, it was going to hurt like a bitch.

When the knife strikes had dulled to a pounding throb, he kicked the top sheet off and rolled out of bed. He needed to do laundry, but managed to find a pair of gym shorts and a white t-shirt that didn't smell too foul. A shower was necessary, but skipped, at least until he knew who was home. Or, more importantly, if Eddie was home.

Out in the hall, the bathroom door stood open, but he could hear the TV rumbling out in the main part of the house. Sly was sitting on a stool at the island that separated galley kitchen from living room, watching the news on the flat screen that was definitely the most expensive item in the home. He had what looked like a bowl of instant oatmeal and glanced up without a smile or acknowledgement.

Drew paused in the doorway, scratching at his short hair with his good hand. "Is Eddie – "

"Just left," Sly said. His mouth twitched in what might have been a smirk. "And yeah, you're on his shit list."

Drew sighed and went to the fridge. "I didn't pop *him* in the face." Every one of his protein shakes was gone, and he had a feeling he'd find the bottles in the garbage. But thankfully, Eddie hadn't looked in the vegetable crisper, so he still had apples. He grabbed a granny smith and went to the cabinet for a water glass.

"No, you didn't," Sly agreed. "But you made him look bad. Ed hates to look bad."

"How'd I do that?" Frustration crept into his voice as he pulled out a stool and sat, eyes automatically going to the TV affixed above the mantle. "When a man pays me to do a job, I freakin' do it. And Eddie's got a problem with that?"

There was a bottle of maple syrup on the counter between their elbows and Sly added some to his oatmeal. "You try hard," he said evenly. "I get that. You're a dumbass, but I get it."

Drew didn't argue on the "dumbass" assertion, but glanced over, curious.

"The thing about Eddie is," Sly continued, "he's basically a chick."

Drew bit back a grin.

"He spends an hour getting ready in the morning; he had to have the master suite. The man wears white shoes; I mean, c'mon, total woman." He stirred his oatmeal and took a bite. "He's got a bigger ego than anyone I ever met, but not for no reason. He's damn good at what he does."

"What? Picking up women in bars?"

Sly shot him a warning look. "Eddie wasn't gonna let anything happen to Lis. Tristan's an asshole, but he's not threatening. But you went in all white knight and trying to save the princess...makes Eddie look lazy. Puts you in the boss's good graces. Makes Eddie very, very pissed off. You see where I'm going with this?"

Drew sighed and nodded, picking up his apple. "You can't make everyone happy."

"Nope."

"Where I come from, it's more important to keep the boss happy."

Sly snorted. "Bet you never had many friends."

"Friends versus money."

"And that's where you're wrong. Neither. Anything ever happens to Lisa Russell, and that's what you'll have: neither."

Three days. They made it three days without any strange happenings. Cars were worked on, customer complaints were lodged due to the slowness of the boys' work, and the family went about its usual routine of drudgery. And then the flowers came again.

Lisa was nibbling at the edges of a piece of pizza, her stomach protesting such solid, greasy food, when she saw the purple and white delivery van pull into the parking lot. Her belly tied itself in a knot and she set her lunch down, her laughter dying in her throat.

"What?" Johnny asked, folding a piece of pepperoni into his mouth.

Rico – his skinny arms smudged with grease, his thick black hair gelled into a nest of spikes – continued to eat, but glanced between them. "What?" he repeated Johnny's question around a mouthful.

Lisa's eyes flitted to the corner where Drew sat, apparently having put himself in time out or some such stupidity, and saw that he'd picked up on her sudden alarm. He'd tailed her at the bar all week, doing a good, if not overprotective job, and unfortunately, she was starting to rely on his presence, much like she did Hektor's. Scolding herself, she looked out the window, took a steadying breath, and watched the deliveryman take a vase of pink carnations out of the back of the van.

Johnny wiped his mouth on the back of his wrist and twisted around in his chair. "Flowers again?" he asked, frowning. "Dude, who did you sleep with to earn all this?"

"I wish I knew," she muttered.

Drew stood and held the door for the delivery guy, scowling in a way that Lisa would have found amusing if she wasn't fixated on the hideous pink carnations coming her way.

"I think we're gonna be best friends before this is over with," the deliveryman said with a chuckle as he set the vase on the edge of the desk beside the pizza box.

Lisa couldn't bring herself to so much as smile. "I'm assuming these were from the same person?"

He shrugged. "Far as I know. But I just make the runs, I never see the customers, so you'd have to talk to the office."

I might just do that. "'Kay. Thanks." She signed for them reluctantly, and waited until he was back in his van before she sank to her chair in a shaking, rattled heap.

"You okay?" Rico asked.

Johnny stood and mangled the pink blossoms as he pulled the card loose from amongst the stems. "It says – " he started, and Lisa cut him off.

"I know what it says."

Drew loomed behind Rico's chair, face a thunderhead. "We gotta tell your dad."

"And say what?" she asked, making a face. "'More creepy-ass flowers'? He already knows that. That's why you're my friggin' shadow all the time."

Johnny and Rico exchanged a look that she took for confusion.

"What? You think he's just hanging out 'cause we're buddies or something?" Drew's face twitched and suddenly Lisa wasn't just jittery with nerves, she was furious too. Whatever her life had turned into, it was *hers*, and it wasn't ruled by anyone else's hand anymore. Whoever this flower freak was, he was taking away her control. Now she had a nervous dad and a dumb-as-a-brick bodyguard keeping such close tabs on her, she couldn't turn around without bumping into someone. Somehow, her mother was handling the situation as gracefully as she handled everything…but Lisa was a Russell, and she responded with anger.

"So who's sending the flowers?" Johnny asked.

158

"I don't know!" She threw up her hands. "That's the problem. And Dad thinks it's some kinda sicko or…or…who knows. He won't tell me. He just saddles me with Captain Meathead over here." She sighed and glanced apologetically at Drew. "No offense."

He shrugged, but couldn't hide the momentary flare of hurt in his eyes, so he presented his back to them.

Johnny's face was scrunched up like a rabbit's. "Like, seriously? You have a stalker? Who would stalk you?"

"I dunno."

"I mean," he went on, "unless you pissed somebody off. You do piss people off, you know – "

"Johnny." Uncle Mark's voice lacked Ray's frigid edge, but it was commanding in its own way. His son jumped at the sound of it, and it cut through Lisa's mounting ire. "You boys get back to work. Hey, Drew, give us a minute?"

When they left, it felt as if they took the tension and confusion from the room with them. Mark deftly moved the flowers to the top of a file cabinet and took the seat Johnny had abandoned across the desk from her. He stretched his legs out in front of him and linked his fingers together over his stomach. The combination of his dirty garage smock and the very serious, sympathetic grooves that crossed his face gave him the look of some misplaced therapist who was living a double life as a grease monkey. He was brimming with concern, but it radiated off him in a way different than that of his brother; he exuded calm. She'd always felt like she could tell him anything without risk of judgment.

"Who is he?" Lisa asked in a quiet, not at all hopeful voice. She propped her chin on her fist and studied her uncle, hoping to find some telling crack in his sedate armor. She found nothing. "My flower stalker? You know, don't you?"

He gave her a little smile. "Your dad thinks he knows, but honestly, sweetheart, no, I don't know who he is."

She believed him, oddly, but it still wasn't what she wanted to hear. "You know," she mused, "I left Tristan six years ago and I've done a very good job of not getting on anyone's stalkery side since then."

159

His smile widened. "Very true."

"This is about Dad." She knew it was true. "Someone wants to scare him by scaring Mom and me."

Mark nodded.

"I want to not be worried, but…"

"Worrying is natural. You're not Wonder Woman."

"Clearly."

"You'll be fine, though. Keep Drew with you. He seems awful…*eager to please*."

Lisa tilted her head far enough so she could glimpse him through the window. He had his good hand in his pocket, his bad hung useless, wrapped in tape at his side. He was trying very hard to conceal it, but she could see the pain flickering across his face when he thought no one was watching; he needed to go to the doctor. "Yeah," she had to agree. "But what if he's the flower guy?"

Mark chuckled. "You think he's smart enough to plan something like that?"

Drew turned toward them, squinting against the sun that reflected off the windows. He couldn't see her, but she could see him, could see the almost naïve, unveiled attention he paid to her. *He's smart enough*, she wanted to say, *but not wicked enough*. "No," she said instead.

18

"It hurts so bad you can't stand it, can you?"

The more time Drew spent at the bar, the more he saw it for what it was: a nightclub that had been renovated on the cheap with mismatched seams along the wooden floors and gaps where caulk and paint had been used to account for ill-fitted moldings. Through the haze of shadows and happy play of colored lights, he saw the water spots in the ceiling tiles. The wine glasses that dripped from the racks above the bar were cloudy and chipped. But rather than disgust him, all the little flaws were comforting; this wasn't a perfect place full of perfect people as he'd worried. It was a scarred, overused place of respite for a gamut of patrons trying to pretend their lives were more fun, and more important, than they really were.

His right hand, bare, its dark bruises looking like blue lipstick marks on his knuckles, lay on top of the bar, and twitched every so often of its own accord. When he glanced up, he saw Lisa with her elbows propped on the bar, loose dark hair tumbling over one shoulder, the ends clinging to the condensation of his beer bottle. Her eyelids battled fatigue, and her smile was tired, but he liked to think that the overall softening of her face could be attributed to more than just the late hours she kept. Slowly, at a snail's pace, she seemed to be thawing. He didn't get the impression she despised him anymore.

"It hurts." He was honest, but flexed his fingers to show he wasn't immobilized. "I can still use it, though."

She snorted. "Did you change your mind about that X-ray?"

"Nope."

"A cast wouldn't make you less of a man, you know," she said lightly, and straightened to unlace the apron she wore over her denim cutoffs.

"Where are you going?"

She rolled her eyes and pulled a can of Coke from the cooler beneath the bar. Drew was off his stool and prepared to follow her when she came around and settled in beside him. "Oh, sit back down, I'm on break," she chastised. "You're taking this all way too seriously." The words were unkind, but her tone wasn't, not truly, and after two weeks of keeping tabs on her, he'd become dead to it.

Lisa popped the tab on her Coke and took a dainty sip, her gaze focused somewhere in the near space beyond the bar. She always gave off the impression that she was comfortable with silence – or in this case, the silence between the two of them, because the cacophony of sound around them was almost deafening. Drew never felt the need to fill up moments with his own voice, but he'd not been around too many females who could bear to be so quiet, and the curiosity was starting to drive him mad. Lisa didn't appear all that shy, or nervous, and she was chatty with her cousin and the Latino kid who worked at the garage. He seemed to be a piece of furniture to her, an object, something that kept her safe, and to which she didn't feel compelled to speak. He was okay with this – he *was* – he told himself that a lot. If anything, it made her more interesting.

He pulled his battered hand in to his chest and leaned his forearm on the bar, shifting closer so she could hear him above the crowd. "You hate working here, don't you?"

She took another sip of Coke. "More than you know." Her reply was flat. "But the money's good."

"Your dad's paying me to just sit here. You can't need the money that bad."

She turned toward him with narrowed eyes. "I might have to live at home, but I don't ask my parents to pay for a damn thing." Her expression became something akin to a glare. "My dad's in credit card debt up to his receding hairline, and since my dumb ass didn't go to college, then yeah, I have to work at places like this. And I do need the money." She snorted. "I'd figure at least *you* would know what that's like – needing money so bad you take sucky friggin' jobs."

162

She had him there: he wasn't proud of the things he'd done for a little cash in his pocket. "Sorry. Didn't mean to make you angry."

"I'm not – " She sighed, and he thought she checked some of the venom in her tone. "I'm not angry," she started again, actually sounding like she was "not angry" this time. "I just – "

"Don't like me?" he offered with a half-smile.

She surprised him by smiling back, and setting her elbow on the bar so she could be more comfortable and continue to face him. "I don't like that you have to be here," she amended. "But seeing as how I don't know you, I can't dislike you."

"I dunno. I think you can dislike someone you don't know."

She rolled her eyes. "But that's not what I meant."

He was strangely relieved to hear that.

"Can you blame me for not wanting to have a watch dog? I mean, I have a literal watch dog at home, but having to bring muscle to work? Don't tell me this is fun for you either."

Parts of it were fun. Watching her was fun…in a non-creepy way…right…

The patrons around them paid them no attention, and the music was like a second pulse in his ears, so he figured it was safe to talk. "Who do you think is messing with you?"

She made a face. "You could probably fill a room up with poor little boys whose feelings I've hurt."

"I thought girls were the ones who always wanted revenge."

"That's true a lot of the time." She shrugged. "But the note doesn't sound like something a female would write. It's very…pathetically creepy. That doesn't scream 'girl' to me."

"Yep, that's guys for ya: pathetically creepy."

Another white, straight, pretty smile split her face. "I didn't mean it like that."

"You say that a lot," he countered, reaching for his beer with his good hand.

Maybe it was a trick of the red and gold and blue lights above them, but he thought her cheeks were tinged with color as she glanced away from him. "I'm not a sweet person, in case you couldn't tell." And it almost sounded like an apology, like she wished she were sweeter.

"Sweet's overrated."

Lisa laughed. "Too bad no one agrees with you on that."

He watched her a moment – he did that so much now that it was a possibility he was sleepwalking at night and that *he* was the creeper sending her flowers – and he thought this threat had to be linked to Ray's sketchy activities, because he just couldn't believe she'd brought this down on herself. She didn't think of herself as sweet, but he was convinced she was. Her mouth was sweet. The way her hair framed her face was sweet. Under her tough outer shell, he had a feeling she was sweet as sugar, and overcompensating for it. She'd been engaged once upon a time. And had her heart broken. A real man could survive the sharp slice of a woman's tongue on occasion; it was like he'd thought all along: this was Ray's doing, this stalker.

"Who'd wanna hurt you?" he asked, surprised by how much gravity he'd levered into the question, surprised that he'd spoken it aloud at all.

Her eyes cut toward him, just white-lined crescents in profile with party lights reflected on them, but he saw fear in them. "Lots of people, I'm sure."

"You scared?"

"I don't wanna be."

And he believed her. He had no doubts that the last thing this girl wanted to be was a damsel. Unfortunately, when it came to her current predicament, she was about a hundred pounds of can't-do-a-damn-thing-about-it.

"Hey, girl!" someone shouted to his left and he turned to see Lisa's blonde, curvy friend whose name he couldn't remember taking the stool beside him. She – was it Jessica? She looked like a Jessica – leaned across the bar, the neckline of her bright blue dress cutting into her breasts and gave him a calculating glance before her eyes went to Lisa. "Total coincidence from *hell*. Guess who I saw pulling in outside?"

Lisa groaned. "Please don't tell me – "

"Tristan."

"What's that asshole want?" Drew asked before he could check himself.

The friend – man, what was her name? – gave him a slow smile, eyes twinkling. "Not a Tristan fan, I take it."

"Have you seen Tristan's face?" Lisa asked, and with another sigh, she hopped off her stool and returned to her post behind the bar. She stopped across from them to tie her apron back on and Drew figured she hadn't taken the break she'd truly wanted...or needed.

"Seconds, Tony?"

The lawyer, dressed down in khakis and a white Ralph Lauren button-up, waved away Cheryl's offer of another round of Key Lime tartlets as she cleared their dishes from the table. "Oh, no. It was delicious, but no. I'm gonna be on the treadmill an extra hour as is."

She rolled her eyes as she turned away from him. There'd been a time when Tony had limped up the stairs to their old apartment in holey shoes with pizza stains on his Fruit of the Loom t-shirts, and now he was the picture of a posh Alpharetta attorney, brand conscious and image savvy. It made her a little bit nauseous, to be honest.

"Dinner was great, baby," Ray said behind her as she turned on the tap and passed their dessert plates beneath it. She smiled, but faintly, because it wasn't just a compliment, it was a request that she leave them alone to talk for a bit.

"Good," she acknowledged, and stowed the dishes in the washer. She didn't turn it on, though, not yet, because as she left them with a smile and slipped into the family room, she didn't want the chugging and sloshing of the ancient old Whirlpool to drown out their voices.

The house, relic that it was, was chopped into small, secluded rooms rather than open, free-flowing spaces like their previous house in Alpharetta. Cheryl had batted at tears with her lashes when she'd sold her furniture – the furniture she'd only dreamed of all her life – but she'd swallowed that ridiculous grief and selected more economical pieces that would be better suited for the antebellum floor plan. The parlor opposite the dining room in the front of the house was full of Russell family pieces: the striped wingback chairs, the leather settee, the secretary she'd refinished the summer before. But here in the family room, deep, cozy corduroy sofas and a chair big enough for two encircled Ray's flat screen. The built-in bookshelves were full to bursting and disorganized, barely enough room to walk between them and the arms of the couches. But it was a homey, comfortable space. And the walls were thin, poorly insulated.

Cheryl picked up her sketch book from its resting place on the sofa table that flanked one wall. The wall that separated family room from kitchen. She had a chair there with a cross-stitched seat full of roses, and a pack of watercolor pencils in a drawer. She sat, flipped to a clean page, and her fingers began to conjure a kitchen while her ears picked up on the conversation.

"…happy here?" she heard Tony's voice.

Ray's response was tepid. She could imagine his accompanying shrug. "Cheryl wants to decorate houses. And God knows what Lisa really wants to do, but it's not slinging beers and keeping books. They're as happy as they can be, I guess."

"You take good care of them."

"I know." Ray snorted. "But maybe if you'd ever get married you'd figure out that women want a lot of things, and being 'taken care of' isn't at the top of that list."

Cheryl grinned.

There was a sound like the bottom of a glass thumping on the table. "*But* it's on the top of *your* list," Tony said. "What the hell are you doing, Ray? I heard you went to see Shilling."

"We had a chat, yeah."

Her fingers stilled on the paper. *Oh, Ray, don't get yourself in trouble…*

166

Apparently, Tony agreed with her. "You told me you weren't going to harass him. I only gave you the intel because you -"

"I never said that," Ray argued.

Tony sighed loudly. "You're not a cop, and you're not even a lawyer anymore, in case you forgot." Cheryl could imagine the look on her husband's face.

There was a beat of silence.

"Fine," Tony muttered. "What've you found out so far?"

Ray's voice was just a low murmur, and she pressed her head back against the wall in hopes of hearing better. "...went by the florist's and they couldn't tell me shit about the guy."

"No description? Not even a vague one?"

"No. Dumbass who was there said he didn't work in the mornings which was when the purchases were documented, and whoever it was paid cash."

"Security tapes?"

"Now how am I gonna look at those not being a cop or lawyer? Huh?"

"Well, I'm certainly not putting lying past you at this point."

There was another lull, and then both men chuckled. Cheryl's hand moved, the pencil gliding across the paper again, but she felt her brows knitting themselves together.

"You know I wanna help," Tony said, "but I'm not in any kind of position to tap into Shilling's life. For what it's worth, I think Mark's right about this one – "

"Aunt Cheryl?"

She gasped and the colored pencils slid off her lap, clattering against the hardwood in a way that she knew made her look guilty. Johnny stood in the doorway between family room and hallway, a plaid flannel shirt held in one hand. His thin, cute little face was screwed up in confusion.

"Oh, I'm sorry."

"No." She pushed a smile across her lips and bent to retrieve her pencils. "It's fine. I'm just jumpy. Whatcha need, sweetie?"

The conversation in the kitchen had come to an abrupt halt.

"One of the buttons came off and I wanted to see if you could sew it back on. Dad called and asked if I wanted to meet him down at the pool hall."

Single fatherhood had left Mark and Johnny with more of a friendship than a parent/child relationship. The nineteen-year-old should have been hanging out with his friends rather than helping his dad pick up women at a damn pool hall, but Cheryl knew that otherwise, he would have been playing video games in his room or spending all night at the shop working on the Trans Am.

You shouldn't have been eavesdropping anyway, she scolded herself, and set her sketch pad aside. "Sure, baby, bring it here."

By the time Tristan made his way to the bar, Lisa was beginning to feel like she'd gathered a small contingency of supporters. Morgan was trying to chat up Drew with little success, and Trevor had come down out of his nest, taking his break with a vodka rocks and basket of hot wings. He was the one who alerted her of her ex's approach.

"Your punkass is here," he said around a mouthful, and Lisa watched his wide, white-rimmed eyes slide over toward Drew in silent question.

She nodded.

Tristan had learned something from the other night, it appeared, because he was alone, and he approached the bar with something like trepidation instead of his usual swagger. The left side of his face was still marred by the lightest traces of bruising. The blood had gone out of his eye, but it was still a little red and unhappy looking. He raked a hand back through his dark, perfect hair and gave the trio sitting at the bar a cautious glance; he knew Morgan and Trevor, and now Drew, and clearly decided to play it safe as he put several stools between himself and the DJ.

168

Holly was working his half of the bar and had already moved in to take his order, but Lisa waved her off. "He'll have a Coors Light," she told the other bartender and earned a murderous look for it that she ignored. "Why'd you come?" she asked once Holly was gone.

Tristan's face lacked its usual mocking grin. "To apologize."

She laughed. "Yeah, that's a good one." A glance proved that Drew was at full attention and looked poised to launch off his stool at the slightest provocation.

Tristan followed her gaze and made a disgusted sound in the back of his throat. "Your new boyfriend has issues. Where'd you find this one?"

"Somewhere besides where I found you. I've learned not to look under rocks."

And there was the grin, full of the nastiness she'd always hated. "You're never gonna learn how to get along with anyone, are you?"

She returned his smile. "No."

He shrugged and slid off his stool. His beer hadn't arrived yet and she assumed, correctly, that he had no intention of paying for it. "You shouldn't still hate me, Lis," he said. "Not if you're really over it all."

Anger swirled in the pit of her stomach because no matter how wrong he was on the matter, she knew she'd never be able to beat back her own stubborn need to put him in his place at all times.

"Watch the mail. Missy's sending you an invitation to the shower." He was gone, slipped away in the crowd, before she could tell him she'd rather have a root canal than attend his wife's baby shower.

Holly returned with the beer and frowned. "Oh, great, you ran another one off. I swear, Lisa – "

"Yeah, yeah, keep on swearing." It was a miracle, she thought, that she hadn't been fired yet.

***

The Double Vision, like all bars, was a desolate, depressing place after closing. After the last of the drunken patrons had been pushed out the door and the mop boy was going around setting chairs up on tables and sprinkling cat litter on vomit; when the fluorescent tubes were flipped on and painted all the after effects of revelry in a hellish light, the hulking, empty place was hideous. Half the girls had taken their tips and were gone; the others were closing out their registers in the back. Drew was still perched on his stool, not enough beer in him to have taken the edge off, but thankful for the quiet drone of vacuums rather than the thump of audio equipment.

DJ Twist – Trevor – crossed the bar, a backpack slung over his shoulder. He'd tied the ends of his corn rows up with a rubber band and slipped a jacket on over his tall, thin frame. "Hey, bro." He extended a hand for Drew to shake as he neared. "Good to meet you."

The shake turned into more of a palm slide. "You too." And it had been. Drew had been so unimpressed with the people in Lisa's circle of friends – including Morgan, whose name he'd finally remembered – that the DJ had been a pleasant surprise.

"Lis isn't so bad once you get to know her," he said with a parting grin as he turned for the door.

Drew didn't think she was that bad anyway – who was honest to God afraid of the girl? – but he kept that thought to himself. Morgan had given him advice along the same lines…only bitchier. *Stare at her all you want, she's not gonna pay you any attention.* Said in a way that implied *she* might be willing to pay him some attention. He'd been concerned by how obvious he must look.

Lisa was another ten minutes or so, and when she emerged, she had put on her cowboy boots and her sandals dangled from her fingertips. Her hair was up in a sloppy ponytail and she'd pulled a hoodie over her halter top. She looked exhausted. "You ready? Well, stupid question I guess."

He fell into step behind her as she made her slow way across the dance floor, dodging the mop being drug across it, and up the wide steps to the catwalk and main door. Her

170

narrow shoulders were slumped and the pointed toes of her boots rapped against the stairs, and Drew understood why Ray was so protective of his daughter: she was in a stupor of fatigue by the end of every night. The dark circles under her eyes, the vinegar in her temper…she wasn't a happy girl, and unhappy, sleepy, preoccupied girls weren't as aware of their surroundings as they should have been. That, and, well, she just wasn't satisfied with the pace of her life, and that was enough to make any dad – a good dad – worry. Drew worried, more than a little, and he had no right to.

The night was balmy; thick and as welcome as a heavy quilt as it wrapped around them and chased away the chill of the bar's AC. Drew kept so close their shadows overlapped, and he scanned the parking lot, scoping out the empty stretch of darkened pavement for anything suspicious. But all was quiet save for the rush of the occasional passing car and the sound of their footfalls on the blacktop.

Lisa fished her keys out of her purse, then fumbled them, and they fell with a metallic jangle.

"You want me to drive?" he offered.

When she stood, keys in hand again, she tucked a stray piece of hair behind her ear and frowned. "No."

"I don't mind," he pressed. "And you're tired –"

"I'm not that tired," she snapped, but then sighed, all the fight going out of her. "Okay, that's a lie." Her eyes flipped up to meet his. "You won't wreck my truck, will you?"

"I think I can manage."

"It's a piece of shit, really, but I'm still making payments on it."

"Like I said."

She pressed the keys into his waiting palm and gave him one last disbelieving glance, chewing at her lip, before she retreated around the tailgate of the blue Ford and headed for the passenger door. "The gas is sticking lately," she cautioned, "and the brake too sometimes, but – "

"Hey." A man's voice behind them stopped her in her tracks.

Drew recognized the speaker before he turned, and when he did, he was not surprised to see that his former roommate, and Ricky's fighter, Josh, looked ready to spit lightning. His eyebrows were two angry blonde slashes meeting over his nose, his hands curled to fists at his sides.

"Josh."

"You know this guy?" Lisa asked, a tremor of uncertainty in her voice.

"Is that how it is, then?" Josh's voice was bubbling with acid. "You flip on us and *steal* from us for some bitch?"

"Whoa." Drew took a step toward him, palms raised in a show of passivity. "Lemme explain."

"We thought you skipped town," Josh said. He twitched and became more agitated, so Drew backed off. "But you fell in with *Russell*?!"

He'd spent all this time worrying about someone who might be after Lisa that he'd missed the guy who wanted *him* dead. Josh had always been a fan of the Double Vision, and Drew felt like an idiot for not remembering that. "Josh, man, it's okay, I just – "

He was ready for the first swing. Josh had been too far away so he'd lunged forward, his sucker punch coming a half breath too late. Drew ducked it and came up with fists raised. He blocked the next two shots with his left, and then threw his own strike. His right snapped out, the jab a glancing blow that bounced off Josh's chin…and fire exploded in his hand.

Oh, shiiiiiit…He remembered his battered knuckles too late, and the pain shot all the way up to his collar bone and snapped his teeth together. It provided just the time Josh needed to overwhelm his defenses, and then everything seemed to happen at once.

A thick hand closed around his throat and a knee caught him in the ribs. As the breath went out of him, he realized they were no longer boxing, but brawling. He grabbed a fistful of Josh's shirt with his good hand, but his right was rippling with spasms and useless. Josh's momentum drove them backward, and Drew's head met the quarter panel of the truck with a sickening *thump*. The world went white and then black; his stomach leapt up his throat.

"Hey!"

Suddenly, nothing was holding him up, and Drew went down hard on his hands and knees, another sharp jolt of pain shooting up his right arm. Color came back to him, but the pavement seemed to tilt crazily, so he shut his eyes.

A loud *click* reached his ears. What was that? He knew that sound. "You think you can get to me before I pull the trigger?" Lisa's voice floated somewhere above him. *Shit*: Lisa and Josh. He had to get back on his feet. "You get the *hell* outta here before I change my mind about calling the cops."

With his unbroken hand on the truck for support, Drew got shakily to his feet in time to see Josh retreating. His vision was a blurred tumble of shapes and shades, but he still registered the image of Lisa standing behind the tailgate of the truck, a revolver in her hands.

Her head swiveled in his direction, and her face divided into two. "You okay?" Her voice sounded like it was coming down a drainage pipe.

He started to nod, but the motion sent his insides catapulting up his esophagus. He doubled over and puked all over his shoes.

"Yeah," she said. "We're going to the hospital this time."

19

They came. Both of her parents. Drew had never met the wife before, but she was brunette like her daughter, and lovely, her face creased with worry as she and Ray stood facing the exam table. By contrast, Ray had a cardboard mask of pleasantry in place and looked like he might dissolve into an angry tirade at any moment. Lisa was on the rolling stool where the doctor would sit when he finally came in, her legs crossed, folded arms and head resting on the counter beside the sink.

Drew wished the floor would open up and swallow him whole. He'd had lights shined in his eyes and his hand had been prodded and poked. After a wait in the ER, staring at his puke-spattered shoes, he'd endured an exam and an X-ray; his hand had been casted, much to his displeasure, and now here he sat again, still staring at his shoes. His skull still felt as heavy and pulpy as a bruised melon, the blood throbbing through his temples, but the nausea had receded…some. He still felt sick. His vision still blurred if he lifted his head too fast.

Ray and his wife – Cheryl, she'd said her name was – had arrived when he'd been brought into the private exam room, but Lisa had been off-and-on the phone with her father the entire stay. Cheryl had brought coffee, which he'd been unable to drink, and he was guessing it had to be dawn by now or close to it. The elder Russells were both dressed and groomed and looked like they were starting a day rather than ending it.

"Why didn't you say anything about your hand?" Ray asked what had clearly been on his mind since he'd first laid eyes on the blue cast Drew wore with nothing short of shame.

"I – I didn't wanna be a bother." He could barely bring himself to say it.

"How is putting a head-shaped dent in her truck not being a bother?"

"Dad," Lisa sighed.

"Baby," Cheryl said quietly. "Let's give the poor kid a break."

Ray opened his mouth, and then closed it again, but his eyes were brimming with questions. *Who did this? Is he gonna try it again? Was it about Lisa? Or you? Are you bringing shit down on my family?*

"I'm real sorry, Ray," he said, his head feeling too heavy to hold upright anymore.

It was Cheryl who consoled him. "It's fine, honey." He heard the light rap of her shoes come closer over the tiles. "We're just glad you're okay."

Ray snorted.

"He got the shit beat out if him," Lisa said, and though it set the world to spinning, Drew had to glance her way because he couldn't believe she might be about to defend him. "Just...leave him alone."

Whatever her dad might have said, it was interrupted by the doctor's arrival. She was Asian and even tinier than Lisa, narrow, rectangular glasses perched on her nose, her glossy hair half-fallen from its topknot. She looked like the last thing she wanted to do was see yet another patient, and given the hour, Drew figured he might be one of her last stops before she went home and fell into bed.

She breezed in on sneakers that squeaked over the floor, his chart in her hand. "Forester?" she verified, giving him a glance.

He nodded.

She had a recap of his treatments that she read in a tired, flat voice, and then the prescription pad came out and he was told when to take the Vicodin – as if he didn't already know – and was cautioned to use Advil if possible instead. He had a mild concussion and would need to be monitored – which he already knew. By the time she'd exited with a swirl of white lab coat, Drew realized he hadn't actually listened to a word she'd said. He knew the drill from previous trips to the

175

ER and instead, he'd been imagining all the ways in which Sly or Eddie or Ray – or all three of them – were going to punish him for this. And he was resigned to the knowledge that, whatever their plans, he was completely at their mercy. He had not a friend or ally in the world.

"Okay." Lisa yawned and stretched and got to her feet. "Let's blow this place."

"You ride with your mother," Ray told her, "and I'll take this one back."

"No," both the women said in unison.

Drew glanced between the three of them, startled, confused, not at all sure why Lisa or her mom might stick up for him. The expression on Ray's face indicated he was thinking something similar.

"No," Cheryl repeated. "You will not take him back to that rat nest and ask Sly and Eddie of all people to play nurse maid." She shook her head. "We'll bring him home with us – he can stay in the carriage house," she said in a rush, hand raised as Ray began to protest, "just until he's feeling better."

Ray grumbled something under his breath that Drew couldn't hear and his wife glared a hole through him. "This isn't up for negotiation. You *will not* tell me I can't invite a guest to stay."

Drew looked over at Lisa and saw that she was trying to hide a smile behind her hand. For all the ways Ray scared the bejeesus out of him, Cheryl Russell looked about as friendly as a cobra at the moment. And she was defending him. *Him.*

He half wondered if he'd fallen into some kind of wormhole when he'd hit his head, because God knew he'd never had a lucky break in his life.

The hardwood planks that covered the floor had long ago lost their sheen, if they'd ever had one, and the wallpaper, once-white with tiny yellow flowers, was faded and peeling up along the ceiling. But there were four walls and lots of space, a sturdy-looking wood bedframe in one corner, a patchwork quilt and white pillows making it inviting. His eyes moved over the café table and chairs, the huge armoire against the back wall, the free-standing floor-length mirror, and felt like he'd stepped into a scene from a movie set fifty years ago.

"The bathroom's just through that door," Cheryl said as she stepped in behind him. "The bathtub faucet leaks a bit, but it's not too loud."

Drew stood rooted to the spot, dumbstruck, maybe because of his still-pounding head, but maybe because he didn't understand, or trust, this sudden kindness. He wanted to, though; boy did he want to.

Fragile, early rays of light passed through the unadorned windows and captured dust motes in their beams. The air smelled of old wood and dryness, like the pages of a library book that hadn't been opened in a long time. When Cheryl had said "carriage house" at the hospital, he'd half-expected to be led to a barn. But the two story white clapboard structure with a drive-under garage below was just as impressive from the outside as the *Gone With the Wind* house that sat in front of it. He'd stared like a fool as they'd pulled around the drive, all the weeping willows and porch columns unexpected. Cheryl had rushed to make apologies, saying they were still fixing it up, that they'd inherited the house and that it had been "a big box of shit" when they'd moved in three years ago. Drew had wondered if those were the things that wealthy people said to make losers like him feel better about their lives.

"Ray's grandmother lived up here for a while, back when his parents were alive." When he turned to face her, he watched guilt flicker across her face. She tucked her hair behind her ears in an almost nervous gesture and walked past him, moving to tidy the pillows on the bed. "It's a little musty, but should be comfortable."

When he compared it to the room at Sly and Eddie's house, "comfortable" was too modest a word. *It's great*, he wanted to tell her, but instead, "Why are you doing this?" came tumbling out of his stupid mouth before he could stop himself.

She tucked her hair back again because it had slid over her shoulders, and when she faced him, a sad smile on her lips, the sun poured across her features and for a moment she looked just like her daughter…only a friendlier, softer version of her. Lisa and Ray shared a strong resemblance, but there was a healthy dose of her mom in there too.

"What can I say," she said, "I'm a mom. And you look like you're badly in need of one of those right now."

He'd felt older than his years for a long time, and suddenly he was a child again. Only, a child he'd never known, because Drew had never had a mom in his life.

"Ray's not a trusting person." She went to the armoire and one of its ornate, carved doors came open with a *pop*. "He thinks everyone in the world's out to get him."

Maybe they are.

She withdrew a plastic shopping bag and sealed the chest. "He's done his best to make Lisa just like him," she said as she crossed the small apartment. "Somewhere along the line, my sweet girl turned into the biggest cynic." Cheryl sighed, but the smile returned, and she pressed the bag into his hands. "Toothbrush and mini toothpaste. Deodorant. Just some of the basics to get you by until you can go get the rest of your things."

All the generosity was making him twitchy. "Thanks, but…I don't plan on staying."

Her smile went all the way up to her pretty brown eyes. She patted his arm. "We'll see."

Drew stood, trying to absorb all of this, and listened to her footfalls retreat to the threshold, then down the stairs once the door was closed. Was he dreaming? No…no, this was just a brief flash of something better. A chance to let his concussion heal, to catch some true rest in a safe place.

But was it safe? Was it really?

He closed his eyes and felt blood pounding at the backs of them. His head hurt so bad, this might very well have been a hallucination. Regardless, the lure of dreamland was too great to fight off anymore. In the car, in the passenger seat beside Cheryl, he'd tilted side-to-side like a drunk. Every pothole along the way had sent his churning stomach halfway up his throat. And he seemed to have semi-permanent double vision.

The shopping bag fell out of his hand and crackled when it hit the floor. He took the lumbering steps necessary to reach the bed and flopped onto it face-first, the tired old mattress groaning in protest. He was asleep almost immediately.

Lisa had reached a point of sleepiness in which nothing existed save the inside of her skull. She sat at the kitchen table, pitched forward in her seat, lying across its surface, fresh sunlight from the window above the sink battling against her oh-so-heavy eyelids. She heard the coffeemaker and the low drone of the washing machine in the mud room, cozy sounds that only intensified the problem of staying awake.

With her ear pressed to the table, the sound of Ray's coffee mug thumping down over a square of the morning paper reverberated like thunder through her head. "Ugh." Whatever she'd wanted to say turned into a wordless groan instead.

Ray sighed. "Just go up to bed."

"No...work," she managed, and made a rallying attempt to sit that went nowhere, and she stared at a spot on the opposite wall instead.

Another sigh echoed above her. "Mark can answer his own phones. Saturdays are slow anyway. It's not like you'd be any help like you are now."

That was true, even if it wasn't easy to hear. With more effort than it should have taken, Lisa pushed up onto her elbows, blinking against the brightness of the morning. She wasn't going to put up a real fight about staying home from the garage, but before she crawled up the stairs and slithered in between her sheets, she wanted to say what had been nagging at her all evening...well, morning, really.

"Dad." He flicked a glance toward her, but his eyes returned to the paper. "I know Drew's kind of an idiot, and I know better than to put any trust in him yet." His eyes returned, and stayed this time. "But don't chew him out over this. I know you didn't hire an underground fighter and think

179

he didn't come with baggage, and anyway…" She stifled a yawn behind her hand. "It doesn't matter 'cause I took care of it tonight. The guy's tried to come to my rescue twice, now. Just…don't rag on him, okay? It's really not fair if we're both shits to him."

A ghost of a smile touched his lips. "Both?"

She made a face and got unsteadily to her feet. "I'm not nice and you know it. Just…please?"

He made a show of deliberating, shaking his head like he argued with himself, but caved with a shrug. "Sure, I won't 'rag on him.'"

For some reason, his promise made falling asleep that morning all the easier.

20

Something touched his shoulder. He was home, back in Augusta, the dry, cracked stretch of red clay in front of the house as hard as pavement under his bare feet. He heard the door slam on its hinges with a sound like a gunshot behind him and didn't flinch; he'd learned never to flinch, because it only made him angrier.

"Boy! Where are you, boy?"

The glass jar in his hands started to slip beneath his now-clammy palms. Within, the praying mantis he'd found in the woodpile tilted its alien, green head and regarded him through the glass. He'd found a nice stick for it to climb on, and a leaf for shade, some dirt in the bottom. His friend at school, Brandon, had brought a jar of crickets for show-and-tell last week. But this week, he was going to bring the mantis, and it was going to be the best thing anyone in his class had ever seen.

"Boy! What the hell did I tell you?"

Something touched his shoulder again, only this time, he knew it was some*one* instead. His father's big hand wrapped around the top of his arm, his cruel fingers digging grooves into his skin until it felt like he would draw blood. He was spun around, and the jar flew out of his hand. It shattered on the hard-packed earth and Drew didn't know what happened to the mantis because his father's face was shoved in his own, his breath sour with onions and meat and bourbon.

No, no, no, no, Drew chanted inside his head. This couldn't happen anymore. He was an adult now, and he *wasn't going to let this happen.*

Never again, he'd promised himself. Never again was he going to let himself be weak.

He bolted upright and realized too late that the old house and Dad, the jar, the hand, all of it had been a dream. A nightmare. He heard a gasp and tried desperately to blink away the fog in his head. His skull was pounding like someone had driven a railroad spike through his temples, and he fought to grab hold of logic.

"Let go of me!" Lisa's angry hiss dissipated the last scraps of the dream and he was on his stomach in the bed up in the Russell carriage house. He'd jacked up on his bad hand, the whole thing numb under its cast as it supported most of his weight. He had a death grip on Lisa's wrist with his left hand, and she was glaring at him with a volatile mixture of fury and terror as she struggled to pull away from him.

"Oh, shit." He dropped her immediately and she backed away, rubbing her arm with her opposite hand. "Oh, damn, I'm sorry. I thought you were…I, ah, shit, Lisa, I'm – "

"Whatever," she snapped. She turned away from him, her loose hair hiding her profile from him, but he saw her shoulders heave and knew she was trying to catch the breath he'd frightened out of her.

How many times had she braved the clutter and stench of her cousin's room to go in and shake him awake in the mornings? More than she'd like to count, and that was why she'd thought nothing of rousing Drew the same way.

Big mistake.

She stood, gulping deep breaths down into her lungs, cradling the slender bones of her wrist that had been ground together in his hand, and told herself that she hadn't been at all frightened, only startled. But where was the line drawn between startled and frightened exactly? She didn't know.

He'd come awake so suddenly, without a sound, his arm striking out of reflex, that she hadn't had a chance to move away. When his dark eyes had found her, they'd been wild and white-rimmed at first. When recognition came, she'd seen the shock and shame in them; he hadn't meant to grab her

But it didn't change the fact that her pulse was an erratic rush of butterfly wings behind her breastbone.

The bed springs groaned and the worn, soft old sheets rustled. "Are you okay?"

Lisa couldn't pretend there wasn't true concern in his voice, and she glanced over her shoulder to see that he was sitting up in bed now, his bare feet on the hardwood, rubbing at his eyes with his good hand. The wifebeater he'd slept in was so full of holes it looked like it might dissolve on its next trip through a washing machine. The hems of his red plaid boxers were frayed. His right hand looked clumsy in its cast. Sympathy welled up inside her before she could stop it.

"Yeah." Her voice was steady. She let both her hands fall to her sides; the one he'd grabbed felt sprained now. "Mom wanted to know if you'd like lunch."

He rubbed at his face, at his hair – it needed a trim, but she liked it longer – and gave her a worried glance. "I don't wanna put your mom out or anything."

"We're just having sandwiches." He frowned. "And my dad's not home."

His head tipped in silent thanks for that piece of news, but the frown didn't leave him. If anything, it deepened, his brows drawing down over his eyes. "You pulled a gun on Josh," he said in a voice like he couldn't believe what he was saying.

"Yeah, I did." Drew's head had punched a dent in the side of her truck and she'd been left with two options: fling up her hands and scream and act like a flustered female who couldn't handle the situation...or *handle* it. *I won't lie to you*, Ray had told her once, *a girl your size can't ever hope to physically overpower a grown man.* And then he'd pulled a .38 revolver from the safe in the back of his closet and taken her to the range where she'd been drilled until she could get eleven out of every twelve shots inside the 10 ring on the target. Until she could make the most of two cylinders' worth. "You getting knocked unconscious wasn't much of a deterrent for that asshole."

He shook his head, then winced. "You pulled a *gun* on him," he repeated, and the look he shot her was full of such comical disbelief she had to bite back a smile.

"We live in Georgia, dude, everyone has a gun."

183

"I know, but – "

"Lunch?"

He closed his mouth, his half-smile guilty and sheepish. "Yeah. Lemme take a shower and I'll be in."

They were sitting at the table when he entered hesitantly through the screened-in porch, and their conversation ended as if the words coming from their mouths had been sliced off with a knife. They'd been talking about him he guessed, but didn't much care because he was busy conducting a visual sweep of his new surroundings.

The porch had probably been separate from the house at one point because the frame for the doors was still in place; it looked like an addition. The floor had been laid with a tight-nap carpet that butted up to the kitchen's open door and the furniture was white wicker stuffed with cushions. Potted ferns and flowers were nestled in beneath the wide bank of windows that could be opened to allow airflow through the screens and into the main part of the house.

Cheryl and Lisa were at a rectangular farm table that floated between two banks of cabinets, light from the window above the sink falling in a halo around them. It was a small space, and not newly renovated, but it was clean, a lamp and calendar and series of decorative jars along the countertop making it apparent this was a lived-in, worked-in kitchen and not a showpiece.

"Feeling better?" Cheryl asked, her smile warm.

He was in the clothes he'd been wearing the day before, barefoot because his shoes either needed to be washed or thrown away, and he was suddenly very aware of the picture he presented. "No one woke me up," he said, kicking himself as soon as he'd said it.

Lisa rolled her eyes, but Cheryl kept smiling. "I've seen my share of concussions and nobody ever thanked me for waking them up every hour to make sure they were still alive."

"Oh. Thanks."

Lunch was thin-sliced roast beef and pepper jack cheese on a toasted bun. The curly lettuce and tomato slices were still beaded with moisture from a rinsing. And Cheryl had *made her own* chips from salted, shaved potatoes. Drew took the first bite and realized he was famished, and that it was going to be a struggle not to cram the whole sandwich into his mouth in one bite.

Cheryl asked him the most carefully constructed, benign questions she could: about boxing, his training regimen, diet, side sports and interests, all while never asking anything probing or awkward about his past or personal life. Halfway through his meal, he'd decided she might be the nicest woman alive, occasional resemblance to poisonous snakes notwithstanding.

Lisa, by contrast, picked at her food and said little, her eyes flitting around the room but never resting on him. She had dark, dark circles under her eyes this afternoon, but he didn't find her any less attractive for it. If anything, he felt a pang of sympathy for a girl who worked herself into exhaustion in the hopes of keeping her family happy.

As Cheryl was clearing the plates, Lisa caught him scoping out the adjoining room via the glimpse through the doorway. "You want the grand tour?" she asked, which surprised him, but he nodded.

The first floor was carved into rooms that were small but comfortable. Some of the furniture was new, but most of it wasn't, and some of it looked like stuff you might see in the backgrounds of old oil paintings. The floor was a symphony of groans and pops and creaks under their feet, and it had the unsteady look and feel of a living museum; an unlived-in plantation whose only guests were day trip tourists. In the foyer, floor-length windows flanked by white sheers opened up onto a wide, deep front porch full of rocking chairs. Through the glass, he could see a long tendril of vegetation curling up around one of the great white columns.

"The parlor's a shrine to my grandparents and their great-great-grandparents." Lisa indicated the sitting room across from the dining room with a wave as they reached the

185

bottom of the staircase. Drew noted stodgy old uncomfortable-looking chairs and sofas and little oval-topped tables, an upright piano against the back wall. A painting of two women in gargantuan skirts hung above the mantle. "Mom wants to redo it but Dad won't let her."

The steps curved slowly up to a wide landing where he could tell a set of French doors led out onto a balcony. A seating area had been arranged with white chairs and a loveseat. The hall branched before them in two halves to the left and right, black-and-white family photos framed and hung in a collage on the stretch of wall ahead of them.

Lisa chatted as they went, telling him that Mark and his son lived with them, and that between all their combined incomes, they'd been able to keep the house from being foreclosed upon. She had complaints, but Drew was left with the impression that the extended family who lived here benefitted from one another's company, and that whatever rich-person life they might have left behind, they were probably better off for being in this place now.

He knew they reached her room when she fell silent and gave the door they stood in front of a little push. It swung inward and he caught a glimpse of an oatmeal colored rug and a yellow quilt over a wrought iron bed frame. Even out in the hall, a touch of fabric softener and perfume touched his nose.

"My room," she explained without necessity. "But we don't need to go in there."

They ended up on the porch, in white rocking chairs, Hektor stretched out on the floorboards at his mistress's feet, a breeze rippling past them. Lisa's brows were knitted together in a way that made him believe she wanted to say something; so he waited, and it came.

"I'm sorry," she said after a long stretch of silence. Her hands were linked together in her lap and she stared at them while the wind played with the collar of her yellow, sleeveless camp shirt. "It's not fair that you have to follow me around. I wouldn't wish that on anyone."

Drew sighed, and, mindful of the massive, tender bruise on the back of it, let his head fall back until it touched the chair. He closed his eyes and winced. "You've seriously gotta stop with that."

"With what?"

"You feel sorry for yourself."

"What?" She bristled. "No I don't!"

"You were just doing it." He tried not to smile. "You wanna act all tough and bitch at me, and then you say 'poor me, nobody likes me.'"

"I..."

He cracked one eye and saw that she was blushing furiously, her lower lip caught between her teeth as she stared across the lawn.

"Well, at least I'm honest," she said at last. Her voice had lost some of its defensive conviction. "It's better than pretending to be well-liked" Her eyes fell to her lap as he watched and she picked at her flaking fingernail polish. She looked embarrassed. Ashamed, maybe.

Drew had been told he was stupid since he was old enough to know what the word meant. And he wasn't especially smart or clever, so he supposed it wasn't unfair, but he knew all too well that if you heard something often enough, you quit fighting it. You shook it out like a cape and wore it. Owned it. Used it as an excuse for all the things you did. Lisa Russell had been told she was an awful bitch until she'd adopted the attitude for herself. Maybe, as he sat on this clean white porch with her and thought about all she had, he shouldn't have felt sorry for her, but he did all the same.

"It's probably smart," he said, closing his eye when she glanced in his direction, "to keep people out."

"Mock me all you want, but it's true," she fired back.

"I'm not mocking you." And he wasn't, because he'd learned the truth of the statement a long time ago.

She snorted. "Tristan's convinced I'm still heartsick over him."

"Are you?" And for some reason, the answer to that question mattered; he wanted to hear it.

When she didn't respond, he opened his eyes and almost laughed at her comically serious expression that dared him to ask again. "Take that as a 'no.'"

"I'm smarter than I used to be," she said, still earnest, "and more careful. *Never again* am I gonna be so stupid I let a man hurt me just for the fun of it."

Drew stiffened in his chair. *Never again*. How many times had he whispered those words to himself? They were his driving force, the thing that pushed him to be faster, stronger, smarter, better. *Never again*, he'd thought to himself the very last time his father's drunken hand had crashed against his face.

"What?" She frowned at him.

"Nothing. Just...good policy is all."

Her mouth pulled to the side like she couldn't tell if he meant what he said or not. She stared at him a long moment, then straightened, head turning toward the yard full of songbirds again. "No one ever agrees with me on that," she said in a quiet voice. "'You'll be lonely,' 'you're missing out,' 'who'll take care of you?' It makes me sick. I don't *need* anything. Getting married, having somebody, that's all about want and not need." Her head tilted a fraction and he could see green in the corners of her eyes as she searched for his opinion, like she dared him to disagree with her.

Drew had a feeling he knew the answer she expected, what she wanted to hear, and what she *thought* she wanted to hear. He shrugged. "You have your family. You need *people*, everyone needs people, but no, you don't need a man that way."

He thought either he wasn't as dimwitted as he'd always been led to believe, or he had some strange ability to read her better than certain other losers who trolled bars looking to harass their exes, because he expected the small frown that turned the corners of her mouth. "Exactly," she said, and sounded so unconvinced it would have been funny if it wasn't sad.

21

"...we got the headlights in today. Found them for a song from a collector in Indiana and had them shipped down."

Drew nodded, pretending he understood the significance of the find. He knew cars needed headlights, sure, but he wasn't a mechanic and had little to no technical knowledge of anything like a '76 Trans Am. Lisa's cousin Johnny, home from work, didn't seem to notice, though, and was happily prattling away about the car he and his dad were fixing up for themselves. Drew felt like a lingering intruder in their house and kept waiting for Ray to come into the family room where he was sitting with Johnny and Lisa, scowling, and order him out.

He'd fallen asleep on the front porch earlier, coming awake with a start to find that the rocking chair's back was digging grooves into his spine and that the sun had made a lot of progress across the sky. Lisa had, surprisingly, been stretched flat on her stomach on the floor, a book cradled in her hands, her dog at her side. She hadn't been aware that he was watching her and she'd smiled at something she read, tucking a stray lock of hair back that had escaped from her ponytail in an unconscious gesture.

"Now, the taillights," Johnny continued, and Drew glanced to Lisa.

She met his glance and twitched a smile, rolled her eyes. *"My cousin has his sweet moments,"* she'd told him earlier, *"but he does tend to bug the shit out of people."*

"...well, hold on, lemme grab the catalogue." Johnny bolted up off the sofa and set out at a jog toward the front of the house, his socked feet sounding like they might punch right through the creaky old floors.

Lisa snorted in amusement when he was gone. "You're fresh meat," she explained with a surprisingly friendly and relaxed smile. Being at home did her good; he had seen her worries fade an inch at a time since lunch. The security of family and the solid, timeless house around her seemed to eat away at the hard candy shell she chose to wear when she was out in the world. "I think he always wanted a brother."

Not that it was any of his business, but Drew lifted his brows in silent question.

"He's got a sister." She made a face as she said it. "Lives in LA with her bitch mom." She'd picked almost all the polish from her nails by this point and put the end of one between her teeth. "What about you? Siblings?"

"No." Did he, though? Had his mother, whoever she was, wherever she was, gone and had herself more children? He didn't know, nor did he care to. "I'd ask you if I was missing out, but I don't guess you know either."

Her smile looked a little sad. "Johnny's been like a little brother most of my life." She shrugged. "I love the idiot, what can I say?"

"You really weren't kidding, were you?"

"About…?"

"Not being sweet."

She chuckled. "Whatever else I am, I ain't a liar."

Johnny's running footsteps on the stairs heralded his return and Lisa smoothed her smile into a benign, pleasant expression. Drew couldn't stop looking at her, even when her cousin came spilling into the room, a huge auto parts catalogue flapping in one hand, talking animatedly. He didn't want to watch her, but he couldn't control his eyes. He was fast becoming infatuated and knew it….and likewise couldn't do anything about it.

"Oh, Ray! Sweet! I was just telling them that – "

Drew didn't hear the rest of what Johnny said because he was too busy trying to keep his pulse to a normal rhythm while he whipped his head around toward the threshold. Ray stood with his shoulder propped in the doorjamb, arms folded over his chest, and though his nephew was the one talking to him, the man's unforgiving green eyes were trained on Drew. Who was struck with the horrific knowledge that he was no

190

doubt sitting in Ray's favorite chair, staring at the guy's only daughter.

Mark brought a woman to dinner. And because he hadn't warned Cheryl in advance, she was furious and flustered and worried her house wasn't clean enough for company. More specifically, *female* company, because she was convinced women paid much more attention to the cleanliness of one's house than did men.

Her name was Ellen and she was surprisingly age appropriate. Fortyish, with a voluminous head of white blonde hair that fell nearly to the middle of her back and had been gelled and sprayed to a plastic consistency, she had the bone structure, posture, but extra poundage of a state fair beauty queen who'd packed on some weight since her pageant days. She dressed well for her frame, though, in a stiff, pink cotton dress that pulled her curves tight rather than clung to them, a wide, black belt cinched high on the narrowest part of her waist. Her finger and toenails were the same shade of bubblegum as her dress, as were the faux crystals that dripped from her silver pendant earrings.

Lisa had smiled and bitten her tongue and forced a polite greeting out around a chuckle when she'd been introduced, and wisely, Cheryl had instructed her daughter to sit down at the foot of the table next to Drew and across from Johnny. Lisa figured they were all wondering the same thing – seeing as how Mark had never mentioned a girlfriend, let alone one who merited a family dinner invite – and after the basket of rolls had been passed around, Cheryl finally posed the question.

"Ellen." Her tone was carefully neutral. "Where did you meet Mark?"

The blonde smiled broadly and set her fork aside so she could lay her hand on Mark's forearm. "I work at the salon next to Poolside."

The not-at-all-creatively-named pool hall where Mark gambled away his paycheck. Which meant Mark had been in during the day because as far as Lisa knew, hairdressers didn't work past nine p.m. She shot a glance to her father's face and saw his poorly-hidden scowl; he was thinking the same thing.

"Oh." Cheryl blinked, her silverware hovering mid-slice above her pork roast. "Well…that's nice."

"I hafta confess," Ellen continued, "I watched him through the window for two weeks before I worked up the courage to step in fronta him on the sidewalk and ask him out."

Two weeks? Ray's glare asked as he stared a hole through his brother.

Lisa felt a pang of guilt, hoping Ellen didn't think they were laughing at her, but was having trouble hiding the laughter that threatened as she watched her dad and uncle's silent conversation of glares and shrugs. Clearly, all the "parts runs" Mark had been making had had nothing to do with the shop. In honor of a guest, they were having drinks with dinner, so she reached for her beer to cover an impending smile.

She met Johnny's gaze across the table. *Why didn't you tell us?* she mouthed.

I didn't know he'd bring her tonight, he mouthed back.

Something touched her arm and she realized it was Drew's elbow when he whispered in her ear: "She's talking to you."

For one moment that she found oddly horrifying, she was too startled by the rush of his breath across her earlobe to grasp what he'd said. She blinked and glanced around the table. "What?"

Ellen was leaning forward so she could see around Drew, her hair not moving in the slightest. "Lisa, honey, your uncle says such nice things about you. You're working at that big bar off 75, right? Oh, what's it called?"

She forced a tight smile. It was painful to know that her job as a bartender was an identifier: that to some people, she was a girl in a short skirt and tight top. Even worse was the knowledge that it was her choice to work there, so the stigma was of her own making. "The Double Vision," she supplied. "Keeping the college students of Acworth drunk for five years now." She took another swallow of beer to wash down the foul taste the words left in her mouth.

"I've never been!" Ellen seemed oblivious. "What nights do you work? We'll have to come in and see you sometime."

"Every night but Monday." Ellen's plucked and drawn-on eyebrows jumped in mild surprise. "Which, reminds me, I need to get ready to leave." Sunlight still fell through the windows in happy shafts and the evening birds were twittering in the willows outside; the thought of putting on her slut outfit and leaving for work was so depressing Lisa could hardly bear it.

"Oh, baby, you hardly ate anything," Cheryl said.

Lisa plucked her beer off the table and forced a smile across her lips before she turned. "I'm fine."

"Oh, I hope I didn't upset her."

"No, no, she's just working too hard."

Drew listened to Cheryl reassure Ellen while he shoveled the rest of his pork roast – which was heaven on a plate – and green beans into his mouth in a haste so he'd be ready to follow Lisa out the door when she came back downstairs. Johnny continued to regale him with tales of his Trans Am, but otherwise, no one spoke to him, and as soon as it looked like it wouldn't be terrible manners to excuse himself, he did so, heading out the back door to grab his wallet off the nightstand in the carriage house.

He didn't realize he'd been followed until he was halfway across the drive and heard the door off the screened-in porch slam shut on its hinges. He paused and turned to find Ray coming after him, not in an angry haste, but not with a friendly smile either.

"You're not hard to sneak up on," Ray said as he drew to a halt in front of him, hands in his jeans pockets giving him a false projection of casualness.

Drew knew he was being baited – he'd been baited his whole life in some form or other – and shrugged. "People don't usually sneak up on me," he countered. "They come right at my face. And I put 'em down."

Ray's sideways smile was full of unspoken threats. "You're not fighting for me. Out in the big ugly world, people don't 'come at your face.'"

He glanced down at the blue cast over his right wrist, his fingers protruding lamely from the plaster. "It's an adjustment," he said. "But I'll get there."

Ray snorted. "I don't have time for that." Drew opened his mouth to protest, but was cut off. "I'm sending Sly with Lis tonight. Somehow I don't think they'll end up in the ER at the end of the night."

It was a fair jab: Drew had screwed up. He'd let his guard down, forgotten that his own past transgressions might be the thing that put Lisa in danger. But as he took in his new employer from head-to-toe, he couldn't help but frown. Lisa wouldn't need a bodyguard if it weren't for whatever her father had done. Drew's poor decisions had shit-all to do with bizarre flower deliveries and potential stalkers. He felt his resolve harden. "Josh wouldn't have hurt her," he said and wanted to think it was true. "But last night, that was my bad, and I get it." He leveled a sharp look at the other man. "But you wouldn't have me tailing her if *you* didn't have some skeletons tryin' to bite you in the ass. Am I right?"

Ray was silent, returning his stare with so much anger shining in his eyes it was a miracle they didn't catch fire.

A foreign thrill licked through Drew's system and he finally knew what it felt like to tell the man pulling his puppet strings "no." Well…if not "no," then at least "back the hell off."

"You didn't hire me because you think I suck," he said. "Call Sly if you want, but I'm going. I don't back out of a job."

And because he wasn't entirely comfortable with this whole insubordination thing, he turned and kept moving toward the carriage house. Ray didn't follow.

The drone of the vacuums was the sweetest sound at the end of every shift. When her knees and feet and the small of her back felt full of needles and she swore she'd dump the next customer's beer in his lap, the static hymn of the old Hoovers up on the carpeted catwalk was downright magical.

Lisa stowed her apron in its cubby beneath the bar and sighed, all her usual pent-up frustration with her job exiting between her teeth. Drew was watching her from his perch on the other side of the bar top, as was now customary, and she had to admit that his eyes didn't bother her anymore. With his cast and his head trauma, after he'd survived family dinner and insisted that he be the one to escort her again – which she knew he must have done – it was hard to find fault with him. She knew she would have been able to if she'd tried, but she didn't want to. And when her eyes had found his throughout the night, she'd almost felt like smiling.

"I'm gonna take the trash around back and then I'll be done," she told him as she pulled the cinch ties on the bag that lined the big can behind the bar where they tossed empties and squeezed lime wedges.

He started to stand. "Should I come?"

"No." She had to grin – he really was a good dog. "I'll just be a sec."

Trying not to stagger against its weight as she hefted the bag up over her shoulder, she gave him a mock-salute and left the bar area via the swinging half-door in the rear. Her ankles threatened to buckle and she cursed her shoes for it as she crossed to the entrance of the short hall that led to the back door. She traded greetings with Miguel and stepped lightly over his just-mopped floor; and rolled her eyes at Holly's glare. Maybe, at some point in her life, she'd work with people she could get along with.

She startled a rat the size of a toy poodle when she pushed through the back door and it scurried, screaming, around behind the dumpster. "Oh, God." Lisa jumped as she felt the thing dart across her feet and caught her breath, feeling stupid, as she watched its silhouette disappear into an even deeper darkness that the one she stood in.

"Dumbass," she cursed herself for being jumpy. She was filled to the brim with fatigue, the beer she'd had with dinner not helping the situation at all; couple that with the straight-out-of-a-horror-movie rear exterior of the bar, she was downright girlish in her jumpiness.

She tried to tell herself it couldn't be helped. Mysterious flowers. Drew getting jumped. The flickering streetlamp at the edge of the parking lot that couldn't make up for the fact that the security light above the back door was missing its bulb. She stood in a pool of oily, rank shadows, the dumpster a hulking monolith of even purer black to her left along the brick façade of the building. The air was ripe with the smell of garbage and stale vomit. The pavement was slippery beneath her feet. And, Lisa noted with a grimace as she heard the latch click into place, she'd forgotten to wedge the loose brick into the door, thanks to the rat's appearance, and now she'd have to walk all the way around to the front of the building and back in through the main doors.

"My life…so charmed," she muttered as she lifted the lid of the dumpster and then nearly gagged as the stench of rotting…*everything*…came pouring out of it. She chucked the bag and backed away, waving her left hand, hoping the wet glob of whatever she'd just touched wasn't as gross as she worried it was. "For Christ's sakes, this is just – "

The air left her in a rush as she collided with something behind her. Her shoulders ran into something hard and her breath left her lungs in a loud burst. "What – "

A hand, its palm clammy and big and smelling of sweat, clamped over her mouth. She hadn't backed into some*thing*, but some*one*. She felt his chin on top of her head; his arms came around hers and she knew he far outsized her.

Panic surged in her chest, a stiff wave of terrified nausea hurtled up her throat. *"You won't ever be able to physically overpower a man,"* her father's voice rang in her head. And her gun was in the glove box of her truck. And her favorite little switchblade was in the bottom of her left boot. Also in her truck.

Oh, God, oh, God, oh, God…

His other hand held both her wrists clamped together, the bones feeling like they might snap at any moment, and he crushed her between his arms, his big fingers digging into her

196

face as he sought to suffocate her. He lurched to the side, and kept going, and Lisa knew he meant to drag her off.

It took half a heartbeat for her to come to the unbelievable conclusion that he was kidnapping her, and then another half for her to push down the debilitating swell of emotions rolling through her to decide that, gun or no, she was not going quietly.

She lifted both feet clear of the ground and kicked him as well as she could, driving the hard, plastic heels of her sandals into his shins. He grunted, but didn't loosen his grip. Lisa arched her spine and tried in vain to throw herself out of his arms.

His hands were damp and she rubbed her wrists together, struggling to –

One of her hands came free and she struck blindly in the dark, reaching behind her, thumping her fist between his legs, but not with the force she'd wanted.

"Bitch!" he hissed in her ear. He released her other hand and she lunged against him. She raked her nails up his arm, clawed at him.

And then he punched her. Stars exploded behind her eyes. Her racing pulse blurred to a steady drumroll that thundered in her ears. Her heart threatened to burst out of her chest and he squeezed her so tight she couldn't draw in another breath. Warm, wet tears slid down her cheeks unbidden because her vision wouldn't clear and she couldn't get her bearings and he was *taking* her.

This sort of thing didn't happen to girls like her. She wasn't a victim, wasn't careless. But still, her mind was flooded with all the horrific possibilities of what this meant, what he would do to her once he took her wherever he was taking her.

Lisa kicked and struggled, and tried to scream at him, fighting her own uncooperative body as much as she did his.

I don't wanna die, I don't wanna die…

And then she was loose, falling, hitting the pavement in a tangle of flailing limbs. Air crashed down into her lungs and she gasped and coughed and levered herself up to a crouch, head spinning, world reeling, as she tried to find some reason that her attacker would have released her.

A dark shadow in the shape of a man was sprinting off into the night across the parking lot, soles of his shoes slapping loudly against the pavement. And Lisa could barely make out someone standing above her, just a shift in the pattern of shadows around her. She gasped, and then covered her mouth, half afraid she'd throw up.

"You okay?"

It was Drew, and as he knelt in front of her, all the adrenaline bled out of her on a trembling exhale. The sense of urgency, the need to escape, left her, and in its place, the frantic notion of what-might-have-been left her shaking and clammy with cold sweat.

"Yeah," she managed, and reached to touch the knot forming on the side of her head where the attacker had hit her. "Holy shit."

Drew made an angry, grunting sort of sound. "When you didn't come back in I got worried."

She'd never been so glad of a man's worry as she was now. She swallowed the compulsion to gag. "Did – did you get a look at him?"

"No. Too dark. You?"

She shook her head, then winced when the motion sent fresh stabs of pain radiating through her skull.

"Here."

"I'm fine." But the protest was lame, and she didn't fight him when he slid an arm around her waist and pulled her gently to her feet. She staggered a step and leaned into his side for support. He felt sturdy and strong beside her, and though in a different moment she might have called herself weak, now, she just wanted to grab a handful of the back of his shirt and let him lead her around to the front of the bar.

So that's what she did.

22

Ray was scared. Drew could see the unmistakable glimmer of fear in the man's eyes as he braced his hands on his kitchen table beneath the glow of the overhead lamp. "You get a look at him?" he asked, his voice clipped.

Drew shook his head and then his eyes slid back to Lisa who sat beside him, staring blankly into near space, her fingertips at her temples looking like all that held her head up on her neck. Recalling the attack as he'd seen it, bringing the image back to the forefront of his mind, filled Drew with his own share of fright, and the knowledge of such worried him. It hadn't been adrenaline or duty or obligation that had sent him catapulting out the back door of the bar. No – as he'd watched the shadow of a man crush the shadow of Lisa back against his chest, prepared to drag her away into the night, a cold blast of terror had rushed through his system. He wasn't easily scared, but he'd been scared for her, and though he accepted the truth of it, it wasn't reassuring. You didn't get *frightened* for your charge, for your boss's kid.

"He didn't hear me come out and I had a clear shot at his face," he explained. A humorless grin touched his lips before he could stop it. "Hit the asshole across the mouth with the back of my cast and he took off. Guess this thing's good for something."

Ray's brows drew even tighter together, if that was possible. "And you didn't see him at all?"

"It was dark, Dad," Lisa defended. "He was just a shadow."

"And I'm pretty sure he was wearing a ski mask." Drew held up his right arm so the dark, knit fibers that had

199

scratched off on his cast were visible under the lamp. He recalled at least a half a dozen episodes of *CSI* he'd watched over the mountain of empty beer bottles in Josh's living room once upon a time. "Should we, you know, call the cops or something? Maybe they could take a sample and they could get the…what do ya call it…the DNA, and…"

He trailed off as Ray's glare threatened to cut him. Lisa shot him a very disapproving look.

"This isn't TV," Ray said with disgust. "What, we let *city of Acworth,*" he spat the name, "PD put out a BOLO for a 'man of unknown age, description or race who might have a ski mask in his back pocket'?" He shoved away from the table with a sneer and began to pace around it.

Cheryl was leaning back against the counter in front of the sink, looking shocked and nauseous, her arms folded over her middle. Without makeup, the grooves around her mouth and eyes were more pronounced, and terror for her daughter had widened her eyes to tear-filled saucers. She met his glance and gave him the tiniest of trembling smiles, though, as reassurance that maybe he wasn't so stupid as Ray thought. A thankful smile. If not for him, Lisa would be…It was heavy stuff, that thought. He felt its weight all the way down to his bones.

Ray reached the threshold between kitchen and back porch and he spun, a dictatorial finger stabbing through the air toward his daughter. "You're done there, you hear me? You *do not* work at Double Vision *one more night!*"

Cheryl put a shaky hand to her mouth, taking the end of one nail between her teeth in the same way Drew had watched Lisa do.

Lisa lifted her head; her hands fell palm-down on the table, and it was such a rallying gesture, the way her shoulders heaved as she pulled in a breath, that Drew thought she meant to defy her dad. But then she swallowed, the muscles in her slim throat moving, and the last, clinging bits of fire in her green eyes died down. She looked exhausted. Defeated. And she nodded before her gaze swept down to her hands. "Okay."

If this was the first time Drew had ever laid eyes on the girl, he might have called her meek. As much as she hated the bar, as much as he thought it was the worst place for her – save maybe a strip club – it was her independence. If she was giving it up, then she was shaken. Badly shaken.

Ray must have expected an argument, because then he didn't seem to know what to do, running his hands back over his thin hair, exhaling in a loud rush. He nodded.

"Babe," Cheryl ventured, "I think we really ought to call the police." Her husband's betrayed look didn't sway her. "This is getting to be more than you can handle."

Which was clearly the wrong thing to stay. The storm clouds that had dissipated reformed over his face. "We have jack shit to tell the cops," he argued in a nasty voice. "We – "

She raised a hand, palm facing him, and shook her head. "I'm not fighting with you tonight." Her voice shook. "I'm just not. We all need some sleep."

Drew glanced over her shoulder and through the window above the sink, noting that the deep indigo of midnight had faded to the pinkish gray of dawn. This would be the second day in a row that had bled into morning. His right hand was throbbing insistently, reminding him that he'd been over twelve hours without a prescription pain pill, and that he needed sleep. He'd been so hyped up with worry over Lisa, and then Ray's reaction to Lisa, that he'd almost forgotten that he felt like dog shit.

"All of us," Cheryl said. "It's Sunday, we don't have to go anywhere. And we're probably waking up Mark and Johnny."

"Mark and Johnny can go to hell," Ray snapped, but he took a step anyway, toward the door, toward the stairs, toward bed, as his wife wanted.

"We'll sort this out when our heads are clear," Cheryl pressed. She pushed away from the counter and set a gentle, motherly hand on her daughter's head. "Come on, sweetie. We'll get some aspirin."

When Lisa didn't jump at the idea, but remained staring at the table, Drew offered, "You want a Vicodin? The doc gave me plenty." He left out the part about already having a stash of his own.

To his surprise, Lisa turned grateful eyes to him and nodded.

He walked through a balmy dawn that had been pinpricked with coolness and drizzled with dew to the carriage house. The prescription bottle waited on the antique-looking nightstand. He paused in the bathroom to cup water in his hand and swallow one of the two pills he'd shaken out, then he returned to the house among the singing of early rising birds.

Ray was gone when he reentered the kitchen, and Cheryl stood behind Lisa's chair, stroking her hair. He didn't really know what a mother's concern looked like, but still, he knew this was what he was watching as he approached the table. He set the white, oblong pill on the table in front of Lisa and Cheryl already had a glass of water in her free hand.

Once Lisa swallowed it down, she said, "I'm fine, Mom," not unkindly. She was the one who'd been attacked, but she was trying to be the brave one. Which, judging by the pained look that flickered across Cheryl's face, her mom thought that was ridiculous.

"Don't stay up," she admonished, then, reluctantly, with slow, lingering steps, she left the room.

The sound of her slippered feet was just fading up the stairs when an electronic chime echoed throughout the room and Lisa groaned. "The alarm," she explained with a slow shake of her head. "Dad's burglar alarmed you into the house and probably not on purpose." The chuckle she forced had not a trace of humor.

Drew shrugged. "I can crash on the couch."

When Lisa didn't get immediately to her feet, he pulled out the chair beside her and sat. Down on her level, he could see the fluttering of her lashes as she blinked furiously at the table top. A shadow of a bruise was forming on her temple and anger tightened like a fist in his gut; the bastard had hit her. It wasn't enough that he was trying to...well, he didn't like to run all the scenarios...but to know that the tall shadow he'd clocked had *hit* someone who he'd clearly outsized and

202

outweighed…That was pulling all sorts of strings Drew hadn't known were dangling inside him.

"You hated that job." He meant it as a joke, but it came out more consoling than that.

She brushed her knuckles over her eyes and when she lifted her head, she didn't look like she was about to cry. If he'd ever seen a situation in which a chick was perfectly entitled to some tears, this was it, but she refused to give in to that. The delicate lines of her face hardened. "This sort of thing doesn't happen to me," she said fiercely. "I'm not the stupid…idiot…stupid" - her cheeks flushed with mounting anger - "*girl* who just lets things happen to her!"

Drew couldn't help it: he wanted to smile. He didn't do it, but the impulse was there, as was the sensation that her anti-girl-ness was endearing in its own way. "I've seen grown-ass men get mugged and carjacked."

"So?!" She threw up her hands.

"So," he explained, "you're not…'some stupid girl,'" he used her words, "because you couldn't fight off a dude who *got the drop* on you and was *much bigger* than you."

Her scowl told him he'd missed the mark.

"Are you mad at me?" he guessed with a sigh, figuring it was true.

The anger bled out of her face as she shook her head. She sighed. Pulled her lower lip between her teeth. "No." Her eyes darted between him and her clenched hands. She always guarded what she said to him, so when she spoke, he was shocked. "I'm mad" - her voice was stilted – "that I…that I needed someone to…come to my rescue."

"Why?"

"Because I don't want to be a bother to anyone."

He bit back another smile. "It wasn't a bother."

"Because my dad pays you."

"Because I like you."

She leaned back in her chair, hands braced on the table, and blinked at him. Her brows drew together and he thought she was trying to be nasty with him, but she failed. "Well, you shouldn't."

This time, he did smile, and she glanced away from him.

"I'm serious," she insisted, but her voice quavered just a little and he knew she was trying to convince herself more than she was him. The girl was all kinds of screwed up.

She stood and he did too, his useless, casted hand hovering at her elbow as she wobbled. And maybe it was dumb to think that she might actually ask for or accept help, he realized, as she pushed her chair in and headed for the door.

She stopped, though, and his senses, though already feeling the first numbing strokes of the pain meds, came to attention as she halted beside him. She stared at the floor a long moment, drew in a deep breath. And then before he could respond, she turned and slipped her arms around his waist in a quick, tight hug. Her whole body was shaking as she pressed it, however briefly, to his, and when she glanced up at his face, her green eyes were slick with moisture and brimming with all the terror she'd been trying gallantly not to show so far. She stretched up on her toes and touched the softest of fleeting kisses against his cheek, and then she was gone, moving away from him, and Drew wondered if he'd imagined the whole thing.

Ray didn't sleep. At a quarter past eight, he was ensconced in the room he'd turned into his office, drowning in a sea of paper.

In the front left corner of the house, set off the dining room in what had once been some kind of parlor or sitting room, his massive, claw-foot desk had been wedged diagonally so that the back of his chair was snugged into a corner of the room. A tall window dressed in wooden, horizontal blinds kept the sunlight at bay, the two lamps on either corner of the desk providing the illumination he needed. The floors were the same bare, creaking wood as throughout the rest of the house and the walls were some vague shade of cream that Cheryl doubtless knew the name of. The only pieces of furniture, save the desk, were relics from some generation of grandparents or other: a spindly-legged, striped sofa and a small, glass-paned cabinet that he used to hold his law tomes.

He'd known sleep would be elusive, but when it proved nonexistent, he'd bent his focus toward productivity: a frenzied, insane sort of productivity. After he'd been expelled from the bar, he'd spent a week in the bottom of a bottle of Jack Daniels. Then he'd realized that the only thing to be done was to try and maintain some scrap of the life he'd built for his family, and so he'd put his more oily traits to the next best use. Now, aside from King Customs, he owned two businesses.

The security firm, which was really just Sly, Eddie and sometimes Mark, was listed in all his accounts under the title RBSS – Russell Business Security Solutions. It was vague and direct at the same time, sounding much more self-important than what it truly was: hired muscle who served as everything from party bouncers to executioners of shady nighttime shake downs. The work was not consistent, but his costs were almost zero save the guys' salary, which, though decent by their standards, was considerably smaller than what he charged his customers.

Adamant was a payroll company that serviced two hundred businesses in Alpharetta that handled many of its clients' HR responsibilities in addition to depositing money in employee pay accounts. Ray had scraped and scratched and fought to get the loan necessary to buy the company, and now his banker blushed at their infrequent meetings because he'd doubted Ray's ability to make payments. Idiot. He always made his payments. Though Adamant was run by a former Russell & Carillo hopeful intern who'd decided he belonged in an office and not a courtroom, and Ray trusted him, he made a point of stopping by at least twice a week, but usually more often than that, to check on things.

And then there were his stock investments, which, given the current state of the economy, added up to shit.

None of the paperwork strewn across his desk was at all relevant to any of his business ventures.

He had photocopied news clippings dated three years ago that detailed Carl Shilling's trial. Ray's very last trial. He had all the old Shilling files he was supposed to have destroyed when he was disbarred. He had printouts of the cell phone pictures he'd taken of Shilling's car at the La Quinta. It was all spread around him and a pen was clamped between his fingers as he hashed theories on a yellow legal pad.

The night they'd gone to "visit" Shilling, Mark had said he thought the man looked shaken. Broken. Afraid of them. And if Ray hadn't known him to be a murderous son of a bitch, he would have agreed. Because it was hard to rectify whoever Drew had described as "trying to snatch" his daughter with the sweating, skinny Carl Shilling who'd just been let out on parole. But it was the only lead he had, the only explanation that made any sense, and he was jotting notes as fast as his cramped fingers could fly over the paper.

He was so concentrated that he didn't hear the door glide open, or hear Cheryl's bare feet move across the planks. He sensed her presence, more than anything, and glanced up to find her with a steaming coffee mug clasped in both hands, wearing khaki cargo shorts and a loose, white, sleeveless top that reached nearly to mid-thigh. She'd showered and applied her makeup; her hair had been dried and fell in loose tumbles over her shoulders. But she looked like he felt: exhausted and wired all at once.

As he watched her, feeling guilty, her eyes fell over what he was working on, and her mouth pulled to the side in a grimace. "Ray." Her tone was gently chiding. "What are you doing?"

It was so obvious a question that he knew it wasn't real. He glanced down at the hard-pressed, slanted letters he'd written across the page in what looked like the harried hand of a madman. "What's it look like?" he said, reaching to gather the scattered papers to the center of the desk.

"What it always looks like," she answered, and he glanced up again and saw her lift her brows in a knowing way. "Like you're taking everything on all by yourself."

He held her gaze until he couldn't, then he sighed. They'd had a version of this argument hundreds of times, and he'd learned it was easier if he didn't argue, but heard her out.

206

He waited as she crossed to the sofa and perched on its edge, took a sip of coffee.

"You're not responsible for taking care of this whole family," she said, as expected, and he felt himself nodding. "Not even from murderers."

His head snapped up, attention snared by this addition to her speech.

Her eyes were full of fear and pleading. But bravery too. "Tell us. Tell all of us. The guys and Johnny and Lisa and me. I won't live inside a horror movie full of dumb teenagers who insist on splitting up and pretending they don't believe in ghosts." Her chin lifted to a defiant angle. "We're gonna sit down and we're gonna figure out who's doing this. And we're gonna make it stop. You hear?"

Even though he felt like he was being slowly strangled, Ray smiled. "I love you. You know that?"

"I do." She returned his smile. "Which is why I know you'll tell us."

23

On her stomach, on the love seat, a pillow that was nearly as big as she was filling up her arms and propping up her head, Lisa could find no shame in her baggy sweats, lack of makeup, or current state ensconced beneath a light blanket in front of the TV. She'd had worse shots to the head, and she'd been to parties more exhausting than her attack the night before. So it was with great reluctance that she acknowledged that it was her nerves – tattered, fried and totally done – that had pushed her fatigue onto a whole new plane of misery. Her head pounded, a vague nausea tickled at her stomach, and her limbs felt weighted down with lead. She wanted to go to sleep and not wake up. Except, as dawn had fallen over the house, as the Vicodin had kicked in, she'd tumbled headlong into a nightmare that had sent her bolting upright in bed, breathing in ragged gulps, sweat plastering her pajamas to her body.

So as noon melted into afternoon, she tried to find some comfort in resting, if not sleeping. At another time, she might have felt like a slug for it, but she was past the point of caring.

There was a Braves game on and Drew was sitting on the sofa, near enough that she could hear the ice cubes shift in his glass every time he raised it to take a swallow. His presence was comforting and she was done pretending it wasn't.

"You ever had one of those?"

Lisa forced her head up and glanced at the TV and the DQ commercial that was playing across its wide screen. A new kind of Blizzard was being advertised and she gathered it involved brownie pieces of some sort. "No." She rested her chin on the pillow again. "You rethinking your diet or something?"

"I am when I watch that commercial."

He'd been striving to engage her in light, benign conversation all afternoon. Rather than annoying, his occasional comments were welcome reminders that she was being watched over. In some part of her brain she knew that she was overly grateful for his presence because she was still so shaken from the night before. But that didn't stop her from clinging to him – figuratively speaking, anyway. If that clinging became physical, she was in for some seriously poor decision-making.

On the floor, half-lying beneath the coffee table, Hektor stretched and groaned in his sleep. The light coming in through the windows was gray and heavy with the promise of an afternoon storm. It was almost the perfect rainy day.

The motion detector chimed as the front door was opened and two familiar male voices echoed off the high ceiling in the foyer. Sly and Eddie were talking about whatever tail they'd picked up at a bar the night before and as their booted footsteps moved toward the back of the house, Lisa twisted around so she could get a look at Drew's face. As she expected, his jaw was clenched in apprehension. As far as she knew, he and Eddie hadn't mended fences.

"Yo," Eddie greeted as he stepped into the family room. He carried an overstuffed black duffel bag in each hand and he chucked them both at Drew. "You left your shit behind."

Clearly, there was no truce.

One of the bags landed with a muffled thump in Drew's lap, but the other flipped over the arm of the sofa and crashed into the legs of the hand-me-down end table, sending the glass lamp it held tumbling into open space. Drew made a grab for it and saved it from shattering against the floor, cursing.

"Hey!" Cheryl protested as she entered via the kitchen. "Who said you could throw things in my house?!"

Sly smacked the back of his friend's head. "Told you, dumbass." Then he turned toward Lisa. "How you doin', sweetheart?"

She sat up and consolidated her pillow and blanket in the corner of the loveseat, her knees draw up to her chest. "Fine."

"Liar." He plopped down beside her but didn't push the issue.

"Who was it?" Eddie asked as he propped a shoulder against one of the built in bookshelves.

"No idea," she said with a sigh. Admitting that was almost as frustrating as racking her brain and coming up empty. She'd tried to recall some tiny, recognizable detail about her attacker, and still, she had no clue.

Sly and Eddie traded a meaningful look and Cheryl sighed. "Oh, no, no more of that secret shit." She stepped back to the threshold and cupped her hands around her mouth. "Ray!" she hollered, "they're here!"

"Dining room!" his answer came echoing back.

Cheryl nodded and motioned for everyone to follow her.

Dread sank like a stone in Lisa's belly. In her memory, every official, dining room-held family meeting was brought about by some negative life change that affected all of them. Like her father's disbarment. Like the news that they'd have to leave Alpharetta and return to Cartersville. And this time, as a little stab of pain radiated up her arm thanks to her valiant struggles, she knew this meeting somehow related to her. Just as she knew that Ray didn't address all of them unless he was out of alternatives.

The dining room table was a Russell family heirloom: sixteen feet long with a scarred, but still shiny mahogany top, legs that were heavy white pillars carved with intricate grape vines. The silver and crystal chandelier above it was original to the house and tarnished despite all of Cheryl's best efforts, but it, like the table, belonged in the room with its sweeping windows and floor-length drapes. As a family, they were transient, but some pieces of history had earned their permanent places.

Ray was seated at the head of the table, facing the windows, and Mark and Johnny joined them all from upstairs as they took their places: Cheryl at the foot, the rest of them in between. Lisa situated herself so she was between her cousin and Drew, the boxer buffered by Cheryl on the other side, and it took her a moment to realize that she'd been willfully shielding him from Eddie. Protection went both ways, she supposed.

Ray worked his hands back over his head – if he kept the habit up, he'd be completely bald – and then faced them with a look that somehow managed to capture all their gazes at once. "I think I know what's going on," he said without preamble, and proceeded to tell them.

"Do you feel better?"

Lisa hadn't intended to wind up on the front porch with Drew again, but somehow it had happened and she wasn't complaining. The rest of the guys were in front of the ball game and her mother was prepping dinner after having refused any of Lisa's help; Ellen was coming over, she'd said, and Lisa "needed her rest." So she sat at the edge of the porch, legs dangling over the side, the breeze tugging at her hair. The roiling clouds overhead were the color of soot, the afternoon was dark around them, and lightning streaked in forked tongues across the sky.

"Not really," she admitted. He was sitting beside her, legs folded, elbows on his knees, and she turned to regard him. He was watching her, like he always was. "I almost wish this was some grudge against me. Now Dad thinks this is all on him."

"Well," Drew said after a beat of silence, "it is on him. He caused this, Lisa. It's not something you have to beat yourself up over."

She forced a chuckle. "Right. Plenty of people to do the beating for me."

He didn't smile.

"Lame joke?"

"Yep."

She blew out a breath that ruffled her hair and watched the lightning tear open the clouds. In a matter of minutes, a curtain of rain would uncurl from the heavens like a bucket tipping over, but for now, it held off. "I'm scared," she admitted, and felt heat bloom in her cheeks. "I feel like a weak-ass," she continued, "and I hate it. I hate someone controlling my life: where I can work, whether or not I can even be alone." Frustration was welling up in her chest and she checked her speech before she started hyperventilating in anger.

When Drew's hand landed on top of her head, she was so startled her spine went rigid. And then his thumb swept down along her temple, over her bruise, and pushed her hair back behind her ear. It was meant to be comforting, but was awkward, like he didn't know quite whether he ought to touch her or not and had settled for patting her head like she was a dog.

But at the same time, the gesture was terribly sweet in its uncertainty and innocence.

Lisa didn't look at him again, not even when he pulled his hand away. She was afraid her smile might be mistaken for making fun of him, and that he wouldn't reach out again after he saw it. And that wasn't what she wanted – him refraining from reaching out.

God help me, she thought, *but here come the bad decisions.*

24

"Johnny," Lisa called through the open door into the garage. "Come here." She kept her voice low because the two windows in the office were open and Ellen was making startling progress across the lot in her peep-toe pumps.

"Yeah?" He entered with a can of Dr. Pepper in one noticeably clean hand – clearly lunch break was still in session.

"What's Mark's girlfriend doing here?" she whispered as the woman closed the distance to the door and reached for the handle. She had a canvas tote bag slung over one shoulder of her bright turquoise peasant top. Her white crops were hemmed in sparkling silver applique that matched the combs sweeping her mass of platinum hair off her forehead.

"Dunno." He shrugged.

A fresh blast of hot air, more forceful than what slipped in through the windows, created a whirlwind of paperwork on the desk. Lisa slapped at it as Ellen swept into the room, pushing her sunglasses up on her forehead.

"Well hey, ya'll!" she said in such a loud, cheerful voice that Drew was startled from his chair nap and came awake with a snort and a flailing of arms. His cast thumped against the wall and Lisa winced in sympathetic pain.

"Hi." So far, based on their two encounters, Lisa liked Ellen in the way she liked all friendly people – she found the woman pleasant, but without knowing her truly, felt she had every right to be cautious. Suspicious even.

Ellen didn't seem to notice. "Hi, Johnny-boy!" she crowed happily, and pulled him into a smothering hug.

Lisa traded amused glances with the now-awake Drew. They were doing that now, since the night before, since her dad's spilling of information and Drew's strange dog-pat to her head. She hadn't taken her walls down, but somehow, he'd managed to throw a grappling hook up and scale his way to the top. And not, surprisingly, by force, but through that steadfast blandness of his. Bland she could grow to like. Bland she *did* like.

"Oh, hi, dear." Ellen had disentangled from Johnny and was beaming at Lisa now, setting her tote bag on a rare free section of desk. "I thought I'd bring the boys a little something from my kitchen."

Hokey occasionally worked, if it was genuine, and Ellen seemed, with that smile that went all the way up to her extravagant smoky-shadowed eyes, to be genuinely hokey. Lisa had to grin. "I think they actually just got done with lunch. If they have double lunch, I don't have a prayer of getting them back to work."

Ellen winked at her and pushed down the sides of the bag to reveal a Tupperware cake plate. "Not lunch. Three layer chocolate fudge cake." She popped the lid and Lisa got a peek of neatly swirled, rich dark chocolate fudge icing. The half a turkey sandwich she'd choked down for lunch screamed for some company.

"Wow, um..."

"I brought plates and plastic forks," Ellen said brightly. "It'll be a fun treat, don't ya think?"

Lisa thought it would be nothing but a distractor that prevented the guys from diving back into work, and that it would be a miracle if Big Tom's Fastback was finished before the year was out. But her uncle Mark had such poor taste in women... She couldn't remember a time when one had brought him dessert at work. His women were petty and shallow and too young and never anything more than a weekend dalliance, so it seemed unjust to rob her uncle of three layer chocolate fudge cake, even if it pushed back their schedule.

"I think it sounds great." Lisa knew she didn't do bright and happy well, and the boys' glances proved that she'd sounded just as wooden in her delivery as she'd felt. Ellen didn't seem to notice, though, and ventured out into the garage after Mark, white pants and all. "Did I really sound that bad?" she asked when Ellen was gone.

Johnny laughed, but Drew's smile was softer, more sympathetic. "No."

Ray wasn't in-shop, off making the rounds with his payroll business, so of course the boys camped out in the office and devoured Ellen's baking. Lisa nibbled her way through half a piece and then went outside, the humid afternoon suddenly sounding less stuffy than the tiny office crammed with humans. She went to the edge of the parking lot, up near the sidewalk, and propped a hip against the shiny, but very empty shell of an old Nova that was slanted across the front corner as advertising. They'd pulled in nearly a quarter of their business thanks to interested passersby who'd stopped to ask if the Nova was for sale.

There was a kid dressed up like a sub sandwich holding a sign on the sidewalk a few dozen yards away, advertising the deli next door. Afternoon soccer mom traffic cruised past sluggishly, the hot breeze generated by the dozens of passing minivans stirring Lisa's hair and filling her nostrils with the familiar smells of motor oil, sunbaked pavement, and whatever delightful things they were grilling at the Longhorn down the street.

The Nova had no windows because it had no interior. Not even a wheel. But there was a glove box and in it, a pack of smokes Lisa had hidden there in case life got too crazy and she decided her clean streak wasn't as important as she'd once thought. She found the slightly smashed pack of Marlboros by feel, and when she straightened, cradling it in her hands, she was startled, but not surprised to find Drew standing behind her.

She saw him scan the street, the sidewalk, and the parking lot before he glanced her way. "You smoke?"

She fiddled with the pack's cardboard top and sighed. "Not for a couple years," she said. "And I shouldn't now, but…"

"You're stressed."

Lisa nodded, ashamed about it but not wanting to lie. Tension was being layered on piece by piece, as thick and dark as Ellen's cake, and Lisa was slowly forgetting what relaxation felt like. She was jumpy, exhausted and sleepless, and she feared a meltdown loomed in her future. That was the thing about pressure: it couldn't maintain a constant level – either things would come to a head with this Carl Shilling person, or Lisa would be pushed over the edge until she went numb, until she didn't feel anything anymore. "I think something bad's going to happen," she heard herself say and wished she hadn't.

When her phone trilled to life in her back pocket, she nearly leapt out of her skin, and was so embarrassed by it that she didn't try to shrug away the hand Drew settled on her shoulder. Swearing under her breath, she slipped her phone out and saw that it was her mother calling.

"Hi, Mom," she said with a sigh.

Cheryl could tell her daughter was caving. "I'm telling you," she pressed, "now couldn't be a better time for this. You and I need something to distract us."

Lisa made an unhappy sound on the other end of the line. "Distract us right into getting kidnapped?"

It was a possibility Cheryl was already planning for. "We charge them for security and bring the boys along."

"Hmm."

"Just say yes," Cheryl urged. "I know this isn't the kind of design job we were expecting, but it's a step in that direction. This is a good idea, Lis."

In truth, Cheryl had decided to take the job whether or not Lisa agreed to participate. Thirty minutes earlier, when Patty Smyth's number had flashed across the ID display on her cell phone, she'd nearly hung up on the woman in her haste to take the call. Patty had sighed and sniffled and sounded like her usual bored self: a former beauty queen and retired middle school teacher whose husband had survived the economic downturn and whose self-entitlement knew no bounds. She was in charge of a very "dignified" book club these days and she wanted to host an "evening garden party" for her "girls" in

216

the "most dignified" of ways. Cheryl had gritted her teeth and suffered through the digs and slights – Patty wasn't sure if after "that unfortunate business" involving Ray's disbarment if Cheryl was still interested in designing, to which Cheryl had gently reminded that she'd offered to do Patty's study only weeks before.

The party was to be a test. Cheryl wasn't truly a party planner, but she knew that if she could pull it off, and if she then designed a room in Patty's house, all of Patty's snooty book club friends would consider using her.

"You're gonna do it without me anyway, aren't you?" Lisa guessed.

"Of course."

She sighed. "Alright. I guess I'm in."

Cheryl hung up with the truest smile to touch her face in weeks. In her head, she was already preparing a list of supplies she would need. Tables needed to be rented, paper lanterns prepared, linens ironed. She conjured and then instantly dismissed a dozen possible tablescapes. Her gardens had reached a point of maturity at which she could clip flowers and use them in arrangements; her hydrangeas would make lovely centerpieces in ceramic bowls. Maybe some tea lights and tapers with mirrors beneath...

"I have a delivery for Cheryl Russell."

Her head snapped up and she went stumbling out of her mental evening-time garden party and back into the current reality of the dental office. The deliveryman who peeked around a vase full of pink carnations wasn't the same one who'd made the previous flower deliveries, but his identity was irrelevant.

"Leave them on the counter," she said, unsmiling, and watched his face fall. Clearly, she hadn't reacted the way most flower recipients did.

As she'd been instructed to do, she snapped a picture of them with her cell and then emailed it to Ray, her stomach churning.

***

217

The fluted glass vase shattered on impact when it crashed against the pavement. Lisa observed it with a detached sort of contained horror, noting that the pink carnations looked somehow sad as they thumped lightly down, their green stems glittering and wet, their pale petals delicate and soft against the asphalt.

Drew's shoulders were jacked up halfway to his ears, his arms bowed out in a display of aggression that had sent the deliveryman stumbling back against his purple florist's van. The guys were emptying out of the office, calling to her, asking what the hell was going on. Ellen had a hand over her mouth in an obvious display of shock. But Lisa didn't respond. She stood rooted, the cigarettes crumpled in her fist, still stunned that Drew had charged the van after its arrival and snatched the flowers from the driver's hands. Here she'd been worried about snapping, and *he'd snapped*.

Something bad's going to happen, she thought again, and realized what that something was. Her dad had ruined Carl Shilling's life when he'd turned over damning evidence to the DA. Criminals like Shilling – wife and daughter killers, sickos and freaks – needed to be out in the world in order to satisfy their sadistic proclivities. Containment cut off their addiction at the source: there were no wives and daughters to terrorize, to *murder*, in prison. The torture of getting caught wasn't being exposed...it was being denied, having his impulsions prevented.

Now Carl wanted to ruin not just Ray's life, but hers too, her mother's. Because what was life if you slept with one eye open and were tailed by a bodyguard?

If he'd wanted to kill them, he would have come and killed them. No...he was toying with them. He was shredding their confidence and sense of safety. He was building them a prison, one bouquet at a time.

Lisa was quiet on the ride home that evening – "home," as if crashing in the Russell carriage house constituted an actual home for him – and Drew kept stealing glances at her from the corner of his eye. He was still juiced from earlier, his sudden

218

burst of inexplicable rage at seeing the florist van taking its sweet time in ebbing, but she had her left arm braced against the window, her right draped loosely over the wheel.

"Tell me something about you," she said at the second red light.

"What?"

Lisa shrugged. "You know all the important things about me – not sweet, being stalked, runaway bride…all the dirty details." She pulled her eyes away from the road long enough to give him a searching look. "What about you? Family? Side interests? Skeletons?"

The ride from Alpharetta to Cartersville was not a short one, and Drew didn't want to spend the majority of it discussing the shitstorm that was his life up till now. But Lisa had a point – he'd come into her life and learned everything about it in short order. He was living in her parents' garage, for God's sakes, but she knew nothing about him. It was only fair…

He exhaled noisily. "I'm from Augusta." He decided on the abridged version. "Mom left when I was little, Dad was always in and out of work." He shrugged. "Nothing special."

He saw her chew at her lower lip and wondered if she was thinking he was full of shit. "How'd you get into fighting?"

"How's anybody get into anything?"

"Okay, Confucius." She snorted a laugh. "You don't have to get all defensive. I was just curious."

She hadn't so much as smiled since he'd sent the delivery guy running, so her chuckle was as effective as twisting his broken arm. "I was good at it," he elaborated. He'd never been tall as a child and had grown into a rather scrawny teenager. But he'd been quick. And quiet – when you weren't running your mouth, you noticed things about the people around you that no one else did: limps, weak left hands, a propensity to overuse a right jab. His first fight had been one of self-defense, and though he hadn't started it, he'd ended it, the chunky, pimple-faced boy who'd attacked him in the cafeteria rolling on the ground, clutching his ruined nose and howling.

219

"Got kicked out of school for it and didn't see a reason to try and do much else."

"Hmm." She made a reflective sound. "You don't really strike me as the violent type."

He was so taken aback, he couldn't help but stare at her.

She shrugged. "What? You don't. I mean, you're fantastic in the ring." He thought a pop of color bloomed in her cheek. "But I can't see you being a bully."

"I wasn't."

"It makes sense. Your ring name." A smile touched her lips. "My uncle took me and Johnny deer hunting once," she said, and he had a feeling this was going somewhere, so he kept silent. "He still takes Johnny, but sitting up in a tree all afternoon wearing deer piss and camo isn't my idea of a fun time. Still...it was worth the experience. Anyway," she continued, "we didn't walk out of the woods 'til late that night. Mark thought it'd be cool to eat dinner up in the deer stand to celebrate our kill." He saw her roll her eyes. "And we had to use flashlights to get back to the truck. We came across a deer carcass probably three days old. It was full of claw marks and Mark said he could tell it had been suffocated. Only cats kill like that," she said meaningfully, sparing him a glance, "and the only cats in those woods were lynx."

"A lynx isn't a big cat," Lisa said, "so it drops out of trees on large prey like that. They're smart. They're skill hunters, not brute strength killers."

"Are you complimenting me?" he asked, not quite believing it.

Her grin widened as she faced the road. "Well, it was really a *bobcat*, not a lynx, but yeah. Showing an appreciation, whatever you wanna call it. The point is, you're a good fighter, not just some dumbass who throws his weight around. You could go somewhere with your fighting. *The Lynx* could go places."

Drew glanced away from her, wondering what had inspired this pep talk. Maybe she was tired of his lingering presence and had decided encouragement might be the thing to drive him away. He watched the road lying before them like

220

a great gray snake and felt the familiar, forbidden pang of longing. Ricky hadn't been the first to promise him wealth and women in exchange for his skill in the ring. He'd entertained his own hopes and dreams about this talent of his turning into a career. And yet here he sat, guarding a rich man's daughter.

"I don't need 'places,' but a car would be nice," he said before he could stop himself. "Health insurance. Maybe a pair of shoes I hadn't hurled all over."

A beat of silence passed and when he felt Lisa's hand land on his forearm on the truck's center console, a bolt of lightning crashing through the windshield of the truck would have been less shocking. "I quit dreaming about things a long time ago," she consoled, her fingers closing over his good wrist in a comforting gesture. "But I don't think things can stay this shitty forever."

He didn't know what she was playing at, but wanted to play along, if only to prolong this sentimental crack in her façade. But he didn't know what to say. "You getting optimistic on me?"

"I'm knocking on rock bottom." She pulled her hand away and raked it through her hair. "I'll be tossing scripture at you 'fore it's all over."

Golden sunlight was washing over the driveway and its canopy of trees like warm, foamy beer when Ray arrived home that night. He spotted Mark stretched flat on the bench swing that dangled from an oak branch as big around as a keg, a thin wisp of gray smoke marking the cigarette that was clamped between his lips. The kids – a duo that was now a trio thanks to the addition of Drew – were in the side yard playing keep-away with Hektor and a tennis ball. Ray watched them as he climbed out of his truck, frowning as he noticed the way his newest employee kept shooting smiles at Lisa; then made his way toward his brother.

"Where you been?" Mark asked without sitting up.

Ray braced a shoulder against the tree's trunk, the bark biting into his skin through the thin barrier of his button-up shirt. "Looking for Shilling."

"Looking for…?"

"He quit his job and according to Tony, his PO can't pin him down."

Mark sat up, taking his cigarette between his fingers, legs swinging off the bench to land on the grass. He didn't need to be explained the significance of this new development. Shilling's behavior had been disturbing, but not escalating up to this point; the flower deliveries were getting downright boring. But quitting his job was a new move, and going off the justice system radar made his next move almost impossible to predict. It had also turned Ray's stomach into a churning vat of acid fear.

"His first kills," he said of the wife and daughter, not knowing if those had truly been his first kills, only that they were the first on record, "weren't identical. All the evidence pointed to the fact that the daughter was the true target and the wife got in the way."

"Lisa and Cheryl aren't together unless they're at home," Mark said, and how sick was it that it was a good piece of news?

"I know. And Drew's with her round the clock."

Mark's head turned toward the side yard and his lips quirked into a frown. "Drew's a nice kid and all, but is he, you know, adequate security?"

"Lucky for us, Shilling isn't especially dangerous to grown-ass men his own size," Ray said bitterly. His eyes tracked the tennis ball's movement from Drew's hands, across the beer-stained sky, under the gilded leaves of a birch tree, and into Lisa's waiting palm. "And focus tends to put a man on high alert. Drew Forester wants to bone my daughter…"

Mark coughed.

"…and that's the sort of thing that creates focus."

25

The Smyths had old money, and lived in one of the well-established, sprawling Alpharetta subdivisions that was situated between two horse farms rather than a new-construction development with postage stamp yards and stripling trees. Their Georgian mini mansion was set well off the road, its backyard ringed by tall, ancient oaks that dappled the gardens with sunlight during the day and provided oily, secluded pockets of shadow after dark. It was a beautiful space, brick-paved paths wending their way through award-winning perennial beds. A koi pond the size of a swimming pool, dotted with water lilies and lined with river stones, stood beneath a white, wood pergola in the far corner of the yard and was the destination at the end of every path.

Beautiful already, Cheryl had transformed Patty Smyth's yard into an art piece. Lisa settled her hands on the hips of her white cotton eyelet dress and surveyed the décor.

The buffet tables had been pushed up beneath the patio alongside the outdoor kitchen, the white linens spotless, the caterers whisking back and forth, laying out trays of low-calorie whatever-it-was that the Smyths' friends ate. The brick patio had been set up as a dining area; café tables draped with more white linen were arranged in purposeful disorder, a wide, water-filled glass bowl full of white rose petals, hydrangeas, and floating tea lights set in the middle of each. Cheryl had run translucent fishing line in a web between the trees and had strung white paper Chinese lanterns that added an understated pop of the exotic. Lisa had spent the night before rolling bundles of silverware – Patty Smyth's real silver because plastic would have been insulting to the guests – and had burned most the skin off her fingers hot gluing cards together that labeled each dish.

223

It was a muted, white and silver and cream, sophisticated sort of affair, and standing back from it, Lisa wondered if their hard work would show. "You nervous?" she asked her mother.

Cheryl, like her, had busted out her Sunday best and wore a gray knit pencil skirt and white sweater set, the pearls she so rarely wore anymore. Mother and daughter had both painted their fingernails white and toenails a dainty pink. Lisa squirmed inside her stiff halter top dress and longed for a pair of jeans.

"Terrified," Cheryl admitted. "Let's just pray Her Majesty approves."

As if on cue, Patty came sweeping through the open French doors at the back of the house. She passed between two caterers who nearly spilled the serving platters they carried in their haste to avoid her, and Patty clipped along without seeming to notice that she'd almost had tomato basil chicken dumped down the front of her silver cocktail dress.

"Hello, girls," she greeted in a voice that might have hinted at a British background...though the woman had never left Georgia in her life. Patty Smyth was tall, upwards of five-seven, reed-thin and harsh-looking. She had an aristocratic, austere face and wore her hair short and slicked back over her ears so that it looked like a blonde helmet. In her mid-forties, she was already hitting the Botox hard and had a certain plastic quality to her tight, infrequent smiles.

She surveyed the gardens, long-fingered, ringed hands on her hips. Lisa saw the twinkle of diamond studs in her ears that matched the choker that glimmered around her throat. For what was essentially a tea party for her close friends, Patty was severely overdressed. "Very good," she said with a sniff and then breezed away on her stiletto sandals.

"Well." Lisa shrugged. "Guess that's better than 'very bad.'"

Two days before, Ray had pressed the keys to Mark's Chevy, a hundred bucks and an AmEx into Drew's hands. "Go get something decent to wear to this damn party we're working," he'd said, and then he'd turned back to the ordered chaos on his desk in the office at the house. And that had been it. No warning, no other directions.

A sane man would have fled and never looked back, maxed out the card, put Ray Russell and his strange family well behind him.

But here he stood at a white garden gate in a new black polo shirt and dark jeans, new belt, new kicks, a touch of gel in hair that he should have buzzed by now, watching the wealthy pretend to eat mini quiches and talk about the funny sounds their Beemers were making these days.

He was too loyal. He'd been loyal to Ricky, to a guy named "Anchor" once who'd nearly gotten him killed, and now to Russell, apparently. But Ray had something that the others didn't, and she was walking toward him now, a champagne flute in one hand, her sandals dangling by their straps from the other.

"I feel so safe," she said with an amused eye roll as she drew closer, stepping into the puddle of shadow where he was stationed. She was in a good mood tonight; she and her mother were good at this. Who'd have thought Lisa thrived domestically like this, but she did, and was clearly proud of what she'd helped put together. "The guests, though?" She lifted her brows and nodded toward two women wrapped in jewel-toned shawls who were staring at them – at him – and grinned. "Pretty sure four guys in all black are giving them the creeps."

"I'm creepy now. Great."

"Definitely not creepy," she countered happily – she really was bubbling with good humor – and turned to put her back against the gate alongside him. She threw back half the champagne in an elegant swallow and then offered the glass to him.

"I'm working."

"Serious," she said with a grin, putting the glass to her lips again. "Not creepy, but sooo serious."

"Are you tipsy?"

"Little bit."

He grinned. Good for her: if he was serious, she was terrifyingly stern. "I've never been to anything like this," he admitted, "not even as security."

"It's pretty," she said, "I love the place, but the *people*...Patty Smyth is the biggest gossip, and the most influential one, in the tri-county area. She's a cold bitch, but for the most part, doesn't exaggerate. Now that one - " She pointed to a plump, gray-haired woman in a teal dress that was belted tight around her thick waist. "Abby Pine? She might as well carry a butcher block around as many knives as she sticks in people's backs."

Drew didn't really give a shit about any of the details, but it was good to see her more relaxed. "What kinda dirt could any of these people have on each other?"

She turned wide, dancing eyes to him. "*Tons*. Three years ago, Patty put out the word that Meredith Childress left a charity function two hours early with the stomach flu. Two days later, Abby over there let it slip that Meredith was actually pregnant, and Meredith's husband had had a vasectomy."

He lifted his brows in feigned surprise.

"Someone's always sleeping with someone else's wife or husband or kid or..." She bit her lip. "Jesus, I'm just as bad as the rest of them." A blush stained her cheeks; he could see it even in the semi darkness, the same as he could see the vibrant green of her eyes, and she turned away, embarrassed.

She lifted her glass again, saw it was empty, and let it fall to her side. "I forget sometimes." Her smile became frozen as she watched the party. "I get off in my little world, in our old haunted house. At the bar, at the shop...and I forget that I used to be a part of events like this. I was one of these spoiled Alpharetta rich girls," she said with disgust. "Manicure, pedicure, name brand everything. I was gonna get married at the friggin' Ritz, for God's sakes! Ugh. I got swept up in it."

Drew couldn't envision her being one of these people, he just couldn't. "It happens," he said and knew he didn't sound convincing.

226

"It shouldn't ha…oh *shit*," she breathed, jerking upright beside him.

He was on instant alert, scanning the dense wall of trees and shrubs behind them. "What?" When he glanced back, he noted her posture: it seemed more resigned than frightened. "What?" he repeated.

"It's alright," she sighed. "Unless you wanna tackle a pregnant woman, I think you can stand down."

"Who?"

She stabbed her champagne flute through the air and toward a tall, blonde, model-looking young woman in a tight pink dress that showed off a rounded, pregnant belly. "Missy Albright. Tristan's wife."

She was on top of them before Drew made the connection that Tristan was the douchebag he'd decked at the bar that night, and then the prospect of gossip seemed to suddenly be much more threatening.

26

Lisa had seen women ravaged by pregnancy: bloated and damp with sweat, sans makeup and forty-some-odd pounds heavier, angry and red-faced. Missy made pregnancy look like a weekend stay at a resort spa.

Her blonde hair was gelled and teased and sprayed into its usual defiance of gravity, her makeup flawless, if not overdone. She was tan, her ankles trim, legs looking miles long in heels. Her fuchsia dress would have looked more appropriate on a high schooler at homecoming, much like all of her wardrobe, and it flaunted her belly. A diamond solitaire necklace gleamed at her throat and her engagement ring flashed as she lifted a hand to tuck a non-stray piece of hair back. Lisa had the small satisfaction of seeing that the ring was the same one Tristan had given her once upon a time, but otherwise, even pregnant, Missy was not a girl who made other girls feel good about themselves.

"Lisa," she said, bubbling over with false congeniality. "I didn't know you put this little thing together." She swatted at the air in an "oh, you" gesture, smiling.

"Missy." Lisa twitched a tight smile. "I see you've finally mastered the art of subtle intimidation as opposed to your usual direct insults. Way to grow."

The blonde's smile seemed to freeze, the humor draining out of her eyes. "You always did struggle with being polite, bless your heart," she said through her teeth. Her blue eyes moved up and over Lisa's shoulder and Lisa knew she must be checking out Drew. Her smile twisted. "Security? I forgot that's what your dad was doing these days." Her eyes returned. "How's he doing? Poor thing."

"My dad owns several businesses," Lisa said coolly. "He's doing fine."

Missy's head tilted to the side, golden hair waterfalling over her shoulder. Behind her, two lackeys approached like actresses who'd been given cues, like beautiful, brunette zombies coming to their leader's defense. Lisa remembered first names, but not last: Brittany and Dani. "That's really good," Missy said, voice laced with the kind of cloying sweetness all the liars in her social circle employed. Her henchwomen fell into place on either side of her. "Good for him."

"Isn't it about time for you to rub some more cocoa butter on your stretch marks, Missy?" a familiar voice chimed to Lisa's left. A glance revealed Morgan beside her, as perfectly coiffed as ever, in a dress that looked like a disco ball but somehow worked on her. Lisa hadn't heard her friend's approach, but was more than grateful for her presence now.

Missy wasn't. Her smile was more of a sneer. "Morgan. You were invited?"

"My mom's in the book club same as yours. Plus, I can actually, you know, *read*."

As had always been the case, Missy could dish it out, but could not take even a little bit of it. Rebuttals were not her thing. With a lift of her tanned nose and a haughty shrug, she swept away – *swept*, despite her ponderous belly – her minions at her heels.

"You looked like you could stand to be saved," Morgan said when they were gone. She glanced over at Drew. "Tall, dark and dumbfounded over there didn't look like he was doing much good. No offense, sweetheart."

Drew shrugged. "Hey, just glad you think I'm tall."

"You didn't tell me you were coming." Lisa elbowed her friend.

"I wasn't sure I was coming." She shrugged. Morgan slid her arm through Lisa's and began towing her away. "I'll keep an eye on her," she promised Drew as they moved back toward the patio.

"I don't need watching," Lisa said, rolling her eyes.

229

"Right, right. That's why your dad hired this crew to watch a damn garden party." She lifted her waxed, pale brows in a knowing way. "You're not, you know, top secret, Lis. I get what's going on here."

Lisa had never ranked Morgan among the people in her life with advanced deductive reasoning, but she felt a jolt of alarm. Lisa scanned the party and, more importantly, its fringes. She found her uncle, Sly, Eddie and Drew all tucked away in their shadowed alcoves beneath the tress. To anyone else, they would have been terrifying: threatening, man-shaped shadows with white, flickering eyes, the darkness providing the illusion that they were twice their actual size. What sort of ordinary girl brought a retinue of guards with her to a function like this? Their presence made it all the more obvious that she didn't belong here, among merry, twinkling lights and finger sandwiches. They were a living embodiment of the resentful, dark contempt she held for the life she'd once attempted.

"You do?" She kept her voice neutral as they reached the patio. She slipped her arm away from Morgan's so she could put her shoes back on.

"Yeah, and I gotta say, it's overkill, girl. Do you honest to God think Tristan's gonna come after you? His black eye's not that bad."

Lisa chuckled. Only Tristan would be so egotistical that he thought she was afraid of him, and only Morgan would jump to that conclusion. She was glad for the misunderstanding, though. "You never know," she said, trying to hide a smile. "I hear angry exes can be pretty dangerous."

Eddie had been thinking the only good thing to come out of this night would be a check. But as he watched the leggy brunette in the bright teal wrap dress break away from her pregnant friend and head his way, a champagne flute in each hand, he began to rethink that assessment.

She was a nicer grade of meat than he was used to: perfectly straight, blindingly white teeth, the expensive kind of fake tan, a haircut that had probably cost more than he made in a week, mani, pedi, designer label dress that hugged every curve. "I didn't take Patty for the type to hide the good stuff in the back," she purred as she slid to a hip-swiveling halt in front of him. She extended one of the champagne flutes in offering. "But that just applies to men. If I were her, I would have hidden you too."

It was exactly the kind of cheese Eddie himself ladled onto his potential conquests at bars; nice to know this one was dishing out charm on her own. She wouldn't take any convincing that way.

Ray had specified no drinking on the job, but really, this was more about some quick cash than an actual responsibility. He accepted the glass, raised it halfway to his lips and offered her a calculated smile. "Trying not to get mobbed, sweetheart. What's your excuse?"

She flushed with pleasure and took a sip of her drink. Her dark eyes made a leisurely stroll up from his toes to the gelled tips of his hair. "There's never anyone interesting to talk to at these things."

He quirked his brows. "You found me though."

"Yes I did."

They measured one another up a moment. If you knew where to concentrate your efforts, there was very little courting that ever had to be done. Eddie didn't hold much with lies and small talk when it came to the ladies. Tonight, he'd found his perfect match, and it had nothing to do with astrological signs or compatibility scores.

"I'm Dani," she said at last, her white, wide smile dazzling.

"Eddie."

"There's a bathroom in the hallway upstairs." She half-turned, like she was prepared to walk away. "If you go in through those French doors, take a right and go up the staircase off the kitchen, it'll be your third door on the left." She gave him one last smile. "Knock twice." Then she threw back her champagne in one long swallow and headed for the house.

"How's it going?"

Drew was doing his job, standing at his post, observing any and everything just the way he was supposed to, but Ray's voice floating from the darkness somewhere behind him was a bit of an unpleasant shock anyway. Ray had that effect on people.

"No signs of anything unusual."

"Any new arrivals in the past hour?"

In truth, Drew had spent most of the last hour eye-stalking Lisa as she and her blonde friend made the rounds, but he wasn't about to admit that. "Some of the husbands – boyfriends – whatever they are." He pointed toward the knot of cigar-smoking men who'd shown up en masse like they'd all been off together having some sort of guys' night while the women had their tea party. Still sporting a green ring of old bruising around his eye, Lisa's ex had an arm around the pregnant blonde, the two of them nauseating in their coziness.

Ray made an acknowledging sound in the back of his throat. "I always hated that little prick. He – "

A scream shattered the muffled chatter of the party. It was female, the kind of terror-borne shriek that burst vocal cords and set dogs to barking. As heads whipped around and guests startled, Ray took off, bolting toward the house, and Drew followed.

In the kitchen, one of the pregnant girl's friends was leaning against the counter, a hand to her throat as she choked on wet, noisy sobs, her face red, tears leaving wet trails through her makeup.

"What?" Ray demanded of her. Guests were pouring into the house, crowding them.

Footsteps came thundering down the rear staircase behind her and Eddie appeared, his eyes wide, face uncharacteristically blank.

"She –she," the girl gasped, "she's…oh, God, *she's dead!*"

27

"She's not dead," Sly told them before the wail of approaching sirens drowned out all other sounds.

Dead or not, Lisa felt a cold shudder move through her as she pressed her heart pendant between thumb and forefinger and tried to control her erratic pulse. In the chaos of finding Danielle, as the guys had leapt into action and startled gossip had gone ripping through the crowd, Lisa had been able to think of only one thing: Somehow, this was connected to them. If not for their presence, there wouldn't be a dead – or, almost dead – girl in the Smyths' upstairs hall bathroom. And her heart wouldn't be knocking inside her chest like a trip-hammer.

An ambulance pulled up at the curb, spinning red lights blasting through the dark. Ray stood in the front yard, hands on hips, waiting for the paramedics; Harold Smyth had been too rattled and white-faced to protest when Ray had taken charge of the situation. Scattered around the yard, alert and tight-faced, tendons standing rigid in their flexed arms, Eddie, Sly and Drew looked military and professional.

Too obvious, Lisa thought. They were much too obvious and involved to escape questioning when the police arrived. And all of them had rap sheets; none of them could afford to get caught up in this.

Ray thought the same thing, apparently. As the paramedics rushed toward the house, he turned and headed their way, expression grim.

"Time for you two to go home," he said when he reached them. "Sly and Drew will go with you."

Cheryl folded her arms beneath her breasts and fired a scowl at him. "What happened to that girl?"

"Later," he dismissed, and started to walk away.

"*Raymond*," his wife hissed. "I'm hosting a party here."

"Your party's dead, sweetheart. No pun intended. Go home."

Lisa found her voice. "I have work."

"You quit that job," he reminded her.

"I took a few days off," she corrected. "I'm not quitting until I have something else lined up."

He gave her the kind of glare that turned men to stone, his meaning plain. If someone had slipped into a party full of guests and nearly killed a girl, then she wasn't safe at work. She wasn't safe anywhere, save at home, under lock and key and armed guard.

But the mystery of it all – the inexplicable chain of events that didn't make a damn bit of sense – left her feeling so helpless that she just couldn't submit to lockdown. This was not a movie. No one was *out to get them*. She hoped…

"You." Ray snapped a look to Drew. "Go with her. If so much as one hair – "

"She'll be fine," Drew said with such conviction in his voice that Lisa almost believed him.

Drew was starting to understand why her fiancé had cheated on her. Lisa was the kind of brave, the kind of stupidly stubborn, that infuriated most men. He wanted to be furious with her now; she had one hand on the wheel, the other propped on the console, watching the road and listening to Pearl Jam through her fuzzy truck speakers.

But he could read the fear in her. The tension. The tremor in her delicate jaw and the nervous flash in her green eyes every time the headlights from an oncoming car washed over her. She looked beautiful, and small, and fragile, and too proud for her own good. Her fiancé had looked at her and then looked elsewhere. Drew looked at her and wanted her face pressed against his shoulder, her nails biting into skin, as she came with him inside her.

He was at that stage: wanting her in vivid, detailed fantasies that he wished more and more had a chance of coming to fruition. He didn't just think she was pretty and he wasn't just watching her for Ray's sake; he liked the girl. He *wanted* her. Tonight had solidified that knowledge, left him more desperate. Someone was strangling girls and if Lisa was on that list – and he knew she was – then she had to realize that she could trust him. That she needed him to keep her safe.

His attention jerked from her profile to the window as the truck slowed and turned up over a curb. They were at King Customs.

"I need to change for work," she explained as she pulled up to the dark office and killed the engine. "You can wait here."

"Like hell."

Her head snapped around, eyes wide. "What?"

"If you think you're going anywhere in the dark by yourself, you've lost your damn mind."

A smile ghosted across her lips. "Look at you, getting some balls."

"I'm not kidding, Lisa. You got attacked; one of your friends almost just got killed – "

"Dani Britton is not my friend."

"*Whatever.*" His voice cracked through the truck, sharper and angrier than he'd intended. She sat back against the window. "Somebody obviously has it out for you, and you aren't taking stupid risks on my watch."

"What do you mean 'out for' me?" She frowned, but he saw the doubt twist her delicate features. "We don't know that what happened tonight wasn't an accident. She could have slipped and hit her head."

"Someone choked her out," Drew said, and her eyes flared big as half dollars. "Does that sound like an accident?"

She turned away from him and released a shaky breath. When she popped her door, he popped his, and she didn't protest. He waited while she gathered up a tote bag and then followed at her heels, close as a shadow, to the door of the garage. When she unlocked it and moved to step inside, Drew caught her by the arm, gently, and held her back while he went first, flipping on the lights and scanning the office for anything out of place.

"Yes," she snapped as she pushed past him. "I'm sure the murderer let himself in and then *relocked* the door."

"He could have come in the back and been waiting in here."

"You've watched too many movies," she complained, and headed for the door that led into the work bays.

His pulse gave a jump to see her in the dark threshold. "Where are you going?"

Her scowl was a fearsome thing. "To change into my hoochie clothes. That alright with you?"

"Be careful."

"Yeah. My pushup bra's gonna push my boobs right up and poke my eyes out. Real dangerous." And she slipped into the shadows of the garage.

She was bluffing, covering her nerves with her smart mouth. It was so laughable he had a hard time being angry about it. But he just wished...

A voice.

Drew registered muffled sounds from the parking lot and the indistinct murmur of more than one voice.

Fuck.

In a soundless rush, he went through the door into the working part of the garage to find Lisa...and then froze.

A shaft of moonlight fell through the high, round window set in the roll-top door and it landed on Lisa like a spotlight. She stood with her pushup bra in her hands, naked to the waist, her cutoffs unfastened. Her tanned skin had turned to alabaster in the blue wash of light, shadows carving the lean contours of her arms and flat stomach. He spotted a flash of dark, lace waistband in the deep V of her unzipped shorts before his eyes went to her chest and stayed there. Her breasts were high and round, her nipples peaked in the cool evening air. Her hair flowed down over her shoulders and

236

brushed the tops of them. No stripper had ever looked so tempting in his eyes.

"What...?" she started, and he shook himself off, went to her and put himself between her and the door, crowding her at the hood of Big Tom's Fastback. She clapped her hands over her breasts and tried to whirl toward him.

Drew grabbed her hips, her skin silk-soft beneath his hands, and dropped his head until his mouth was even with her ear. *"Be quiet. Someone's out there."*

They both stopped breathing. Drew could hear his own pulse. Could smell her perfume, and something else that was just her skin. Was more aware, than anything, of her almost naked in front of him.

The voices floated through the door.

"...I've told you that at least a hundred times..."

"...sorry...next time..."

Lisa released a deep breath. "I know them. They own the deli next door."

Her hipbones were sharp against his fingers; she didn't eat enough. "What are they doing here this late?"

"I don't know. I don't *care*."

As his fear-fueled adrenaline faded, it was replaced with a different kind. One that swirled hot and hungry through his veins. Lisa, he realized, was going to have to make the first move if she wanted him away from her. He'd watched and wondered for too long, and he was too invested at this point, to pass up an opportunity like this; he might never get another.

She didn't move, though. He heard her take a deep breath. "You're touching me."

"Yeah. You want me to let go?"

Another deep breath. "Not really."

His hands left her as she shifted and turned, and the moonlight sliding over his shoulder turned her big eyes to emeralds. For the first time that night, all her guards were down and every ounce of fear was showing. "Someone's playing games with us," she said, and he waited. She blinked. "I am so damn tired of playing."

Her hands fell away from her breasts and she spread them over his pecs.

"Tell anyone and I'll kill you," she warned.

He kissed her.

It was the gentlest thing, like he was afraid of her reaction. His lips touched hers and they both went still. For a moment, Lisa held her breath and wondered if, inside the rippling body leaning over her, Drew was tentative and skittish. She'd watched him watch her, had thought – had hoped, even – that beneath his quiet, careful exterior, something vibrant and hot-blooded waited to be turned loose.

But maybe she'd been wrong.

She eased back, hands sliding down the hard swells of his pecs to the ribbed stretch of abs below, a shiver starting in her fingertips and rippling all the way up her arms just at this bare contact through his shirt. It was a shame it wasn't going to go further. She became aware of her nakedness, and pulled back further. Such a shame…

"Wait." His good hand caught the back of her head; his other stayed at her waist, his cast rough against her skin.

The moonlight was behind him, and she couldn't read his face, saw only the outline of his head limned in silver.

You have to step up, she thought, a desperate twinge pulling at her insides. *I need you to be the man here.*

She heard him take a deep breath. His fingers threaded through the hair at her nape; they felt solid and strong, just like the rest of him. She wet her lips. "Drew -- "

He cut her off with another kiss, and this one was nothing like the first. This one slanted hotly across her mouth; it pressed her head back into his hand, made her feel small and vulnerable, and…wanted. She hadn't been wanted like this in a long time.

Her lips parted beneath his and his tongue flirted between.

Oh, thank God.

238

She hummed a quiet note of pleasure in the back of her throat and he reacted; he cracked her lips wide and went in deep. The kiss became a frenzied, artless thing, all tongues and teeth and shattered breathing.

His hand left her head; it slid through her hair and half-curled around the side of her throat. Their lips came apart and his mouth trailed across her cheek – he pressed a kiss just beneath her ear – and went to her neck. He held her to him as he sucked at her skin, grazed her throat with his teeth.

Her fingers were knotted in the front of his shirt and that wasn't enough. She gathered it up and slipped her hands beneath the hem, flattened her palms against the washboard flat of his stomach. *Damn*. To hell with her dignity; Morgan was right: he was *hot*. And his lips were sweeping down to her collarbone. And his hand was sliding down the curve of her breast and cupping it from beneath.

Her breath caught at the contact and her chest lifted against his touch. His fingertips played across her, working inward until it was her nipple he teased to distraction. With only one good hand, he had her shivery and breathless. She raked her nails lightly through the deep grooves of his abs, knees liquid, trapped in the dark silence with this intense and quiet shadow of a man tweaking all her senses.

His head lifted and she thought he meant to kiss her again; she stretched up on her toes in anticipation…

But instead his face hovered over hers and his hand went flat against her belly, slid down into the open waistband of her cutoffs and cupped her through her panties.

Lisa staggered back and the Mustang's grill caught her across the backs of her thighs. She let her legs go limp, let the car support her, as Drew's fingers found just the right spot through her lace bikini bottoms.

"Mmm." She hooked her fingers into his belt and held tight, hips tilting as he stroked her. The window was bright as a spotlight, the blue moonbeam falling across her, them, giving her a visual that doubled her pulse. His face was still in shadow, his breath rustling against her hair. But she could see herself – her naked skin pale in the surreal moonlight, her

239

nipples peaked, her breasts covered in gooseflesh – and his vein-laced arm going all the way down to where his hand worked against her through the open, parted fly of her cutoffs.

Feeling selfish, feeling so flushed she thought her ears would burst, she leaned back and braced her hands behind her on the car's hood, watching the spectacle of his hand in her pants, hips lifting.

Then his fingers swept her panties aside and he made contact with bare, slippery skin.

Lisa closed her eyes, her head fell back on her neck, and she let it happen.

With hands that had seen such violence, he balanced her against the car and delivered her nothing but pleasure. His middle finger slipped inside and went deep, crooking, sending a shudder through her, while his thumb worked magic on her clit.

She shocked herself; she let go of all her tension and committed to the moment. Let him push her all the way to climax. She came with a little gasp, and then a sigh, and then she lowered herself back across the hood and went boneless as his hand withdrew.

The moonlight was on her; it pushed at the seal of her eyelids. She didn't care.

"Come here." She cracked her eyes and reached for him, ready to return the favor.

But Drew hung back in the shadows. He was breathing hard, but his voice was even when he said, "That was probably a bad idea."

Lisa groaned. "Why? Please do not tell me you're thinking of my dad right now."

"Well, he – "

"He doesn't have a say in this!" She jackknifed upright. Her old friend shame began a slow-build in the pit of her stomach. "If you don't want to be with me, then just say so, but don't use my dad as – "

As she made a move to stand, he blocked her in, hands on the polished steel on either side of her hips. She could see his eyes now; they looked black and wild, white-rimmed and

240

glinting. "I'm thinking," he said in a quiet voice that left her skin prickling, "that you'll hate me if things go any further. And I don't want *that*."

"You're an idiot," she accused.

"No argument here."

He was a sweet idiot, though. Lisa laid her hands on the taut cords of his neck and kissed him like he'd kissed her.

He responded, easing her back down onto the car, crawling up over her. She unbuckled his belt, thumbed open the button of his jeans, unzipped them. When she took hold of him through his boxers, his whole body gave a great leap: all finely sculpted taut muscle moving against her. Their lips broke apart and his breathing was ragged as he reached between them with his good hand, the other braced beside her head, and tugged her cutoffs down her hips. She braced her heels on the front bumper and lifted up, taking them the rest of the way down and then kicking them free. In a rush, her legs went around his lean hips and his boxers were pushed down, his erection springing free between them. She wrapped her hand around him, guided him to her entrance; they both caught their breath.

And then he was pressing in, and she was already slick and hot and ready for him, primed by his fingers.

Lisa murmured a wordless thanks as he sank deep, filling her up. Her thighs gripped tight and her spine lifted and she basked in the sensation...and then he started to move.

His belt buckle rattled as he withdrew and plunged in again, his thrusts deep and sure; there was no need for delicate pretense and he seemed to know it, setting a pace that rocked the Mustang on its struts.

Lisa gripped tight, her nails sunk into the smooth skin of his back; she lifted and strained beneath him, chasing another release like he'd given her before.

Above her, inside her, he was nothing but leashed power and sleek, flexing muscle, pinning her to the hood of the car, taking her body in an almost desperate way.

She could tell when he grew close – the pace intensified, the soft insides of her thighs were rubbed raw by the jeans he still wore. Climax gripped him; he thrust in *hard*, and she followed.

They clung, panted, waited, as the end came with a great crash.

Then Lisa became very aware that she was almost totally naked on top of a customer's car, her bodyguard's cock inside her. The harsh sound of their breathing echoed in the empty garage bay, almost obscene. Regret…it was what she should feel – what she *wanted* to feel, on some level – but it was drowned out by the pulsing that echoed through her limp body. Her heartbeat thumped wildly and it knew only pleasure, not shame. Not yet, anyway.

With a deep breath, Drew withdrew and rolled away from her, lying back against the car beside her.

"That was…" she started.

"A mistake?" he wondered.

"I was gonna say 'good.'"

She rolled her head to the side and thought she could make out his eyes on the other side of the moonbeam that played between them.

They stayed still a long moment, until finally, she eased upright. "I guess I gotta get to work." As she leaned forward to retrieve her cutoffs, he pushed off the car and walked toward the office. The door shut behind him.

She sighed. "Thanks," she muttered. "You couldn't even say *that*?"

28

"Danielle Britton," Ray told the oldest, most in-charge-looking nurse at the station, and was rewarded with a blank stare. Beside him, Eddie made a noise that might have been a squelched laugh.

The nurse – a gray-headed thing with an *I don't think so, young man* look on her lined face – propped a hand on her hip. "Danielle Britton *what*?"

"A strangle case that came in about a half hour ago. We need to see her."

Other nurses were looking at them now – young, furtive ones. The gray one gave him the up/down routine and her gaze shot to Eddie with veiled interest; the guy couldn't seem to help drawing female attention, even from the fifty and over crowd. But then her eyes snapped backed to Ray and the frown lines in her face grew deep as harrowed rows in a crop field. "Her father's with her," she said, "so you can't play that card. You two cops?"

"Detectives, actually," he said, and leveled a frown of his own that had her reconsidering; her brows gave a little jump.

His poker face – his *lawyer* face – was impenetrable. She realized that. "ICU," she said, finally, and Ray grabbed Eddie by the elbow and towed him that direction before she could change her mind and call security.

They weren't alone as they stepped into the elevator car. Two women in track suits stood in the back corner; Ray took quick stock of them – both dabbing at their faces with tissue and talking in low, rushed murmurs – and judged them harmless, putting his back to them.

"How," Eddie asked, "are you gonna get us into the ICU without badges, *detective*?"

He hadn't figured that out yet; as it turned out, he didn't have to. They stepped off the elevator and nearly collided with Arthur Britton.

"Art." Ray sidestepped to avoid a head-on and blocked the guy in with outstretched palms. Eddie stepped to his other side and they had him cornered as the elevator doors slid shut behind them. "We were coming up to find you."

Arthur was in some sort of boring, number-crunching branch of a downtown marketing firm and held some seven word title that made him, more or less, an accountant. He and Ray had never been close, but the girls had gone to school together once upon a time; if Ray remembered right, Lisa had once stuck gum in Danielle's hair and been given a day of ISS for it. Mrs. Britton had looked outraged and Arthur had looked bored to tears at the meeting with the guidance counselor.

Now, the man looked pale and slippery as paste, about one good cough away from vomiting. His hair was receding worse than Ray's, and too many summers on the golf course had pressed heavy lines around his eyes and mouth. Normally, the grooves looked healthy; today, he looked ancient. His white oxford was rumpled and half-untucked from his gray Dockers. He pulled to a sharp halt, scrubbed both hands down his face, and passed a blank look between the two of them.

"Art," Ray said again, "Ray Russell. I was at the garden party; Cheryl was hosting. I wanted to come check on you guys."

Arthur swallowed hard, and the fact that they weren't friends in the least didn't seem to matter much in light of what had happened. He nodded; glanced back down the hall toward the sealed doors that led into the ICU waiting room.

"How's Dani?" Ray pressed.

"Carla's with her." He licked his lips. "She was conscious when they…when they brought her in. But she was screaming her damn head off. They sedated her."

"Is she still awake?"

"Sort of." Then his eyes narrowed and snapped to Ray's face, focused for the first time. "You came all the way to the hospital to ask that?"

244

There were times – even dark, stressful, impossible times – when he missed the courtroom charade: luring witnesses into trusting and believing him, spinning stories and building rapport, working toward something. He'd always loved that, even if it made him a bastard. "I know the girls were never close," he said, and Eddie rolled his eyes, "but we traveled in the same circles. We're the same kind of family." Eddie's eyes were going to roll right out of his pretty head. "I've got a daughter and I'd hate to think" – he threw in a grim face for effect – "well, God forbid I ever had a crisis like this, I'd like to think I had friends looking out for me."

Arthur was too strung-out to argue the bullshit of the statement, so he nodded.

"I don't practice anymore, but I've got friends on the force," Ray lied. "Have the cops been by?"

"Yeah. She was sleeping, so they said they'd come back."

If he pleaded, he'd come across as creepy; it'd be better to forge ahead with feigned authority. "Let me talk to her. A familiar, non-threatening face. If she can tell me anything, I can put some calls in, get the ball rolling with the five-oh."

Arthur's brows gave a jump. "You could do that?"

"Absolutely."

He considered a moment, then tipped his head toward the doors. "Go ahead. Carla's there. I'm gonna run home and get some things for her."

Ray gave Eddie a look that told him to stay put in the hall; he would fire off a text if the cops showed back up. "Can you buzz me in?" Ray asked, and just as simple as that, he was in the ICU.

Carla Britton had expensive taste, but she hadn't grown up on a fish farm with boy-short hair, and she lacked Cheryl's warm worldliness. She was a redhead, her hair in a blunt, shiny bob that swung forward in front of her face, diamonds glittering from her throat, hands and earlobes that peeked through the curtain of her hair. Her dress was expensive and better suited to a younger woman; she sat in a plastic chair at her daughter's bedside, heels tucked beneath her chair, bare

245

toes quivering on the tile, arches flexed. She was shivering and Ray didn't know if it was nerves, or the sixty-eight degree hospital air.

Her head snapped around at the sound of his footfalls and her eyes were deer-in-headlights startled. "W-w-who…"

"Ray Russell," he said, and didn't offer a handshake because he figured she wouldn't accept it. "I'm old friends with Art. My wife was hosting the party tonight and I wanted to come check on Dani."

She accepted the explanation without question, which irked him. What if he'd been the strangler coming to revisit his victim? She didn't know that; she should have at least called her husband to verify. But she said, "Oh," and turned to glance at her daughter, reaching for her still hand on top of the blankets.

Danielle was a beautiful girl: well-defined, aristocratic features, full lips, high, winged brows and rich, chocolate hair. He thought he remembered some of Lisa's ranted chatter about her having had a boob job after high school. Except for being a little pale, and having the darkening blue prints of fingers around her throat, she looked peaceful. There was an IV that he guessed delivered pain meds, sedatives and fluids hooked in her left arm.

"If it's possible," he said, and Carla Britton gasped like she'd forgotten he was in the room. "I'd like to wake her and ask a few questions about the attack." He wasn't going through his fake explanation again. "I have police connections," he said.

"Oh." She blinked at him, then said, "Oh," like she actually comprehended. She made a face. "They had to sedate her; she's been so upset."

"I'll keep it short," he promised. "If I can tell the police what I know, send them in the right direction, it'll save her a real interrogation."

She must have agreed because she reached up and smoothed her daughter's hair back. "Dani? Sweetie?" She patted her hand. "Can you wake up for me?"

Danielle rolled her head on the pillow and murmured something.

"Dani? Honey?"

Her fingers twitched and her brow furrowed. Her eyes came open one at a time, slowly as if the lids had been glued together. Ray had to give her credit for fighting the sedation; her eyes – brown and bloodshot – drifted across the monitors, the curtain, her mother…and then came to him and locked hard with terror. A man had attacked her, without a doubt.

"Danielle," he said, and she pressed back against her pillow, her pallid complexion going sheet-white. "You're okay. I'm your dad's friend. Can you tell me what happened?"

Carla looked up to him, brows plucked together. "She looks upset. I don't think – "

"No," Danielle said, and her voice was a rusty croak. She shook her head, hair rustling against the pillow.

"You don't remember?" Ray pressed, ignoring the girl's mother. "Or you don't want to tell me?"

Her eyes – even under sedation – brimmed with the wild, mindless panic of a prey animal.

Ray had made a career of questioning victims, but suddenly, there was a cold finger of fear tracing down his spine. Without courtroom and Sunday best, a gallery of jurors or the civilized safety of procedure, he was just a guy in a room talking to a girl with handprints around her throat; and all he could think of was: what if it had been Lisa?

Could he really be this stupid? Drew had always known he wasn't gifted – hell, he wasn't even sure he was *smart* – but was he really so stupid as to find himself in this position?

"*A mistake?*" he'd asked Lisa afterward, in the moonlight, in the panting silence. And he'd said nothing since. He'd laid her over the hood of a car, without condom, sweet talk, or promise, and had then been mute their whole drive to Double Vision. Now, he watched her serve drinks from a bar stool, and he watched the fine tremors of intensifying anger go dancing across the taut muscles in her arms. She smiled, she even forced a laugh or two for her customers, but underneath her glittery lip gloss and smoke gray eye shadow, she was seething. At least…he thought so. He had no other explanation for the way her face snapped back like a rubber band when she thought no one could see her; her lips thinned and her eyes flashed and she was a little bit terrifying as she pulled glasses and poured shots.

He had to say something.

"Lisa," he tried as she passed in front of him. When she ignored him, he waited for her to pass back the other way and said, "Lis," with a pleading note in his voice.

She halted like she didn't want to – arms still reaching out ahead of her, legs mid-stride and off-balance – and darted him a glance from the corners of her eyes, refusing to give him her full attention. She said nothing.

"Can we talk?" he asked. "Maybe when you go on break?"

In answer, she snatched her apron off, fumbling with the strings and cursing under her breath; she headed for the back hall at a march and Drew slipped off his stool to head after her.

Down the wood-paneled, fluorescent-flickering corridor that led to the exit, the din of the bar dulled to white noise, the music a hot pulse that came up through the floor. Lisa's angry strut reminded him, for some reason, of a cat, and her dark ponytail whipped as she ducked through the door of the employee locker room, a warning toss of sleek hair that told him to follow at his own risk.

He paused a moment, his casted hand on the doorjamb, and asked himself what he would say. Was he afraid of her? Of what she would expect now that he'd touched her – been inside her? No. There was guilt, and regret, and worry, but there was no fear. And under the others, deep down and fragile, was even a kernel of hope – hope that her skin was still tingling the way his was, that she wanted a chance to try again. Because he was a dumbass prize fighter with nothing but a duffel of clothes to his name, and Lisa Russell was the best thing to happen to him since…*ever*. And because of *that*, he had a feeling that, whatever he was to her, it wasn't good, and didn't even begin to hedge toward *best*.

Steeling himself against her eruption, he pushed through the swinging door.

And wasn't prepared for the scene that greeted him.

Lisa sat on the same long wooden bench where she'd bandaged his hand before, her platform sandals tucked together on the floor, an arm around her middle, thumbnail clenched between her teeth, lashes batting a fast rhythm against her cheeks. In the moment between the door closing and her eyes snatching up to his, guarded and closed, he could have sworn she was about to cry. There were tears in her voice, but not on her face as she launched her offensive.

"*Never again*," she said with such force that it catapulted her to her feet, her body rigid with the tension of conviction that crackled through those two words. Her eyes had a wild, animal shine to them, and her straight, white teeth were bared like fangs. "I said – I've been saying – that I would *never* let some guy compromise *anything* about me ever again!"

Drew hadn't expected this; he blinked stupidly. "Lisa, I asked you – "

"Oh, fuck your asking. I knew better. I let you – " She spun away from him and paced down the length of the bench, little hands balled into fists at her sides.

He sighed. Even worse than having a female with hurt feelings over his silence, he had indignant, don't-need-a-man Lisa on his hands. He could have apologized for his silence – soothed with empty platitudes – but he had no idea how to fix this, whatever it was. After a long moment of watching her narrow back – and wishing he'd had a chance to see the skin beneath her yellow halter top in warm lamplight – he said, "I'm not going to tell anyone."

Her head whipped around.

"Remember? You said, 'tell anyone and I'll kill you,' so I wasn't gonna say anything. I figured we were gonna pretend it never happened."

Something went rippling across her face: pain, regret, guilt, something. She pulled in a deep breath and let it out in a rush. "Right."

"Right," Drew repeated, studying every twitch of her lashes, waiting for the moment when she let slip what was really bothering her. "So we don't have to do this" – he gestured between them, at the empty air charged with what they weren't going to say – "if you don't want to. We can honest to God pretend nothing happened." That wasn't what he wanted, but she did…

Maybe she did. She did, didn't she…?

Her eyes moved over him, sharp and attentive, assessing. He remembered the breathy sound of his name on her lips in the garage, the seeking way her fingers had probed through his shirt. Her invitation had been unmistakable then. Now – this new invitation – was unbelievable.

Realization slammed into him: she didn't want to pretend, she wanted to acknowledge, and she wanted him to be an obnoxious ass about it. She wanted him to stake a claim.

"Yeah," she said, and blinked hard again. "Yeah, we should do that." She shook her head. "Sorry I jumped all over you about it."

She didn't look at him as she moved to the door, but she hesitated. It was only a second, but it was long enough to confirm his suspicion: *never again* was sounding like a long damn time all of a sudden.

Sly looked like he thought he could have somehow gotten better answers from Danielle Britton. "Nothing?" he asked over the Bailey's spiked coffee Cheryl set in front of him.

"Nothing." Ray blew the steam off his own mug and frowned over the top of Sly's head where Cheryl stood at the stove "not listening." He couldn't keep things from her, true, but he didn't have to be happy about it. "She was scared shitless."

"Yeah," Sly said, "but now she's scared shitless and we know nothing."

The guy wasn't big on backtalk, and Ray shot him a look that told him he didn't expect any now.

At the stove, Cheryl turned and put her back to the counter, brown eyes colliding with Ray's. "You know he's violent," she said levelly, not betraying the brave face she was trying to maintain. "And you know he isn't picky; he'll hurt anyone who gets in the way. Danielle got in the way somehow." She passed a glance over all of them. "So that's not nothing."

Sly stared down into his coffee.

Ray sent his wife a mental thanks that she accepted with a nod and turned back to the stove.

"You know what I think you should do?" she asked over her shoulder. When he didn't ask, she continued: "I think you should have Lisa talk to the other girls at the party. My guess is that one of them knows something; what they won't tell your grumpy face, baby, they might tell her."

It was three by the time she'd gone slipping through the slumbering house, showered, and fallen across her bed to the sound of Hektor's snoring. Her body was exhausted, but her mind was spinning, and what she wanted most was the last thing she should.

Somehow, she'd expected – wanted – a fight from Drew; she'd wanted him to be insistent and invested, had wanted him to argue against her shoving him away. But he'd gone along with her wishes, no questions asked. Their mutual lapse in judgment at the garage was going to be just that – a lapse, one they would both forget and from which they'd move forward and not look back. Morgan would have applauded her: she'd had a meaningless tumble with a hot guy. But Lisa wasn't applauding anything, save her own naïve conviction that *never again* had truly meant something.

Drew, she decided, was the world's most passive boxer.

With a reproachful inward scowl, she flipped back the covers and pulled a tattered old flannel shirt on over her pajamas. Forgoing her flip-flops because they made too much noise, she slipped from her room, leaving Hektor behind, and moved back through the house, silent as a ghost.

251

Idiot, she scolded herself as she punched in the alarm code. This was a bad idea on so many levels. Her dad, the guys...too many people stood to make her life hell over this. She reset the alarm and flitted out the door before the countdown on the keypad reached zero.

The driveway was a mosaic of the lace-edged shadows of oak limbs. The concrete was still warm from the day's baking beneath her feet, the grit sharp on the pads of her toes. A breeze tossed the branches together and they whispered; she pulled her flannel shirt tight and picked her way between all their trucks, heading for the carriage house. It was too dark to see the steps, but she knew them by feel, and the red door waited at the top, black in the night, foreboding in its solidity. She could still turn around, could still decide that Drew was right after all and that forgetting was the best thing for both of them. But instead, fueled by a need that had nothing to do with sex and that scared her breathless, she tested the knob, found it unlocked, and let herself in.

It took her eyes a moment to adjust to the shadows that were sliced with the moonbeams that played through the windows. The shadows took shape: the armoire, the door to the bathroom, the bed, the telltale lump beneath the covers. Drew was asleep already, snoring softly.

Cautiously – because the last time she'd startled him awake, he'd nearly snapped her arm in two – she tiptoed to the edge of the bed. "Drew." He was on his stomach, face turned toward her, and he shifted under the covers, the sheet slipping low over his bare back. "*Drew.*"

He came awake with a start, levering up onto his arms. She was prepared, but even so, the suddenness of the motion startled her.

"It's me," she said before he could react more violently.

His eyes swung up to hers, bright with moonlight, and the tension went out of him. "Lisa." She had an ordinary name, but she liked the way he said it. He frowned. "What are you doing in here?"

There were a thousand things she could have said: *I'm lonely; I'm confused; you don't really want to pretend, do you?* But she said, "Does it matter?"

His answer was to move over and push the covers back.

She let the flannel shirt slide back off her shoulders and felt – though he'd already seen her naked in the dark – self-conscious as she climbed in beside him in her camisole and shorts. The old bed frame creaked and the sheets rustled, and as her head hit the pillow beside his, she was flooded with worry; what if he –

He rolled into her and his good arm went around her waist, heavy and muscled and pulling her in close against his chest. He smelled like soap and his skin was warm and smooth beneath her hands – beneath her face as she settled it against his chest, his chin tucked over the top of her head. She released a breath she hadn't known she was holding and let the long day's tension go bleeding out of her; suddenly, she was exhausted. Her eyelids flagged. The even thump of his heart against her cheek was a lullaby.

"So," Drew said, and his hand settled between her shoulder blades, holding her to him. "How are we gonna explain this?"

Her age was irrelevant, as was the fact that she'd been engaged before; her father would treat her exactly like an errant sixteen-year-old when he found out where she'd spent the night. She sighed. "I figure we can either try to hide it – which won't work; or we can admit it – which will involve some yelling."

She held her breath while she waited for his response. He said, "I can handle yelling."

She woke him up in the black hours of early morning, her little hands gliding down his stomach and launching him to full awareness. When he sought to roll her onto her back, she braced her hands on his shoulders and said, "Let me on top." And he did, and was rewarded for the concession.

253

She was intense, this girl; she didn't speak and didn't scream and her nails raked down his chest as she took him in with a welcoming, hot hunger that he could *feel*. He'd been with the kind of women that dripped sex – suggestion and promise and hooded looks creating an aura around them that was unmistakably inviting. But those women were no different in bed than out of it, detached and impersonal. Lisa was focused, she was all action and no talk, and it felt intensely personal. When he eventually drew her down and rolled them, trapped her beneath him in their cocoon of scratchy sheets, the sex was slow, languid, and if he dared think it, sheltering. They were damp skin and mingling tongues, shared air and matched rhythms.

Afterward, he held her, because he wanted to, and because he thought she wanted it too. Their skin glued together – her forehead to his chin – and their breathing evened out in the first gray strokes of dawn.

"Do you think," Lisa started, and she took a deep breath that stirred against his throat. "Do you think that whoever attacked Dani is connected to the flowers? You think it's the same guy?"

He thought a moment, wanting to phrase it in a way that didn't frighten her. She'd never admit it, but she was scared – it was what had led her to his bed, even if he wanted to think otherwise. "Ray thinks so. But there's no real proof."

"But what are the odds that someone at a party I worked just happened to get attacked?"

"Slim."

A thin finger of watery light sliced across the floor; they were running out of time.

"This guy," Drew said, "Shilling? You really think it's him?"

"Dad was his attorney and he turned evidence over to the prosecutor," she reasoned. "He has every reason to hold a grudge against him."

"Yeah, but he did his time. He's out, right?"

"Right."

"Why the hell would a guy who got a second chance risk going away again just 'cause of a grudge? Your dad wouldn't even know he was out if it weren't for…" He didn't know what to call this bizarre *Criminal Minds* episode he'd been sucked into. "The flowers. A guy gets a second chance, he isn't gonna blow it."

He felt her shrug. "He killed his own wife and daughter. Nothing he does could make sense."

"Still…"

Lisa pulled back and tipped her head; he saw the liquid flash of her eyes as she scanned his face. "You don't think it's him, do you?"

There was something soft about her face, a warm, trusting stillness that made him uneasy. She was looking to him, asking him, wanting to know what he thought – about something this important, no less. He didn't trust himself to give her the right answer.

"Drew," she prodded. "You don't?"

He rolled onto his back and she propped up on an elbow, staring down at him. He lifted his eyes to the ceiling and kept them there. "Not really. I mean, I don't have any idea who it could be, but I don't think it's Shilling."

"Did you tell the guys that?"

"No."

"You should."

He sighed, and glanced sideways at her; she had a stubborn set to her little jaw. "What good would that do? They aren't gonna listen to me."

"They don't listen to me," she said, "but I still say what I need to say."

He had to grin. "I noticed." He reached up with his good hand and touched his knuckles to the side of her head, against her glossy dark hair. "But your head's harder than mine."

She made a face. "Yeah, but if you're gonna be – " She cut herself off, eyes widening, looking shocked.

"If I'm gonna be what?"

255

Her gaze skittered away and then she flopped down onto her back beside him, sheet tucked up over her breasts. Drew swore he could hear her reprimanding herself in her head. "If you're gonna...stick around." She sounded like she phrased things carefully. "Then you've gotta learn to speak up."

Okay, he thought. *Starting now.* "You want me to stick around, then?"

It was silent a beat before she said, "Yeah," and in just one word, her voice lost all its strength and sounded laid-bare and vulnerable.

It was the sweetest thing he'd ever heard.

29

The first thing that greeted Lisa on the driveway an hour later was her dog. Hektor was trotting excited circles behind her truck, nub of a tail wriggling, tongue lolling. She was walking toward him, smiling, a greeting on her tongue, pavement cold beneath her bare feet, when she lurched to a halt. Hektor wasn't out by himself; someone had let him out. And that meant someone knew she was missing. And that meant –

The door off the screened porch slammed back on its hinges and her heart gave a terrified leap to see her father on the steps sliding a flat look across her and up over her shoulder where Drew stood. "Inside. Both of you. *Now*." He retreated and let the door crash into its frame; inside, Cheryl reprimanded him for it, her voice just a murmur from a distance.

Lisa caught a deep, trembling breath and twisted around to glance at Drew. She almost didn't recognize him: his jaw was set and a cold, crystal glaze had slipped over his eyes; he stared at the house and the cords at the base of his neck danced. If she dared think it, he looked ready to fight, protective. He was, she realized with a strange thrill, going to stand up to her dad.

No boy had ever dared do that for her.

No *man*. If he was going to challenge Ray, then he was a man.

Seeing him in this new light bolstered her courage. "He won't actually do anything," she said, hoping it was true. "Just yelling, remember?"

His gaze dropped to her face, eyes softening, a muscle in his cheek twitching. "I'm not worried about that." He was worried about her – about how Ray would treat her. She really couldn't take any more of this or she'd start to turn into one of those jelly-kneed, doe-eyed girls in novels.

They walked to the house without touching, Hektor between them. Drew held the door for her and followed her through the screened porch into the kitchen. Ray was waiting for them at the head of the table, hands braced on the ladder back of his chair. His head lifted at the sound of their approach, his eyes glacial. Cheryl was prepping breakfast, seemingly oblivious to the scene that was about to unfold.

Lisa felt her throat closing up in an old, familiar reaction. At the mercy of her father's stare, she was sixteen and stupid again, making the kinds of short-sighted mistakes that wrecked her reputation and shattered her parents' trust.

At the stove, Cheryl rapped her spoon neatly against the edge of her skillet and sent her the fastest of reassuring looks: *You're fine.*

Lisa took a deep breath. She *was* fine. She wasn't a kid anymore; they'd never been a religious family and there was no sense pretending she'd committed some egregious sin. If anything, Ray was to blame. He'd forced them together all these weeks; what had he expected?

She took another breath and squared up her shoulders, stood tall in her pajamas, on bare legs. Something stirred at her back – Drew's fingers as he toyed with the ends of her hair. *Come on, Dad*, she thought, meeting his implacable gaze with one of her own. *Call me a slut. I dare you.*

Ray opened his mouth –

She braced herself for the tirade.

- and he said the last thing she'd expected. "I went to the hospital to see what I could get out of Danielle Britton last night."

Lisa blinked. "You did?"

"Yeah. She knows who attacked her – I got that impression – but she was too scared to squeal."

"So." Suddenly light-headed, she fell into the nearest chair and braced her elbows on the table. "You're thinking she would recognize him? Or that she *knows* him?"

"Knows him, is my guess, well enough to be worried he could get to her if she ratted him out."

She let that sink in a moment, studying her chipped nail polish. "Well, I didn't exactly think some random strangler wandered into the Smyths' party."

Ray frowned. "Not random. Shilling could have – "

"How would Dani know Shilling?"

Cheryl nodded in agreement and kept stirring home fries.

"It was a high profile case," Ray said with a dismissive wave. "She could have seen his picture somewhere and – "

"Actually, sir." Drew's voice was as shocking as a gunshot through the kitchen. "I don't think it was Shilling either."

Lisa had never before seen the look of bafflement that slid across her father's face. Cheryl whirled to give Drew a desperate, you-shouldn't-have-done-that glance.

"You don't?" Ray said, emotionless. "You've got a *better* theory, then?"

Drew must have known it was a trap; he seemed to choose his words carefully. "I don't think a man who thought he was going away for murder – and got off on some kinda tax charges – would risk going back in again. So, no, I don't think it's him. That's all the 'theory' I've got."

Ray's fingers drummed on the back of the chair; a vein along his temple – just a thin trace of a shadow from across the table – pulsed. "Boxer's intuition tell you this?"

"Oh, Christ, Ray," Cheryl said with a sigh. "Leave the boy alone. He has an opinion – we all have opinions – and he's entitled to one."

Ray didn't react to her. His eyes came to Lisa. "You better go get dressed. Mark says he's gonna give Ellen your job if you don't get there on time."

The remark was unnecessarily cruel; it was her reprimand, she knew, as she slid out of her chair. He'd decided, for some reason, not to ream her out about Drew, but she was going to suffer all the same.

He watched Lisa leave – the unconscious sway of her hips, the light sound of her bare feet on the floor, hair swinging between her shoulder blades – and waited for the hammer to fall. Ray was hiding it well – as well as any father could, Drew supposed – but he was livid, and it was only a matter of time before –

"So that's how it's going to be, then?" he asked, and Drew felt the back of his neck prickling as he gave the man his full attention. "All we've done for you, and you're going to repay us by sleeping with our daughter?"

A week ago, he would have denied the allegation; after all, Ray didn't know anything had happened, and was only guessing. But after the night before, his indignation felt justified; Ray Russell was a conceited, overbearing asshole, his daughter more like a favored pet than an emotional, intelligent girl whose opinions he valued. He took a deep breath. "Sir, no offense, but if you were worried about Lisa's sex life, you'd pay her enough so she didn't have to work at that bar dressed up like a Hooter's girl."

Cheryl spun to face them, no longer feigning disinterest.

The vein in Ray's temple looked ready to burst; a high, hot flush rose along his cheekbones and his jaw clenched tight. "Are you calling me a bad father?"

"A scared one," Drew said, "who's so caught up in fixing his mistakes he doesn't see what it's doing to his kid."

"Oh, but *you* see?"

"I see *her*. You told me to watch her, and I do. I dunno what else you've got going on, but I've just been watching Lisa."

It was, probably, the most dangerous conversation of his life. The stakes – Lisa's sleek arms curled around his neck; the tickle of her hair against his nose; the angry flash of her eyes right before they melted and swallowed him up – suddenly seemed higher than those of any fight. A man without anything to lose made the most frightening of opponents, and he'd always been that man. But in this too-calm fight across the kitchen table, he couldn't bear the thought of losing what he'd just gained, whatever it was.

"She's scared," he continued, "and lonely, and she's got this thing about not disappointing you."

Cheryl cleared her throat and said quietly, "He's right, Ray."

Her husband ignored her, gaze never wavering. "And let me guess: you're all too happy to play Prince Charming."

"She's twenty-four; she makes her own decisions about that sort of thing." Drew swallowed hard, already cringing at what he was about to say. "It's stupid for you to think you can – or should – control her like that."

The summer air went artic. Cheryl wasn't breathing.

"Sir, I would never hurt Lisa on purpose, but not because you told me not to. If you want to fire me, fine," Drew said. "But I honestly don't care what you think at this point."

"Oh…" Cheryl said, hand going to her throat. She probably needed to sit down, Drew thought.

In a voice that belonged to a *Die Hard* villain, just a threatening whisper of sound, Ray said, "The moment – the instant – Lisa wants you gone, you're gone, and not a second later. Understand?"

"Perfectly."

Footsteps came rapping down the staircase and Lisa appeared a moment later, in cutoffs and cowboy boots and a Mötley Crüe t-shirt with the sleeves cut out of it. She'd tied her hair up in a messy knot, washed her face and put on fresh makeup. Her cheeks were flushed. "Ready?" she called.

Ray was still holding his gaze, murder in his eyes. "Yeah. Coming."

"Sweetie," Cheryl said in a choked voice. She gestured toward his boxers and wifebeater getup. "You might want to put some pants on first."

***

"I should have taken a shower," Lisa said. There was a breeze coming through the open office window and she could smell a night at the bar and...other activities...on herself.

Drew, reading a car magazine in one of her visitor chairs, said, "You smell like sex."

She made a face at him. "I know."

He lifted his head and grinned. "I wasn't complaining about it."

Her stomach somersaulted and she glanced away, cheeks suddenly hot. *Stupid boy. Stupid accepting, understanding, dumbass boy.*

A knock at the garage door pulled her attention. Mark was braced in the jamb, eating a Snickers with greasy hands. "Hey, doll." He stepped in and closed the door behind him, garage noise dying away. "I've got a job for you."

Drew was alert in an instant; he didn't move, but she could see tension lock him in place.

"Job?" she asked, caution stealing through her.

"Yeah. It's for your dad, actually." He held up a hand when she frowned. "Now just hold on a sec. Hear me out." She sighed and sank back in her chair. "He went up to the hospital last night to talk to Danielle Briton, but she wouldn't say much. He thinks you might be able to find out who attacked her, girl-to-girl."

"Um...Dani and I are not friends. Not even close. She won't talk to me."

"Girls lean on other girls when shit gets scary," he reasoned. "Friends or not, she's more likely to confess to you than any of us."

She snorted. "How progressive of you, Uncle Mark: all girls gossip with all other girls."

He sighed. "You know that's not what I'm getting at. Come on, Lis. We could use your help."

Her gaze went to Drew; he gave her a little eyebrow shrug. This was what she'd wanted, wasn't it? Some trust and responsibility and a chance to help her family.

"Take the rest of the day off," Mark said. "Take as much time with her as you need."

She took a breath. "Okay. Where is she?"

With a vase full of stalker-flowers in hand, Lisa was directed at the nurse's station to Dani's room. "Try not to look bodyguard-ish," she said to Drew as she knocked on the indicated door.

It eased open a fraction, and Lisa pushed it wide, Drew crowding in close behind her. There was a purse and a sweater in the chair by the bed, but the room was empty save Danielle. She was watching the TV, half-asleep, and her eyes sprang wide as they entered.

Without hair and makeup help, she was pale and sallow, hair stringy across the pillow. The panic that streaked across her face was unmistakable. Her gaze went to Drew and stayed there. Her arm flopped out of bed, hand going for the nurse call button.

"Whoa." Lisa ditched the flowers on the dinky table and held out both hands in a slow down gesture. "Hold up, Dani. It's fine. Drew" – she turned to him over her shoulder – "is stepping outside, right?"

He nodded and backed out of the room fast. His shoulder appeared in front of the door's window: he was setting up sentry.

"Okay, he's gone," she said, turning back to Danielle. The girl was shaking all over, breath wheezing in her throat. Her covers slipped down and Lisa could see the angry dark marks a pair of hands had left around her neck. *Shit.* "See? He went out in the hall. It's just you and me."

Dani blinked, and some of the scared-animal shock faded. She pushed herself up higher in bed. Her brows snapped together. "Lisa?" Her voice was a mangled, hoarse mess. "Lisa Russell?"

"Yeah." There was an empty chair over against the wall and she slumped down into it. "None other."

"Your dad was here last night," Dani said, suspicion tightening her eyes. They were red with burst vessels from her near-strangulation. "He was asking me about what happened."

263

Lisa nodded. She had no idea how to play this. Did she act helpful? Or conspiratorial? A mixture of the two won out. "Yeah, he told me. His guys were working security last night at the Smyths' party. They're, like" – she applauded herself for remembering to use "like" – "freaking out that they missed somebody sneaking into the party."

Dani swallowed, throat working, making her wince as the bruised flesh constricted. A definite fright came into her eyes. "Yeah."

"They had a whole perimenter set up." She drew a rough diagram of the Smyths' yard through the air with a finger. "There was Dad, Sly, Drew, Eddie…Drew's the one outside. Did you meet him last night?"

Dani shook her head, but she chewed at the inside of her cheek.

"Eddie, then? You met Eddie, right?" Lisa flashed a knowing smile for effect. "He's always scoping out the ladies when he's supposed to be working."

Her eyes made a fast, uncertain dart for the door and returned; a shudder moved through her.

"Okay, look. I know you were supposed to meet Eddie in the bathroom. So sue him; he can't keep his mouth shut about his conquests." Dani's meager color abandoned her. "But he's not the Alpharetta Strangler. He didn't do this to you."

Slowly, she shook her head.

Lisa scooted her chair up closer to the bed. She had no idea how long she had, how long it would be before the owner of the purse and sweater in the other chair returned. Dani gathered her gown tight around her shoulders as Lisa neared: she was scared out of her mind. "I'm gonna be straight with you, Dani," she said, putting on her sternest, most mom-like voice. "I know we're not friends. I can't stand any of those girls who were at the garden party last night. But someone, over the last couple of weeks, has been trying their best to scare the hell out of me."

That got her attention. Dani's eyes came dangerously close to leaving their sockets. "What-what do you mean?"

God, this was probably a mistake… "Someone's been sending my mom and me flowers, with a creepy-ass note attached. Someone jumped me outside the bar one night. My dad's on high alert, and that's why the guys worked security at the party last night."

She digested that, and then a blush popped in her white cheeks. "Is this *your* fault?" She gestured to her throat. "Is that what you're getting at?"

"If this guy – whoever tried to choke you to death – was only after me, why waste time with you?"

It was taking an effort, it looked like, for Dani to maintain a semblance of anger. The wild fear was shivering through, breaking to the surface.

"You know who did it," Lisa pressed. "And I know you're scared. But I need to know – my Dad needs to know – so we can make him stop."

"S-stop?" Dani stammered. "You guys aren't the police."

"No we're not."

"So what are you…*what*, are you just going to….*bump him off or something*? Oh my God. Like in some old gangster movie?"

Lisa frowned. "Dani, you got *strangled*. Doesn't that scare you?"

"It terrifies me." Her lips trembled. "And so do you."

And wasn't that a resounding slap to the face?

Lisa dug a pen and old napkin out of her purse and wrote down her cell number. She set it on the nightstand. "If you change your mind, call me." She made meaningful eye contact. "I'm serious. When you're ready to talk, give me a ring."

Dani's gaze was mistrustful, and quivering with fright. But she took the napkin, balling it into her hand. Lisa didn't know if she meant to trash it or keep it; either way, there was no sense staying any longer.

Drew was standing so close she hit him with the door on her way out. He spun around, face so concerned she had to bite back a smile. "What'd she say?"

265

Lisa eased the door shut and started down the hall; he fell into step beside her. "Nothing. She's freaked out of her mind about whoever it is, and doesn't want to tell me."

"So she knows who it was."

"For sure."

"And she wouldn't think twice about sending someone like Shilling back to prison."

"For sure, also," she agreed. "No, this is someone closer to home for her than that."

They rode down the elevator in silence, and the closer they came to the ground floor, the further Lisa's mind drifted from Dani and this new twist in their "case." Alone together in the small car, both of them smelling like day-old sex, her muscles sore in a long-unused way, her thoughts attached themselves to Drew.

When they left the hospital for the parking deck, she said, "So after I left the room this morning…"

Drew tensed; she could feel the energy shift between them as they walked.

"Did my dad say anything to you?"

He was scanning the surrounding cars, power coiled in his arms. "No."

"Liar."

He slanted her a sideways look without turning his head. It struck her, for a moment, as a very Sly-like thing to do. She didn't know if that comparison was cute, or disturbing. "I can handle your dad," he said. "Don't worry about that."

Before she could catch herself, her fingers curled lightly around his wrist. He glanced down at her hand, then at her face. "I have the rest of the afternoon – I vote we go home and snag showers."

He smiled.

Cheryl suppressed a shiver as she shut off her engine and glanced up at the brick façade of the shopping center in front of her. The purple marquis for the florist's shop was a logo she'd become more than accustomed to over the past couple of

266

weeks. The place – one of the most popular in the area – was the same that had been sending her flowers at work. *All the pretty colors for a pretty girl...*

It wasn't Tansy's, she knew: the shop wasn't responsible for what was happening to them. In fact, it had been featured in both *Southern Living* and *Better Homes & Gardens* as being one of the chicest places to buy arrangements in the Deep South. But sitting in front of the shop left her clammy nonetheless. So much for conquering her fears.

With one last deep breath, she climbed from her car and went in.

At the chime of the bell, the two employees working behind the counter called, "Hello!" and the heady scent of gardenia assaulted her. The shop was dressed like an old-fashioned apothecary – lots of dark wood and heavy secretaries full of drawers along the walls; they contained seeds and ribbon and florist foam and other trappings for sale. Display arrangements of apricot roses in heavy urns flanked the counter and Enya floated from overhead speakers. It was a narrow little space, with just enough room for two patrons to navigate around one another at the register. Cheryl settled in behind the girl at the counter, and it was then that she recognized her.

Missy Albright's voice – "I need *four* of those, not five" – was unmistakable.

"Missy?"

The blonde turned, hair settling prettily over her shoulders. She was in a loose white sundress cinched over the highest point of her baby bump with a red leather belt. She was as stunning as always, mouth curled in a frown as per the norm. Cheryl didn't think the girl cruel – not the way Lisa did – but it riled her maternal side to see a young woman so dissatisfied. And that's what it was, that attitude – it was all dissatisfaction and unhappiness, masked with bitchery.

Her face was blank a moment before she blinked and said, "Mrs. Russell," in an emotionless voice.

Cheryl recovered first. "How are you doing? After last night, are you – "

267

"Disturbed? Yes." She lifted her slender nose and gave a little sniff. "I can't *believe* what happened."

"How's your friend?"

Missy coughed a tight laugh. "Um, not good. Tristan and I are on our way to the hospital to see her."

Tristan: now there was a name she could do without hearing for the rest of her life. "You're on your way there now?"

Missy looked at her like she couldn't believe she'd dared to ask it. "Yes."

"I was actually picking some flowers out for her. Would you mind taking mine with you? If you can wait just a second, I'll have them ordered." She gestured to the display case of pre-arranged bouquets.

Missy pretended to think long and hard about it. She accepted her credit card back, signed the receipt, and finally said, "I guess so. Let me check with Tristan. He's waiting in the car." She whipped her cell from her purse and dialed.

30

The ceiling fan twirled in lazy arcs overhead, blowing the wispy, drying tendrils of hair down the sides of her head. The sheets were cool beneath her warm, still-damp body. She smelled shampoo, and soap, the clean cut of fabric softener from the pillowcase. She wanted a smoke, a sandwich, and a nap; but more than that, she wanted to stare at the ceiling fan.

"So," Drew said. He was stretched out beside her, good arm propped under his head. "This is what it's like to sleep in the big house."

In the shower, his cast held out of the spray, she'd passed her soapy hands across all the hard, lean contours of his body: the wide shoulders, the narrow waist, the landscape of muscle between. Up the back of his neck and through his hair, nails scratching shampoo against his scalp. He'd leaned into the attention like a starved, grateful dog, eyes closed, not shy about enjoying the rub down. When she'd finally curled her fingers around his cock, he'd been all too ready to return the favor. Her body still hummed. She could still taste soap on her tongue. Her pulse was sluggish and satisfied...and waiting, dormant for the moment, ready to leap again. He was young and strong, and she was fast realizing she might not be able to get enough of him.

"Aren't you impressed?" she asked with a low laugh.

"Yeah."

She kept waiting for it to feel awkward, but so far, that sensation hadn't arrived. She rolled onto her side and rested her head on her fist. "What did my dad say this morning?"

"You already asked me that."

"You didn't answer, though."

Drew sighed. "The usual angry dad crap," he said to the ceiling. "I don't – " he started, and then sighed. "Nevermind."

"No. Tell me. You don't what?"

He frowned; she saw lines form at the corners of his eyes as they crinkled. "I don't like the way he treats you."

A note of something like pure delight chimed inside her ribs. She pushed up on an elbow so she could see his face better. "You know you're going to have to explain that, right?"

His eyes slid over and attached themselves to hers. The brown irises were amber in the flood of afternoon sunlight. "You're twenty-four, not ten," he said. "And you work hard. I mean...I get him being protective. But the rest of it..." He shrugged. "Not like I have experience with good dads or anything. Forget I said that."

"You been on the wrong side of a father's shotgun a time or two?" she asked, smiling. The smile faded, though, when he didn't answer. "Or," she said carefully, "you're talking about your own dad."

He swallowed.

"What's he like?"

His expression was so serious. "Like no one you'd ever want to meet."

He was such a good guy. The thought slammed into her and she reached to lay her hand along the side of his face. His jaw clenched under her palm. "It's safe to say you're nothing like him."

She withdrew her hand and his lifted; he tapped at the swinging heart pendant around her neck.

"You wanna talk about it?" she asked.

"Not really."

A beat passed. "Parents are tough," she said, at last. "Dads, especially. In a lot of ways, I admire the hell out of mine." The way Drew watched her made her brave. "But I don't know how to make him proud. Honestly, I'm sick to death of trying." She shrugged. "But I owe him – him and Mom both. And as long as I do..."

"You'll do what they want."

She shrugged again. "It's not such a bad deal."

"You're not happy, though."

She searched his eyes, wondering how a damn prize fighter could read her so well. "That has nothing to do with them."

His hand ghosted up the side of her neck, around to her nape, fingers spearing through her hair. It was exactly the kind of moment that terrified her. That moment, before he pulled her down and kissed her – not the forbidden dark of the garage, not stealing into his bed the night before: It was the daylight, and this slow, deliberate slice of afternoon that frightened her breathless.

He brought her face in close to his, until her lips hovered over his, and then he waited. He made her close the distance. And she did, pressing her open mouth over his as a shiver stole through her. His fingers curled in her hair. His tongue slid between her lips, between her teeth.

Without breaking the kiss, Lisa shifted, straddling his waist, palms flattening against the hard expanse of his chest. His hand traveled down the curve of her spine, to the small of her back, holding her to him.

She could have stayed like that, kissing him, for the rest of the afternoon. But it was still too soon, this was still too fresh, and her patience was no match for the clawing need shredding her insides. She was wearing nothing but an ancient t-shirt that hung past her knees and she pulled away from him, breaking their kiss, so she could gather it up and pull it over her head. His casted hand settled on her hip. His eyes raked up her, leaving her flushed. And his good hand skated up her stomach and closed over her breast.

She pressed her lips together against a happy sigh as he lifted her, his thumb passing across her nipple again and again until it was hard and straining. Her hips rolled. He gave her nipple a light pinch – her breath caught – and moved to her other breast, fingers kneading, palm cupping.

When he started to move away, she pressed her hand to the back of his, holding him to her. She squeezed his warm, rough fingers around her breast, chest surging against the contact.

271

"What?" he asked with a chuckle. "You like it slow all of a sudden?"

"Sometimes." Her voice was a soft purring sound she didn't recognize. She guided the tip of his index finger to her nipple. He complied, circling the tight bud. "You in a rush?"

"Not especially."

She closed her eyes and basked in the sensation a moment. She'd gone so long without...and even then, it hadn't been good. This was *good*. Everywhere he touched came alive, heat shimmering deep in the pit of her belly.

He stroked her breasts – alternating squeezes with feather light touches of fingertips – until her hand fell away from his. Then he moved south, fingers trailing down the flat of her belly. Around her navel. Between her legs. He just teased her, flirting along her most sensitive skin until she was grinding lightly against his hand, hungry for more.

"You're a tease," she finally muttered, and moved backward on her knees, away from his hand, until she straddled his naked hips. He was hard, erection reaching proudly toward her. She watched his abs leap when she wrapped her hand around him, and she grinned. A fast, fleeting grin, that faded as she lowered herself onto him, taking his cock inside her, and the intensity of the sensation demanded all her attention.

His hands locked on her hips, his cast rough against her skin. His eyes went to the action where she lifted...and then eased down again.

She did want it slow, for whatever reason. Her hips circled in easy, deliberate swirls, almost lazy, like a dance. The incoming, warm sun on her back and the feel of his taut stomach beneath her palms grounded her as the slow rotations did amazing things to her building pleasure. Her eyes closed; she leaned back, spine arching. She was barely moving now, gently grinding. She reached between them and found her clit, stroked herself. Settled in for the gradual onslaught of orgasm.

Drew murmured wordlessly. She cracked her eyes a fraction and watched him watch her touch herself, his cock sheathed to the hilt. His face was harsh with restraint, all hard planes and angles.

With her free hand, she reached and cupped her breast, lifting and kneading it, tight nipple thrusting forward. She couldn't remember the last time she'd been this turned on. And yet...

She leaned down, low, hair spilling over her shoulders; her breasts landed against his chest. "You wanna trade places?" she asked.

His answer was to jackknife off the bed and flip her over onto her back, safe within the cage of his arms. A startled laugh tore out of her throat as her head hit the pillow.

"You – "

And then his hips flexed and she didn't say anything else.

Her body leapt against his, more than ready for his hammering rhythm. His thrusts were hard, and deep; she sank her nails in his biceps and welcomed the rush. All that easy patience of his evaporated now that he was the one in control. Hot color moved beneath his skin, along the planes of his face, as he leaned down to seal his lips to hers.

The kiss was an assault. His tongue plunged into her mouth and his teeth scraped at her lips; and it overwhelmed her, turned the world to a blur of pure sensation behind her closed eyelids. It felt like he was searching her mouth as deeply as his cock moved inside her wet, writhing body, and the comparison, the mutual invasions, set off fresh fireworks in her bloodstream.

When she came, it was absolutely melting, heat and light and bright white sparks surging through her, lifting her shoulders off the mattress. Their lips broke apart and she gasped...and then sighed...and then murmured a wordless thanks.

He wasn't done, though, and he rode her through her crescendo and beyond. His breath sawed out of his lungs, rushing against her ear.

Lisa trailed her hands down the lean, flexing cords along his ribcage, and then lower, to the smooth dip at the small of his back, nails teasing. Limp and satiated, still rippling with aftershocks, she brought her knees up and sank her fingertips into the hard curve of his ass, tilting her hips, urging him deeper, taking him in further. His next thrust moved all the way through her; she felt it in her stomach and chest and at the base of her throat. She gasped again, stunned anew by how strong he was. He –

"*Jesus*," he hissed against her ear. It could have been a curse...or a prayer. And then thought left her as he came, and sent her over the edge again.

To be chronically single, the girl had a hell of a lot of underwear. Drawers full. Drew paused in the middle of tugging on his socks to admire the view. Lisa stood with her back to him at her dresser, in nothing but lacy, leopard print panties, rifling through a neat row of bras in the top drawer. She had finger-shaped bruises on her hips. And with her hair in a ponytail, he could see the red mark he'd left on the back of her neck in the shower. She had an uneven, natural tan. He watched the play of light down her slender legs as the muscles shifted, admired the curve of her ass and the way her waist narrowed tightly just under her ribs.

She finally picked out a black bra, slid her arms through the straps and fastened the clasp. Just that small, domestic, intimate gesture was something he'd file away in his memory, to replay later, when she'd decided he was a piece of shit after all and didn't want anything else to do with him.

She turned to him, a clean white tank top in one hand. "What?"

He was still staring, he realized, and shook loose. "Nothing." He pulled on his other sock.

"Uh huh." When he lifted his head, he had an eye-level, up close view of her bellybutton and the lean planes of muscle around it. The black lace waistband of her panties. "Right." She was smiling when he glanced up at her face, green eyes bright with sunlight. "You are the furthest thing from subtle," she said, still smiling. "Eyes popping outta your head and shit. Should I turn back around so you can stare some more?"

"Yeah. That'd be good."

She laughed – it was a light, easy sound - and as it died, a softness came over her face. She set her hands on his shoulders. "You're stupid," she accused, and kissed his forehead.

He curled an arm around her waist, holding her to him a moment. She still smelled faintly of soap, her skin warm and soft. He could have stayed like that, but her phone rang, and she stepped away to answer it.

"She wants to talk to me in person."

Ray made a face she couldn't see and stepped out of the garage, into the blistering sun turning the asphalt into a griddle. "You already saw her."

"I know," Lisa said on the other end of the cell pressed to his ear. He could hear an engine running; she was driving. "But something's changed her mind since then. She sounded like she was crying over the phone."

He frowned. "I don't like this."

"Dad, you don't like anything."

"You're not alone, are you?"

"Of course not." She sighed. "You bought me a new guard dog, remember?"

All too well. "Yeah, well don't get too attached. That one's going to the pound before this is all over." He hung up before she could make a smart remark.

His phone rang before he had it back in his pocket. "Damn it," he murmured, pressing SEND and snapping it back to his ear. "What?"

It wasn't Lisa's voice that greeted him.

"Ray."

On the baking parking lot, he went cold all over. He knew that voice, whispering against his ear while they leaned together at the defense table in the courtroom.

"Carl," he greeted, his own voice hardening. "I've been looking for you."

Shilling took a fast breath. "We need to meet," he said, shakily. "As soon as you can."

The cold feeling grew icy. First with Danielle Britton, then with Shilling. Ray took a deep breath and smelled something nasty brewing, as pungent as ozone in a storm. "And why would I do that?"

"You want to. Trust me."

"Trust you?" Ray barked a humorless laugh. "Yeah. I'll be sure to do that."

"Ray…I'm serious."

Against his better judgment, he said, "Where?"

"Him again?" Drew asked, voice tight.

Lisa was turning down the volume on her cell and glanced up to see who he was talking about. They were walking toward the elevators and coming toward them were Tristan and Missy Albright. Her stomach contents curdled on sight. Missy looked as beautiful as always, in dress and heels, her hair flawless. Tristan still wore the faint shadow of the bruises Drew had put on his face, and that eased some of Lisa's insta-tension.

"Maybe they won't see us…"

But they did. Missy's brows plucked together with obvious distaste and Tristan flashed a tight, unhappy smile.

"Keep walking," Lisa said under her breath, and felt Drew's hand settle at the small of her back.

But Missy called, "First your mother and now you. Are you Russells stalking me?"

Lisa pulled up to a halt in front of the pregnant blonde, Drew looming solid and comforting behind her. Her shoulder touched his chest; he must have been half-curled around her. The support was fortifying. She kicked her chin up. "Considering the obscene amount of detail on your Facebook page," she said sweetly, "half the country's probably stalking you."

Missy pulled a disgusted face.

"Where'd you see my mom?"

"Ask her yourself." Missy flipped her hair. "Come on, Tristan."

Her husband slid an arm around her waist. "Don't let her upset you," he said with a nasty glance at Lisa. "It's not good for your blood pressure."

As they walked away, Drew leaned down and said, "Don't let them upset you; it's not good for my hand," in her ear and a laugh bubbled up in her throat.

"Poor hand," she said, reaching back to brush her fingers along his cast. "Alright, let's go," she said, and continued toward the elevators.

In her room, Danielle was sitting up in bed, ten shades whiter than she had been that morning. Her eyes – wide and wild – locked onto Lisa the second she was through the door, and she pulled her hand from her mouth; she'd chewed her nails ragged.

Lisa grabbed Drew's t-shirt and hauled him in after her, closing the door behind them. "What?" she asked, some of Dani's fear touching her nerves. She'd never seen anyone so outwardly frightened in her life. "What's wrong?"

Dani gathered the blanket in her fists and squeezed hard. She pulled in a fragile, trembling breath. "He-he…It…"

"Who?" Lisa pressed, stepping up to the bed. "Who was it?"

"It – " She swallowed hard and tears sprang to her eyes, shiny under the hospital lights. The marks around her throat had darkened with time, and were ghoulish. She whispered something Lisa couldn't hear.

Lisa sighed. Her pulse was thumping hard in her ears and she had zero patience for this whispering bullshit. "I know you're scared," she said, trying to keep her voice calm, "but I need to know who it was, damn it, so – "

"It was Tristan," Drew said behind her. "Wasn't it?"

Lisa whipped around to look at him, and saw nothing less than hatred etched in the harsh frown lines bracketing his mouth. "*What?*" She turned back to Dani. "Was it?"

Danielle's eyes dropped. She swallowed hard. She nodded.

Before his disbarment, when the family coffers had been stupid with money, they'd lived in a neighborhood in Alpharetta called Astor Farms. It wasn't a farm, but a tasteful subdivision full of McMansions, lined with sidewalks and trees. There was a playground down at the clubhouse, between the pool and tennis courts, and that's where Shilling wanted to meet.

The balls on the guy: picking Ray's old neighborhood, and a spot by kids, no less.

"I don't have any cell reception," he said, and skidded his phone across the dash of the truck. It hit the windshield with a satisfying *thump*. "Great."

"You've got me, though," Mark said from the passenger seat with a half-grin.

"You're not funny."

"And you're not handling this well. Come on. I got your back."

They left the truck and fell into step out of mindless habit, their strides matched as they started across the dry grass toward the playground. The slides, swings, and jungle gyms were teeming with children, their mothers sitting on the benches around the perimeter.

*One of these things is not like the others…*Ray spotted Shilling right off. He sat alone, at the end of one bench, hands knotted together in his lap, watching a woman smear sunscreen on her little boy two benches over.

"Fucking creep," Ray said.

Mark murmured a disagreeing sound. "Look at his face," he said.

Reluctantly, Ray did. It was narrow and harsh, too-thin and lined prematurely. The deep grooves in the corners of his eyes tugged down hard, melting into the lines that framed his mouth. And his gaze lingered – almost…sadly – on the plump blonde mother applying sunscreen to her tow-headed kid's face.

278

"I've seen predators," Mark said. "He doesn't look like one."

Ray pulled up an image of Drew's defiant, puffed-up expression from that morning; the daughter-screwing prick had said he didn't think Shilling was behind any of the chaos that had befallen their lives. What did he know? He was just a punk. A daughter-screwing punk. But if Mark thought the same thing...if he thought Shilling was innocent...

"Stay here," he said, and struck off toward his quarry alone.

"*Tristan?*" Lisa didn't recognize her own voice. She leaned down in Dani's face, not caring that the other girl shrank back, quivering. "Tristan did this to you? Tristan Albright?" Her pulse throbbed in her ears. Her breath caught in her throat. There was no way this was true...Just no way...

"Yes," Dani said in a small, choked voice. She dashed at her tears with the back of a trembling hand. "It was him."

She didn't realize she was swaying drunkenly until Drew's hands landed on her shoulders. Then she knew that he was all that held her up. One of his hands – the one with the cast – lingered between her shoulder blades and he dragged a chair over with another; he eased her down into it not a moment too soon. There wasn't an ounce of blood left in her head, all of it fast draining to her feet. He lingered behind her chair, hand circled loosely around the back of her neck. She leaned into the touch and let it anchor her; took a deep breath, and then another.

"Okay," Lisa said with a huge exhale. "Okay. Okay, okay." She closed her eyes a second and Drew's fingertips rubbed tiny circles along the sides of her throat. God bless the man.

"Okay," she said, eyes opening. "Dani, I'm gonna need you to tell me *exactly* what happened."

Her own reaction seemed to fortify Danielle a fraction. She nodded and sucked in a deep breath. "Please don't tell Missy," she pleaded. "Or anyone. I just – "

279

"I won't. You think I even talk to those bitches?"

Another nod. Dani wet her lips, took another shivery breath, and began. "I was in the yard," she said, staring at the ridges of her legs under the covers. "That guy – Eddie – he was cute and well…" A blush rose along her cheekbones. "I told him to meet me upstairs, in the hall bathroom. I went in first. I didn't know anyone was inside" – her eyes widened as she remembered – "but I heard a voice when I got to the top of the stairs. Someone was standing in the hall, outside the bathroom door. His back was to me." Her breathing picked up with an unhappy hitch. "I could tell it was Tristan. I recognized his voice; he was talking *loud*."

"Who was he talking to?"

"He was on the phone. He said, 'You keep your fucking mouth shut, or I'll step things up.' He said" – she took a breath – "'What do you think Russell will do to you if something happens to one of his women? Huh? If you think he's on your ass now, wait till I…'" Dani's eyes flashed to Lisa's, bright and terrified, the pupils just pinpricks of black under the fluorescent lights. "'Wait till I put my hands around his bitch daughter's throat,' he said." Tremors overtook her. "He said he was going to kill you, Lisa."

Drew's hand was all that kept her upright. Lisa took a breath and made herself say, "Then what happened?"

Dani shuddered hard. "He turned around. I guess he heard me – and his face…God, his face looked awful. He didn't look like himself at all. It scared me." She swallowed. "I started to turn around, but he caught me by the hair. I tried to scream but he put a hand over my mouth. I had no idea what was going on, or what he was doing, or why he'd even *said* those things – " The tears started to fall. "This was *Tristan*. This was my friend's husband! And he pressed my face up against his shirt so I couldn't scream and he…he tried to *choke* me to death!"

Lisa blinked. "And you're telling me the truth?"

Dani looked scandalized. "Of-of course!" she cried.

Logic. I need logic. If *Tristan* had been behind the flowers – if it had been *Tristan* trying to frighten them – and *Tristan* had been the one to choke Dani, then that meant he was getting spooked. He was escalating the violence. Becoming paranoid. He was starting to feel trapped. And he –

"He came with Missy to see you," Lisa said woodenly, and Dani nodded.

"The way he *looked* at me…Missy was in front of him and couldn't see, but his *eyes*…Oh, God. If he knows I told you anything– "

"He won't." She lurched unsteadily to her feet and Drew grabbed her arm, holding her upright. "I have to go."

"But wait, Lisa – " Dani's voice became panicked. "I – "

"Call your parents," Lisa said, "and tell them to come sit with you. Then call the police and tell them exactly what you told me. Tell them it was Tristan."

"But – "

"Do it, okay?" She stepped around the chair. "I have to get out of here." And she left the room without looking back. Drew followed, hand curled around her upper arm, as she shuffled down the hall and turned into the alcove where the restrooms were. She didn't question Drew's presence as he went into the ladies' room with her. He let go of her when she staggered into a stall and lost what was left of her breakfast. It was just bile and spit, but she heaved until her stomach ached. When she flushed the toilet and backed out, Drew was waiting for her at the sinks, his concerned frown putting one of her mother's to shame.

"Someone's gonna freak about you being in here," she said in a raw voice as she pulled a paper towel from the dispenser and dampened it.

He didn't comment.

She rinsed her mouth and then pressed the damp towel to her neck, the coolness easing some of her nausea. When she finally forced her gaze up to Drew's, she had trouble handling the way he was staring at her. It was intense and protective and tender all at once, and it made her want to cry.

She turned and put her back to the counter so they were side-by-side. "I almost married him," she said in a small, scared voice that she hated. "I slept with him. I – oh, God – "

She battled a fresh wave of nausea and pressed her knuckles to her mouth, fighting the urge to gag.

Drew's solid arm went across her shoulders and she sagged against him, too distraught to be ashamed. She felt his face against the top of her head. "You didn't know," he said, voice just a whisper.

"Some taste I have. Aren't you proud you got to bang the ex-fiancée of the Alpharetta Strangler?"

"Do *not* say that."

"God," she breathed. She wiped the towel down her face. "It – it doesn't even make any sense, though. Yeah, Tristan's a Grade A douche, but this? And the flowers and – "

She stiffened and shrugged out from under Drew's arm. She spun and her eyes went to his face. "You don't think he'd – "

"I think he'd do anything," Drew said, face hardening. "Which means you're not getting out of my sight."

"Oh, big overbearing man now?" Lisa asked, but his words were reassuring as she pulled her cell from her purse and mined through her contacts for Missy's number.

"Nice afternoon for a little parole violation, don't ya think?"

Shilling started as Ray dropped onto the bench beside him. His eyes flared – feral as a cornered fox's – in the instant before recognition landed, and then all the fight drained out of him with one long, exhausted breath. He looked like shit. Worse than shit. "Ray," he said, voice defeated. "I'm glad you could make it."

Ray scanned the playground through his sunglasses. The kids, in their colored t-shirts and shorts – running, yelling, dodging – looked like bright little beetles zipping around in the afternoon sun. "Yeah. I'm sure the rest of these concerned parents are glad too."

Shilling sighed, a bone-weary sigh. "I don't want to fight."

"No?" Ray asked, feigning innocence. "I guess you did always prefer picking on women and children."

"No I don't!"

Heads turned in their direction. Two kids coming down the slide were startled and tumbled off the end into the sand. One started to cry and her mother ran to her.

Shilling wiped his mouth with his palm and stared at his toes. "I don't," he repeated. The glance he slanted up at Ray was ragged and wet, totally defeated. "I don't expect you to believe me," he said, and Ray felt a prickling go up the back of his neck. Something – some invisible shift in the wind – was badly wrong. "But I didn't kill Rene. Or" – he swallowed hard – "our girl. I know who did."

Ray felt the hair on his arms stand at attention. He still didn't believe the asshole – how could he? – but his curiosity was good and piqued. "Who?"

Shilling took a pained-sounding breath. He watched the children. "My son."

"Your *son*?"

"I had a boy out of wedlock," Shilling said sadly. "A long time before I was married. I never acknowledged him. I think maybe that's why he was so angry with me. Why he – "

"Hold on." There was an electric current, supercharged with doubt and anger, coursing beneath his skin. "You have a bastard son – who killed your wife and daughter – and you choose to tell me now? Not when I was trying to keep you out of prison?" Ray started to stand, and Shilling stayed him with a desperate, flailing hand motion.

"I know. I know. But…I was trying to protect him. I didn't know" – he swallowed hard, Adam's apple jackknifing in his throat – "that he would try to do it again. I didn't know – "

"Look, you've got about fifteen seconds to explain this shit. Otherwise – " He let the threat hang.

Shilling took a breath. "I had this girlfriend in my younger days. She was wild. We both were. We were into coke and heroin and God knows what else. Everything. She was a looker, and a good time, but she wasn't anyone I'd ever take to meet my mother. I was never going to marry her.

283

"When she turned up pregnant – shit, I'm not proud – I gave her some money to go get rid of it. With her drug habit, I figured there was probably something wrong with the baby anyway…but she had it. I paid her off and didn't think anything else about it. At least, not till…"

"And your son is…?"

"The girl I got pregnant was Gretchen Albright."

And Ray knew of only one Gretchen Albright: beautiful, but haggard with age, bottle blonde and married to a retired banker twice her age. She had one child: a son.

"And my son," Shilling said, "is Tristan Albright."

"Missy," Lisa sighed. She hit the gas as the light turned green and rapped her nails against the back of the cell phone she held to her ear. "Can you please, for once, stuff our bullshit feud up your ass and just listen to my question?"

"Oh, you're a bitch – "

"Don't hang up! Please! God." She sighed again, and didn't hear a dial tone. "Missy." She changed lanes, glancing over her shoulder and across Drew in the passenger seat to check her blind spot. "I just left the hospital. Do you know who attacked Dani?"

"Um, no – "

"Tristan did."

There was a beat of silence, and then Missy snorted. "Wow. This is a new low for you. I mean, seriously."

"Believe me or not, I don't care. But he did it." She had only so much emotional room at this point, the shock too severe to digest. She couldn't hold onto her disgust at the moment, and it was fast being replaced with a high-burning panic, the kind that left her chest tight and her heart pounding. "Where is he? Is he still with you?"

Missy made a disgusted sound. "I'm not telling you."

"*Missy!*"

Drew flinched.

Missy sucked in a breath on the other end of the line.

284

"I'm telling you," Lisa said through her teeth, "that your husband tried to kill one of your best friends! Now where the hell is he?!"

She must have yelled louder than she thought, because Missy took a rattled breath and said, "I-I don't know. He dropped me off at work and then left."

"If he comes to pick you up," she said, "don't go with him." And hung up before Missy could say anything else.

It was a hot afternoon, too hot for the truck's air conditioning to do much more than swirl her loose scraps of hair. Heat mirages shimmered between her bumper and that of the Mercury in front of her. They were well out of Alpharetta and driving through the sleepy farmland that lie between it and home – Cartersville. The house wasn't too much further. Just past that big cattle operation and through downtown, then down their tree-lined street to their own personal Tara.

And worry was gnawing at her, for reasons she didn't understand.

"Did you call my dad again?" she asked.

"Straight to voicemail," Drew answered. "He must be out of network."

"Call Sly," she said, "and tell him what's going on."

"And what is going on?"

"I don't know."

"He came to me, about eight years ago," Shilling said to his clasped hands while children played and screamed around them. "Before his mother married that ancient old bank crook. He wanted money – a lot of it. He wanted to go back to school. Get a new degree."

Tristan had been dating Lisa at that point, this sophisticated older guy with a head of dark hair and an easy smile.

"I gave it to him. But he was back two months later, wanting more. He hounded me. Called my secretary and scared her. He came by the house and scared Rene one

285

afternoon." He shook his head. "I gave him one last payoff, and told him to get out of my life."

"He was your son," Ray said, without emotion.

"He was a spoiled prick. And he was drunk. And he wasn't right in the head." Shilling's smile was twisted and broken. "That's what I thought. And I didn't want him in my life."

"And he killed your family for that?" Ray's voice had become the steady, non-judgmental tone he'd used at court. His attorney voice. But inside, he was boiling.

"He said afterward that it was an accident. He went to see Rene and it just – he was sobbing when he told me. He left notes, he said, and flowers, so it would look like a serial killer did it. It would look like some freak – God, I should have killed him then. I should have." His hands balled into shaking fists. He blinked hard, his face red. "But I'd just lost my wife and daughter and he was a kid – "

"You let everyone think you killed your wife, to protect him."

Shilling didn't answer. "When I got out on parole, he started – I dunno why, but, Jesus, he thought I'd come to you. Tell you that it had been him all along."

"And he starts sending flowers to Lisa and Cheryl."

"If I violate parole – if I reach out to someone like that – the old case could be retried with new evidence. I could go away for good."

The sun had shifted, the shadows it threw across the grass long and distorted. Ray could feel his pulse shooting through the veins in his ears. "This," he said carefully, "sounds like the biggest load of shit."

Shilling closed his eyes and made a whimpering sound.

"I'm supposed to believe Tristan Albright killed your family, suckered you into covering for him, and then is so stupid he thinks coming after *my family* will keep you silent about him?"

"I'm not asking you to understand it. I don't understand it myself. But you have to believe it. You have to believe me."

***

"I don't know where you are or why you won't pick up your phone," Cheryl said into her cell. "But I sent Eddie to the store for me. Ellen's coming over for dinner and if you boys get done playing detective, give me a call and tell me how many to set the table for." She hung up before Ray's voicemail cut her off and sighed. Her key wouldn't fit in the back door and the weight of her purse and shopping bags dragging down her arm wasn't helping. Through the window in the door, she could see Hektor waiting for her, beating his nub of a tail.

"I'm trying," she said, and finally managed to turn the key. "There. This old house and its old locks…"

The Doberman bounded around her as she entered. She dropped her purse at the back door and heeled it shut; the door rested against the jamb, but didn't seal. "Damn," she muttered, stroking the dog's head, shuffling toward the kitchen table with the rest of her bags. She had a ham and enough green beans to feed an army. The plastic shopping bags were cutting into the skin of her forearms and she hefted them onto the tabletop with a grunt. "Alright. There." Hektor nosed her hip. "What? You want a handout?"

Her phone rang and she disentangled her hand from the bags to answer it. "Hello?" she asked, stepping toward the island and the jar of dog treats there.

"Mom," Lisa said on the other end of the line, sounding breathless. Cheryl felt the back of her neck tingle immediately. "Where are you?"

"At home – "

A fast flash of movement caught her eye: a shadow on the screened in porch.

"It's Tristan, Mom. He's the one who strangled Danielle."

There was a man on her back porch. And the door was open a crack.

"He's sending us the flowers."

"Oh, God."

287

Cheryl threw herself at the back door. Hektor snarled low in his throat and leapt. Her hand hit the door and she pushed – but it flew open, striking her in the face.

"Mom?!" Lisa said. "What's – "

"No!" she yelled, and everything went black.

"Mom?" Lisa pulled the phone away and stared at it. There was a sharp clatter, a rustle, and then a sequence of muffled sounds she didn't understand. She heard Hektor snarling. "Mom? *Mom!*"

"What?" Drew sat up against his seatbelt beside her. "Lisa, what?"

"Oh my God...Oh my God..." Her hands shook uncontrollably on the wheel as she stomped the brake and spun down their street. The interlaced branches overhead threw dappled light on the windshield that made her squint. "Oh God." Her heart was leaping against her ribs; her stomach liquefied and panic seized her, took her breath.

Her brain still worked, though. In a way. In a rampaging, red way. "Open the glove box," she said. "*Now.*"

He did, and she lunged toward it, the truck veering. They hit a mailbox with an awful screech.

"Lisa, what the – " She was aware of his hand on the wheel, steadying them, but all she cared about was her own hand – it was curling around the grip of her revolver.

She turned the truck into the drive, seatbelt already disengaged, door already flying open. She managed to throw it into park and tumbled out onto the driveway, hitting the pavement at a sprint.

"Lisa!" Drew shouted at her.

She ignored him. He might be quick in the ring, and he might be strong, but she had blind fury fueling her. She had her keys in one hand, gun in the other, as she streaked across the front lawn, the world a tumbling blur of green around her.

Tristan.

She didn't understand any of the hows or whys, but she *knew*. She knew in her bones. And she knew what she was going to do to the bastard...once and for all.

Her key slotted in the lock, the front door gave way, and she was pounding through the hall while Drew yelled somewhere far, far behind her. When she hit the living room, she could hear Hektor. He sounded like a hell dog. Her boots rapped against the hardwood, sharp as gunshots. She forced herself to slow the last corner, lifting her .357 in both hands, leveling it at the kitchen as she swept into it.

"Mom?"

Cheryl was under the table, clutching the side of her face in one hand, blood trickling between her fingers. She had an arm hooked over the seat of a chair. Her eye, the one that wasn't covered by her hand, came to Lisa in panicked shock. "Lis, no – "

Tristan was on the floor beside the table, just inside the back door, Hektor on top of him.

"Hektor, heal!" Lisa commanded in a voice that defied every ounce of her terror. He obeyed, coming to her, putting himself between her and the intruder, growling low in his throat, hackles raised.

Tristan struggled back against the door.

"Don't move."

He froze, and his eyes pinged up to hers. Hektor had savaged his arm and the side of his throat. There was blood all over him, glossy and crimson, throbbing from deep punctures along the soft inside of his arm. Red foam dotted his face, cast off from the dog's snarling muzzle. There was no malice, no hatred, nothing but naked fear on his face, his eyes wide and white-rimmed.

"Lisa," he said, and bright sparks of hatred shot through her head.

"Don't talk."

"Lisa!" She heard Drew. He sounded a world away. Car doors slammed in the drive. Someone else was here. Sly, probably.

Sly: *"Not everyone has the stomach for killing."*

289

She pulled the hammer back with her thumb and adjusted her aim, the barrel of the revolver aimed at Tristan's chest. "You might bleed to death from the dog bites," she said. "Or I might kill you first."

"Lisa," Cheryl said from under the table. Chair legs scraped against the floor as she pushed them back.

Tristan was pasty-white and slick with sweat. He licked his lips. "You can't do it, Lis."

She took a step closer, so she had a clear shot over the top of Hektor's back. Tristan's eyes widened.

"Lisa!" Drew shouted again. It was definitely him. She heard his sneaker treads in the hall.

She didn't have much time. She looked into Tristan's face; how had she ever looked in that face and seen anything worth wanting? God, she'd been stupid. God, she'd put her entire family in danger.

"You bet I can," she said.

He screamed.

She pulled the trigger…and her arm went spinning up to the ceiling, the gun kicking in her hands, a larger, stronger hand locking around her wrists, as the shot went into the plaster overhead, and not into Tristan's heart.

"No!" left her as a long, pitiful wail as she fought the grip that held her. She tried to wrench away, but couldn't. She twisted her head and saw Drew behind her, drawing her back against him. He pried the gun from her hands as if he were taking a toy from a child, his face grim.

And then she saw Sly, and Eddie, and her dad and uncle. All of them. The sound of distant sirens pricked her ears.

"No," she said again, to no one.

31

She was going to throw up again. Her stomach churned and her eyes throbbed and her pulse was killing her, choking her down at the base of her throat. "Let go of me," she hissed, and Drew's hands finally released her. She staggered to the edge of the porch and heaved over the bushes. She didn't have anything to bring up, but she gasped and gagged anyway, eyes running, tears falling down onto the pine straw.

The police were pulling up on the front lawn, sirens wailing, and she hated the sound. It meant that she'd lost.

As her retching subsided, she heard Drew step up behind her. His hand landed in the middle of her back and she ducked away from him, spinning so they faced one another. She leaned back against one of the heavy white porch columns and saw the cops coming up the front steps from the corner of her eye. She ignored them and they proceeded into the house. The sirens had been shut off and it was quiet now, out here on the porch and away from the chaos of the kitchen.

Lisa was shaking she was so furious. Her teeth chattered as emotional tremors overtook her. "Why?" she demanded.

His brows lifted in what might have been an incredulous stare. He was breathing hard too, she noticed, t-shirt clinging to the perspiration on his chest. He'd had to wrestle her out of the house, kicking and arching like a snake. "Why? You mean, why did I stop you from getting charged with murder?"

"It was self-defense," she hissed.

"He was lying on the floor after your dog almost ripped his ear off. How is that self-defense?" His eyes were dark, flashing with anger, glittering as the evening sun turned molten.

"My mom – "

"Is a little beat up, but she's gonna be fine."

"Fine?" She bristled further, pushing away from the column. She still felt like she was choking, a hot, painful lump stuck in her throat. "She was *attacked* – "

"Lisa."

"What?" Her voice was a terrible screech that scraped her throat raw. Tears rolled down her cheeks and she swiped at them, not wanting him to see, not even understanding them.

"I was trying to help you. Trust me, you don't want that on your conscience. You don't want to remember killing him – "

He'd been inching toward her across the porch and he stopped when she lunged, slapping both palms ineffectually against his chest. It was like slapping a wall, a sharp sting shooting up both wrists. It made her cry all the harder. She shoved him. "You don't know that! You don't know anything!"

He reached up and caught her arms, face gentling. She hated it – the way his eyes softened. "Lisa, baby – "

"Don't call me that!" she shrieked. She was sobbing now, great shuddering sobs that left her breathless. "I'm not-not-not your anything! If you cared about me e-even a little – "

His brows snapped together. "Oh. If I cared about you, I'd let you go in there and kill him right now? In front of the cops?"

No, a tiny voice whispered in the back of her head. But she was too enraged, too full to bursting with senseless emotion, that she couldn't make sense of her buried urge to throw herself in his arms and cry against his chest. "*Get away from me!*" She hit him with both fists and spun away from him, crying messily, hugging herself to stop the shaking.

He lingered; she could hear his shoes on the floorboards. Half-turning, she shouted, "Go!" over her shoulder.

She heard him sigh, and then retreat, steps heavy on the porch as he went to the stairs.

She shoved him out of her mind, more effectively than she'd been able to shove his wide chest, and went inside, mopping her face with her hands.

***

"Let me see."

Cheryl was shaking like she had palsy. She pulled her hand away from her face and it was all Ray could do to keep from snatching Lisa's gun up off the counter and chasing the paramedics out the front door where they were toting Tristan to the ambulance. She had a deep laceration along the ridge of her cheek, bleeding like crazy, and the eye was already starting to blacken, the lid swelling.

She licked her lip; it was split in the corner where the door had caught her. "I'm fine," she said, voice unsteady. "Just a little rattled."

"Hey." He snapped his fingers at one of the lingering paramedics. "See to this," he said, pointing to his wife's face. Then he turned back to her. "You should go to the ER and get checked out. You probably need stitches."

"I don't, and I'm fine," she said, voice strengthening. "Where's Lisa?"

"Here," came the answer from the kitchen threshold.

They both turned, and there was Lisa, looking ten pounds and two feet tall, holding herself around the middle, trying unsuccessfully to staunch the tears pouring down her face.

"Oh, sweetie," Cheryl said. "Come here."

Instead, Lisa's eyes came to him. "What will happen to him?" she asked in a voice that he found, if he was honest, frightening, coming from her.

Ray put a hand on Cheryl's shoulder and squeezed. "We'll have to see how the facts stack up," he told his daughter. He frowned. "Where's your guard dog?"

"Heading back for the pound, probably." And she turned away and shuffled into the next room like something from a horror movie.

"Sir?" The paramedic was standing at his elbow. "I need to take a look at your wife's face."

293

Ray didn't look at him. He ran his thumb down Cheryl's uninjured cheek and she smiled bravely. "Sure." He told her, "I'll be in the dining room," and ensured the fire rescue guy was going to be gentle enough with an iodine swab for his liking.

Sly and Eddie were waiting for him, standing on opposite sides of the table, still and silent as stone. Mark was by the window, watching Tristan get loaded into the first ambulance.

Ray's head was a mess of snarls, each more tightly knotted than the last. The shock of Shilling's revelation – and what had happened in the minutes afterward – was still too fresh for him to make any kind of sense of it. He would, eventually, but not now. Now was one of those times when he was thankful his brother had talked him into hiring a pair of court martialed Navy SEALs. He needed them for moments like these.

He looked to Sly. "Find out why," he said. "And make sure it doesn't happen again."

Sly's blue eyes were glowing in the evening sun. He nodded.

"What if he won't let me in?" Johnny asked, raking a hand through his dark hair and looking doubtful.

"That's not the point," Sly said, patience ebbing. Johnny was a good kid, a sweet kid, but sometimes… "He just needs to come to the door."

He nodded. "And then you guys will – "

"Go knock on the damn door."

"Yeah."

Sly watched from his position two long strides down the hall as Johnny approached the apartment door. On the other side of the door, pressed flat to the wall, Eddie waited, electric with coiled energy. It wasn't a pulse-pounding, excited sort of energy; it was more visceral and less pleasurable than that. It was an alertness. Preparedness. An exact knowledge of what was about to be expected of his body and an anticipation of every move, the gliding of every muscle. It was an energy that had been trained into them, and they shared it.

Johnny rapped twice on the door and waited, fidgeting. He'd been pushing lately to have a role in the security business, not understanding that, at times, it was more like a "security" business. The kid had to grow up sometime, Sly figured, and in this family, that needed to be soon.

They'd waited out in front of Nick Morrow's building until an elderly woman with an armful of laundry had come out; they'd helped her, earned profuse thanks, and snuck in while the door was open. Now they waited, gambling that Tristan's closest friend would know something.

Sly tensed as the door opened a crack and a wedge of pimply face appeared. "What?"

"Nick," Johnny said in a high, too-friendly voice. "Hey, man."

The door pulled wider, all of Nick's greasy face visible. Everyone like Tristan had a collection of friends designed to make him feel better about himself. He had dumb jocks and gutter rats and this: the unfortunate looking one with a personality to match. "What do you – " Sly saw his eyes widen as he finally recognized Johnny. "Oh, shit – "

Sly and Eddie moved in seamless unison, landing on the door with a speed that left Johnny gasping and Nick cursing. It flung wide. Sly grabbed Johnny by the shirt and shoved him in the direction of the apartment's tiny kitchenette before he went after Nick. Behind him, he heard Eddie lock the door.

"No!" Nick protested, making a mad lunge across his living room.

Sly caught him by the back of his shirt and yanked him back hard, slamming him to the ground. The wind left his lungs in his rush and his eyes bugged. While he was still gasping, Sly flipped him onto his stomach, pulled both his hands behind his back, and zip-tied them together. He wore dirty, smelly socks without shoes, and Sly bound his ankles too, not because he was afraid of the little shit getting loose, but because it would up the terror.

295

When Sly glanced up, Johnny was staring at him in wide-eyed shock. Eddie was moving around the kitchenette.

"You got any salt, Nick?" Eddie asked. "If I'm gonna have to force feed you saltwater, I'd just as soon get started now."

Nick squirmed impotently on the floor, testing his bindings. "What-what..." He gasped down at the floor. "What do you want? Just take it." He wasn't far from crying. "I'll do whatever you want, but please – "

Sly dug a knee into the small of his back. "You'll tell us what we want to know?"

"Yes!"

Eddie braced his hands on the kitchen counter and sighed. "Well that wasn't any fun."

Sly cut the tie securing Nick's ankles and hauled him upright, setting him back against the side of the sofa. He stood and found a kitchen chair, dragged it over in front of their captive.

Johnny was sitting in a recliner over by the TV, dumbfounded and frightened. Nick looked worse, white as paste beneath the red blots of his zits. He was trembling.

"Alright," Sly said, sitting and bracing his legs out in front of him. "You know why we're here?"

"About-about" – Nick licked his lips – "Tristan."

"Good doggie," Eddie said.

Sly asked, "So you know that he was planning on killing Cheryl and Lisa Russell?"

"Whoa. Whoa, man, no way."

"Oh, I'm sorry. Murdering. Did you know he was planning on murdering them?"

"Dude, he wasn't going to – "

Sly leaned down into his pimple-covered face so quickly Nick threw his head back against the sofa, gasping. "Do I need to tell my friend to keep looking for the salt?"

"N-n-no, I – "

"I'm not here to listen to you justify your friendship with some sick bastard," Sly continued. "Don't pretend you don't know exactly what's been going on these past few weeks.

You can rat on your friend, or you can keep testing my patience."

Nick swallowed, Adam's apple bobbing in his skinny throat.

"Now," Sly said, "let's start with the easy stuff. Was Tristan sending the Russell girls flowers?"

"He – "

"It's a yes or no question, Nick."

He swallowed again. "Yes."

"Why?"

"To – just to mess with them. To scare them a little. Them and Tristan's dad."

"And his dad is…?"

"Carl Shilling."

"He told you this?"

"A couple months ago. He was drunk and he wasn't making much sense, but yeah, he told me."

"He was trying to make it look like the flowers were from his father?"

Nick nodded.

"Why?"

"I don't – "

"Why would he want them to think that?" Sly pressed. He lifted the toe of one boot and just that sent Nick cringing away from him.

"I dunno." He was sweating. "'Cause of that business with Russell turning on his client. Why wouldn't Tristan's old man want revenge? Tristan said – he said they'd think it was his dad automatically. They'd never know it was him sending the flowers."

Sly pretended to think it over, silent and still a long moment until Nick started to squirm. "You didn't think that was really fucked up?"

Nick shrugged as best he could with his hands bound, avoiding eye contact. "I dunno. I always knew Tristan thought Lisa was a bitch. I mean, *she is.* So I thought – "

"So you thought, what's the harm in terrifying her and trying to kidnap her and – "

297

"Whoa!" Nick said. "I didn't do that. That shit behind the bar? That was Will."

Sly looked to Johnny. "Will?"

"Part of Tristan's group," Johnny supplied. The kid was, thankfully, getting his color back, a more suitable, harder look claiming his face. "Big ex-football playing loser."

Sly turned back to his prisoner. "He attacked Lisa behind the bar?"

"Yeah. Your friend did a number on his face. It looked like he had road rash."

Sly suppressed a hint of a smile. Good for Drew. "What was Will supposed to do with her?"

Another shrug. "Get her in the trunk."

"And do what?"

He shrugged again, and squirmed, cheeks coloring. "Bring her to Tristan."

"So you could do what with her?"

Sly's voice had been so low, so innocuous, and yet the most acute kind of penetrating; it invited confessions, lured them out of people. He'd used it so many times, always with results, so he was forced to believe Nick when he lifted his head, features pinched, and said, "I don't know."

Sly leaned back. "Did you ever stop and think," he drawled, "that you were all about to do something that would get you very arrested?"

"Not really."

They exacted Will's address from Nick, shoved a sedative down his throat, waited until he passed out, then cut his wrists free and left. "We don't want him giving Will a heads up," Sly explained to Johnny, who nodded and absorbed it like it was the most important lesson of his life.

As it turned out, though, Will wasn't at home. His landlord said he'd been found by a neighbor, unconscious and bleeding out of his ears not but an hour ago; he'd been taken to the hospital.

"Drew?" Eddie asked as they walked back to the truck.

No one had seen the guy since that frantic moment in the kitchen with Tristan.

Sly nodded. "That'd be my guess."

"I can make some coffee," Cheryl said, and started to rise.

Ray laid a hand over hers on top of the dining table, keeping her beside him. "No. We're all fine and you're not."

She murmured a note of disapproval, but stayed in her seat.

It was dark, the night heavy and black, the air thick as a quilt. Nightfall had brought with it a kind of relief: this nightmare of a day was almost over.

"Okay." Ray glanced around the long dining table. The chandelier cast diamond-shaped glimmers across the faces: Mark, Sly, Eddie, Johnny…and Carl Shilling. Sly had poured a round of Jack; they were all working on round two. "You've been to see the friends?"

Sly nodded. "Even Will, who's got a mother of a concussion." He almost smiled. "Drew was missing those speed bag workouts, apparently."

"How did Drew even know to get to Will?"

"I talked to Lisa's DJ friend at the bar. Drew stopped by this afternoon, wanting a rundown on all of Tristan's friends." He shrugged. "Will was the ex-baller. He would have been my bet on the attempted kidnapper too."

"Huh." *Perceptive*, Ray thought of the kid, and then shoved it aside.

"They all had the same story," Sly said. "They knew Tristan was messing with Lisa and Cheryl, but none of them saw a reason to put a stop to it."

"Sweet kids." He looked to Shilling. "Carl, how are we going to stick the little bastard with murder charges?"

"My testimony won't be worth much."

"I'll talk to the DA. By the time we factor in what happened today, it won't be much of a stretch to tie him to the previous murders."

Shilling's smile was sideways and humorless. "Thank you. I guess."

299

There were a thousand curses Ray wanted to lay on the man. If he'd told the truth straight off, none of the rest of this would have happened. His girls wouldn't have been in danger.

Beside him, Cheryl's fingers stroked against his.

So his girls were okay. It didn't make the danger they'd been in any less real.

"Thanks for coming forward," he relented. "Finally."

Shilling ducked his head and stared at his hands. Ray had no idea, if he was honest, what it felt like to be him at the moment. One of his children was dead, and the other was an absolute sociopath. It didn't get much more fucked up than that.

There was the softest of knocks at the front door and all of them tensed. A half a second later, when the knob turned, Ray cursed himself for not having locked the door behind the police. They were all half out of their chairs when Ellen stepped in. She was in a red dress belted tight around her waist, big Wilma Flintstone fake pearls at her throat and both wrists. Her hair was truckstop waitress big tonight, and the sight of her made Ray want to laugh…in a good way.

She turned to face them after she closed the door, smile bright. Her gaze moved over all their tense faces, and for a moment, before her eyes settled on Mark, she sent Ray the most subtle of looks. A fast, careful question. She knew – under that truckstop hair, she was sharper than he'd given her credit, and she could read the vibe in the room.

She didn't say anything, though, but smiled, and said, "I brought two kinds of salad."

Cheryl dashed a hand under her nose and got unsteadily to her feet. Ray wanted to protest, but she squeezed his shoulder. *We need this*, he swore he could hear her think. *We need to pretend things are okay.*

And they did. She was always right about these things.

***

It had taken an embarrassing amount of time to get her tears under control. Her eyes were so sore as a result that they throbbed in time to her heartbeat, swollen and bruised-feeling. The dark helped. Her room was bathed in darkness, an ambient glow from the security light filtering through her window. She could feel more than see Hektor's sleek head resting on the edge of her bed. He was worried about her. And he probably still had blood on his mouth.

They were all downstairs talking, and for once, she didn't care that she was left out. This anger was too thorny and devastating for her to be able to manage it and hold up the threads of a conversation. The hot, red, murderous fury had faded, tainted blood leaking from her system. And in its wake, she struggled to understand how she was even capable of that kind of rage.

It wasn't about revenge.

It was about her family.

About the thought of anyone hurting any one of them.

Her sheets still smelled like soap and sex from that afternoon. God, that had only been hours ago. It felt like her whole life had changed since then. It hadn't changed as fully as it might have, because that stupid, brave boy she loved had intervened.

Loved.

Holy shit.

There was a soft knock at the door and, thinking it was her mother, said, "Come in," in a voice just audible to her own ears. She heard the door crack and a heavy, careful tread started across the rug. Not her mother.

She sat up and twisted around, saw Ray easing down onto the edge of the bed beside her. The mattress dipped; Hektor went and nuzzled his hands, asking to be petted. He scratched the Dobie's ears in an absent, fond sort of way, murmuring, "You're a good boy." He'd come for a reason, so Lisa let him reveal it himself, keeping silent.

In the dark, his eyes were bright as they lifted to her. "I think this bone-headed dog and you are twins," he said. "But thankfully, he's the one with the sharper teeth." When she

301

didn't comment, he said, levelly, "You were going to shoot Tristan dead."

"I was."

"I gave you that gun for self-defense."

"And according to Drew, that's not what I was doing."

Ray sighed. Heavily. His shoulders sagged. "And what do you think?"

"I think…" She took a deep breath, suddenly shaking. "I think I'm not right in the head."

"Sweetheart." His hand reached through the darkness and settled on her hair, like when she'd been a little girl. "There's nothing wrong with your head."

She shuddered hard, breath catching. "But I – "

"You live in a world I never wanted for you," he said. "And you've dealt with things I never wanted you to see. The reason I keep you out of the loop, Lis, is not because I don't want you around. Or because I don't trust you. It's because I never wanted my daughter to have to decide if a man should live or die."

"Because I'm a girl?"

"Because that's not the kind of decision a man wants on his conscience for the rest of his life. I know what it feels like. I don't want you to know it…unless you absolutely have to."

She was crying again, fat tears flooding her tender eyes. "Did I – Did I make the wrong decision today?"

His fingers rustled in her hair. "You made the exact decision I wanted you to," he said, voice sounding thick, "because you're a strong, brave young woman. I couldn't be prouder of you."

She let him gather her up against his side like she was a child, her arms going tight around her waist. "I love you so much," he murmured against the top of her head.

She cried, too exhausted to try and stem the tears. When she'd calmed, racked with hiccups and shivering, she asked, "Where's Drew? I made a mess of things with him. I should apologize."

It was silent a beat and she felt Ray's arm stiffen around her.

"What?"

"Drew's gone. His stuff's gone. We have no idea where he went."

And as it turned out, she still had some tears left.

Tristan's friend Will with the kidnap-happy hands hadn't been hard to find. Trevor at Double Vision had been helpful. And Will hadn't been able to fight anything that wasn't a hundred-and-two pound girl. Drew hadn't even broken a sweat. He hoped Will had permanent brain damage.

The street was quiet in the sinister way of every bad part of town in every part of the country. Dogs barking and being silenced with a whimper. Quick, scurried snatches of conversation through windows. Dark doorways. Rustle of uncut grass. It was nothing like the manicured, tree-lined drive of antebellum relics where the Russells lived. It was nothing like home.

But he didn't have a home.

He hoisted his duffel up higher on his shoulder and quickened his pace. There was a single light on in Ricky's front room, and if he hurried, he might catch the bastard before he drank himself into his nightly stupor.

Ricky wasn't alone, though. In the heaving shadows of the front lawn, a long finger of black broke away from the trees and moved toward him. "What the fuck do you want?" Josh's angry voice floated out of the darkness, and then he breached the puddle of light from the streetlamp, face twisted with cruel lines.

Drew held his ground. He was, once again, the guy with nothing to lose, and that was still more dangerous than anything Josh wanted to dish out. "I wanted to apologize," he said.

Josh hawked and spat on the ground. "Fuck you."

"I'm serious. I wanna apologize to you and Ricky. And..." This was the hard part. "See if I can get my job back. I don't have anywhere else to go."

"What happened? Your pretty little princess bitch got tired of you?"

He ground his teeth, anger flickering at the edges of his calm at the insult. But he said, "Something like that."

Josh's grin was nasty. "Job back, huh?" He chuckled. "Yeah. I bet Ricky'll be *thrilled*."

32

Two Months Later

Murder case reopened was a headline across the top of Ray's Wednesday paper. He skimmed the piece: *New information has come to light on the brutal slaying of Rene and Anna Shilling four years ago…Husband, Carl Shilling, was accused of the murder…Shilling's estranged son…expected to go to trial…*

"You're not listening."

Ray lowered his paper and spared his brother a glance over the top of it. They were in the garage, Ray on a camp chair, feet propped on the work bench in front of him, Mark black all over with grease and toweling at it ineffectually. He was grinning, white teeth flashing in his dirty face. "No," Ray agreed. "I'm not."

Unperturbed, Mark swept an arm toward the sleek length of car parked beside him in the bay, grin going idiot-big. "I said, have you seen her?"

"How could I not? That goddamn gold eagle blinded me when I walked in the shop."

Mark laughed, and in the spirit of being a brother who was worth a shit, Ray got to his feet and jammed his hands in his back pockets. "Do I get the guided tour?"

"With headsets and everything."

The Trans Am, completely revamped and taking up valuable garage space, would have earned a Burt Reynolds seal of approval. Mark had painted it black, and revived the eagle on the hood; the seats were tan leather and all the parts, down to the knobs on the radio, were vintage, ordered and bartered and pilfered from other Pontiacs.

"She's beautiful," Ray had to admit. "But." He gave Mark a flat look. "In the meantime, how many customer cars have you guys finished?"

Mark's smile didn't slip. "No comment."

"Yeah," he sighed. "I figured."

Behind him, a whistle drew his attention. He turned and found Sly coming in out of the sun, garage shadows falling over him. He plucked the last inch of his cigarette out of his mouth and ground it out on the sole of his boot.

"You guys take two hour lunch breaks these days?" Ray asked.

Sly ignored the jab and braced a shoulder against one of the ceiling support poles, arms folded. "I was doing a little recon on a lead I got last week," he explained. His eyes were an eerie color in the shade, almost colorless. A muscle in his jaw ticked and it might have been a substitute for a smile or a scowl; it was anyone's guess. "I found Drew."

Ray expected a reaction; he expected to feel a hard rush of hate and disgust go punching through his gut just at the sound of the boy's name. He'd never had even a fleeting affection for the boxer, and knowing what he'd done to Lisa should have ensured a visceral recoil at news of him.

Instead, he felt...nothing but a warm slide of interest. A piqued curiosity. A moment of *Huh. How's he doing, by the way?* There was no hate, no contempt, and maybe...maybe even...damn, was he *concerned*?

"He's back with Bullard," Sly said. "Bare knuckle boxing for shit money and probably boosting electronics too."

"Damn," Mark said. "He went back to Bullard?"

"He didn't think he was wanted anywhere else," Ray said grimly.

"What happened with all that?" Sly asked. "He just took off that night."

His stare made it clear he knew exactly what had happened, and Ray frowned. He was wrong this time. "I dunno, really."

"He's not a bad kid," Mark said. "Quiet. Respectful. Not afraid to get hit." Ray could feel his brother's gaze against his profile and it was accusing. "Far be it from me to try and run your business, brother, but he's – "

"A good fit. Yeah, I know."

"He's fighting tonight," Sly said. "At Dunbar's."

Which meant they could go pick him up, if they wanted to. If they wanted to pull him out of the shithole of his life a second time and tell him to stay for good. And what would that picture look like? Where would he live? How much of a charity case was he going to be?

He didn't have those answers, he realized, because it wasn't his decision to make. He sighed. "Ask Lisa what she wants to do."

Sly's brows gave a little jump.

"It's her call," Ray said. "I won't hire him if she doesn't want me to."

But he'd let the punk live in the house with them if that's what his little girl wanted.

She'd heard, via some nebulous web article or other, maybe at church – she couldn't remember – that following a crisis, a person looked at her life in a whole new light. She was thankful for every boring, mundane day after she'd stared down the barrel of true terror.

Lisa wanted that to be true, but unfortunately, it just wasn't. It wasn't that she *wasn't* thankful – she was clinging to her family and to her job, her best friend and her dog and every moment they got to exist, alive and well. And it wasn't that she wished for a charmed life. But each time a nightmare slithered through her brain, bringing with it Tristan's face and the terrible thing she'd almost done, she woke with a start and reached out through the sheets…for nothing. Because she was alone. And she'd always been alone. Being alone wasn't the problem; being without Drew was. And it was dreadful. When she thought about Rene and Anna Shilling, and what might have happened to her mother, and to her, she shivered and wished her silent, thoughtful boxer was staring at her. She wished like hell that she didn't still want him, but she did, and she tortured herself with the last wounded look on his face before he'd walked out of her life. He hadn't failed her, not once; he'd saved her from her own stupid self. And he'd blasted her mantra – *never again* – to bits.

Work was dead and she was doodling aimless patterns around the edges of the desk blotter, thinking she needed to invest in a radio that wasn't so scratchy-sounding, when the door from the garage opened and Sly made dropping into the chair across from her look a calculated move. She spared him only a glance and kept at her doodle – it was a little bird with a pointed head, a round berry in its beak; a cardinal, she thought.

"Big Tom's got a new baby," she said, conversationally. "A Chevelle. It'll be in next week for you guys to take a look at the transmission."

He was silent, and she finally gave him her full attention. "You're creepy, you know?"

A small grin plucked at one corner of his mouth. "I thought you liked strong silent types these days."

Even a veiled mention of Drew squeezed her heart. She blinked and hoped it didn't show. "There's silent, and then there's *you*."

He gave a facial shrug and pulled one ankle up on the opposite knee, scraping at something on his boot sole with his thumbnail. "Eddie and I are thinking about going to watch a fight tonight." His voice was neutral, but the back of her neck prickled. He flitted a fast, blue glance toward her face. "You wanna come?"

She started to answer, and realized she couldn't. She swallowed. "Why would I wanna do that?"

He met her stare unflinching. "Drew's fighting tonight."

Eventually, after another dozen years of decay, Double Vision would become Dunbar's. Because every honkey tonk in the South eventually crumbled and dissolved into Dunbar's.

West of the city, two miles off the interstate, the place sat right at the corner of Hillbilly and *Deliverance*, a debauched warehouse strung with party lights and pulsing with Skynyrd's greatest hits. There was nothing around it save a few ill-kempt single-wides and an abandoned used car lot, all the power poles choked with kudzu, the pavement faded and cracking. There were dive bars, and then there was Dunbar's. It had been a barn once, or so the story went. Between the Christmas lights, industrial fluorescent tubes flickered along the exposed ceiling beams. A bar made of plywood and old barrels ran the length of one short wall and the beer was warm, kept in cardboard boxes. If it didn't come in a bottle or a can, they didn't sell it. The floor was dirt and sawdust. There were a handful of pool tables, an old Pac-Man machine, a series of upholstered sofas if anyone felt like getting lucky on top of years' worth of other people's fluids and filth. And in the center was the ring, a spotlight beaming a sharp halo across the fighters.

It smelled like sweat and piss and Lisa wanted to gag. Sly and Eddie walked on either side of her, the three of them arm-in-arm. The crowd was pulsing and screaming and filthy, and the last thing she wanted was to get separated from the guys. They found a spot up close to the ropes and the guys staked a claim with feet planted apart and shoulders rigid. Lisa shrank back in her hood and waited, breathing cigarette smoke and praying like crazy that Sly had been wrong, and that Drew hadn't subjected himself to this.

But then the next fight was called, and there he was.

His trainer – a fat slob with a sweat ring around the neck of his shirt – leaned on the ropes and took hold of Drew's shoulder, shouting something through the din of the crowd. Drew nodded and flexed his fingers.

He was thinner than he'd been, which didn't seem possible. Under a rippling layer of muscle, he was nothing but bones, ribs pressing against his skin, shoulders sharp. His shorts threatened to slip down the sharp points of his narrow hips. Under the lights, the entire right half of his face was a mosaic of purple and green healing bruises. And his broken hand was no longer bound in a cast, but wrapped in white tape like the other, ready for his match.

"He looks like shit," Sly leaned down and whispered against her ear.

Her stomach turned over.

The fight started like every other she'd seen: the men circling one another, searching for openings, finding their footing. Drew's opponent struck first, darting in with a fast jab that was deflected. Drew countered, landing a glancing right off the side of the other guy's head. She couldn't hear, but could read lips as the opponent cursed. He lit back into Drew with a fast combo, the sick thump of fists against flesh ratcheting up her nausea.

Drew did more shielding than hitting. And then, before the end, he took a great swing with his right...and she could *see* the pain going up his arm from his ruined knuckles, hitting him in the skull, taking the breath out of his lungs. She shut her eyes so she didn't have to watch him fall.

"Don't fuckin' tell me it's broken again!"

In the garish light of Dunbar's locker room, Drew could already see swelling. He cradled his hand and probed the knuckles with his thumb, grinding his teeth together against the fresh needles of pain.

Ricky had been the one to take his cast off, soaking it in water first and then scraping it away. The hand had felt better than it had before the resetting, but he needed surgery. Every fight put him just that much closer to irreparable damage. His fighting days were over, but he would keep fighting, until his use-of-his-right-hand days were over too. And then he didn't know what he'd do. Bag groceries maybe.

"I don't think so," he lied, and glanced up to find his boss snarling at him.

Ricky was flushed and sweating, like he'd been the one in the ring. He mopped his face with the towel slung around his neck. "It better not be. After the shit you put me through." He shook his head and paced away, breathing through his mouth. "Have you got any idea how much money you cost me?"

Drew kept his head down and said nothing. Without an answer, disgusted, Ricky left the locker room. "I need a drink," he muttered to himself, and the noise of the bar crashed through the swinging door.

For a long moment, Drew sat on the bench, head leaned back against the cool metal of the lockers behind him. The room was dank and rancid, everything covered in some kind of brown sludge that had long ago dried and cracked like old varnish. There was a dripping sound coming from somewhere. And yet, it was the most peaceful moment of the past week; of the past two months, really. His bed at the house was a sleeping bag. The nicest thing he owned was a toothbrush: a Colgate number with a varied sequence of bristles that had felt like an unnecessary splurge.

He would have liked to shut his eyes and fall asleep there, dripping sound and smell and all. But Ricky would be waiting, so he heaved to his feet and pulled a gray muscle shirt from his bag, shrugging into it and wincing at the pain that shot through his hand and up his arm.

There was another raucous spill of sound as the door opened, and he turned that direction with a sigh. "I'm coming. I – "

Sly Hammond stood in the threshold, a slight shape tucked under one of his arms. He made eye contact – his eyes were the exact terrifying shade of blue that Drew remembered – and gave him a single nod. "I'll wait outside," he said, and backed out, the door swinging shut and leaving only the slender little thing in a hooded sweatshirt inside the locker room.

Drew knew who it was straight off. He saw her in every dream, both waking and asleep. When her slender hands reached up to push the hood back, he started to shake, and couldn't get control of himself.

Lisa was in cutoffs and cowboy boots, her legs slender and tan as always. Her hair was loose around her narrow face and shoulders, her expression hitting him in the backs of the knees and making him want to sit back down. Her big green eyes were wide open and welcoming, laced with sadness. She took a hesitant step forward. "Hi."

311

He glanced away from her, not trusting himself. "Hey." He concentrated hard on shoving his water bottle into his bag. "Does your dad know you're here?"

She came to his side, all reticence gone, boot heels striking the concrete. He wanted to smile, glad to hear her usual attitude, but that would only make things more difficult.

"My dad doesn't own me," she snapped, right beside him, close enough for him to smell the light brush of her perfume just above the stink of the locker room. "He doesn't get to make big, life-altering decisions for me."

A chord plucked inside him, humming in the dark, secret corners where the tiniest bit of hope remained. He risked a glance at her furious, beautiful face. He took a breath. "Are you ever *not* angry?"

He expected a fight, and instead, she softened completely, eyes going liquid and warm, lips parting as she took a deep breath. "Drew, look at me. Look at me for real."

He turned his head, heart starting a steady knock against his ribs. He didn't want to be so effected, but he couldn't slow his pulse.

Her hand landed on his arm, her fingers smooth and cool, her touch light as thistledown. "Why'd you leave?" she asked, and her tone tugged at his conscience, stronger than any physical pull.

He was honest. "Because you never really wanted me around anyway. And after what happened…you were so upset…"

She rolled her eyes and heaved an agitated sigh. "Yeah, I was upset. That situation was *upsetting*. But that didn't mean I wouldn't cool off."

"You don't sound cooled off."

"Damn it." She squeezed his arm, hand pathetically weak, and she seemed to know it, releasing him and taking an angry lap around the locker room. "You can't just run away like that. When things get tight, and people get 'upset,' you can't bail."

He folded his arms and leaned back against the lockers, squaring off from her. "And what would have happened if I'd stayed?"

"I would have apologized!" she exclaimed, demonstrating wildly with her arms. "And thanked you, you dumbass, for…for thinking clearly. And keeping me from – " She glanced away and took a deep breath. "You can't bail," she repeated, voice suddenly quiet. "You can't do that."

"Why not?"

She charged him, eyes wild, hands landing on his chest as she leaned up into his face on her quivering tiptoes. "Because I love you!" she snapped, and he felt like he'd been punched. A good punch. An amazing punch, sending sparks of sensation through his bones. "You can't," she went on, "come into my life, and get under my skin, and – and…*look at me* the way you do, and make me *fall in love with you*, and just leave! I won't let you!"

His hands found her narrow waist. "You love me?"

She looked horrified by what she'd said, eyes falling to his chest. But then her lashes fluttered and he saw the fast glimmer of tears. Her fingers curled into the thin cotton of his shirt; they curled tight, her knuckles resting over his wildly-thumping heart, muscles of her throat working as she swallowed. She nodded.

Drew snatched her to him and spun, setting her back against the lockers, not trusting his legs to hold them both upright. She clung to his shirt, her thighs clamping tight around his hips; she fitted herself to him and held on for dear life, eyes liquid and dangerous. They were the kind of eyes that could drown a man, and they were looking up into his face, doing their best to pull him under. She had no more walls and no more roadblocks. She'd taken them all down, emotionally naked in front of him, and it was the sweetest thing he'd ever seen.

He slipped his arms around her and gathered her even closer against his chest, his forehead resting against the cool steel of a locker front, his nose in her hair, the smell of it flooding his senses – what few senses he had. This was stupid;

he should turn her loose and send her on her way. But he felt the fragile rise and fall of her ribcage as she breathed and held her instead.

"You shouldn't be here," he said quietly.

"Neither should you," she countered. "You're killing yourself." Her head lifted and he felt her breath against his cheek, her lips to his skin as she spoke. "Come back with me."

He closed his eyes against how wonderful that sounded. Not Ray's dirty looks or Eddie drinking his shakes or Sly sneaking up on people. Not the shifty work and distrust. But he thought of the sagging old mattress in the carriage house, and Cheryl's cooking. And Lisa. Mostly of Lisa.

Something warm and wet slid against his face: her tears. "Please," she whispered.

"Will...will you say it again?" he asked, and didn't have to explain.

She kissed the line of his jaw. "I love you."

He swallowed. "I love you, too."

It was almost one when they reached the house, but the lights were still on, and the kitchen still smelled like food when they walked in the back door. Cheryl wrapped him up in a gentle, motherly hug and told him how glad she was that he was back. The sentiment – it felt so natural and true from her – hardened the lump in his throat until he wasn't sure he could talk. She sat him down and offered a bowl of beef stew so good he almost used his hands just to shovel it in faster. Lisa sat with him, keeping up a stream of one-sided chatter that he understood didn't need his input; she just wanted to talk. It was light, everyday stuff: the Trans Am was done, things seemed to be getting serious between her uncle Mark and his new girlfriend, Johnny had decided he wanted in on the security business too.

And then, as she was clearing his plate away, Cheryl said, "Ray's in his office," and Drew was aware that there'd be no reprieve tonight. Straight into the lion's den.

Ray's office was at the front of the house, in a room with tall, narrow windows draped in pale blue, shelves lining the walls, his desk wedged into the corner so he had a perfect view of the door. A pair of brass and marble lamps flanking his workspace shimmered a warm yellow light through the room and painted sinister triangles of shadow beneath Ray's eyes.

The Russell patriarch lifted his head at the sound of the door latching, expression expectant and less than friendly. He linked his fingers on top of his blotter and pinned Drew with a squirm-inducing stare. Drew held his ground, though, shoulders straight. He was quivering inside with exhaustion, but he'd be damned if he showed weakness to this man.

"Did you win tonight?" Ray asked.

Drew kicked his chin up a notch. "No."

"How fucked is your hand?"

"Pretty fucked."

Ray's eyes went to it, like he could see the damage to the bones beneath the skin. His gaze skipped up again, harder than before. "You went back to Bullard." Not a question.

"Yeah."

"After what we did for you, after we took you in, you go crawling back to that asshole?"

"Sir," Drew said with a sigh, signing his own walking papers, "you didn't want me around from the start, and no offense, but you know I'm right. You don't like me. You don't want me to be with your daughter." Ray's face had become unreadable, carefully blank. Drew took a deep breath and kept going. "But I care about Lisa a lot, and she was in trouble...she was the only reason I stuck around as long as I did. When I thought she didn't want me to be here anymore..." He shrugged. "What would you have done, if you were me?"

To his utter and complete shock, Ray's mouth curved in the slightest of smiles. "I probably woulda decked me, if I were you."

Drew blanked his features, not sure how elaborate this trap was.

"You know," Ray went on, "Lisa's always had trouble with boys. She's too opinionated for them, you know? She's got a mind of her own and she uses it. I always figured she'd find somebody one of these days - somebody she really wanted. And I knew when that happened, I wouldn't have a say so."

Drew was silent.

Ray sighed, and his gaze moved up and down the length of him, a frown forming. "You look like shit, son."

It wasn't the insult, but "son" that reached over the desk and slapped him. Drew took a fast, startled breath before he recovered his surprise. "Yes, sir."

"Did Cheryl feed you?"

"Yes...sir."

"Good." Ray nodded to himself and pulled open a desk drawer, beckoning him closer with a wave while he dug for something. "Come here."

Still not trusting the situation, Drew complied, and an index card filled with cramped all-caps handwriting was slid across the blotter toward him. He asked first, brows lifting in question, and picked it up only once Ray had given him a nod. It was hard to see in the lamplight, but there was a name and number there, a shorthand list of days and times.

"There's a gym down the street from the garage," Ray said. "TKO. It's one of those places where the yuppie boys learn how to fight so they can impress their douchebag friends. It's newly renovated; all the equipment's new and the manager's a decent guy. Nothing like your Bullard."

"Okay..."

"They're looking for a new boxing instructor, someone who can do one-on-one client sessions six days a week. The pay's not anything to write home about, but for you, it'd be a real step up in the financial department."

Something else came out of the desk, something printed on letter quality paper. "Rico drew you up a resume," Ray explained, sliding it across the desk too. "If you don't flub the interview, the job's yours."

Drew's eyes pinged from the card in his hands...to the resume...to Ray's face, his stomach a churning ball of emotions, the lump in his throat threatening to choke him. "Are...are you serious?"

"As a heart attack."

"But...why?"

"It's not completely selfless – I could use your help with the security gigs. A strong arm shouldn't ever go to waste." Something subtle shifted in Ray's face, a tiny softening. "And because of Lisa. I want my little girl to be happy, and for some reason, she thinks she will be with you."

Drew swallowed, struggling to find his voice. "I won't...I won't disappoint you," he said, waving the card. "I swear."

"Don't disappoint her," Ray said, "and you and me won't ever have a problem." In an undertone that hedged toward dangerous, he added, "She's my little girl, Drew."

He met the man's stare. "She's the best thing that ever happened to me. Ever."

Lisa didn't ask permission and no one stopped her when she dragged her favorite pillow and comforter across the drive and up the carriage house steps. There was no one there to protest when she climbed into bed with Drew amid the shadows and they tangled together in the dark.

They lay on their sides now, molded together, his arm encircling her waist. She played with the back of his good hand, tracing the veins that wound around the curve of his wrist and across the base of his thumb. She could feel his breath stirring her hair. Could smell soap on his skin from the shower. His thighs were braced under hers, her hips cradled inside of his. She'd known she missed him, but hadn't understood how acutely until now, while they were glued together like this.

The silence was a comforting darkness draped over them, filling up the corners of the loft space with a warm sort of blackness that defied all laws of shadow. Branches rubbing up against the wall were somehow soothing. That new-life, post-trauma perspective was in perfect focus now.

"I quit the bar," she said, voice just a breath of sound; she didn't want to disturb this silence of theirs.

317

His arm flexed, drawing her back against him another fraction. "You did?"

"Mom and I are starting up our own design business." She huffed a laugh. "I think we've finally lost our minds."

"Nah," he said against the back of her neck. "You'll do great. That party was a hit...up until that whole attempted murder incident."

She started to laugh, and turned her head toward him instead, feeling his nose against the side of her face. She lifted her arm in an upward curl and found the top of his head over her shoulder, fingers massaging at his scalp through the prickles of his hair. He was so sweet. So loyal and supportive and all these things she hadn't ever thought she'd been missing out on. "Don't leave again," she pleaded, voice raw and shaking in the sheltering dark.

"As long as you want me, I'll be here."

Epilogue

"I gotta give it to you, honey. You know your shit," Ray said, and slipped an arm around his wife.

The backyard was awash in light, a whole great net of rounded garden party bulbs strew overhead, like a pavilion of fireflies. Autumn was fast approaching, but the lawn and gardens were still lush, the green washed gold under the lights. Cheryl had transformed the place into a fairy garden. White chairs, an arbor of roses, a linen-covered buffet heaped with Southern fare. Someone – Rico, probably – had rigged up a stereo system and as the first strains of "Sweet Home Alabama" flooded the yard, and the bride snatched up her groom's hand and tugged him toward the patch of grass serving as makeshift dance floor, Ray smiled.

"All I did was decorate," Cheryl said, resting her head against his shoulder. "It's Lisa who lights it up."

That was true. In a short, swinging white dress that showed off her cowboy boots, a wreath of laurel and white roses on the crown of her head, Lisa was glowing, her cheeks bright apples of happiness, her smile bashful and thrilled all at once.

Drew had put a little much-needed weight on. His skin had a whole new vitality to it; his brown eyes were brighter, speckled with beads of light from the bulbs overhead. He wasn't the worse dancer: the boxing had taught him the footwork.

It was a small wedding: the guys, Mark and Ellen, Lisa's friend Morgan, Lisa's somewhat new friend Danielle. It was a far cry from the Ritz, and twice as beautiful. Lisa had stretched up on her tiptoes, her arm through his, and kissed his cheek right before he'd walked her down the aisle. "I love you, Dad," she'd whispered, and her smile had eased the ache in his chest; it had told him that this was nothing like that first wedding attempt. She was in love. In love with a boy who was twice as in love with her. Walking her up to the arbor had been the hardest thing he'd ever had to do…but watching her now made it worth it.

Ray and Cheryl stood at the edge of the yard, by the railing of the screened porch, and Ray caught a glance of someone walking toward them. It was Father Morris, still in the robes he'd worn while officiating.

"Father Morris," Cheryl said, easing from beneath her husband's arm, "can I interest you in a slice of cake?"

The clergyman smiled at her, one of those warm, all-the-way-to-his-eyes smiles. "That would be lovely."

She gave Ray's hand a last pat and slipped away, giving them a discreet moment of privacy.

Morris drew up beside Ray and mirrored his stance, watching the proceedings. "It's a beautiful wedding," he observed. "Maybe the most charming I've ever attended."

Ray twitched a grin. "Tell that to my girls. They planned the whole thing."

They were planning a lot of things these days. Their design venture was fast evolving into a self-sustaining business that didn't need a cent of financial support from him. He was immeasurably proud of the two of them.

"I was glad to conduct the ceremony," Father Morris said. He offered a smile. "It was the least I could do as thanks."

"The Church hasn't had any more problems, has it?"

"No. Our donation program is stronger than ever. I can't tell you how appreciative I am of what you did for me. For the Church."

Ray acknowledged him with a grunt.

After a long moment of building silence – Ray could feel the cleric wanted to say something – Father Morris said, "What you did for that boy" – his gaze was on Drew as he twirled Lisa around – "that was quite the charitable act."

Ray snorted. "I didn't do it for him; I did it for my daughter."

"Either way, the motive was love." His head turned, gaze sharp as flint and totally out of place on a man of the cloth…or, at least, that's what Ray had always thought. He'd never put much stock in religious types. But the penetrating way Father Morris studied him was beginning to alter that opinion. "You know," Morris continued, "our methods are different." He smiled. "Extremely different. But our causes aren't so different." His look was approving and assessing all at once. "The world needs more men like you in it, Ray."

"The world's a scary place."

"And only going to get scarier."

Ray let his gaze rove across the party, across his family. "Yeah," he agreed. "And I intend to be ready for it."

Other Titles from Lauren Gilley

Shelter

Whatever Remains

The Walker Family Series:

Keep You
Dream of You
Better Than You
Fix You

For updates on the next Russell novel, visit her blog:
Hoofprintpress.blogspot.com

And look for *God Love Her*, coming soon.

324

About the Author

Lauren lives in Georgia, taking care of her horses and daydreaming about the lives of imaginary people. She's the author of six contemporary novels, including the Walker Family Series four-book saga. She invites her readers to visit her blog for updates, social media connections, and bonus material: hoofprintpress.blogspot.com. She loves to hear from readers, so don't hesitate to leave a comment and follow along.